Praise for Muriel Bolger

'Engaging and perceptive … a great read'
Patricia Scanlan

'A perfect, escapist beach read with a serious edge'
Irish Examiner

'Bolger weaves a tale of rags and riches, love and tragedy …
I didn't want to put it down. A perfect holiday read'
New Books

'An engaging piece of work from one of
Ireland's foremost travel writers'
Sunday Independent

'Expect twists and turns, heartbreak and tragedy'
Books Ireland

'Evocative … a most engaging story'
Dublin Duchess

D0268580

Muriel Bolger is a well-known journalist and award-winning travel writer. She has written four books on her native city, including *Dublin – City of Literature* (O'Brien Press), which won the *Travel Extra* Travel Guide Book of the Year 2012, *Darting About, Statues and Stories* and *Dublin's Magical Museums* (Ashfield Press). *The Captain's Table* is Muriel's third novel. She is currently working on her fourth.

Also by Muriel Bolger
Consequences
Intentions

The Captain's Table

Muriel Bolger

HACHETTE
BOOKS
IRELAND

First published in 2013 by Hachette Books Ireland
First published in paperback in 2013 by Hachette Books Ireland

Copyright © Muriel Bolger 2013

The right of Muriel Bolger to be identified as the Author of the Work
has been asserted by her in accordance with the Copyright, Designs and
Patents Act 1988.

A CIP catalogue record for this title is available from the British Library.

ISBN 978 1444 743 357

Typeset in Bembo and Coronet by Bookends Publishing Services.
Printed and bound by Clays Ltd, St Ives plc.

Hachette Books Ireland policy is to use papers that are natural, renewable
and recyclable products and made from wood grown in sustainable forests.
The logging and manufacturing processes are expected to conform to the
environmental regulations of the country of origin.

Hachette Books Ireland
8 Castlecourt Centre
Castleknock
Dublin 15, Ireland

A division of Hachette UK Ltd.
338 Euston Road
London NW1 3BH

www.hachette.ie

When we were about thirteen Mairéad Wilcox
wrote in my autograph book –
'In your golden chain of friendship regard me as a link.'
I'm delighted to say, a lifetime later, that link and friendship
are as strong as ever, so Mairéad, this one is for you!

One

HER TRIP HADN'T BEGUN AS PLANNED BUT, then, little was going according to plan in Jenny's life this year. The flight to Athens had been uneventful – until the announcement from the cockpit just before landing had told them that, due to another general strike, the airport was closing at nine p.m. and there would be no public transport. No taxis either. That would have given Fergus a laugh, if he'd known that she'd left Ireland.

She had booked a budget hotel room near the port for the night, a small establishment that would not have sent transport to collect her, and by the time she had collected her bag she was prepared to negotiate with anyone to get her there.

She was lucky: a party of three asked her if she'd like to share their taxi. Admittedly it was a limousine and the driver insisted they each pay an additional ten euro for toll charges. She wasn't even sure if there were toll charges on the way but there was little option. She wasn't going to miss her cruise. He gave them a tirade on the state of the economy and pointed out the piles of rubbish at every corner, decomposing in the heat. The refuse collectors had been on strike for four days and the smell wafted in through the car's air-conditioning. That night Athens looked nothing like the capital of ancient civilisation, despite the floodlit Acropolis on its distant hill.

The driver told her that her hotel was in an unsuitable part of town, where he wouldn't have let his sister stay. Once he had given her time to digest that gem, he suggested another establishment, owned by his brother-in-law. She was resolute. She was a seasoned traveller and wouldn't fall for that ruse. She had already paid for her room, and told him she had no intention of wandering anywhere tonight.

The place was basic, but a friendly porter took her bags to a rickety lift. She killed a few mosquitoes in her room, and almost knocked herself out with insect repellent before falling into an uneasy sleep. She couldn't wait to join the ship the next day.

*

Down at the port, check-in was streamlined and quick, and she was glad to be out of the city, with its rubbish and flies. She followed directions, found her stateroom and discovered an unexpected invitation to go to the bridge for the sail-away.

Her cases were yet to be delivered so she wandered about, finding her bearings and meeting others doing the same. She had a salad in one of the restaurants and listened to occasional announcements preparing the passengers for the mandatory emergency drill that would take place before their departure.

'You'll find your muster-station number on the back of your stateroom door and on your key card. Staff will be stationed along the routes and at the top of the stairways to offer directions and assistance to anyone needing it. You will not be allowed to use the lifts.

'You'll hear the ship's signal – seven short bleeps and one long one. Take your life jackets, and make your way to the muster stations.' The message was repeated in several languages.

A little later the signal sounded around the ship and everyone obeyed the drill with good humour. Some of the women remarked that the rigid orange jackets must have been designed by men, to be worn by men, as they certainly didn't take bosoms into account. They listened quietly to the ensuing information.

'When we have to anchor off certain ports that are too small to accommodate large ships such as this, we use the lifeboats to tender you back and forth, so there's no need to panic if you see us lowering them into the water from time to time. We use them for crew-training sessions during some voyages too, so if you see us in them you'll know that we're not abandoning ship.'

'Well, that's reassuring,' a man beside her muttered, and Jenny smiled back at him.

*

About an hour later Jenny made her way to the bridge and was surprised to find she had to be frisked before being admitted to the inner sanctum.

'It's just routine,' the female security officer said as she ran the electronic wand over her.

Inside Captain Douglas Burgess welcomed the handpicked guests as old friends, before leading them towards a side table on the spacious bridge and telling them to help themselves to the array of canapés. A uniformed waiter served champagne.

'Isn't it wonderful to be allowed up here?' Jenny said to a woman beside her. She knew that the task of choosing who should be there had fallen to someone in an office, whose job it was to work on such special lists.

'It's a real privilege – our son is working on the ship. How did you manage it?'

Jenny knew her invitation had come via her sister, whose husband's brother was an engineer with the company – he must have put a word in. Before she could explain this, the captain was making a speech.

'You might have noticed that we don't shake hands here, but that doesn't mean we're unfriendly.' He beamed. 'We knock elbows or touch hips as we pass. It's just a little precaution to avoid passing on germs. If you get sick, we'll feel sorry for you. If we go down with something, it's not sympathy we'll get because no one will be going anywhere.' That got a reaction from everyone. 'So, before we hit the high seas, why don't you get a bit of practice at the how–de–dos and say hello to each other?'

He walked over to the two people nearest him and they bounced hips. He knocked elbows with the next person. That was the cue for them all to begin raising elbows or gyrating – 'Hello, hello, hello.'

'Now, after that icebreaker, I'm going to ignore you for a bit. We've work to do,' the captain told them. 'Although you may not see much of us around during your time with us, we're a bit necessary up here, especially First Officer Kurt Svensen over there. He can read the maps and the dots on the radar screens. Meanwhile, I'd like you all to be very quiet for the next few minutes, and not talk to any of us until we clear the harbour. This is a pretty tight one and, as you can see, there's lots of traffic about so we need to concentrate. After that we're all yours.'

They nodded, as though they understood just how intricate the operation was. Although the guests numbered about fourteen they took up hardly any space in the vast expanse that stretched the width of the liner. The control centre was manned by several crew; behind them, open cupboards held rolls of charts and flags.

'There's a nasty wind blowing up out there. It's nothing to worry about, we'll soon leave it behind, but as the verandas on these ships act like individual sails, catching all the gusts, we need to keep our wits about us. And,' the captain emphasised, 'the officers on the bridge need to be able to hear the communications from the pilots and from those guys you can see outside on the two platforms. Well, that's my lecture over. When we're out on the open seas I'll answer any other questions you want to ask.'

Jenny stood beside a couple who had earlier introduced themselves and whose names she had already forgotten. She was too distracted by the efficient activity all around.

Through the panoramic window she could see two small pilot boats ahead of them in the channel, guiding the liner though a maze of ferries, yachts, a police boat and some cargo vessels. Behind, at the various piers, they left a clutch of even bigger cruise ships, some resembling tower blocks at the water's edge.

Hush descended, broken only by disembodied static communications and jargon being conveyed from one officer to another. Jenny felt like a bit of an imposter in this hallowed sanctum. She'd never imagined herself up there, among the gleaming consoles and knobs, computers, charts and nautical maps or, indeed, amid these uniformed officers with gold stripes on their epaulettes. She looked at the other guests. They were probably frequent sailors or voyagers or whatever the nautical equivalent of frequent flyers was. Maybe they all had family working on board, or perhaps they were simply friends of some of the crew. She wondered what had brought them on this voyage and if any of them, like her, were trying to escape their past.

Once clear of the harbour the pilot boats broke rank and turned back. Athens retreated very quickly and the sea shimmered before them. The youthful-looking Captain

Doug, as he had told them to call him, came back to join them. It was obvious that he loved what he did.

'I believe we have a couple celebrating a forty-fifth wedding anniversary. Rose and Matt.'

A sprightly pair stepped forward. 'That's us.'

He smiled at them. 'You must let me into your secret.'

Matt laughed. 'Loads of patience and a bit of selective deafness.'

'And,' Rose said meaningfully, 'that works for me too.'

'It sounds like a good compromise,' Doug agreed. 'I believe you have a load of family with you too, for the celebration party.'

'Eleven more – lucky thirteen altogether. We've been planning it for ages.'

'I look forward to meeting them. And if we can do anything to make it even more special, let me know.' He turned to the others and said, 'And my spies have informed me that at the other end of the scale we have some honeymooners among us too.'

A flamboyant male couple grinned.

'Congratulations and welcome aboard.'

'Thank you. We're Bud Harris and Sonny Carpenter Junior, from the United States. And, yes, we've survived two days of wedded bliss so far. I have to say I thought it would be much more … well, more frantic up here. It all seems so relaxed and quiet.'

'Well, it helps when everyone knows what they're doing. We do have a little help from the radar, GPS, and a few pairs of good eyes.' He made it seem very simple. He showed them how they recognised the various shapes on the radar, and when they highlighted a dot, which proved to be another ship, it came up with the other vessel's vital statistics – type of craft, passenger or cargo, number of crew and passengers.

'You mightn't think it, but the sea is full of roads, just like on land, which come with traffic rules and regulations we all have to obey.'

He took time to explain various instruments and gadgets. When they dispersed about half an hour later, Captain Doug had managed to make them feel that, as guests, they were the important ones on board, not the crew.

Jenny still had to unpack properly. When her case had arrived earlier she had taken out only the essentials before the bridge visit. Now she had time to settle in and arrange her bits and pieces. She was looking forward to wearing summery things again: the autumn had come in with a cold snap at home and the clocks would be going back in a few weeks' time. She unfolded each item, stopping for a second to admire some of the new wardrobe she'd bought for the cruise. She'd left most of her clothes in her old home when she'd walked out, and she'd never gone back for them. She'd changed her hair too, lightening it and going for a layered gamine cut that was easy to care for and made her almost-forty-year-old face seem much younger.

She pushed her cases under the bed and smiled as she

took the bottle of champagne out of the ice bucket. Nice, she thought. I'll share that one evening when I've met some people. The bowl of fruit on the table gleamed, and she broke a few grapes off a small bunch. Popping one into her mouth, she sat down with the daily News and Pursuits bulletin. This charted their course, and gave the weather forecast and a list of events and activities for the following day at sea. Glancing through it, she thought, there'll be no time to get bored.

Seven a.m. Walk a mile. Thirteen and a half times around the deck, it stated, was a nautical mile. That was a bonus: a regular mile was 1,760 yards, but she knew that was shorter than a nautical one so maybe she'd avoid the average cruise weight gain of a pound a day that a friend had warned her about. The stresses of the past few months had taken their toll and she'd lost weight. Now she wanted to make sure she didn't put it back on. She vowed she'd do a mile every morning and another in the evening. It would give her the chance to meet some new people as well.

She noted that the Destination Lecture, which would take place later that day, focused on the attractions and the history of their first port of call. There was the Savvy Traveller Trivia quiz in the Mosaic Lounge at noon. She pencilled a 'D' for definite beside both. I'll have to pace myself when sunbathing anyway, she thought. The sun doesn't have much respect for my skin and the roasted-tomato look isn't appealing. Now, what about this? A Solo Travellers' Lunch, hosted by the cruise director.

Jenny dismissed it at first – forgetting briefly that she

qualified not only as someone travelling alone but also as a single woman. Solo traveller … It had a much more wholesome ring to it than Singles' Event. After all, travellers could be on their own for all sorts of reasons, couldn't they? Maybe they had a spouse or partner who hated sailing, or a fear of flying, or a dependant at home who would rather stay behind watching golf on television or the grass grow. There could be any number of reasons. Maybe, like herself, they were running away from someone. She didn't see herself ever doing a singles' thing – they smacked of desperation and she certainly wasn't desperate. She had a small library with her, and there was the balcony if she wanted to be alone. She marked another 'D' on the sheet. I'll go to the lunch, she decided.

She slid open the patio door. The voile curtains caught the warm wind and lapped around her legs. Untangling herself, she stood for a while at the rail and looked out to sea. The only sounds she could hear were of the waves slapping the side of the ship, way below. She sighed and went back inside. She'd go and have a look at the sail-away buffet.

✳

Further along Jenny's corridor on deck seven, Hamish Macleod arrived back at his cabin some time after five and carefully made space among the papers on the dressing-table for his glass of red. He'd brought it from the dining room where he'd done justice to the all-day sail-away buffet. House wines were complimentary. He'd come on the cruise to get some sun and take time to think. He had business decisions that needed to be addressed and he hoped the distance between Scotland and the Mediterranean would make things clearer in his mind. If he decided to sell up, he could start a new life wherever he wanted to. If he didn't, he'd be going back to more of the same, in what he now recognised was a very humdrum life of work, which no longer gave him any sense of satisfaction.

Earlier he'd decided to leave his unpacking until after he'd eaten. Now he set about putting his trousers on the hangers. Hamish was a broad, stocky man. He eyed himself in the full-length mirror. Not bad for a man of almost fifty. Not quite over the hill. Not quite overweight either. His relationship with good whisky over the years had rearranged his waistline, and now he pulled in his stomach. He was fresh-faced and his hair had turned to distinguished silver while he was still in his thirties, a family trait. That was when he'd decided to grow a matching moustache, believing it gave him a rakish look. He unfolded his collection of colourful shirts and cut-off shorts. He shook the creases out of two linen jackets and his dress suit, and draped them over padded hangers. Then he liberated the two bottles of Famous Grouse whisky he'd packed in his check-in luggage and slid them into a drawer beneath his underwear and socks. He knew he wasn't supposed to bring booze on board.

During the meal he'd eyed up the talent among his fellow travellers, but it was a bit early to decide if there were any prospects of a fling. The Filipina bar server was a beauty.

Flirtation, he knew from past experience, was not vetoed, but a dalliance with any of the staff was out of the question.

In the Mistral Suite on deck eight Bud Harris, a film producer and director, and Sonny Carpenter Junior were still a little jet-lagged after their transatlantic flight from New York.

'It's hard to believe it's over, after all those months of preparations,' said Sonny.

Bud agreed. 'I'm glad it is, although it was terrific, even though it took almost as much stage-managing as a Broadway musical.'

'And it cost about the same.'

'I can't wait to see the photographs and who picked up on them.'

The previous few weeks had been a whirlwind of preparations in the run-up to their civil marriage. They had been to a few other such ceremonies for friends, but Sonny, 'style adviser to the stars' and personal shopper to the rich and often famous, had been determined that theirs would outshine them all. It had gone without a hitch, as he had promised. Now it was all behind them and they were settling in to enjoy their honeymoon together.

'I still can't believe we got up on the bridge,' said Sonny, the shorter of the two by a good eight inches. 'That second officer was a looker, wasn't he?'

'You know it annoys me when you comment on good-looking guys.'

'And you know, as I'm always telling you, that it's you I'm with, so stop being a divo. You're better-looking than any of them.'

Sonny reassured him regularly, but Bud could never see himself in that light.

They'd decided to retire early that first night and be ready for the gym and the sun the following day.

'These sunbed tans are all very well but I can't wait to feel the real thing on my body,' Bud said, while Sonny rearranged things. Their butler had done their unpacking, but they liked to have everything just so. The man had also refreshed the ice in their champagne bucket and removed the untouched plate of canapés and cheese that he'd placed there earlier, with some chocolate-dipped strawberries. Their king-size bed had been turned down and there was a marzipan fancy on each pillow.

Sonny popped the champagne cork. 'Let the honeymoon begin,' he said. 'But, please, no more geography lessons, or history ones for that matter. I'll learn everything I need to know on the tours.'

Bud laughed. He loved all the strategic planning, deciding what they should see and what to avoid whenever he travelled anywhere.

'Just remember I'm not a movie in the making. I'm not a project, and I don't need constant stage direction. I'm your spouse now,' Sonny added.

'OK. In that case, let's go to bed.' He opened the door and slipped the 'Do Not Disturb' sign in the slot outside.

Two

GUEST RELATIONS WAS ALWAYS BUSY WITH passengers wanting to change money, needing advice on shore excursions or the doctor's consulting hours, looking for lost property, postcards stamped with the local issue and asking myriad more improbable questions.

Marina and Jack had worked there for a few years and knew how to handle pretty much anything. They knew as soon as a guest opened their mouth to complain if they were genuine or not. They could also tell who would be back again and again with spurious grievances and threats of letters regarding their treatment to head office when they returned home. There was always one on every cruise.

Already on this trip they had met him and his family: an English couple with their adult sons. They had scarcely arrived on board before appearing at the desk. Marina and Jack laid bets on who would make the first complaint. As the family arrived *en masse* they exchanged a look that said, 'Here we go!' Marina had a theory that if the woman was going to do the talking she'd go straight for Jack, assuming she could charm him. His dazzling smile, though, belied a steely intolerance of time-wasters and chancers, and he could spot them a mile away. If a man were complaining, he'd make for her, thinking that because she was a woman she'd be easier to talk round. This time she was wrong. The man ignored her and addressed Jack.

'We're not very happy.'

'I'm sorry to hear that, sir. What's the problem?' asked Jack, smiling at each of them in turn. Another cruise had begun.

Three

THE SUN FOUND A CHINK WHERE THE curtains didn't quite meet and woke Jenny. She looked at her clock, got out of bed and peeped through the opening, her eyes adjusting to the breaking dawn. In front of her she saw a horizon union between a serene sea and an equally serene yellow-tinged sky. She opened the sliding door and went out. It wasn't yet hot, but the promise was there. She stretched and inhaled the salty air, appreciating that there was a certain freedom in being able to stand on her own balcony in her nightie. She felt almost as if she owned the world.

Freedom was a state she was getting used to after eight years of captivity. Not captivity in the sense of being locked up, although there had been times when she had longed for the solitude that that might have afforded her. Instead her shackles were the sort that came with being a possession, an exhibit. She had been relegated to that status very quickly after her marriage to Fergus Ruddy, although it had taken her a while to realise it. She could have been a portrait slotted between her husband's Le Broquy and his dramatic Charlie Flanagan land and skyscapes, which fitted so well in their home, with its acre of gardens and the right postal address. Exhibit five: elegant wife, accomplished and charming hostess.

Her friends had envied her, but they hadn't known the truth: the awful truth. Her husband, soon to be officially her ex, had never allowed her any freedom of any kind. They had met through work. A linguist, Jenny spoke German, Mandarin, Spanish and French, and worked as a translator for an international publishing house on a freelance but almost constant basis. She was also on various panels and was frequently called on when interpreters were needed, both at legal and at official levels. She had met Fergus when a trade delegation was being put together to target the possibilities of Chinese investment in Ireland. The ensuing mission had thrown them together, and when they had returned from the Far East they had become an item. The assignment was deemed a massive success. Millions had been secured in foreign deals and potential alliances, and Fergus was lauded by the press and the government alike for the part he had played.

She admired the masterful way he could sway an argument,

or turn a conversation in the direction it needed to go during difficult negotiations. He had a presence that made people notice him when he walked into a room. He was almost ten years older than her, but she had never seen that as a problem. Now, when she looked back, she realised he was everything her father hadn't been, strong, forceful and decisive. She hadn't equated those traits with domination and violence. Because of the nature of their work they had often travelled together, before and after they had married. As a government adviser to the Department of Overseas Development and Enterprise he was away a lot and she continued with her translations. She worked from their spacious home, often sitting in the garden she loved.

A charmed life, her friends agreed. Little did they know that Fergus treated her like the hired help, measuring out his affection and money. He left cash for her on a table in the kitchen. If she wasn't available for him when he decided he needed her, he often withheld it. In the beginning she had pretended not to notice, but it had got worse. *I should have done something about it then, but I didn't know what to do. What a fool I was.* She felt disloyal even thinking that. She had wanted her marriage to work, desperate not to end up as her parents had, only communicating through their children. It had got to the stage when he hadn't even liked her having her friends to the house, only his. That hadn't happened overnight, but had been a slow progression, ensuring that she felt so uncomfortable when her friends visited that it had been easier not to invite them and meet them elsewhere, while he was at work, pretending that she needed to get out of the house – working from home was too solitary. She had never told anyone about his behaviour, hoping he would change.

When they entertained his contacts and friends at home or at official functions he was the perfect host and spouse – attentive, charming, complimentary and kind. Oh, yes, Fergus could certainly put on a good show when it suited him and when it might help towards his ultimate goal. He left his bonhomie at his golf club and rarely talked to Jenny when no one else was around.

She still got the shivers when she thought of the first time he'd hit her. She'd just stood there in horror, not believing it was happening. He had said sorry instantly and she had screamed that if he ever did that again she'd go to the police. That would put an end to his career and his political aspirations. His reaction to that had been a stream of expletives and door-slamming. Then he had driven away, and hadn't come back until the next day. She had never found out where he'd stayed.

If she had told Leslie then, would he have changed? But that would have meant letting her sister know more than she had wanted to volunteer at the time. Maybe they should have gone for counselling – but Fergus wouldn't have done that in case anyone recognised him.

He had been so different when they had first met and married. He had been genuinely thrilled when she had told him about the baby too, just like his old charming self, showering her with flowers and attention.

When Jenny had finally decided to leave, she'd known she should have done it a long time before. After he'd gone to the office she had taken a case from the attic, packed some clothes and gone. She had a fair bit of money put aside from her own work: her running-away money. It wouldn't last forever, but it would tide her over for a while. She drove to her sister's house and told her what had just happened, the reason why she had left Fergus and wouldn't be going back to him. She had returned once more to the house she had called home for eight years, and only because she'd read in the paper that he was abroad, with some delegation or other. She had collected some more of her things, dropped her keys on the kitchen table where he used to leave her allowance, and driven back to the furnished apartment she now had in Castleknock, thanks to her brother-in-law Richie.

In typical Celtic Tiger fashion, no expense had been spared in doing it up. It had been 'dressed' by an 'interior artist', as Flavia Cantinella liked to call herself, although Richie had been convinced she was from Leitrim originally, one of the Cantwells, who used to have a forge way back. She denied all connection, saying her grandfather was Italian. Whatever her lineage, she had flair and claimed she sourced her pieces to showcase 'an aspiration, a life you'd like to have'. That heralded the arrival of overpriced pieces of Swedish glass, flamboyant Graham Knuttel coffee and tea cups, and tasteful Ceadogán rugs. The silk curtains pooled on the floors throughout, adding several thousand euro to the cost. The bespoke dining furniture had been made by Klimmek-Henderson, the bedrooms were Rolf Benz and the kitchens SieMatic. Everything, from the elaborate security system to the solid-block wooden floors and triple-glazed windows, shrieked affluence. Jenny had never lived in an apartment before – student flats didn't really count – and she loved it.

'Some day I'll get one just like this for myself and do it up the way I want it,' she told her sister. 'My own den, beholden to no one!'

'Talk nicely to Richie and he might let you have it for the right price after things are settled between you and Fergus.'

'I wouldn't hold my breath if I were you,' she replied.

Richie was a good sort, if you ignored his ever-expanding theories on the universe and eternity, which seemed to get wackier with the years. He believed his first dog, Boss, was the conduit between here and there, wherever 'there' was. He was his special messenger who had guided him, when he was asleep, on the big decisions in life.

'Ah, now, Richie,' his wife often teased. 'Why hasn't he given us the lotto or the Euro millions numbers?'

'You may laugh, but he's never yet let me down.'

'Yet being the operative word!'

If it were true that Boss had inexplicable supernatural powers, then his dog's forecasts had been a positive influence because Richie, an astute businessman at the best of times, had made several wise investments and got out of others before the collapse in the noughties – if you didn't count the apartment that Jenny was occupying temporarily.

His wife argued, 'That old canine guide must have lost the scent along the way because he didn't tell you that if you bought three penthouses you'd have no bother getting rid of two but you'd be stuck with the third.'

'Well, dearest, you may scoff but we made a healthy killing on the first two, so I don't mind sitting on it, and it'll help Jenny get settled.'

'Why couldn't she have found someone like you?' Leslie asked her husband.

'I never liked that fellow. Too smarmy by far. I'm just glad we can give her a dig-out until she gets back on her feet.'

He had insisted that Jenny move into the penthouse, as an unofficial caretaker, and he wouldn't hear of her paying rent for it.

'See, ladies, Boss was telling me something all the time. I knew I'd invested in that place for a reason.' The sisters didn't believe him, but they had no arguments against that. 'It would just be lying idle, with things as they are at the moment, so you'll be doing me a favour, keeping it heated and lived in. Stay as long as you like. It was the show apartment so it's furnished. Feel free to put anything you like into it. Make it home and homely.' She protested, but he stopped her. 'You can sort me out when you've taken that arrogant coward to the cleaner's.'

But Jenny had no intention of having any more to do with her husband and told Richie so. 'You can't put a price on how liberated I feel now.'

'Yes you can, and you will!' he insisted. 'That conniving

sod won't want the Ruddy name dragged through the courts. It won't do his political ambitions any good.'

'I don't want revenge. I'm just happy to be free. Besides, he'll never sell that house. It belonged to his parents.'

'Who left him very rich, thank you very much. The scumbag can find other ways to release funds. He has investments, probably an overseas bank account or two, I shouldn't wonder. He's nothing if not canny and, as we all know now, those advisers were making almost as much as the barristers in the tribunals did. Are you OK for money in the meantime?'

'I am, really. I still have my translation work, and now that I'm sorted out with somewhere to live I'll survive very nicely, thanks to you both.'

Leslie told her later, 'You can have my running-away money to fall back on if you need it. I'm not planning to go anywhere just yet.'

She was lucky to have such a family, Jenny mused now. Cruise veterans themselves, they had insisted on giving her this trip. Between them, they seemed to know people everywhere. She'd liked the ship when she'd seen the brochures, especially because it wasn't too large. She wasn't keen on the floating high-rises that you could get lost on and never be found again. The itinerary had appealed too. She'd never been to Israel, or to some of the Greek islands where they would call. She'd have a chance to collect some new memories – ones that didn't include Fergus.

She shivered. Forget him, she told herself. The past is the past. This is a new beginning. She went back inside, excited again. She'd do the deck mile before showering and breakfast. It was a sea day, which meant no ports, and it stretched out invitingly before her.

Up on deck ten, several people had already gathered and two very fit-looking figures were already zooming away, extending the course at one end by climbing up a flight of steps, running around the bow and back down another flight to maximise the benefits. Jenny, a people-watcher, was always fascinated by how easy it was to spot some of the different nationalities. American men, if you couldn't hear them first, were identifiable by their uniformly tidy haircuts, and the women had perfectly matched glow-in-the-dark teeth and long straight legs. The roly-poly ones, like you saw on the *Steve Wilkos Show*, limited their exercise to pilgrimages to the all-day buffets and usually had logos emblazoned across ample bosoms and bottoms. The British were usually colour co-ordinated, with discreet initials on their polo shirts and matching cut-offs, socks and footwear. The Scandinavians were lean, toned and usually out-lapped everyone else in a quietly confident way that seemed to say, 'We do healthy things all the time so this is no big deal.' The Latinos were absent from exercise of any kind, as Jenny would observe over the next few days, other than ambling across deck nine to climb the seven steps to the Jacuzzis by the swimming pool.

Everyone greeted each other, stating their names and promptly forgetting them. One woman, a few feet away from Jenny, didn't introduce herself: she was stick-insect thin. From behind, her bob made her look like a knitting needle, the large wooden type with a rounded knob at the top to stop the stitches falling off. They did a few stretches, then set off to snake around the fitness track thirteen and a half times. The sea was calm, the sky dotted with a few clouds. The ship was moving slowly. There were some fishing boats trawling the waters and another cruise liner in the distance, gleaming white. Otherwise they had the world to themselves.

Now, let me consider my options, thought Hamish, on his way to eat. Room service, the dining room or al fresco from the buffet? It's got to be outside: I've paid for sun and more sun. He piled a plate with fruit, added some yogurt and found a table at the back. That's more like it, he thought, as he watched the ship's wake stretch out behind. This is just the stress buster I need.

He had decided to take the cruise to put some distance between him and the office. His haulage business had sailed through several boom years and now, although it was not doing as well as it had been, it was in no danger of failure. There were other options on the table, options that would allow him to live comfortably somewhere else. He'd always said that he'd like to retire by the time he reached fifty. Now he found himself in the enviable position of having the opportunity to do just that. Making the final decision to hand over or sell up was the difficult part.

He was procrastinating about relocating to the south of England. Facial neuralgia and the biting winds that continually whipped around Edinburgh didn't make happy bedfellows.

Ideally he wanted a place in the sun, probably in Cyprus, but that meant he'd have to find a space for his classic-car collection. If he sold his business he could afford to garage them and hop back and forth when he wanted to. His thoughts were interrupted as the plummy, clipped tones of the couple at the table behind him cut through the air.

'I left my sun hat in the suite before I did that deck mile. I'll come out in a ghastly rash if I sit here,' she said.

'You only had that and your glasses to think about,' he said.

'Oh, Will, darling, do fetch it for me.'

'Why can't you go? It's only one level down,' he said.

'Precisely,' she said. 'And here's my breakfast.'

'Oh, all right, Heather,' he said reluctantly, as a waiter placed carrot juice and an egg-white omelette with mushrooms in front of her.

'So you should,' she said, and added, as an afterthought, 'Thanks, Will.'

By the time he came back with the straw hat the ship had altered course and the sun no longer caught their table. 'You don't need it now,' he said.

'I do,' she said. 'It means I can hide from some of these tiresome people and pretend I haven't seen them. You can take yourself off to the pool, though why you want to expose yourself like that I'll never know. I suspect it's probably so you can eye up the talent.'

The man laughed. 'How well you know me, darling.'

Hamish had to restrain himself from turning to look at

them – it could have been a scene in a situation comedy. He smiled to himself and went in search of some other goodies to eat. After he had polished off a ham omelette he gathered his belongings and headed for the upper deck, away from the main drag, where he could sizzle happily until lunchtime and do his own eyeing up of the talent. I think I'll pop along to that Solo Travellers' Lunch and see what, if anything, it has to offer, he decided.

Around the pool the large sunloungers were filling, many bagged by early risers who had come out to put down their books and belongings, laying claim to their preferred spot. There was no need for that as there were always spaces in abundance, but it seemed to satisfy some basic need: people had to stake out their territory. Jenny settled down and took in her fellow passengers while pretending to read. Not as many British as she'd expected, lots of Americans, some Brazilians, Russians and God only knew who else. An interesting mix, she decided. So far she hadn't heard any Irish accents and was glad. She hoped that no one from home would recognise her as Fergus's wife because she didn't want to have to explain and make excuses for him. She knew that sooner or later it was bound to happen and she also knew she couldn't prevent it. He had put his name to countless organisations and causes and was now instantly recognisable – his mug was everywhere. Lately, however, it had appeared in association with questionable dealings.

Jenny shook away the thoughts and returned to her book, but her concentration was broken by snippets of conversations wafting around her.

'Your thirty-third cruise? Wow, you're veterans.'

'Pete just got the all-clear again, so we decided to celebrate. We had to cancel last year. He was too ill.'

'Isaac and I are celebrating our ruby wedding anniversary.'

'We always go with Azamara or Celebrity after our calamitous experience on …' The name of the offending line was lost in the shrieks of someone who found the water in the pool too cold for their liking.

'The staff are exceptional – can't do enough for you – but that comes from the top down. The captain is a very affable guy, quite young and very dishy too.'

'Never! I'm a cruise virgin. This is my first.'

'Oh, I'm sure you'll love it.' A well-endowed woman with a high ginger hairdo had interjected with that reply. There was nothing virginal about her or the way she was making a show of spreading her towel on her lounger. She straightened and tugged at the top of her leopard-print swimsuit, which had slid perilously close to exposing her breasts. 'Oops,' she said, with a giggle, to the men on either side of her. 'That could have been serious.'

'Did I miss something?' one joked. The other put his sunglasses back on and, from the angle of his head, Jenny reckoned he was still gawking at her, until the woman at his side, probably his wife, gave him a prod in the ribs. He settled back with his e-reader.

Later she wasn't sure if she had dozed or not, or had simply imagined those insights into her fellow travellers' lives. But no, the redhead was still there and she was still flanked by the same men. Jenny was now too hot and moved to the shade. This time she did doze and woke up too late for the lecture she'd planned to attend, and realised that the Savvy Traveller quiz would have begun by now too. She went back to her stateroom to freshen up, before heading towards the main dining room. She wasn't hungry, but she was curious about the other solos on board.

In an area above the main staircase the quiz was still in progress so she sat in a chair at the back. Several of the guests were arguing good-humouredly with the question master as he read out the answers. He was a young man from the entertainment team, with words at will and lots of cheeky banter. He admitted that he didn't actually know if the Spanish Steps were in Rome or the Vatican City. In the end he decided to award points for both answers, which seemed to annoy an elderly pair, who insisted that they were in Rome. 'We've been there four times.'

The gathering dissolved, heralding the start of lunchtime.

Four

NOT WANTING TO APPEAR TOO EAGER, JENNY loitered before making her way to the main restaurant. She was shown to the designated table at which some of the other solo travellers were already seated. The cruise director was standing by to welcome them. 'I never know how many will turn up but it looks like a good few today,' he said to Jenny.

An attractive man with a great smile stood up as she found a chair. 'Hi, I'm John, from England, and you are?'

'Jenny, from Ireland, on my first cruise. Didn't I see you running bright and early this morning, out-lapping everyone?'

'That was me, all right. I like to get it done before it's too hot. This is Hamish,' he said, indicating a silver-haired man with a matching moustache, whose Scottish accent she loved immediately.

'I'm Ben.' He was an older man and was sitting beside the busty redhead, whom Jenny now recognised from the poolside theatrics. She introduced herself as Sylvia.

Beside her a petite lady announced, 'I'm Betty and, although I can't believe it, I've just celebrated my seventy-eighth birthday. All my friends are dying off, so I decided to go on a cruise. I've told my children that if I die while I'm here, they should have me tossed overboard. My first daughter was delighted – much cheaper than a funeral and a burial plot so there'd be more for her to inherit. She's mean, that one, unlike the others – I have four. They'd be happy to pay for a good send-off. They like me.'

More introductions followed those revelations and they were given menus. Each time the waiter came to take the orders, no one had looked at them, still too busy chatting. Eventually Sylvia said, 'Don't go away, because if you do we'll just start yakking again.'

He had just about managed to go around to everybody when the arrival of another man, with a neat beard, had them shuffling up to make space for him. 'I'm Marcus and I'm from Copenhagen.'

'And I'm Sylvia, from London,' she gushed, her gold bangles jingling as she pulled the strap of her revealing sundress back up on her shoulder.

With the candour of people who had never met before and who might never meet again, each explained why they had decided to travel alone and go to the solos' lunch. Hamish had got that rolling when he'd said, 'Right, let's get down to the demographics of the table. In no more than five words your name again, as I'm hopeless at remembering them anyway, and your status.'

'Status? In only five words?' said Betty, the oldest of them all. 'Married, widowed, partnered and single again and I've overrun the word count so I can't tell you about my lovers.'

Ben merely said, 'Widowed, just last year,' and glanced at Betty for sympathy.

'No point in looking back. We have to look forward,' she said, and turned to John. 'I bet a dapper young man like you has a colourful past.'

'John, divorced, only once so far.' He laughed.

'I'm available and I'm Sylvia,' the redhead announced.

Hamish replied, 'So am I. I was divorced, but widowed now, and I'm on the market as well.'

'Too many words,' said Betty. 'What about you?' she asked Jenny.

'I'm separated.'

'And available?' urged Hamish.

'Definitely not,' she replied.

Marcus the Dane told them, 'It's all very recent and I'm not sure what I am – a divorcé in waiting, perhaps, if there is such a thing.'

Well, this is certainly different, Jenny thought, as she looked around the table. They were such an unlikely mix of ages and backgrounds. She noticed that, of them all, Ben seemed most ill at ease. He kept referring to his late wife. Each time he did so,

Betty changed the subject with an ease that suggested she was used to old men telling her their life stories.

The other tables emptied and still they lingered. The maître d', attracted by their laughter and no doubt anxious to release the staff, came over to them. 'You seem to be enjoying the conversation and each other's company, so you may like to continue this evening, with our compliments, in one of our speciality dining rooms. We pride ourselves on our steakhouse. It serves the best beef on the oceans, or you could try the Japanese cuisine. We also have a Mediterranean restaurant.'

They chose the steakhouse, and that was how the improbable group began to form improbable friendships.

When they eventually finished lunch and went their separate ways, Jenny already felt at home on board. She ambled around, familiarising herself with the geography of the ship. She passed the computer room, where several people were ensconced catching up on their emails. Her family had made her promise not to contact any of them unless there was an emergency. They'd said they'd leave her alone too. She studied the list of treatments available outside the spa and decided she would definitely indulge herself, but later in the trip. For now she was happy to let solitude, sun and sea work their magic.

She crossed the upper deck where she'd walked that morning and found herself beside the Drawing Room. She went in to investigate. It had the air of a refined country house, with a fireplace, mahogany cabinets and bookcases, arrangements of armchairs, and circular tables with glossy picture books positioned artfully on them. She noticed printed sheets of puzzles and Sudoku and picked one up. As she turned, she collided with the skinny woman she'd seen on deck at the morning walk. She was half hidden beneath a straw hat and loads of eye makeup.

'I've been traipsing all over the ship looking for those,' she said. 'Must have my fix or I'd die of boredom.'

'It's only one sea day,' Jenny said.

'Oh, it's not being at sea that bores me. It's my husband. He doesn't read, yet he always beats me at Scrabble. How unfair is that? He's more interested in horses and yachts than anything else.'

'I don't know too much about either of those,' said Jenny.

'Sit with Will for half an hour and that'll change, trust me. I'm Heather, by the way,' she said, extending her hand. 'Heather Pembry-Travers. Are you travelling with anyone?'

'Jenny Rahilly, and, no, I'm on my own. I—'

'Lucky you. If you get lonely we're in the Sirocco Suite.'

'Thank you.'

'Better still, come have a sun-downer with us later on. You can meet Will then.'

After that build-up she wasn't sure she wanted to, but she didn't know how to refuse. 'That sounds lovely.'

'See you at five. God knows what sort of motley assemblage he'll have found by then – he's a great one for gathering strays and misfits.' She swanned out of the room, leaving Jenny feeling as though she'd been ambushed.

She took a book on Haifa from a shelf and flipped through it. They'd be there first thing tomorrow morning and she knew very little about the place. She went back outside and settled down to read. Again, distracted by disembodied voices, she found it hard to concentrate, but she was enjoying herself. Day two, a deck mile, a fascinating lunch, a dubious sun-downer date, and dinner with the solo set. She was dying to text her sister and some of her friends to tell them, but instead she lay back with a sigh.

Betty rounded the corner at the ice-cream station, helped herself to a frozen-yogurt cone, turned away and almost crashed into Ben.

'That looks nice. What flavour is it?'

'Vanilla.'

'What's that? Vanilla?' he shouted, cupping an ear with his hand.

'Yes,' she bellowed. 'It's lovely – you should have one.'

'I shouldn't. If Esther, my late wife, were here she'd warn me off because of my diabetes.'

'I'm sure she would,' said Betty, 'but at my age I have fewer days left than I've lived so I'm going to eat, drink, and be as merry as I can. Go on, spoil yourself.'

'You're absolutely right. I will,' he said, with a determination that suggested he'd decided to press the red button that would launch the first manned British space shuttle.

'I'm off to read my book. See you later,' she called. She saw him smile as he licked the forbidden treat. Maybe he wasn't that bad – if he'd only stop talking about his late lamented Esther. He hadn't said much else at lunch. Maybe he just needed to loosen up.

Five

A DISTINGUISHED-LOOKING MAN OPENED THE door to the Sirocco Suite. 'I'm Will. Who do we have we here?'

Jenny introduced herself, explaining she'd met Heather earlier.

'Oh, you're the puzzle lady.'

'Well, I'm not too sure about that, but I believe doing them keeps the brain active.'

'Don't believe a word of it. I have a friend – we were at school together – who used to set crossword puzzles for one of the national papers and was completely doo-lally by fifty-four. Away with the fairies now. Very tough on his family.

Recognises no one. Never laughs or smiles. Expressionless. Just sits there reciting Humpty Dumpty, the bits he can remember. Anyway, no place for gloom, this, go on through. The others are on the balcony.'

She had to restrain herself from commenting on the wide hallway and the spacious sitting room that led outside. She was thrilled with her own stateroom and balcony, but this was palatial. She passed a well-stocked bar and a half-played Scrabble game on the coffee table. She had to stop herself looking at the words on the board. What was it about Scrabble that brought out in her the compulsion to see whether she would have done any better, and the level of play. She refrained but he had noticed.

'Do you play?' he asked.

'It's the only board game I really enjoy. I played competitively in college and I've been hooked ever since. '

'Me too. We'll have to have a game one day. I'm addicted, I'm afraid. Heather goes mad when I pack the board, but I can't stand those fiddly travel sets.' She followed him onto the veranda. The Sirocco Suite's was much larger and deeper than those on the deck below and wrapped around one corner of the ship's stern. There were already six other people out there.

Heather greeted her.

'This is really luxurious,' Jenny said,

'Yes, it is rather,' Heather responded. 'Everyone, this is Jenny. She's Irish ... Oh, I should have made name-tags for us all. I'm hopeless at remembering. Tell each other your names again, will you? We're drinking champagne. Would you rather have something else? Will, get Jenny a drink, will you? There are canapés too. Do help yourself.'

Will obliged and handed her a glass of champagne. He'd met the older couple at the buffet earlier and they had fallen into conversation as they'd inspected the aisles of food..

'Do you sail?' he asked, addressing his question to everyone. No one did.

'We keep a yacht on the water in Cornwall. *Diva* she's called. She's a thirty-footer. Get down there as often as we can unless it clashes with the races, you know. Does anyone follow the horses?'

'I hate racing. The only good thing about it is that I get a new hat every time,' a woman said. She pointed to a man who was now talking to Will. 'That's my husband over there, Paul. He never objects to what I spend on my racing outfits, so I go mad, tossing in an extra pair of shoes or a bag.'

'Whatever they cost, it's probably not as much as he loses, if he's anything like Will. We take a box at Ascot every year,' Heather said.

'We're not that serious about it,' another woman said, 'but we do have a sweep once or twice a year in the office, on the Grand National and big ones like that. I once won nearly three hundred pounds.'

'It's a matter of studying form if you want to be serious about it,' someone else said.

'I don't know about that,' the glamorous woman with him joined in. 'I think it's pure luck. I always pick my horses by the colours of the jockey's racing silks and I never do spots.'

'That's true,' her partner said. 'And she has more luck than any of us.'

'What about you, Jenny?' Heather asked. 'You Irish are renowned for your bloodstock.'

She laughed. 'My ex-husband once had a share in a horse. I think he owned a foreleg, but it never came anywhere except last. I think they described it as the also-ran.'

'It's not a game to be in any more,' Will said. 'Damned Inland Revenue take most of it from you, these days, anyway. I feel I'm working for them. What kind of business are you in?' he asked the older man.

'I'm a consultant in nephrology, and my wife teaches history.'

'Ah, you boys can salt away all those private consultation fees.'

Heater interrupted him: 'Don't be such a bore, Will. Do you ever stop thinking about money?'

'Sometimes.' He smiled at her lasciviously.

The history teacher tactfully changed the conversation. 'I've been looking forward to this for ages, seeing the sun for a change and some of the places I've never been to before.'

'Oh, I never do the sun – Irish skin. I inherited it from my mother with Catholic guilt,' Heather said. 'And I hate those excursions – flocks of people being herded about like sheep, the only difference being that the shepherds have an umbrella instead of a crook.'

Taken aback, the other woman muttered, 'I can't agree with you there.' She looked at her husband for support. 'We find the trips informative and fascinating, especially if the guide is good.'

'And we've never been to Israel before,' he agreed. 'I've been reading up on it for months.'

'How tiresome. It's our first visit too, but I'll watch the video of the lecture in my stateroom. Less chance of meeting a sniper there than on land, eh?' She laughed. 'Are they still at war or is that just the Syrians? I can never keep up with these things.' The others smiled at her.

Jenny was glad she was on her own because if she'd still been with Fergus he'd have launched forth on the Palestinian–Israeli conflict and he hated to lose an argument.

'Well, darling, I'll go ashore,' Will said to his wife. 'Can't go to the Holy Land and see nothing of it.'

The guests talked of their travels, the books they were reading, the ship and where they had cruised before. Jenny was quickly realising that cruisers seemed to have an insatiable need to know where everyone they met had already been, how often and with which lines.

As the hour passed, Jenny was surprised by how easily everyone seemed to fit in, as though they had known each other for ages. It had been the same at lunch. She also knew, from past holidays, that she'd leave the ship after two weeks and probably never contact any of them again, much less remember them a year from now. But for the moment their worlds had intersected and she was happy to be part of that coincidence.

'Do you come to London often?' the nephrologist asked Jenny.

'Yes. We – I come over several times a year, on business mostly. I do a bit of work for one of the publishing houses there, but I have some friends there too and try to tie it in with some pleasure.'

'Are you a writer?'

'A linguist.'

'That's impressive,' another man said. 'Are you travelling on your own?'

'Yes.'

'Is that difficult?' the one she remembered as Paul asked.

'Well, I've done a lot of it in my professional capacity, especially in Asia, China mostly, but I haven't gone on holiday alone before. If today is anything to go by, then, no, it's not! It might be different when I go on the day trips, but there's always the guide to annoy if I get lonely.'

'Well, you know us now,' he said. 'Feel free to annoy us any time.'

'I might well take you up on that.'

'Why not join us for dinner tonight?' his wife suggested.

'Oh, I'd love to but, believe it or not, I have an arrangement already. Perhaps another night.'

'We'll keep you to that,' Paul said. 'I'd love to hear more about China. We have it on our list.'

'It's fascinating'

'Top-ups before the sun sets,' Will announced, and went round with the bottles.

They stood by the rail looking out to where a solitary cloud shared the open sky with the fast-disappearing orange globe.

It coloured the bubbling wake that spread out behind them as the engines churned the water and they moved closer to their first port of call.

'Well, that was worth seeing,' someone remarked, and the others agreed.

'Here's to many more just like it,' said Heather, clinking glasses with Jenny.

Six

THE LIGHT CHANGED SUDDENLY, NOT THE gentle gloaming Hamish was used to in Scotland but rather a hasty retreat from daytime. He stood up. He'd been enjoying the solitude on his balcony where he'd been studying some brochures he'd brought him – properties in Cyprus. He already owned two in Ayia Napa and was dithering as to whether he should buy another or offload those and invest the lot in a new hotel that some friends were building in Paphos. It seemed a solid bet and Cyprus was always at the top of the winter-sun destination lists. He'd make sure there would always be a room for him there too.

I could always pass on the running of the business to that ruffian Mark, he thought. He knows it'll probably come to him some day – and he's the only one who's shown any interest in working in it. I could even let him run it for a while and oversee it from afar. Or I could make a clean break and take the offer from McDougall Brothers. That wouldn't please Mark, though. He's family and we Macleods are a bit sparse when it comes to kin … He splashed a measure of whisky into a glass and ran the shower.

Marcus still got mad every time he thought of Malena with a lover. He hadn't seen it coming and that maddened him too. How could he have been so blind? Everything had seemed so right, so normal, until April. Before April he'd always known where he was heading and why. And Malena was always by his side. If they had been rowing or he had sensed something was wrong, it might have been different, but it had come out of nowhere. Now it was September and, just six months after his wife had left him, he was on holiday on his own, feeling very lonely. If he were honest with himself, he was feeling more than a bit lost and helpless too. Why had he booked such a long holiday? A week would have been enough. Although he wouldn't admit it, it had become apparent to everyone he worked with that he had become manic since Malena had left, working every hour of the day and into the night. That was his way of dealing with the loss.

He opened his laptop, clicked on his diary and saw

nothing but delivery dates for shipments that he wasn't there to oversee.

Marcus knew he'd left the company in good hands and the last thing they'd want was him interfering. I'm turning into Dad, he mused. I used to hate it when he did this after he'd supposedly left me in charge. But he'd had things to hide and resented me finding out how bad things really were.

Marcus had known something was up when his father hadn't let him look at the accounts. He'd become a master of deception by then. Marcus's only brother had had no interest in the business and had emigrated to the States immediately after qualifying in computer sciences. When Marcus had finally taken control, the company had been on the verge of bankruptcy, despite full order books.

He thought back to the phone call from the bank that had been put through to him by mistake. He'd always believed that that was the worst thing that could happen to him, and would never forget the look on his father's face when he'd told him he'd taken legal advice and the only way to keep the business going was for him to retire with his honour intact. But losing Malena had been worse.

Marcus had been determined to salvage the business and had done so with a lot of hard work, long hours and a supportive wife who understood what was at stake. Some nights he'd even slept in his office, too tired to drive home. He had found great goodwill out there for him and his errant father, who had been gambling away the profits for years. He had managed to cover his tracks pretty well until a series of heavy losses had come to the attention of his bank. It was only out of allegiance to an old friend and sailing companion that his bank manager had kept him afloat, but when Marcus's salary cheque had bounced it had rung the alarm bells. And then he'd taken that phone call.

Marcus had turned the company around and had become a very successful businessman, but he still had niggling doubts. When he wasn't around, he feared that if he took his eye off the ball things might slide again, and he couldn't afford to let that happen. It was a much more competitive and tough business world nowadays and there was no place for sentiment.

I'm not really checking up, he thought, just reassuring myself that everything's running according to plan. I'm not used to being on my own. Before, I always had Malena, even when I was away on business.

In later years his diary had usually been full of appointments, work-related and social engagements, which he had attended with his lawyer wife. Several high-profile cases had come her way early in her career and brought her into focus on the corporate front. Now she had a waiting list of clients who would not go to litigation without having Malena Nielsen on their team. Her reputation also attracted the serious criminals, who were prepared to pay anything to have her defend them.

Marcus was very comfortable with her lifestyle and achievements and took great pride in her successes. What with their new cars every year, bespoke tailoring, summer house, boat and holidays in Santa Monica where his brother lived, he had hankered for nothing. With client meetings and keeping to schedules, thrashing out contracts and the satisfaction of clinching the next deal, he had been contented with his life. He had thought she was too.

Thinking of Malena and the hopelessness he felt made him angry again. He closed his laptop and went outside to look at the sea as the sun was setting. He thought of other sunsets he and his wife had shared on their yacht, on holidays, and at their weekend cottage, nearer home in Klampenborg, where they often used to walk at weekends, discussing her cases and getting excited over one of his new clients or orders.

Where had the time gone? They had been teenage sweethearts, sharing their first kisses. He hadn't known then that they'd get together again after university. *And we knew as soon as we did that we'd end up married to each other.* If they'd had children, would it have made any difference? She'd not have left then, would she? Maybe she would.

His sister had stepped in, making sure he was surviving. She appreciated the efforts he had made to save the family business and now felt she had a part to play in minding Marcus through the dark days, inviting him to dinner, and even trying a bit of matchmaking with some of her separated friends. He knew what she was up to and vetoed that. Just days after he had mentioned to her that he was considering a cruise, she had showered him with brochures that included itineraries from South Africa to India. The more of them he had read, the more he had liked the idea of getting away.

Once he'd made up his mind, it had happened very quickly, and here he was, planning to dine with the people he had met for the first time earlier that day.

Going to that lunch had been a spur-of-the-moment decision. He had been reading the newsletter by the pool when he had come across the notice. He had scarcely had time to get back down to his cabin, spray on some deodorant, pick out a polo shirt and slacks and head to the dining room.

When he'd realised the table was full, he'd almost walked on, but the cruise director had noticed him and they'd made space. Now he was dressing again, this time in a smart open-neck shirt and chinos. He took his phone and key card and left for the restaurant.

'Darling,' Sonny called to Bud, who was just stepping out of the shower, 'shall I wear the velvet or the linen jacket with these pants?'

'You look fabulous in either,' Bud replied, wrapping himself in a towelling bathrobe.

'I know I do. So do you, darling, but I don't have your long legs so I have to go for maximum effect on the top half. What are you wearing?'

Choice was not a problem: choosing was. These fashionistas had paid for excess baggage to ensure they would have the right belts, shoes, shirts, ties, tops, shorts, swimwear, bags and dinner jackets for any occasion. They also wanted to be sure their outfits wouldn't clash.

'Come here and make me happy before we go to dinner,' Bud said, throwing off his robe and jumping onto the squashy bed.

'If I give in to you all the time, you'll start taking me for granted.'

'You know that won't happen, you clown. Now, come over here – or do you want me to chase after you down the corridor buck naked?'

'That'd give our neighbours something to talk about.'

It was another hour before the pair emerged from their suite, dressed impeccably, the taller one in subtle shades of cream and mustard, the shorter in lavender and plum. They were accessorised with highly polished shoes and designer belts. They walked hand in hand to the dining room.

After the sun-downers in their suite Will and Heather stayed outside on their balcony while the glasses and the remains of the canapés were removed. At times like these Will yearned for peace and quiet, time to digest the conversations and register the people behind them. He knew, however, that Heather's acerbic and almost clinical dissection would begin at any minute. She rarely had a good word to say about anyone.

He was surprised when she announced, 'That Irish woman is quite interesting. I overheard her saying she speaks several languages. Did you notice she got flustered, began a sentence with "we" and then changed to "I"? She says she's often in

London. I wouldn't be at all surprised if she's having an affair with someone. Maybe he's on the ship. I must keep an eye open.'

Will let her witter on. He had managed to persuade her to go ashore with him the next day when they docked at Haifa and was reluctant to rock the proverbial boat just now.

Seven

JENNY SAT IN THE LOUNGE, NOT WISHING to be first in the restaurant where the maître d' had made their reservation. John and Marcus arrived within minutes of each other. Both self-assured and urbane, they gave the impression of being very comfortable with themselves, John long-legged and confident, Marcus more rigid and formal. Ben and Betty followed. It was then that Jenny stood up and made her entrance. Seconds later Hamish appeared. He reminded her of some film star in western movies, and she felt he wouldn't look out of place in a cowboy outfit and ten-gallon hat, the silver moustache adding gravitas to his sardonic grin.

By the time the wines had been decided upon and the orders taken, Sylvia was the main attraction. If she had been eye-catching at lunchtime she was now shamelessly alluring. She had exchanged the sexy sundress for a figure-hugging number that left little to anyone's imagination. She was artfully made up and her red hair was carelessly arranged with wispy tendrils curling around her face. An assortment of gold bangles on both her wrists jingled as she waved her arms about when she spoke. She did this a lot.

'I managed to get rid of my reprobate eventually, but it was hard work. He was never cut out to be a husband, but he was a great boyfriend and father. He wasn't suitable in my parents' eyes and maybe I should have listened to them. If I had, though, I wouldn't have had my lovely daughter. I was just nineteen and unmarried.'

'That must have been difficult,' Betty said.

'It wasn't what my respectable Jewish parents had envisaged for their only offspring. They had made sure to separate Immanuel and me and he was sent off to Israel to study before I discovered I was pregnant. They wanted me to give the baby up for adoption, but I refused. When we met up again seven years later we got married. Now I sometimes think we did it as revenge on our parents. They all went to the same synagogue. They had conspired against us and we were determined to get back at them. But we had good times together.'

'When did you separate?' Jenny asked.

'Unofficially about two years ago, after almost ten years, but officially earlier this year.'

'Did it take you long to get used to being on your own again after being married so long?' asked Marcus.

'I'll let you know at the end of the cruise.'

'What about you, Jenny? Did you slip back into being single easily?'

She laughed. 'Like Sylvia, I'll let you know at the end of the cruise.'

'It's that recent, then?' said John.

'Just two months. Right now I'm in the twilight zone that I'm sure some of you have experienced, not really knowing how to behave and feeling odd when I'm among couples. It's kind of weird. I still say "we" when I mean "I".'

'You'll soon get over that,' said John. 'I did it for ages. You might change your mind after being away and get back together when you go home.'

'I won't. It's over.'

'I've been single for a good while and I love it, most of the time, but I'd like to have someone special.' Hamish smiled mischievously at Jenny. 'I've never had much luck with Irish lasses – so far.'

Ben jumped in to announce, 'I'm a widower. Just over a year now. Esther and I were married for more than forty years. Don't hold with all this divorce, open marriages and wife-swapping.'

'I see he's read the how-to-win-friends books,' Hamish muttered to Jenny.

Betty broke the ensuing silence: 'I don't think anyone does, dear. No one walks up the aisle deciding that it'll do until something better comes along. Well, maybe some men do, but do you, ladies?' she asked, and added impishly, before they could answer, 'Perhaps we should try to find a new lady for Ben before the cruise is over.'

'Maybe it'll be you, Betty,' said John. 'Are you on the lookout?'

'If that's an offer, you'll do nicely, thank you, John. I've always fantasised about having a toy-boy and you're very easy on the eye.'

'So have I,' said Sylvia, leaning back to give him a closer once-over. 'Although he may be too old to qualify for me. I'd need someone in his late twenties. But let's not flatter him. It doesn't do, does it, Jenny?'

'I haven't tried. Obviously I'm totally out of practice. I haven't flirted with or flattered anyone for a while.'

'Wasn't it Eleanor Roosevelt who said she was very flattered when they named a rose after her?' said Marcus.

'I would be too,' said Jenny. 'What a lovely tribute.'

'Well, I believe she was,' Marcus continued, 'until she saw it listed in a horticultural catalogue and its performance was described as "no good in a bed, but fine up against a wall".'

'Is that true?' asked Sylvia.

'I think so,' he replied.

'I met a wonderful partner on a cruise, and we had great years together,' Betty said, 'but he was a few years older than me and I think I wore him out.'

'Oh, I am sorry,' said John.

'Don't be. He's not dead. He just acts it. He opted out of

life. He stopped travelling and going out. We never moved in together, thank goodness. We always kept our independence. He lives with an equally fossilised cousin in Manchester now, I think, or maybe it's Coventry. Zimmer frame races are the highlight of their lives, and growing tomatoes. Their only conversation is about joint replacements, fertilisers and, of course, funerals. I mustn't forget the funerals. They love them.'

'I still miss my wife, Esther. We were married for more than forty years. She had a hip replacement—'

'Yes, dear, so you told us,' said Betty. 'That's a long time.'

'Gutsy old bird,' whispered Hamish to Jenny.

'I may have white hair but I'm not deaf,' she said across the table to him.

'I am a bit,' said Ben. 'So was my wife.'

Hamish ignored that. 'Well, Betty, I wasn't saying it as a criticism, more in admiration. I think you're great, and young John here might have a bit of competition from me for your affections, although I'm unlikely to fit into the toy-boy box.'

'But that Scottish accent would melt butter,' said Jenny, laughing.

'And a few hearts,' Sylvia put in. Hamish's eyes fleetingly scanned her low-cut front.

'Predatory' was the word that sprang to mind as Jenny observed Sylvia flirt easily with all the men. It made her feel decidedly rusty in the charm department. Hamish was trying hard to keep his eyes off Sylvia's cleavage and failing hopelessly. Marcus was more circumspect while John seemed far more interested in the conversation.

The cruise director had appeared. 'May I intrude on your evening and add another lady to your party? This is Kathy Troy. She's looking after our guest computer room for a few months. It's her first trip with us and I found her sitting all alone.'

'She should be happy with this table of delightful misfits,' said Hamish, standing up to pull out a chair for her.

'I'm Jenny. Don't let him frighten you off. Some of us are actually very nice. Where are you from?'

'Brisbane,' she replied, and that was the height of her conversation. She said hardly anything else all evening, except to answer Ben's questions, which he repeated several times.

'Can I use the Internet room any time? I want to keep in contact with my daughter and she works in the day.'

Kathy told him the opening hours were in the newsletter and that they were also pasted on the window outside the room. 'Usually people just send their messages then and read the replies later, what with different time zones and suchlike.'

'But there's only an hour's difference,' he protested.

'Yes, but the ship goes to Asia and South America at other times, so we go into other time zones too, you know.' She turned away from him, ending the conversation.

Looking across the table at her, Jenny wondered what had enticed her away from her home for a whole season on the seas. She didn't seem to be outgoing enough to fit into such an environment. Most of the crew Jenny had met, from the waiting staff to the entertainment team, were confident and oozing with personality. Maybe Kathy, too, was running away.

Jenny's speculation ended when she realised that Betty was in the spotlight, continuing to entertain them with details of her love affairs and lovers. It seemed she had had plenty of both.

'You meet all sorts as you go through life, if you look about you,' Betty said. 'Some brighten up your world, even for a little while, but others drag you down. I've learned to avoid them. Toxic vacuums, I call them – they suck the energy out of a room the minute they open the door. I've met too many of them. They're the only regret I have, for the time they wasted, yet if I hadn't met them I wouldn't have been able to appreciate the good ones.'

'Very sensible. Love them and leave them is my motto,' Hamish drawled.

Everyone had comments to make on that remark, and eventually other conversations began as the empty dishes were removed and spaces cleared for the next course. Marcus tried to draw Kathy out about Brisbane, where he had business connections he visited, but she wasn't very forthcoming.

John told Jenny he was temporarily retired.

'You can't be. You're far too young.'

'That's why I said temporarily. I'm taking a year out of the rat race – time for myself. I was a bit of a workaholic, and although I loved what I did and it gave me marvellous opportunities to see the world, I lost out on other things.'

'That seems to be a problem of our times. It's difficult to get the balance right,' Jenny agreed.

'Is anyone coming to the casino after dinner?' Hamish asked.

Marcus said a definite no, which carried with it implications of hell and damnation, as though the casino were the deepest pit into which anyone could descend. When he saw that his answer had raised eyebrows, he added, 'I don't gamble.'

'Neither do I,' said Jenny. 'Well, not seriously. The company needn't order another vessel in anticipation of what I'll lose. In gaming terms it would hardly constitute a bet at all. I'm going to play the machines – a penny a pop!'

'I'm going to go to the theatre to see the show. It's the musicals tonight,' Betty said, and Ben nodded. That was his plan too, and she didn't look overjoyed.

Hamish said, 'Well, I'm heading to the den of iniquity because I noticed they stock some very good malts in the bar.'

'Are you into your whiskies?' asked John. 'I used to be the brand manager for a well-known distillery from your neck of the woods in Scotland. It involved lots of travel and tastings, so by the time I moved on I'd acquired quite a fondness for the stuff.'

'Nice job! I like to think I'm a bit of a connoisseur,' Hamish replied. 'I've spent enough money acquiring that status.'

'What about you, Jenny, Sylvia? Are you whisky drinkers?'

'Yes.' Sylvia was, and Jenny was willing to learn. 'Right,' said John. 'Then let's go and begin Jenny's education.'

As she stood up, Hamish was already escorting Sylvia ahead of them while Ben was waiting for Betty. They left Kathy at the table talking to Marcus about the broadband packages on board.

The corridors to the theatre ran past both sides of the casino so you couldn't avoid it unless you went down a deck, walked along the corridor to the next bank of lifts or stairs and came back up again. Cleverly located, to attract unsuspecting punters, it was ostentatious and bright, in complete contrast to the rest of the vessel.

Hamish and John had an animated debate on the virtues of one single malt against another, engaging the barman in their observations. Sylvia whispered, 'I'd prefer a gin and tonic,' but Jenny just laughed and Hamish ordered his recommendation for them all.

From their bar stools the dinner companions observed the goings-on around them. Already knots of people had gathered by the blackjack and roulette tables, and every so often loud murmurs erupted as someone won. The one-armed bandits were fully automated and required only the press of a button to activate them. Two ladies of a certain age sat engrossed side by side. Lost in anticipation of a big win, they pressed their index fingers down with deliberation and sat back between each move, waiting as the dials spun. Others moved around, trying different games. The occasional win was accompanied by flashing lights and hurdy-gurdy fanfares as the coins fell merrily into the cup below. The women smiled at each other when they were successful and went on playing the same machines. Such winning symphonies attracted other players who hoped to have the same luck. Jenny noticed that invariably when someone had exhausted their credit or pot of coins and left a machine, the next person to sit there would often win the big one that their predecessor had been convinced would be theirs.

'That's very strong and I imagine something of an acquired taste,' Jenny said as the first sip of malt took her breath away. 'Wow.'

'Add some spring water,' advised Hamish. 'We purists say it should be from the same source as that used in the making of the spirit, which might be a problem in the middle of the Mediterranean. Don't ever use tap water, though, as that's probably been chlorinated or treated with chemicals and it'll ruin it.'

'Can I have soda with mine?' asked Sylvia. 'That's the way I like it.'

'Sacrilege,' Hamish replied. 'It'll mask the aroma and the complexity of the flavours.'

'It's really a matter of preference,' John told her. 'If you don't like that, Jenny, we'll try a different one next.' He slid his key card discreetly to the barman, telling him to put the tab on his bill.

After a while Hamish and Sylvia left Jenny and John at the bar. They took their glasses with them and wandered from table to table, watching the expressions on the faces of those with serious intent and those who were happy to wager a fixed amount and enjoy the fun, win or lose.

The colourfully dressed guys who seemed to be on a winning streak at the roulette table had caught Jenny's attention. The one dressed in shades of lavender favoured evens. He told the croupier and the onlookers, who had gathered to enjoy the spectacle, that they had a system. The taller man stacked the increasing hoard of chips in front of him, while the other scooped his into an untidy pile.

'It's not a system. It's based on our superstition. If we start on red then we won't change to black or vice versa. It worked for us in Vegas, so we're sticking to it here,' the taller man told them all as the game stopped while the cameras over the table were called in to clarify whether someone's bet had been placed too late for payout.

'Have you ever been to Vegas, Juan?' the lavender man asked the croupier, who wore a name-tag.

'Not yet.' The bet had been valid: the punter was paid and the game restarted.

The taller man lost the next spin and his two subsequent ones. His friend kept winning. He smiled as Juan shoved another pile of chips across the table. 'Way to go, man! Keep it coming, Juan.'

The taller man was gathering his winnings. 'I'm cashing in,' he said, depositing some in the tip slot.

'I don't want to go just yet. I'm having fun.'

'Obviously! Well, I'm not!' the other retorted, pushing his way through the onlookers and flouncing out. The shorter one stayed at the table.

'Trouble in Paradise,' Sylvia whispered to Hamish.

'Looks like it. Do you want to play?'

'I'll give it a miss tonight.'

'I wouldn't mind going up to the nightclub to see what sort of music they play. We could have a nightcap up there.'

At the casino bar John and Jenny were still chatting. She tried to suppress a yawn and failed.

'Am I that boring?'

'Not at all. It's been a long and lovely day, but I think I'll go outside and enjoy some sea air before turning in.'

'Do you want to be on your own or …?'

'Of course not. I want to take full advantage of these balmy nights. We don't get enough of them in Ireland.'

Outside they climbed the stairs to the upper deck where Jenny had taken her early-morning walk. They strolled to the other side of the ship where the moon spread a silvery path across the water.

'Isn't this fantastic?' she said. 'I thought I'd find it difficult to unwind, but I'm totally relaxed already, and after only one full day.'

'I used never to be able to relax. Work was all that mattered. I didn't realise that then, and now that I do, it's too late to change some things.'

'That's because of technology – we're available around the clock now by text or email. Even if I ignore them they'll pop into my mind just as I'm about to go to sleep and nag away until I have to get up and attend to them. Sad, isn't it? I've been forbidden to text or email anyone on this trip and they promised they'd not get in touch unless a tsunami hits Dublin.'

'Well, that's not likely to happen, is it? Are they trying to tell you something?'

'Probably, although I think their motives were altruistic – they just want me to switch off from everything and everyone and have a good time.'

'It's not so easy to switch off. Wouldn't you think with all the communications we have now that we'd have been able to eliminate a lot of business travel? The fact is that people like to see you and look into your eyes before committing to anything,' John said, 'so we're constantly on the go.'

'I fall into that category, I'm afraid. I like to see who I'm dealing with.'

'I have enough air miles to fly me around the world several times, yet when my mother died a few years ago, I was away, and I have to live with the fact that I never got to say goodbye to her.'

'I'm sure she'd forgive you.'

'I'm sure she would, but I see the unspoken accusation in my old man's eyes every time I go away. He can't get his head around the madness of flitting around the globe and living out of suitcases. He thinks my newly developed passion for cruising is insane, a waste of good money. As for my retirement, well, that always elicits a good rant. Too young to retire. Surely I should look ahead to the next rainy day. He grew up in a large family and money was very scarce. He was in the one job all his life. He was always putting his cash away for something.

Now that he has enough to live on comfortably he doesn't because he never learned how to spend.'

'That's sad. Would you take him with you on one of your cruises or would you drive each other mad?'

'He wouldn't go. He doesn't like travelling, and since Mum died, he hasn't gone anywhere other than the Lake District with his darts club and for the odd weekend to see my brother in Manchester.'

'I bet he's very proud of you.'

'If he is, he wouldn't say it. He never could.'

'Aren't families funny? He probably tells all the other darts guys what a terrific son you are.'

'I wouldn't be too sure about that. It's not his way.'

They stood quietly, leaning on the wooden rail. In the distance two other cruise ships sailed in the opposite direction.

'He blames my lifestyle for my marriage break-up too, and there he's probably right, not that he approved of my Oriental choice. I hadn't even noticed it was in difficulty. The first inkling I got was when a strange family came to the door just after I'd arrived back from a conference in Kuala Lumpur. They were calling to collect the dog – my dog. I didn't even know he was looking for a new home!'

'Never!'

'I promise you. We met in Malaysia – not the dog, my wife and me – and after a few years we moved to the UK. She spent a lot of time on the phone and online to her family and she decided to go home. She didn't like the weather, the food or me very much any more, but she had overlooked telling me that. I swear the dog knew more about it as he trotted off without a backwards glance. Man's best friend, how are you? I think now, on reflection, that his betrayal was worse than hers.'

'How long ago was that?' asked Jenny.

'About four years. What about you? Are you happily single?'

'You don't really want to know about all that. My story's not nearly as interesting as yours,' she answered, unwilling to share it with anyone yet, still embarrassed at what had happened in and to her life.

'I doubt it,' he said, smiling at her. 'Maybe you'll tell me another time.'

'Maybe I will. Now I'm off to bed.'

He leaned over to kiss her lightly on the cheek, and she smelt the merest hint of citrusy cologne.

Eight

IN THE BEGINNING HE HADN'T BEEN CRUEL.
His infrequent outbursts of temper had frightened her. The
first time Fergus launched out she'd tried to excuse it as an
accident, although she knew it hadn't been. The punch had
been aimed at her stomach. When he came back the next day
he promised, 'I'll make it up to you. We'll go out for dinner
tomorrow night, to the bistro. I'll never do anything like that
again. I'm so sorry.'

'My brothers would kill you if they knew you'd done that,'
Jenny said. 'If you ever lay a finger on me again, I'll tell them.'

He never hit her after that until … She pushed that event
away. But she recalled how his temper surges had seen him

smash decanters, take a fire iron to a mirror, sweep dishes off a table and throw plates of food across a room. He was always remorseful, but each episode eroded and eventually killed whatever feelings she had had for him.

He had started going on and on about her inability to give him a son. She didn't want to have his child so she took her contraceptive pills out of their foil wrappers and hid them in an old vitamin bottle in the bathroom cabinet. He never suspected anything. She must have got careless, though, because she conceived, and Fergus became again the solicitous man she'd thought she had married.

He couldn't do enough for her. He went with her for the first ultrasound scan and put the grainy images in his wallet to show to anyone he could. He told the doctor he couldn't wait for the next ones, which might just reveal whether they were going to have a boy or a girl. Jenny didn't care what it was and didn't want to know. The secret and anticipation were all part of the mystery of pregnancy for her. She didn't tell him that the father determined the sex. The medic told Fergus that the scans weren't always conclusive, and he wouldn't be the first father to go home to a blue nursery with a little daughter in his arms.

They had just got home from that appointment when a reporter from the *Daily Tribune* tracked him down on the home phone. Until then, Fergus had managed to keep his private life away from the media glare, except when it suited him to be seen. He had kept Jenny in the dark, too, about what was really happening. She hadn't known the press were after him.

He had been as fascinated as she was by the dodgy bankers and politicians who were finally being jailed for scams of fantasy-writer proportions. Because of his involvement as an adviser, his name had come up several times, and that morning it had been mentioned again, in the High Court, in relation to a payments-to-politicians inquiry. Now the reporter wanted a statement.

She watched him blanch as he took the call. He was cocky and spoke too quickly – he always did when he was wrong-footed.

'I'm clean. You don't have to worry about anything,' he assured her. 'Just some little prick trying to make a name for himself with his editor.' He had had a few brandies, which was unusual for him on a week night. He reassured her that nothing could be traced to him: there would be no paper trail, no chain of contacts and no written communications.

'That reporter's a persistent bastard. He thinks he has a story that'll make headlines but, by God, I'll make sure he won't use my name to get them.'

Jenny recognised the signs that heralded one of his irrational outbursts and used her pregnancy as an excuse to go to bed early. He stayed downstairs, drinking.

She'd known something was wrong when she woke. She'd looked at the clock and it was five past four, but the bed beside her was empty. She got up to go downstairs, and felt stickiness between her legs. She had been lying in a wet bed. She switched on the light and saw blood. She didn't know what to do. If she moved she might make things worse. She called his name, several times, but she knew he wouldn't hear her: the bedroom was at the front of the house, the sitting room at the back. She dialled his mobile but he didn't answer, so she called for an ambulance.

Then she rang the house phone and eventually woke Fergus sufficiently from his stupor to get him to open the gates and the hall door to let the paramedics in. He had just come upstairs when she saw the blue lights flashing and heard wheels on the gravel outside.

It was too late, even before she left for the hospital. There was too much blood. The ambulance crew were kind and efficient. Fergus kept telling them he wanted a son. He also wanted to drive behind the ambulance, but one of the attendants stopped him. 'You're way over the limit, mate. Come with us, or you'll be off the road much longer than one night.'

As the vehicle left the house, no one noticed the car slipping into the lane behind it. Whatever had happened, the reporter who had been sent to shadow Fergus knew it was too late for the morning edition of his paper, but he'd have an exclusive anyway for the morning radio programme.

Jenny was in shock. The baby had been a girl. She had often heard people say that a miscarriage was nature's way of disposing of an imperfect creation. 'Do you really believe that?' she asked her doctor.

'I like to think so, but we have no answers. Sometimes a baby can't survive because the conditions in the womb aren't compatible with its needs. Whatever the reason, you must allow yourselves time to grieve for her,' she told them. 'The death of a baby, even at sixteen weeks, is a real loss. It's not easy to put it aside, because we're all surrounded by friends and families with babies. Please allow yourselves time to deal with it.'

Fergus was genuinely devastated and she found herself consoling him instead of the other way around. When he had gone home to shower and change, her sister, Leslie, had arrived.

'I never really felt pregnant,' Jenny told her. 'I'd had no symptoms and no morning sickness and I felt nothing as I lost her. It was all over before I even realised it was happening. I thought I hadn't bonded with her, yet now I feel as though I've just lost a part of me.'

'But you have. I think what you've described is a very normal defence mechanism. Mum never told anyone she was pregnant until after twelve weeks, just in case. Stop trying to analyse yourself. It's a lot to take in and it's a huge shock to your body.' Leslie hugged her. 'I know I'm not supposed to say it, but you'll have other children.'

'I won't.'

'That's just how you feel now. Look, get some rest and come to me for a few days when they let you out.'

✳

It had been a black day for Fergus and it was about to get worse. He was sad that Jenny had lost their baby, and he was annoyed with her because she hadn't managed to hold on to it. How hard was it to have a baby? Teenagers did it all the time. Women in Africa had them in the fields and continued working. Yet his wife couldn't even get that far.

He was driving to the office when he saw the evening paper's headline, *Personal Loss for Government Adviser – Wife Loses Baby*, beside a huge mugshot of himself.

He had to wait until he had gone through two more sets of lights before he could thrust a five-euro note into the hand of a newspaper vendor and grab a copy. He almost rear-ended the car in front as he tried to read the piece while driving:

Personal loss for political adviser — but is he about to lose much more than his baby?

It seems as though the perfect world of Mr Squeaky Clean Fergus Ruddy is about to implode. In the early hours of this morning his linguist wife, Jenny, was rushed to the National Maternity Hospital where she miscarried. The couple have no other children.

Meanwhile at the Commercial Court the name of Fergus Ruddy has been bubbling beneath the slime and grime of dirty deals and backhanders for quite a while. It looks as though it may be time for him to put his head above these murky waters before he has to hang it in shame. It appears his strategy of keeping his friends close and his enemies even closer to him has failed him this time.

One of those heavily involved in the development of enterprise collaborations in eastern European countries has turned state's evidence and promises to reveal all about his dealings with Fergus Ruddy, including releasing some papers he has kept hidden in a London bank vault for several years.

How much longer will the slippery snakes of subterfuge and stratagem be able to hide in the long grass?

Such revelations may put an end to more than Ruddy's political aspirations.

When Fergus reached his office, his heart was pounding. That sleazy bastard was still out to get him but he wasn't going to take this lying down. How had he found out about the baby? Could his phone be tapped? He'd sue the paper and have him fired.

His normally unflappable PA was in a flap. The Taoiseach's office had been on, and so had the Department of Commerce and Enterprise, two top union representatives, all of the newspapers, national radio and television, one of Jenny's brothers and his solicitor.

That was the first call he returned.

'I want you to roast that guy,' he began, but he was interrupted.

'Fergus, this is serious stuff. Are you being straight with me? I told you from the outset that I'm not interested in representing you, no matter what the fee is, if you are or were involved in any of these scams. This country is sinking fast because of the shysters who took those obscene backhanders and pushed through phoney land and bank deals. My own parents have lost everything.'

'You can't do this to me. I need you. We go back a long way—'

'Forget that, Fergus. This goes way beyond the old school tie and the golf club. You have until tomorrow to decide. If I'm not satisfied that you're being honest with me, you can find another law firm to handle your business. I've no intention of wasting one second of my life defending anyone who has destroyed things for so many. I've nothing else to say to you. Have a think about it and call me first thing tomorrow.'

Shocked, Fergus sat at his desk. He couldn't quite believe this was happening. They'd been friends since primary school.

Next he was fobbed off by his PR company, which was owned and run by Trevor Jones, who had also been at school and college with him.

'I'm afraid Mr Jones is out this afternoon.'

'You think I don't know what that means? He's just told you he's not in if I ring. Get him on the line for me.'

'I'm sorry, he's not available. '

'What do you mean "not available"? I pay that bastard through the nose to be available twenty-four seven. Get him for me. And tell him to get around here, pronto, or I'll drag him down with me.'

He got so caught up in the web that he forgot to phone Jenny. He did, however, call one of the business moguls he'd had dealings with over the years, the one who had funded the annual replacement of his BMW convertible and part of the property portfolio he had managed to conceal from everyone, even his wife. Normally all communications were done through third and fourth parties, but if Fannaghy was going to spill the beans, this was no time to hang around.

The next day Fergus got into the office very early, but his PA was there before him.

'This arrived for you a few minutes ago. It's registered so I signed for it.' He wanted to tell her to sign for nothing but knew that would seem irrational. He took it into his office and slit the top. He paled when he read the contents.

> We regret to inform you that as and from this day, date shown above, Tyson and Morgan, Solicitors, are terminating all dealings with Mr Fergus Ruddy and with any companies and/or concerns belonging to or with the involvement of the aforenamed. A public notice to this effect will appear in the national newspapers today.

He grabbed the phone to call them, but at that moment his PA knocked and quietly handed him the morning newspapers, folded in such a way that he could see the items she had circled in red.

'How did you know about this?'

'The phones haven't stopped ringing with enquiries about it, and I'd like to give my notice.'

'You can't do that. I'll clear my name, you wait and see. You'll be glad to work for me after the next elections.'

'No, thank you.'

'I won't give you a reference.'

'I won't need one. Besides, I don't think it would have much value.'

'You won't get another job without one.'

'I already have one. Our PR company has offered me a position. Oh, and when Mr Jones was on he asked me to tell you they're no longer representing you. Now, if you don't mind, I'll clear my desk before I go.'

He managed to contain his anger until she'd left, then flung the phone across the room.

Later he told Jenny that his neglect of her that day and his preoccupation were down to a libellous feature in one of the red tops. 'But don't worry, I'm going to take them for every penny they have. No one libels Fergus Ruddy and gets away with it. Now, how are you doing?'

Jenny spent the next two days in hospital until they had stabilised her blood pressure. She knew from the way her sister and brothers were pussyfooting around her that they had more on their minds than her, but she hadn't the energy or interest to ask what it was.

Nine

JENNY SMILED. IT WAS ONLY DAY THREE AND already she had abandoned her plan to do the deck mile when she saw it was almost eight o'clock and realised that the ship was not moving. Her balcony now offered her first glimpse of Israel: rows and rows of neatly stacked containers of various colours stamped with their owners' names. She was on the wrong side of the ship. She'd have to go to starboard to get a view of Haifa. She had read it was dominated by Mount Carmel. First, though, she had to shower and dress.

Before she went ashore there were formalities to be dispensed with – like bringing her passport to a pre-assigned spot on the ship to be checked by the Israeli authorities, who had already boarded and set themselves up at various stations. There she received her permit to enter Israel, not, as she'd expected, as a stamp in her passport but on a separate piece of paper that she would have to surrender on her departure from Israel in three days' time. While she was waiting to see the official, she met one of the couples from the sun-downer party.

'We haven't booked anything for today. Have you?' asked Paul.

'I thought I'd just explore the town as we're docked so close to the centre.'

'We're going to hire a taxi, fix a price, and let him show us around. We've done that before and found the driver's often more interesting than the official guides.'

'Why don't you join us?' his wife asked.

'I wouldn't like to intrude.'

'You wouldn't. We'll have to be nice to each other if you come along.'

'Then I'd be delighted to.'

'The guidebook says you have to go to the top of Mount Carmel to get the best view of the gardens,' Paul said.

'He does all the homework in advance and knows what we should see,' his wife added.

'Half an hour at the bottom of the gangway? Will that suit you?' he asked.

'Definitely. See you then,' said Jenny.

She went back to her stateroom to smother her arms, the exposed parts of her legs and her face with high-factor sun cream, wiped the residue off her hands, collected her camera and hat, then went to grab a coffee while she waited for the others. From the deck she could see an enormous golden dome shining in the sunlight. It nestled amid the tiered terraces of the shrine to Báb, the grass emerald against the sand-coloured landscape. She spotted Ben and Betty walking off together to a waiting tour bus, but there was no sign of her other dining companions. They'd made no arrangements to meet today, but she was sure they'd run into each other.

She hoped Paul and his wife, whose name had slipped her mind, would want to stop at *Exodus*. If they didn't call at the ship, she'd go there on her own later. Years ago, when suffering from a mysterious virus that had kept her confined to bed for weeks while she was still at school, she'd read about the ill-fated vessel. Its unfortunate refugees had been sent from Cyprus to Palestine for asylum. Once they arrived there they had been refused permission to land by the British, and were sent to France, but not allowed off their ship. They were kept incarcerated for weeks, and eventually, after enduring incredible hardship, were allowed to return to Cyprus. Jenny had just discovered that the actual ship had been turned into a museum, right here in Haifa.

Checking she had her permit and passport, she finished her coffee, then went down the gangway to the dock and showed them to the officials who were installed beneath big umbrellas at a scattering of desks. Then she went to join Paul and his wife. She spotted Will and Heather ahead at a row of taxis. Heather seemed to be floating in a tent of cream cheesecloth, topped by a wide-brimmed straw hat. As they passed each other, Heather said, 'Do you know anything about this Báb fellow? Apparently he owned the big house up there on the hill.'

Before Jenny or her companions could answer her, Heather had floated away. The next they saw of her, she was tucking her dress around her in the back of a car.

Paul laughed. 'I hope she's not expecting the Báb fellow to invite her in for tea at the mausoleum.' He and his wife, Tina, negotiated a fare with a driver further down the line. He assured them he'd show them all the highlights and give them two full hours.

'I'd like to contribute,' Jenny offered.

'We wouldn't hear of it. You can buy the coffee later,' Paul said.

*

Marcus was up early and had done three-quarters of an hour in the gym before breakfast. Then he headed off to explore on his own. He took one of the main arteries from the seafront and was stopped short by a cluster of traditional German-style buildings, with red-tiled roofs and inscriptions over the doors in old-fashioned German script.

His grandfather had been German, although he was never talked about during Marcus's childhood. He had been a commander in the army in the Second World War and was killed in action. That was what they'd believed. But Marcus was a curious child and had discovered that his grandfather had served in the SS and that his death, never mind his wartime activities, had been inglorious. He'd turned his pistol on himself shortly before the Allies had arrived, just weeks before the end of the hostilities. There had been no photographs, medals or decorations to hand down to his family, only shameful secrets that everyone wanted to bury.

He headed back to the main drag and found a coffee shop. He could just about make out the road sign through the traffic, Ben Gurion Street. He knew from history that this founding father of Israel had absorbed Jews from all over the world into the new country, and Marcus found himself wondering if any of his grandfather's war crimes had led anyone here, directly or indirectly.

This country was steeped in conflict and hardship. For some it offered refuge, the fulfilment of dreams; for others it had been an exile too far, a flight that was too often the culmination of persecution, torture, loss and heartbreak. For whatever reason, Marcus felt uneasy there. As he drained his coffee he watched the world go by. It was noisy. Music blared from cars, and motorbike exhausts emitted sounds that were not unlike machine-gun fire. He counted out the unfamiliar shekels, left them on a saucer and headed back for a swim before lunch.

Many of the ship's guests had opted for the organised tour around the city. The guide in Betty's coach was enthusiastic, explaining everything in four languages as they drove past the various landmarks, but by the time she got to the last translation, in Spanish, they were already halfway past the next point of interest. Ben, who was sitting beside her, had forgotten to put in his hearing aids and kept asking Betty what the guide was saying, so she missed parts of the commentary. Still, the bus was air-conditioned and they were going to get out halfway up the hill to go into the gardens. She was trying to be patient with Ben, but resolved to have a bit of time to herself when they got back to the ship.

They left the bus and had their bags checked before they were allowed into the gated gardens. Hamish was there ahead of them. He'd taken a taxi and was chatting and laughing with a dark-haired woman and a security guard. As Betty proffered her open bag she was watching the exchange a few feet ahead of them, where an official, carrying a large gun, was saying to Hamish's companion, 'Madam, could I please ask you to fasten your blouse a little higher?'

The guard didn't miss Hamish's muttered aside to her – 'I bet that's the first time a man ever used that line on you' – and was clearly not amused, but he said politely, 'This is a holy place for some people,' and let them pass.

Hamish acknowledged Betty and Ben with a wink, before heading off in pursuit of the dark-haired woman, who was already taking the steps to the Temple, two at a time.

✽

It was after lunch when John returned to the ship. He went straight to his suite to get his gym things. He worked out every day. After years of expensive memberships at London health clubs, he'd built his own gym in his split-level penthouse. There, from his treadmill and stepping-machine, the view rivalled that of the seagulls swooping and diving along the Thames.

The ship's gym had a horseshoe of treadmills and bikes positioned inside the floor-to-ceiling windows facing towards the sea. It was only ever used by a tiny percentage of guests, usually the steadfast and fanatical. A bronzed, toned and muscular instructor began moving Pilates balls and other pieces of light equipment into a circle in preparation for the next session of afternoon limbering.

'Eat Yourself Slim,' a large notice shouted. In smaller print it said, 'It's easier if you exercise!'

John laughed when he read it. 'Well, that's an oxymoron if ever I saw one,' he said to no one in particular. 'It's easier if you don't eat at all.' A twig-thin woman joined in. She looked as though she lived on grass and water and would be far more attractive with another stone or two on her, he thought. 'A cruise is definitely not the place to start a diet,' he added, but she raised her eyebrows and he knew she didn't agree. Grinning, he made his way to the weights. 'Not too many takers for the class today?'

'Only the really dedicated,' replied the instructor. He cast his eyes in the direction of the woman, who was now pounding a treadmill as though she were trying to outrace it. 'It's always the same after a sea day. Everyone wants to get off and have a look around. It'll get busy before dinner when they decide they need to work off their lunch.'

John knew the feeling. He loved his food and enjoyed a drink too, neither of which was kind to his waistline, so he knew all about compensating and discipline. Fortunately he got a buzz from exercise and never found it a chore.

When Jenny got back to the ship, she found an invitation in the slot on her door, asking her to join the captain and some of his officers for cocktails in his quarters before dinner. It was printed on stiff card with his name and the company crest embossed in gold. She also found an envelope from John, saying he hoped she'd join him for dinner if she had no other plans. 'Meeting up in the cocktail bar first. I bumped into Sylvia and Hamish (not together!!),' he had added, 'and they've agreed to come too.' He'd scribbled the name and number of his suite on the little card. She called and left a message that she'd meet them there, as she had to do something first.

She had been looking forward to a nap, unused to the heat and the amount of wine she and her new-found friends had consumed after their tour of the city. She'd been to *Exodus* too, and her head was buzzing with the emotions it had aroused in her. She couldn't know what the Holocaust had meant to those who had lived through its atrocities, but she admired their stoicism and determination.

She knew that if she lay down now she'd conk out, so she took her book out onto the balcony. Instead of reading, though, she became absorbed in the activities of the harbour beyond and on the pier below. She watched the ship's passengers filing back in little groups, showing their documents, sanitising their hands, taking a drink of water or fruit juice from the welcoming party, before disappearing up the gangway.

When she went back inside, she took her mobile out of the drawer and texted her sister: *I just wanted to say thank you both. It's fantastic so far! Xxxxx*

Ten

DOUG BURGESS LEFT THE BRIDGE TO GET ready for the cocktail party he was hosting. 'I'm off to make myself presentable,' he told his second officer.

'I don't know how you do it all the time, being nice to everyone.'

'It's not that hard if you like people and, besides, if I don't like some of them I can hide up here.' He grinned. 'Like you. I haven't been at it long enough for it to bore me. When it does I'll go back on land.'

'I can't see that happening any time soon.'

'Nor can I.' He raised his forefinger in a mock salute.

He walked along the corridor to his quarters where a

fresh dress uniform was laid out on his bed. He enjoyed the interaction with each new wave of clients he had to meet and greet. It was no hardship to be affable and he believed that if his crew and passengers were happy he must be doing something right. Some of his counterparts hated this part of the job, but not Doug. He revelled in it.

Not that evening, though.

He was heart sore after the latest email from his wife. It had simply said, *Try to take Lewis away from me and you'll be sorry. I've had enough.*

Doug told himself to forget it until later. He had a job to do. His guests were here to enjoy themselves. They were not interested in his domestic problems. He fastened the buttons on his jacket, straightened his shoulders, took a look in the mirror as he passed it and went into his lounge to check that everything was in order.

The food was laid out on platters on a side table and two bar staff were manning the drinks table. One poured champagne into tall flutes; another was in charge of other wines and soft drinks. When the guests arrived, waiters would pass around the canapés.

'Everything looks good. Well done, team,' Doug said as some officers arrived.

*

Jenny took a cerise linen dress off its hanger, put it on with a necklace and matching bracelet, stepped into some strappy shoes and left her stateroom. She met her steward outside. He was working his way along the corridor, turning down beds and changing towels. She asked him for directions, and as he was explaining where the captain's quarters were, she heard a door open and saw the two elegantly dressed men she'd observed in the casino coming along the corridor.

'I couldn't help overhearing – you're going to the party too,' said the short one. 'You must be a VIP – a film star, a frequent traveller? We saw you on the bridge in Athens when we set sail.'

'Pay no attention to him. He's nosy. I'm Bud and this is Sonny. We're from New York.'

She introduced herself, shook hands and let them lead the way.

'We love Dublin.'

'Yes, we do. Shame about the weather, though. Isn't this divine?' Sonny said, waving his arms about, talking and walking sideways until they got to the bank of highly polished lifts. 'We're on our honeymoon.' He held his right hand up to show off a gleaming gold band.

'Congratulations,' she said. She hadn't realised such unions were legal in the States. 'I heard the captain say there was a honeymoon couple with us, but I didn't know who it was. How exciting. When did you get married?'

'Last weekend. We had a fabulous wedding,' Sonny said.

'He wanted it to be the talk of New York so it was totally OTT. We had so many fights we almost didn't go through with it,' Bud told her.

'Oh, that's not true. I just wanted everything to be perfect, and it was,' Sonny said. 'It was *not* over the top but tasteful. Wasn't it, darling?'

'He had a wedding planner who would have had me dress in feathers if I'd allowed him to. We had feathers on the tables and at each place setting, feathers in the flower arrangements and, of course, feathers flying about from the white parakeets in their white cages. He even had feathers around the cake stand and on our bed in the honeymoon suite. I'm amazed I didn't develop an allergy.'

'Oh, stop it already, will you? You do exaggerate, Bud. You make it sound as though we got hitched in an aviary.' Then he turned to Jenny. 'We married in matching dove-grey suits.'

'They were pink.'

'They so were not! Besides, doves have a pinkish hue on their breasts, or is that pigeons – or flamingos?'

'Our suits had more than a pinkish hue. I left the arrangements to him because I was in post-production, working at the studio day and night. I'm in film. That's where I went wrong, leaving him in charge.' He chuckled.

'Well, you certainly seem to live exciting lives.'

'Oh, we do, but admit it, Bud, it was a great day,' Sonny said, stroking his arm.

'Yes, it was. It was memorable in lots of ways, good ways. And we're exhausted after it. Are you on your own, Jenny?' he asked, and she nodded.

'Then you must let us take care of you, mustn't she, Bud? We can be your escorts. We'd love that, wouldn't we?'

'I'd be the envy of all the women and men on board.'

Taking her arms, they squeezed her along the passageway between them.

'Do you think they'll let us take pictures up here? I brought the camera just in case,' Bud said.

'Why not ask?' she said. 'Everything seems very relaxed. I haven't seen anyone jump to attention when a uniform appears and the staff seem to gel really well.'

'That comes from the top down. If they felt they were being watched all the time they'd lose their spontaneity. I would anyway,' said Sonny.

The corridor leading to the captain's quarters was lined with certificates; there were photographs of officers and famous faces too. When they reached an open door, Doug Burgess came forward to greet them. She managed to disentangle herself from her new-found minders and put out her hand to shake his when he reminded her, 'No hands up here – only hips or elbows. So nice to see you again.'

They did their new form of greeting along the reception line, which was heavy with gold braid. The chief engineer, the ship's surgeon, the hotel director and others were all introduced before they were offered a drink. 'The captain's cocktail is rather good. I can recommend it,' the food and beverage manager said. It had a very definite pinkish hue, thought Jenny.

'I thought his quarters would be special. This is just like any ordinary lounge,' whispered Sonny.

Jenny whispered back, 'It's not like mine – I don't have a row of liveried staff on standby and champagne on tap!'

'Neither do we, only Martha, our Polish help – she comes in a few days a week – and Martin, our dog-walker. Well, he's not exclusively ours. He's a dentistry student, and he walks others from our block too. Makes a great sight, our Bernese mountain dog, Mrs Feinstein's Afghan hounds, the Joan Rivers lookalike's poodles and Old Scrooge's mongrel all walking out together. Scrooge is our concierge. We call him that because he scrounges everything he can. Practically asks for our clothes while we're still wearing them. I reckon he even goes though our garbage.'

Jenny glanced around, hoping John might be there. There was an air of opulence in the room, the sort that is always accompanied by expensive scents and colognes. It was obvious that everyone had taken care with their appearance – there was no trace of the shiny-faced, high-factor, windswept look that had been on-trend earlier by the pool.

One couple told her they were going to cruise again, later in the year. 'My husband,' his large wife began, 'and I are running away from home for Christmas and New Year.'

'Any particular reason? The tax man, gambling debts?' enquired a man with a bald head that reflected the lights above. In contrast, the backs of his hands were positively furry.

'None of the above. Our adult children have given us permission to break with tradition and go away. We've always had them, and then their small ones, to stay with us in the country for the holiday, but this year we've been given a dispensation! Freedom!'

'Pay him no heed. He's as free as a bird. I'm the one who does the cooking and the preparations.'

'I know, and you're great at them, but that's why we're running away this year – together.' He laughed pulling her towards him.

'Where are you off to?' asked Hairy Hands.

'We start in Rio, sail to Uruguay and end up in Buenos Aires for New Year.'

'That sounds marvellous. I'd love to go to South America. You could adopt me if you think you'll get lonely without your family,' said Jenny. 'I could do light duties, like fetching drinks from the bar and reserving seats by the pool. I'd be no trouble at all.'

They laughed.

Sonny popped up at her elbow. 'You will join Bud and me for dinner tonight, won't you?'

'I'd love to but I already have an arrangement. Maybe we'll meet up afterwards. Are you going to the casino later?'

Bud came back into their group at that point and answered pointedly, looking at Sonny, 'No. We're not.'

At that moment, the captain wound things up, wishing them a pleasant evening and a good dining experience, wherever they were going to eat. People started leaving.

'That's an elegant way of telling us to move it,' said Hairy Hands. 'I believe my grandfather used to stand up and start winding the clocks when he wanted folk to leave.'

There was more hip-swivelling and elbow-knocking, and everyone departed in good spirits.

The Boys, as Jenny already thought of them, relinquished her, and she went to meet John and the others. She spotted them immediately: Sylvia in leopard print, her outsized jewellery seeming to consist of what looked like an assortment of animal teeth and yards of gold chains. Her wrists were festooned with gold bangles. Hamish and John stood up as she approached.

'We're on G-and-T, but would you prefer something else?' asked John.

'I've just been quaffing cocktails. Maybe some sparkling water for now.'

'Where have you been having cocktails without us?' asked Sylvia.

'In the captain's quarters.'

'Wow! What's your secret?'

'I feel a real fraud, even being invited, but it was fun. I just wish I could remember names. I'm hopeless at it, but I've acquired two minders, a gay honeymoon couple from my corridor. They want to be my escorts for the cruise.'

'I think I saw them in the casino last night. One small and the other very tall? They were on a winning streak and suddenly the tall one went off in a huff. Remember, Hamish?'

Hamish nodded. 'I can't quite get my head around gay marriage or civil partnerships or whatever they call them. My Scottish Presbyterian upbringing falls just short of saying they'll be damned for ever.'

'You can't believe that in this day and age,' Sylvia said.

'It just makes me uncomfortable, that's all. I'm entitled to my opinion,' Hamish said.

'Of course you are – so where do your extreme beliefs leave you on extra-marital sex, intimate dancing and immoral thoughts?' she asked coquettishly. Jenny wondered if he'd tried it on with Sylvia the previous night after John and she had seen the pair head for the nightclub.

'The jury's still out on those.' He grinned wickedly. 'I don't really believe in eternal damnation, but all that gay and lesbian stuff, it's just not for me.'

'I don't think it's a life choice for the vast majority of them either. It's who they are,' said John. 'We all deserve to find happiness where we can, so good luck to them if they've found it with each other. Now, shall we go through?'

The dining room was warm and inviting. Crystal shone and silver gleamed while delicious smells emanated as waiters carried tempting dishes to the diners. A string quartet played softly in one alcove.

Sylvia told them she had met up with an old school friend from London who now lived on the outskirts of Haifa. 'We headed off to the beach for a catch-up and had a picnic there. It's been ten years since she married and moved to Israel, so we had a lot of catching up to do. Isn't it great with real friends, the way it doesn't matter how long the gap is between meetings, you can just pick up the pieces as though it were yesterday?' They all agreed with that.

Hamish had seen Betty and Ben briefly during the morning. He had had lunch with the woman he'd been pursuing earlier and told them, 'She neglected to tell me one little thing until we were approaching the ship on our way back. Then she dropped in that her husband had had a migraine and had decided not to go ashore that morning. She had a husband! She thanked me sweetly for my company, and for lunch, then disappeared to be at his side. That, folks, is the story of my life.'

'But you were married, weren't you?' pushed Sylvia.

'Yes, but that seems like for ever ago now. I met my wife at Edinburgh University. I dropped out and went to work in the family business. It seemed the logical thing to do as I was destined to end up there anyway. She had it all – a flaming redhead like you, Sylvia – beauty and brains, and she qualified easily as a secondary-school teacher. After we married she discovered counselling. She became fanatical about it, reading every self-help book that was ever published before she decided to go back to do further studies in it. Somewhere between then and qualifying as a practitioner, she changed from being a sweet, accommodating, thoughtful and kind lass, who liked being minded and cosseted, into a hard-nosed, selfish bitch, whose mantra was "Look after yourself before anyone else". I didn't need looking after, although I'm not denying that I'm a crass Scot, and that I don't take any prisoners in business, but that wasn't the way I was reared or the way I'd imagined my marriage would be. I thought it involved give and take, sharing and caring, loving the other person more than yourself and all those old clichés.'

'It should,' said Sylvia.

'That was what I thought, but I was wrong, it seems. I was soon moved to the back burner. I was nice to have around when she wasn't doing courses, driving through the glens to Zen or some other such retreat, or taking time out to find herself, again. Then she began holding counselling sessions in our home. We converted the garage into a consulting room for her and I had to get out of the way whenever clients called for fear I might recognise them and break the confidentiality she needed between her and whoever she was treating. That meant watching the matchbox-sized telly in the dining room in case they saw me in the front room where the wide-screen lived.'

'That does sound a bit one-sided,' said John.

'It was. In the end I entered an appointment in her diary, using my mother's maiden name. When she opened the door she told me to get lost. I just walked into her room, sat down and said, "I'm your client, so you have to listen." I put fifty quid on the table to pay for the session. I told her straight that I was tired of being brushed aside and wanted out of our marriage.'

'Wow.'

'What did she say?' Jenny asked.

'At first she acted as though I was being irrational, and then she trotted out, "You must do what's right for you and no one else." That was when she told me she'd become involved with one of her mentors from the university and she'd like us to be over too. She had to move on to be true to herself. She added that she didn't expect anything from me. I could keep the house and everything else, as if that would make it all right. She even handed me back the fifty-pound note! Apparently the weasel had a bigger and better home in a more fashionable suburb, just waiting for her to put her feminine touches to it. That was it, a swift drop of the guillotine and the marriage bonds were irreparably severed.'

'It must have been devastating,' said Jenny.

'It was. I think she'd managed to brainwash herself. She believed that doing what was right for herself was the right thing to do. It absolved her of any responsibility to me as her husband. There were no reconciliation talks or mediation sessions. Nothing. I often wondered if that was the sort of advice she meted out to her clients, although she used to assure me that she never gave advice. Her job was to listen. Well, that conniving weasel must have been playing a sweeter tune than mine as I didn't stand a chance in that contest.'

'Where is she now? Do you ever see each other?' Sylvia asked.

'She's dead,' Hamish said dispassionately.

That brought them up with a bang. They all made sympathetic noises.

'She died about six months after we split,' Hamish went on.

'How awful.'

'It was. She slipped and fell getting onto a boat in Vietnam, when they were off on one of their soul-searching retreats. She was unconscious for three days before she died and the creepy bastard didn't think to let me know. I found out from the local newspaper about two weeks later. He had her cremated over there and scattered her ashes on top of some spiritual mountain they'd been meditating on a few days earlier.'

'How sad,' Jenny said. 'Do you still love her?'

'I did still love her then, and it was a horrible way to end. But now I'm not so sure; I tend only to remember the good bits and have blocked out the bad. Maybe that's a coping or self-analysis thing. God, I can't believe I'm saying these things. What's in this wine?'

'Has there been no one else since?'

'Hundreds.' He laughed. 'So many I've lost count. And I've not finished yet.' He smiled knowingly at Sylvia. 'Now, give me another glass of that red.'

'We're last at the table again,' Jenny remarked, a while later, moving her chair back. 'We'd better drink up and let the staff go off duty before they throw us out.'

John asked, 'What was the nightclub like last night?'

'It had a DJ, but there's live music there tonight,' Sylvia told him. 'Why don't we all go up? We met Marcus there. He hadn't gone to bed after all when we went to the casino.'

'He was bopping when we arrived,' said Hamish.

'Where is he tonight?' asked Sylvia.

'He probably ate earlier or he may be dining at the buffet.'

'I didn't see him all day. Maybe he prefers his own company.'

Eleven

IT WAS MEXICAN NIGHT AT THE CLUB. THEY found a curved booth from where they had an uninterrupted view of the dance floor. It wasn't very busy when they arrived, but as soon as the show was over in the theatre the crowd swelled. A group of musicians, dressed as troubadours, played a familiar Latin-American medley. In the midst of the couples swaying and moving to the hypnotic beat, Sonny and Bud were dancing with all the enthusiasm and intricate moves that you'd expect to see on *Strictly Come Dancing*. People stopped to watch them, and they played up to their audience, with even more melodramatic gestures. Picking Jenny out in the dim light, Sonny gave an exaggerated wave and blew a kiss in her direction. She waved back.

'They're my new best friends.'

'I see what you mean by colourful,' Hamish said. 'But they have a bit of footwork competition from Zorro over there.' He indicated an older man with gelled hair in a quiff. He saw them looking at him and came over.

'Hi, folks, I'm Chad Tayloe-Stuart, one of the dance hosts on board for this voyage. Would any of you ladies like to dance?'

'They're with us,' John said pointedly.

'But they might like to dance,' he said hopefully. He looked at Sylvia and stretched out his hand. She stood up and he moved aside to lead her onto the floor. His footwork was old-fashioned and he held her in a grip of iron, willing her body to dip, swirl and bend when he wanted her to.

He was one of three dance hosts on the ship. The men, it seemed, didn't need any.

'How did you get to do this job?' Sylvia asked him. 'Were you a dancer?'

'No,' he replied. 'I was a history professor in Wyoming and I always wanted to travel. I wanted to be a cowboy and an astronaut when I was young and I didn't do those either. The circus wasn't an option and later on, when I outgrew those ambitions, I was too taken up with trying to make the kids' college fees to think about much else. When I retired I went on a cruise. There were some hosts on it and I thought, well, that's right up my street, so I got talking to one of them and here I am. This is only my second time doing it and I'm really taking a lot of pleasure from the experience. The other guys have been at it much longer than me. One was a professional dancer and the other was in real estate, I believe.'

The tune finished and he escorted her back to the group. She thanked him and sat down again.

'He's an interesting fellow,' she said to Hamish, 'a history don, no less.'

'Dancing his way through retirement and seeing the world – that's what I call using your talents,' he replied. 'It's a shame I can only stand there and wriggle about.'

'He looks vaguely familiar. Does he do this all the time?' asked John.

'No, this is only his second cruise as a host, I think he said. I found him hard to understand – I couldn't quite make out the accent.'

'Don't they say we all have a double somewhere?' Jenny said.

'A doppelgänger,' John offered.

'Well, I pity mine,' said Hamish, 'but wouldn't it be fun to meet yours and find out what sort of life he had, whom he'd married, what he worked at?'

'Not if he was having a better one than I was,' said John.

'That's highly unlikely in your case, young fella. You seem to have it all going your way from where I'm sitting,' said Hamish.

'You won't hear me complaining.' He smiled, signalling to the waiter. 'More drinks, anyone?'

'Not for me, thank you,' said Sylvia, who had just spotted Marcus. He was sitting on the other side of the room with the computer woman. They were deep in conversation and apparently oblivious to the activity around them.

'She's a mousy little thing, isn't she?' Sylvia said. 'Do you think he needs rescuing?'

'Do you?' Hamish asked. 'He looks quite happy to me.'

She didn't answer, but stood up and glided across the floor before the musicians struck up again.

John laughed. 'Methinks the damsel is a mite put out, maybe even a mite jealous.'

'And I thought women were supposed to be the gossips,' said Jenny. 'Give them a chance. They hardly know each other,'

'Maybe not yet, but I think she'd like to get to know him better. Didn't you notice her looking around for him earlier? She strikes me as a lady who'd like to win a cultured and not-short-of-a-bit-of-dosh Danish industrialist,' John said.

'I don't think she's short of a bit of dosh herself – she lives in Knightsbridge, one of the most expensive areas in London – but I'm inclined to agree with the lad here. She seems taken with him, all right. She's a bonny woman, but I'd imagine she'd be very high maintenance. Way out of my league.' Hamish laughed. 'I could buy a classic car with all that gold she's wearing tonight.'

'Remind me not to leave the table. I can't imagine what you'll say about me,' laughed Jenny.

'And I was just going to ask you to dance,' Hamish protested.

'That's all right, then. One of you on your own can't get up to much mischief.'

Sonny and Bud joined them as they moved to the hypnotic

rhythms and were followed by Marcus and Sylvia. As they danced by, Hamish winked meaningfully and muttered, 'Our redhead's like the cat that got the cream.' The computer woman was dancing with one of the other hosts and smiled as they twirled past.

When there was a break in the music Jenny made the introductions. The Boys turned on the charm and only moved away when the music started again.

'Did you have a nice day, Marcus?' Jenny asked.

'I had a strange one, but I don't want to talk about that tonight.'

Jenny wasn't sure whether it was his way of speaking or his direct way of answering that made him seem a little forbidding. She noticed Sylvia didn't try to draw him out as she had done with Hamish over dinner. It had been almost as though she were interviewing him – as a prospective suitor, perhaps. Was it Marcus's turn now? She didn't get a chance to find out because John said, 'If you'll all excuse me I'm going to turn in. I'm off to Jerusalem tomorrow and I leave at eight, but I want to get to the gym first. I shan't be back tomorrow night as I'm staying in the city, so I won't see any of you until Wednesday. Maybe dinner together then.'

Jenny was disappointed. She had hoped to dance with him and maybe enjoy his company the next day.

'I won't be around tomorrow either,' said Sylvia. 'I'm taking the opportunity of the stopover to stay with an old friend who lives outside the city.'

'What are your plans, Jenny?' asked Marcus.

'Oh, I've booked the walking tour of Jaffa and Tel Aviv.'

'So have I,' Hamish said, 'so we'll probably bump into each other along the way.'

'It looks like you might have me for company too,' Marcus said. 'Now, what about a dance before bedtime?' Jenny followed him onto the floor.

It wasn't quite eleven when she made her way back to her cabin. She was pleasantly tired and chuckled to herself at the idea of going to bed so early on holiday. Even at home she rarely retired before midnight. But she was tired. The sun always affected her like that. She was enjoying the company of her new friends, and wished she were the sort of person who kept a diary because she knew she'd have forgotten so much about the cruise by the time she got home. Leslie's embargo on phone contact was having the desired effect: she had switched off completely and didn't want to think about home at all.

Down the corridor Betty was twisting and turning in her double bed. She couldn't settle. She got up and opened the sliding door to her balcony, thinking the sound of the water might induce sleep. It didn't. She'd swallowed her tablets. Usually they took the pain away pretty swiftly, but tonight they seemed ineffective and lying down seemed to exaggerate it. She had been given stronger ones, but she was holding off taking them for as long as she could.

She'd had dinner with Ben, and he was driving her mad.

He'd stuck to her like an Elastoplast all day and suggested eating at six thirty. She had hoped to meet some of the group from the previous evening, but the ridiculously early meal had put paid to that.

'I don't sleep if I eat any later,' he told her. 'It's my diabetes. Esther always had my dinner ready when I got home from work at half past six and she did the same when I retired, so I find it hard to break with the routine.'

'How boring,' she muttered.

'What was that?' he asked, leaning closer to hear her reply.

'I said, I prefer to eat later than that.'

'I'm a little deaf.' This wasn't news to her. She was convinced that he didn't know how to turn on his hearing aids, and if they were on, that the batteries must have been flat. Poor Esther. He talked about her so much she wondered if he had really loved her or was feeling guilt, selfish loneliness and longing for the things she used to do for him. And that seemed to be just about everything. He'd also mentioned his daughter Rachel frequently too. Then Betty felt bad for thinking such things.

Her first husband had died unexpectedly, taken by an unheralded heart attack on his way home from work, but she didn't feel the need to prefix every sentence with his name. He had given her four lovely daughters, whom she'd had to raise on her own. In truth, she hadn't missed him much. He hadn't been kind, but back then you didn't really know a man until you were married to him and then it was often too late: you did your duty and stayed with him, no matter what.

Courtship was long walks and hand-holding, no chance to find out what someone was really like. Now she had friends of all ages, with different interests, and she had moved on, always looking ahead, not back. Perhaps Ben had no friends. Perhaps he was genuinely lonely, despite the much-mentioned daughter.

Several times during the day and over dinner, he had said, 'This is my first cruise. Esther didn't like the sea, but I always wanted to take her on one. I'm sure she would have enjoyed it.'

'Are you enjoying it?' Betty had asked, and his reply set alarm bells ringing.

'I am now that I have you to go around with.'

She smiled at him. Oh, no, you haven't.

She closed the door and got back into bed, determined to give him a wide berth the next day when they docked in Ashdod. She hoped he didn't like getting up too early. She thought about ringing room service and ordering breakfast to her stateroom: that way she could go straight ashore without bumping into him on the way. Then she thought, No – I'll just tell him I've made arrangements and I'll catch up with him later. If I hang around with him, I'll have no chance of meeting other people.

Although she was in her late seventies she still fancied she might meet a suitable gentleman for fun and companionship, or a bit of both, but time was running out. Ben most certainly did not fit into those categories. She began to remember her first encounter with her partner of nine years. They had met on a cruise ship too, but the chemistry had been there from the minute he had been introduced to her. She could still recall how his face had lit up with a smile that reached his eyes and how he had called her Little Beth. She was all of five feet two, and he was a good foot taller. He had made her feel safe, and he had been full of life back then. With those thoughts in her mind Betty finally fell asleep.

Hamish stayed on in the nightclub with Sylvia and Marcus until long after the others had left. He knew what she was playing at as he observed her flirting outrageously with both of them, flattering them, pandering to their egos and keeping her options open by dividing her attention evenly between them. She oozed sexuality and he had always liked big-chested women. He wasn't too sure that she hadn't had a bit of surgical help, though, and the feel of silicone wasn't a turn-on. And she was a tad too obvious for his liking – but if it was on offer he wouldn't refuse. He wondered about Jenny, but felt he might have left it a little too late to get in there. He thought there was definitely chemistry between the Irish lass and John. They seemed very comfortable with each other.

The three of them left together. Hamish gave Sylvia a peck on the cheek and headed towards the stairs.

Sylvia and Marcus walked on together. Marcus had to pass her door to get to his suite.

'Would you like to come in – for a nightcap?'

'No, thank you,' he replied. 'I hope you have a good time with your friend tomorrow. Good night.'

She felt a bit taken aback by his curt reply. It was a long time since she had felt so rebuffed. Inside her cabin, she removed her jewellery, slotting the necklaces into a felt roll-up pouch, the rings into another and her bracelets into a third. She looked at her reflection in the dressing table mirror, she was sure she had put on her fob chain earlier. She always wore it with this outfit, she thought, as she put the rest into her safe and keyed in the code. She'd look for it in the morning. And as for you, Mr Marcus, she said out loud, you can make the next move. I shan't chase after you again.

Twelve

IT WAS DAY FOUR ALREADY. THE CABARET Lounge was the assembly point for those taking tours. Stewards pointed them to various groupings where they sat until called. Those who had booked long-distance excursions to the Dead Sea, or to Bethlehem, had departed much earlier and breakfast had been brought forward to facilitate them in the different venues. When group eleven was called they collected their coloured stickers at the desk and followed their leaders off the ship.

Jenny heard, 'Wait for us, darling,' and recognised Bud's voice. 'We're going to Jaffa too.'

'Lovely,' she replied. It certainly wouldn't be a dull outing with this pair for companions. Both were in matelot mode – Bud in navy slacks, striped matching T-shirt and a red spotted kerchief around his neck, while Sonny's trousers were white, topped with a red sleeveless, collarless linen shirt, and he carried a straw boater. Both had brown leather man-bags. Jenny felt understated in her beige linen cut-offs and matching top. Her floppy straw hat travelled everywhere with her. It was years old and only kept its shape because she always stuffed the crown with her underwear when she packed it to keep the brim flat.

She noticed Hamish and Marcus in the other group and felt slightly disappointed that she was in a different one.

Heather's plummy accent carried across to her: 'I refuse to wear a label on my chest. I'm not five years old, you know. Do they think I'll forget who I am?'

A young crew member was trying to explain that it made it easier for the guide to distinguish his party from other groups when it came to finding the right buses at the rendezvous points.

'Well, that's his job. Not mine,' she retorted, and made a point of sticking the orange circle inside her bag. Will was obviously used to his wife's contrariness, because he said nothing and appeared not to notice her behaviour. Hamish and Marcus were following them. They raised their eyebrows in a don't-let-that-woman-near-me-on-the-bus signal.

'If she doesn't like conforming what's she doing on a tour?' muttered Hamish.

'I think perhaps she just likes the sound of her own voice,' Marcus suggested.

Off the ship, a row of coaches was waiting to take them to their destinations. There were a few off-duty staff in her group and Jenny recognised one of the young men who worked in the casino. When they took a break from their guided walk later on, she fell into step with him. Juan told her that the captain encouraged them to see and explore the destinations they visited. 'It's a real perk. Not all captains do that. I majored in history, so this particular cruise is like going on field trips that I'd never in a million years be able to afford to do. I'm from Peru and we don't usually get as far as Europe.'

'That sounds like a terrific opportunity, doesn't it?' Jenny turned to Sonny, but he ignored her. She knew he had heard her so to cover the slight, she asked Juan, 'Have you been here before?'

'Yes, but unfortunately that stop didn't coincide with my shore leave so last time I got to do Haifa instead. I'd always wanted to visit the *Exodus* museum ship.'

She noticed Bud take hold of Sonny's arm, say something to him and usher him unwillingly to the front of the line. 'So had I,' she said, turning back to the young man, 'yet most people I mentioned it to didn't know what I was talking about.' The guide moved on and Jenny and Juan followed together, drawn together in easy conversation.

The old town was intriguing, with houses in mellow stone matching the cobbled roads and twisting alleyways. Every so often an open gate gave a tantalising glimpse into an inviting courtyard, where water trickled in a central stone fountain.

'Do you think they deliberately leave the outer doors open to show off to passers-by?' Jenny wondered.

'Most probably.'

Old Jaffa was full of short flights of steps and winding pathways. There were art galleries and jewellery shops tucked away at every corner. They had tiny front windows and surprisingly sophisticated interiors that stretched away inside. One shop's signage boasted Archaeology Centre, Licensed to Sell Ancient History. Other doorways were shielded by decorative wrought-iron screens. Buildings straddled arches. Many had precarious wooden bays added, extensions to capture the light and give the occupants a view of the comings and goings of their neighbours.

'Many of these alleyways in the old town have been restored and given zodiacal names,' their guide told them, pointing to vivid aquamarine-tiled nameplates on the corners. Each showed a different symbol, the names written in Hebrew. Jenny spotted the ram, her sign, and read 'Mazal Taleh'.

'That's Hebrew for luck and Aries,' the guide said.

'Well, I already have the luck in being here.'

'That's what we like to hear.'

Later their walk took them over the Wishing Bridge. 'Here, local legend has it that if you find your star sign, and they're all along the top of the guard rail facing the sea, and make a wish, then the wish will come true.'

'Do you believe that?' Juan asked her.

'I don't know but I'm happy to give it a go.' She was already looking for the ram.

'I'm off to find Gemini,' he said, leaving her.

Jenny looked out to sea, then to the north, to the nearby skyscrapers of Tel Aviv, which had almost subsumed Jaffa in their urban sprawl, and she considered what to wish for. She thought about her future and what she'd really like, and realised she didn't know. She was open to new beginnings. She ended up wishing unimaginatively for health and happiness in the hope that they'd be accompanied by unspecified nice things along the way, and a bit of colour too.

Further along the bridge, Sonny and Bud were holding hands, their other hands on the Gemini plaque. Whatever had gone on earlier seemed to have been sorted, and Bud bent down to give Sonny a kiss. When Juan stopped at the same place, she saw Sonny smile at him. Bud turned on his heels and walked away.

The guide led Jenny's group on to a restaurant near the landmark clock tower, where they met Heather and Will's group, who were just leaving.

'They know how to make this place work. We've been fed and watered in thirty minutes flat,' Will said, as he passed Jenny. 'Once those queues for the loos are gone you'll never know we'd been here. They must be making a fortune.'

A little later, after they'd eaten, the guide brought the group together. 'You have free time now to go off on your own.' He told them at what time they should be back at the clock tower.

Jenny was happy to wander off through the labyrinth of streets. The old Jaffa flea market was waiting to be explored. She meandered in and out of shops and marvelled at the most eclectic mix of junk she had ever seen. What on earth would she do with a German Army helmet, a BSA scooter – with its own original sidecar – or one of those old wooden television sets? Why did people sell all these things? And whoever owned these must have liked entertaining, she thought, as she fingered the monogrammed handle of a heavy soup spoon, part of a boxed set of twenty-four silver placings.

She ducked to avoid hitting her head on magnificent crystal chandeliers, and tiptoed over hand-knotted carpets, wondering if they had made their way from Europe at some stage. She stopped to inspect a display of printers' trays and letters.

'You like to buy?' a grizzled old man with a beard and skullcap asked.

'No, thank you. These remind me of something my grandfather had in his garage when I was very small. I didn't understand then why the letters were backwards.'

'The punctuation marks too. These are mostly in Hebrew and Arabic, but I have some English ones too. Printing was a great skill. It's redundant now with computers, but people love to collect these things. What happened to yours?'

'The tray is on the wall in my brother's home. His wife keeps thimbles in it.'

'I have a smaller one you might be interested in.'

She wasn't, but didn't know how to refuse when he shuffled behind a curtain in search of it. He came out dusting it off. As she held the ink-stained wooden frame in her hand it brought back long-forgotten memories and she knew she had to have it. 'I'll be looking for a new home when I go back to Dublin and this will be my first purchase for it,' she told him.

'Then let me give you something.' With gnarled fingers, he fiddled in the various compartments of one of the other trays, searching. He handed her some characters. 'They spell good luck in Hebrew, and I hope they bring you lots of it.' He wrapped them carefully and chatted as he taped them to the tray. He refused to take any money. 'You put a smile on an old man's face and brightened up his day.'

'But I can't take it.'

'You can and you must. Never refuse a gift.' She gave him a hug as she left his shop.

She continued ambling in and out of the shops. There were china sets and soup tureens, mahogany wardrobes, standard lamps, musical instruments and tradesmen's tools. No one else tried to sell her anything. The skullcapped vendors sat quite happily on kitchen chairs along the edges of the path, watching the world go by.

'Isn't this place fascinating? We adore it.' Jenny was startled and turned to come face-to-face with Sonny and Bud.

'I'd love more time here.' Bud said, shifting an odd-shaped package under his arm. You get a great sense of how fashions have changed over the years and of the people who owned this stuff. I find myself wondering if they brought it from Russia or Poland, or wherever, when they arrived in Israel. My family came from the Ukraine originally, but they fled the pogrom in Kiev in 1919 with nothing, only what they were wearing.'

'It's so awful to think about that,' she said.

'The women sewed their rings into the hems of their dresses for safekeeping.'

'Let's not dwell on the past, Bud. This place is fantastic. Did you buy anything yet, Jenny?'

'It's terrific, and yes, I've got a bit of nostalgia. You two must have big suitcases.' She laughed.

'You should travel with Bud. He has so many unused air miles that we always get to go business or first class and they don't mind so much there. We always have extra bags everywhere we go.'

'That's quite a perk. When I was married – I haven't got used to saying that yet – I often enjoyed that luxury too, but I suppose I'll not be doing too much of that kind of travel now.'

'Of course you will, darling,' said Bud. 'We'll find a gorgeous man for you.'

She laughed. 'I just met one, but he's about ninety. What did you buy?'

'I just had to have this – it's a piece of Murano glass and it'll be perfect for our pad in LA,' he replied.

'I love Murano. I had a lovely piece I bought in the factory.'

'Did you break it?'

'I didn't take it when I left my husband,'

They exchanged glances.

'We have quite a few pieces. You'll have to come to New York, visit with us, Jenny, and see them for yourself,' Bud said. 'We'd love that, wouldn't we, Sonny?'

'We'll show you the town. Or you could come to LA – we go there for Hanukkah unless Bud's on location somewhere.'

'I'd love to, but you might be sorry you asked me when I turn up on your doorstep,' she said.

'We wouldn't. Why not come for Thanksgiving? I'll definitely be in New York then.'

'We always have a big party and we could introduce you to lots of new people. Not all our friends are gay, you know,' said Sonny.

She felt she was being swept along in a current of bonhomie and unreality, and she liked the sensation. There was nothing to stop her going to New York, or anywhere she fancied.

'We'll have to buy you something to remember us by,' said Sonny.

'I wouldn't hear of it,' she protested.

'Well, lady, you don't have any say in the matter. Come on, there's loads more to see.'

They met the rest of the group an hour later, and the Boys told the guide they'd skip the rest of the tour – the weight of the Murano glass was defeating them in the heat – and take a taxi back. In a snap decision Jenny decided to call it a day too. The leaflet about the tour had described it as 'gentle walking' but after four and a half hours, under a hot sun, she would be happy to sit down too. And an hour or so by the pool sounded very appealing.

Thirteen

DOUG BURGESS SAT IN HIS QUARTERS. Although his vessel was at anchor for two days there was a lot of paperwork to be attended to. On days like this, most passengers left the ship to investigate, especially in places like Israel, where there was so much to see and so many significant tour opportunities. Even the frequent cruisers almost always went ashore in ports where they could stroll into the town centre and return at leisure.

For the crew, days like this were an opportunity for department heads to have meetings and for routine maintenance to be carried out. The staff relations officer had been bombarded by requests from those wanting to be allowed to join the various excursions, and Captain Doug was known as a soft touch when it came to such perks. He remembered being in interesting ports on almost deserted ships, knowing that half of those forced to stay on duty were superfluous to requirements. What was the point of working for one of the world's prestigious cruise lines and never seeing the places you visited? He had always promised that if he ever made it to command he would change that. Company policy remained the same, but he exercised his freedom to choose in such matters. The crew loved him for it, and worked twice as hard because they felt valued. He knew instinctively where to draw the line between being the boss and being an ogre, and it paid off.

Doug was troubled. He knew he was deliberately keeping busy to distract himself. He had an on-going situation at home that he couldn't handle while he was abroad and he wasn't due shore leave for another month. Despite modern communications, some things were best handled in person, and he hadn't yet decided if an irrational alcoholic wife was one of those.

He had met Andrea while they were working for a rival shipping line. She had been a concierge, the life and soul of every party, always outgoing, and the first for a laugh and a bit of mischief. She was also efficient to an almost manic degree. Cliché though it was, her smile really had lit up a room and it was one of the things that had first attracted him to her. That, and her almond-shaped green eyes.

After they had started seeing each other, he'd told her, 'When I was little my dad used to take out the atlas and show me places he'd been with the Merchant Navy. I can honestly say I never thought I'd get to any of those places, and here I am under the stars in the Indian Ocean, with the only woman in the whole world that I love or have ever really loved.'

Theirs was a fairy-tale courtship and they soon gave up trying to hide it from their shipmates. They had moonlit dinners in the Caribbean, Singapore and Cape Town, ate exotic fare in the street markets of Penang, strolled along the marinas in Monte Carlo and Marbella, and admired the colossal yachts and beautiful people who inhabited that other world. They bought each other jewellery in the gold souks in Dubai. He'd proposed in the cable car on the way up Sugar Loaf Mountain in Rio. When she'd accepted, he couldn't believe it. Their colleagues had thrown one hell of a party for them in the staff quarters the next night. It was a double celebration as he had been promoted and was moving to another cruise line at the end of that tour of duty. Occasionally they'd find themselves in the same port and might manage a meal together ashore. It had been a great time.

But along the way it had all gone horribly wrong.

Now here he was, verging on helplessness, facing a situation that could force him to give up his career, which he had studied and striven so hard to achieve. The career he loved.

Should be apply for compassionate leave – again – or should he sit things out and hope? He knew one of the staff at HQ. In a quiet phone call he might find out whom he could approach to take over command of the ship so that he could go home and try to sort out the mess. If he left it for another month, it might be too late.

✳

The Boys escorted Jenny to dinner. Hamish and Marcus were already seated when they arrived in the restaurant. Then Betty arrived. 'Oh, thank the Lord, a few younger men!' she remarked as she approached their table.

They all laughed.

'Does that include me?

'Yes, Hamish. Anyone under sixty-five will qualify.'

'It's a long time since I've been called a younger man,' he replied.

'Believe me, you are!' Betty said. 'Can I join you? I'm exhausted – I've been playing hide and seek with Ben all day, but I think I've lost him at last. He's like a leech – once he's attached it's very hard to dislodge him.'

'Of course you can join us. There's no need to ask. But we thought we'd be needing new outfits for a wedding,' said Jenny.

'Listen well to what I'm telling you now. You won't. I'm not even sure he'll be talking to me tomorrow. I bumped into him at dinnertime – his dinnertime – six thirty. He asked me to join him and I lied sweetly. I can be sweet sometimes. I said I was meeting some of the people from lunch the other day. I told him that we were going to try the Italian restaurant tonight so please don't land me in it. I'd better have pasta so I can describe it to him if he asks!'

'What a wee minx you are. Poor men like us haven't a chance against such womanly wiles. And he looked so hopeful too. Are Danish women so devious?' Hamish asked Marcus.

'They're more direct. Betty spared his feelings, but in doing so she's probably given him false hope. I predict that he'll be waiting for her again tomorrow.'

'Heaven forbid!' She groaned. 'So how do I let him down? I need help here.'

'Honey, you have to tell him straight out that this is your vacation and you want to meet lots of new people, not just hang around with one person all the time,' said Bud. Sonny nodded in agreement.

'Ask him straight if he wants to marry again. That'll scare him off!'

'Oh, that's cruel, Marcus,' Jenny said.

'It might be, but it could work,' suggested Hamish.

'Or he might take the hint if you're busy all the time. That's how my wife gave me the brush-down – I mean the brush-off – but I didn't notice,' said Marcus.

Good old Betty, she'd got him to talk. Jenny was intrigued. He was a man of the world, yet he seemed gauche around women, as though he wasn't entirely at ease in their company. It didn't seem a good fit with his lifestyle.

'How do you mean?' asked Betty.

'She has a very successful law firm and a very busy social life. She took on partners so that she could still sail and golf. I shared her enthusiasm for sailing. We have a modest yacht, but I never came to terms with golf. I could never see the point in it. It always seemed too tame. Give me the challenge of nature, the wind and the waves, any time.'

'I'm with you there,' said Hamish. 'Forget golf, it's for

sissies – and, believe me, for a Scot to say that is a hanging offence.'

'My wife moves in lots of different circles. I think you would describe her as a society … no, a social butterfly, and when the law faculty decided to have a twenty-year reunion of her class, Malena, that's her name, was the obvious one to bring them all together. They were very busy with the committee they elected, and they were very busy arranging a venue and making contact with everyone. Our house became the planning hub, where they met to discuss progress and plan the event. I stayed out of their way, offering drinks and coffee whenever necessary. But I was too blinkered to realise that only two, Germund and my wife, were conducting this reunion business. They are arch rivals in court, often coming up against each other, so I found it amusing to see them laughing and plotting together. It was very different from their public image. The week before the big reunion she told me she was leaving me to be with him, and he was leaving his wife and two sons. They had already rented an apartment together in Copenhagen.'

'Just like that?'

'Yes, more or less, Hamish, just like that. I didn't believe it. Except that they told me together in my home. Then she said goodnight and left with him. She made no excuses, no apologies. She just said she had gone out with him briefly at college and they had always liked each other and now they felt they were being given a second chance.'

'When did all that happen?' Jenny asked him.

'Not quite six months ago so, please, you'll have to forgive me if I seem ill at ease with being single. I'm finding it a bit strange. For more than seventeen years I had a wife I loved and who I was sure loved me back. Now I feel a little as if someone had cut my anchor adrift, or however you say it.'

'Join the club. I know exactly what you mean,' Jenny agreed. 'I feel disloyal being here, as though I should get someone's permission to go somewhere on my own. Do you think being married takes away some of your identity?'

'I hope not,' said Sonny. 'We're novices, and I hereby publicly ban him from ever holding a college reunion anywhere on this planet!'

Bud laughed. 'And that edict is hereby reciprocated.'

'We ought not to be cynical. My marriage was good for a while, and when it was good it was very, very, good and when it went bad it was horrid!' laughed Hamish.

'Then we have to make sure ours is always good,' Bud said quietly.

'How does it work with you types? Is one of you the wife or what?' Hamish asked.

If he had lobbed a grenade across the table the reaction might have been milder, Jenny thought as she searched for something to say to ease the tension that followed that remark. The Boys stared at him with incredulity.

Betty said, 'Hamish, that was offensive.'

'It wasn't meant to be. I'm just curious. I'm a straight talker. I never met a pair of married homos before and just wondered if there's a dominant or butch one and a submissive one.'

Jenny had often wondered the same, but had held her tongue.

'If there were no ladies present I might just have an answer for you,' Sonny said, pushing back his chair as he stood up. 'This homo seems to have lost his appetite, so please excuse him.'

He looked at Bud, who threw his napkin onto his half-eaten main course. 'So has this queer.'

'That was a bit full-on,' said Betty, when they were out of earshot. 'You should go after them and apologise, Hamish.'

'Why? I was just being honest.'

'And perhaps a little personal and insulting, I think,' ventured Marcus.

'They didn't deserve it, Hamish,' Jenny said.

'Well, I don't think it's – well – normal,' Hamish said.

'And I'm quite sure it is. The abnormality is that it has to be hidden. We've had gay marriage for a long time in Denmark and there nobody comments on it. It's a private matter and no one else's business. I think you are very homophobic.'

'I make no apologies for that.'

'Then perhaps it might be prudent for you not to voice your opinions out loud, especially now that you know they can be so insulting,' said Betty. 'You spoiled a perfectly pleasant evening for us all.'

'I'm sorry—' began Hamish, but she interrupted,

'It's not me you should be making the apology to.'

They all declined dessert and went their separate ways when they left the dining room. Hamish had managed to fracture the easy camaraderie of the group with his tactlessness.

Fourteen

THE FOLLOWING MORNING JENNY MET HAMISH
on the way to the Cabaret Lounge.

'I feel like the naughty boy who was put in the corner.'

'You put yourself there, remember?'

'So you're still talking to me after last night?'

'Well, you have to admit you were a bit out of line.'

'Aye, I suppose I was. Are your two chums coming on the
Jerusalem tour?'

'I'm not sure.'

'I'll find them and apologise anyway. Can't have them
thinking I'm prejudiced, can I?'

'What else would you expect them to think?'

'I don't get out much,' he replied, grinning, 'and they do actually seem like quite nice chaps. I like riling people.'

'I noticed, and they're much nicer than you were to them.'

'Are you going to make me suffer for the rest of the cruise, young lady?'

'Maybe, and we're in the right place for you to do a bit of penance.'

He put an arm around her shoulders. 'You're a good one, Jenny. I like you, a lot.'

'You can try your flattery out on them instead.' She smiled and pushed him gently in the direction of Sonny and Bud, who had just arrived. 'Go and make your peace with them. I see from your number you're on a different coach from me.'

'I'll catch up with you later. Enjoy your day.'

She found a seat by the window and was happy no one sat beside her as she settled in for the hour-long journey through this ancient land, which had seen its share of conflict through the ages.

The day ahead was going to be busy, visiting numerous historic sites in Jerusalem. Convent-educated, she had been a committed Christian until her teens, maybe even a little longer. It wasn't until she began to travel that she realised other cultures and creeds couldn't all be wrong. Now she was moving through the dusts of time, she wondered about the zealots and bigots who had killed and were still killing in the name of their creeds and deities for supremacy and ownership of these holy places. Were some enjoying eternal their reward in the great blue yonder? Did it even exist?

She'd first had doubts when she was fifteen or sixteen after one of her classmates had asked their religion teacher how she knew there was an afterlife.

The teacher, whom Jenny regarded highly, had answered simply, 'I *don't* know. I'd like to think there was something more, but I'm afraid I can't answer that. It's a very personal journey. If you believe, go for it. If you don't, don't beat yourselves up over it. Just be good people. That's the best truth there is.' After a few minutes she'd gone on, 'In my day we were discouraged from even asking such questions.'

They'd loved it when she'd started off with 'In my day' or 'When I was at school' as it usually meant a startling revelation was coming.

'I know it's hard to believe, but when I was at school, like many pupils in all-girl schools where nuns reigned supreme, I flirted with the notion of becoming one myself.' There were gasps of disbelief from some of the girls, but she had continued, 'Then I joined the local tennis club and discovered boys.'

They wanted more. This was far better than learning about the seven deadly sins, or acts of simony.

'I was banned from playing hockey for two weeks when I quoted something about reincarnation. I had only read it so that I could ask awkward but intelligent questions. I was told that I should not be reading about "infidels and heretics" and was given long passages from the Acts of the Apostles to write out instead.'

Miss Moriarty's frankness had always been revealing and refreshing, and if she had taught Jenny anything, it was to be resilient. 'It's not what comes to you in life that matters but how you deal with it. Don't put life on hold while you wait for things to change. Sometimes they don't. When life is good, girls, jump up and down and embrace it. It's been my experience that when it changes, it changes for ever, and not always for the better, and you need to be able to deal with the knocks.'

Their tour guide promised not to talk on the way to Jerusalem or on the way back as they'd be overloaded with facts by the end of the day. Sitting on the air-conditioned coach, driving through the arid countryside of the Holy Land, Jenny wondered what her mother would have made of the turns her life had taken since then. She had loved her sons' girlfriends and wives, and when Leslie had brought Richie home it had been mutual admiration all the way. She would probably have approved of Fergus. On paper he passed with straight A's. He was witty, suave, refined and successful, and had seemed to care for Jenny back then. Perhaps, mused Jenny, as the countryside swept past, it was as well her mother wasn't around to see what had happened. She'd never have forgiven him.

She wished she was still around to talk to. Although she had Leslie, and they were very close, it wasn't the same. She often yearned for the chats she used to have with her mother, and their days in town. Her father was a one-man show – the P. J. Rahilly show – and he hadn't been a hands-on dad. When he wasn't teaching in the College of Art and Design, he was painting in his rooftop studio in Temple Bar. He had made quite a name for himself, showing annually at the RHA and private galleries.

Once Leslie had married, he'd told his daughters, 'I've put money aside for you, Jenny, to finish in college and that'll be my duty done. I no longer feel I have any responsibility towards you girls or your brothers. Besides, they'll look out for you. That's what siblings do.'

It was what parents usually did, she thought, but said, 'Have you spoken to the boys?'

'No, you can do that.' Then he'd taken off, wintering in the Caribbean and summering between the Côte d'Azur and Morocco. He didn't keep up with them through social media, emails or texts, but sent the occasional Christmas or birthday card. Now and then they read about him in the press because some well-known name had bought one of his works for a vast sum. Recently he'd featured on the arts channel.

'He's just the same,' Leslie had said as he was interviewed, his sun-bleached floppy mane now tinged with white, but as luxuriant as ever.

'And it looks as though he's still with Sophie,' Jenny had remarked. He had remarried just sixteen months after his wife's death, much to the astonishment and shock of their families and friends. Sophie was an artist too, only a few years older than Jenny.

'If he'd waited a little longer, and given us time to get over Mum, or at least get used to not having her around, it might have been different. It was all too quick.'

The coach stopped at a checkpoint, manned by military men and women garlanded by bullet belts and serious weaponry. Jenny realised they were already in Jerusalem.

She'd wondered before this trip if she would have a St Paul Damascene moment when she was walking in the footsteps of Jesus and his followers. Hours later, after visiting Mount Sion, the Garden of Gethsemane, the Via Dolorosa and other such holy places, she hadn't.

As Jenny was walking away from the Wailing Wall she had met Hamish, the Boys, Ben and Marcus. They were wearing cheap white satin yarmulkes, provided so that they could visit the holy shrine. Sonny asked her to take a picture of them together and it seemed the tensions of the previous evening had been smoothed over.

'Isn't it incredible to be here?' Bud said. 'I keep telling Sonny we'll have to come back and film. A friend of ours in New York has come across a great book and he's working on the screenplay right at this moment.'

'That sounds interesting,' Marcus said. 'What's it about?'

'Love across the religious and political divide, but with a meaty and true back story. Obviously a lot of it would have to be studio-based, but I'm sure we could get the necessary permissions to film some of it here for real authenticity.'

'Is there a part for a devilishly handsome wee Scot in there somewhere, and a ravishing Irish leading lady?' Hamish asked.

Before Bud could answer, Ben enquired, 'Have you seen Betty? Is she on your coach?'

'No, she's not. I think she may have gone on the tour to Jaffa today, or Nazareth.'

'What's that?' he said, cocking his head to one side. 'She's not with you? I looked for her this morning, but I couldn't see her anywhere.'

'No doubt you'll meet up later on,' said Hamish loudly, winking at Jenny.

'I hope so,' he answered.

'And I thought you were going to behave yourself today,' Jenny said to Hamish as they walked back towards their coaches.

'I've been a model of decorum. I apologised to your chums, who were very gracious about it all. They asked me to their suite for drinks some evening, and I even offered to go and buy batteries for Ben's hearing aids, but he refused. I bet he can hear everything perfectly well, just pretends he can't so that he can switch off if he wants to. Or else he does it so he can lean closer to the ladies when they talk to him!'

'You're incorrigible.'

'Why don't you come back with us? Too many men on our bus.'

'No, thank you, I'm perfectly happy with my own company. I'll see you at dinner.'

Walking back she fell into step and conversation with an old man she had met on the bus. His wife wasn't very mobile and hadn't got off at any of the stops they'd made. They had been taken to a kibbutz for lunch and Jenny had held her bag while she was helped inside. She limped badly and was obviously in a lot of pain. Jenny had sat with them.

They looked time-weary, yet they obviously cared deeply for each other. Why can't I have that? she thought.

'How long have you been married?'

'Sixty-five years last March,' they answered together.

'That's fantastic. And you're still holding hands.'

They looked at each other and the woman smiled. 'Sometimes. We've been here before, but never on a cruise. Isn't it lovely?'

He continued, 'It hasn't always been sweetness and light, but there have been good times, lots of good times. Elizabeth was seventeen and I was eighteen when we married, and together we've survived a lot.'

'I could have listened to them all afternoon,' she told the others over dinner.

'You fared better than us,' said Marcus. 'We had Ben wondering aloud all day where Betty had got to and how he could have missed her.'

Just then John joined them, back from his couple of days' exploring on his own. Jenny was delighted to see him and willed him to sit beside her. He did.

'Tell me all the news and the gossip. Did I miss anything?'

'Nary a thing,' said Hamish. 'What did you get up to?'

They were surprised at how much they all had to tell each other. 'I was intrigued by the old men with their tightly curled ringlets and the assortment of clothes they were wearing,' Jenny told Sylvia.

'It's not usually as busy as it was today. It was a Jewish festival and you'd have seen fathers and sons going together to services all dressed the same.'

'I did, and the little fellows looked really cute, but what are those enormous fur hats about, in this heat, and the knee-length breeches?'

'It's traditional that the men copy the attire of their rabbis, and a lot of the clothes date back to where they originated – in Russia, Poland or wherever. And those fur hats have hollow tops.'

'I wedged a list of names of those dear to me into the Wailing Wall.'

'That's a given if you visit it. We believe that the wall is part of the original western wall of Temple Mount.'

The Boys were dining in their suite that night. There was no sign of Ben or Betty. Sylvia flirted with all the men at the table and Hamish flirted back with her. Jenny could sense an element of competition between him and Marcus. But when Marcus asked Sylvia if she'd like to go to the nightclub with him later, he asked in a way that suggested no one else was included. She seemed embarrassed, as though she didn't know how to reply, and hesitated a fraction too long.

John rescued her. 'I hear tonight's band is very good, rhythm and blues, I believe. I'll certainly be going up. What about the rest of you?'

'I hadn't intended asking the whole table. I was simply asking Sylvia if she'd like to come dancing with me,' Marcus said, in his direct way.

'Sorry, Marcus, I hadn't realised …' She looked at John and Hamish for assistance.

'We'll all go, and if you get tired of Hans Christian Andersen here,' Hamish slapped Marcus on the back, 'we'll give you a wee twirl on the floor.'

Jenny marvelled at how he got away with saying such things. His Celtic humour seemed to give him licence to charm and offend in the same sentence.

Soft lighting and lively music transformed the nightclub. By day it was the least-used space on the ship, a place where you could sit and relax, with nothing to impede your sea view. It was busy tonight and the dance floor was crowded as the band played a tribute set of Little Richard's hits. Hamish was in his element doing a rhythmless cross between the Gay Gordon's and rock and roll as he sang along with abandonment. He manoeuvred himself between Sylvia and Marcus and took her off in a swirl, leaving Jenny in front of the Dane, who was looking none too pleased. When he was reunited with Sylvia at the end of the number he made a point of escorting her to the bar and eventually to a booth away from the rest of them.

'You'll just have to share us,' John said to Jenny, seeing what was happening, 'I thought you said I hadn't missed anything. Is this the start of a romance?' he asked, but Will, who seemed to be on his own, came across the floor at that moment and asked her to dance.

'Where's Heather?' she asked. 'Is she dancing?'

'No, she doesn't like it. Much prefers to get her exercise in the gym. She's probably got her head buried in a book.

I prefer bopping any time. It's the only chance I get to grab hold of a pretty girl, these days.'

He drew her closer to him and she felt he'd had more than his fair share to drink. As soon as the music speeded up, she said, 'I love this one,' and detached herself to dance on her own. She was glad when the song ended. Will reminded her of discos where inebriated guys made a desperate grab for any woman if they hadn't managed to score in front of their mates.

She made her way back to John and Hamish, bought them nightcaps and said, 'I'm whacked after today so I'll take this back to my stateroom. I'll see you both tomorrow.'

Fifteen

WHEN HE GOT BACK TO THEIR SUITE, WILL found his wife in bed. She insisted on separate beds while cruising: 'I can't hack all that air-conditioning and it's just too hot to sleep with you.' He grudgingly agreed, but knew he'd get it when he wanted it and thought that might be now. He knew she'd never fancied him sexually, that theirs had been a business arrangement rather than a love match. They were good mates, most of the time, and Heather kept her side of their bargain and never refused him.

'If I agree to marry you, I'll do my duty, but not if you're drunk, and you can put that in the pre-nuptial agreement too,' she'd told him, when they'd got engaged.

He'd laughed at her straightforwardness. He liked it in her. She wasn't a pushover like his last wife, who was a giggler. She'd even giggled when they were having sex. She hadn't known who the prime minister was, or which party was in government. The only things she had taught him were what a WAG was and that his next wife would need to be more of a challenge, an intellectual equal.

He'd known when he'd met Heather that if she came into his life their relationship would never be pedestrian. She loved beautiful things and haunted auction houses and country-house sales. She dismissed popular magazines and television as a total waste of time. She could spend hours listening to classical music, lost in her own world. Her form of pop was Verdi.

'He speaks to my inner soul,' she'd told him early on. 'He makes it soar and dive. If only you could make me feel like that when we make love, I'd never stop!'

'I do my best.'

'I know you do.'

Will had known they'd be able to discuss world affairs, politics, sailing, racing. They had many shared friends and acquaintances, knew who should not be put beside whom at dinner tables. Heather was unique, eccentric certainly, but life with her would not be dull. Besides, he'd had the hots for her when she'd been married to that bore, chinless Clive or Clement or whatever he was called.

He walked over to the bed and unbuttoned his shirt. 'How about it, darling? You're not still in a huff about that drunken grope with the groom?'

'You've used up your one and only chance there,' she replied, moving over to accommodate him. 'If anything like that ever happens again, I'll chop it off and then I'll fleece you. There'll be nothing left for Mrs Pembry-Travers the fourth, if you even manage to find her.'

That was his Heather at her best and he found it a great turn-on. He laughed and climbed in beside her. He drew her nightdress slowly up over her legs, stomach and breasts, before lowering his lips to her nipple.

Jenny sat on her balcony, listening to the water slapping the side of the ship. The sea was very calm and she could hardly sense any movement. She found it hard to believe there were so many people on board yet she could feel so alone. Not lonely, just alone. There were people everywhere. Below the public areas there was another world where the staff spent their time. Were there on-board romances, illicit and otherwise, going on down there? There had to be. One of the bar staff had told her they had their own disco and bar and partied hard when they could.

It was a floating cosmos, where everyone was out to enjoy themselves. John intrigued her, debonair, divorced and delectable – mysterious, even. How had he managed to retire before he was forty? He hadn't given much away, but then she hadn't either. If she told anyone the story of her marriage, they'd feel sorry for her. She'd seem miserable and as if she'd had an awful life. And that was so far from the truth. They wouldn't see the real, optimistic Jenny, about to stumble into the future with no road map.

She liked Hamish. He was like an overgrown schoolboy and just as unpredictable. He got away with that acerbic wit because of his velvety Scottish voice. She liked the way he made no secret of trying to notch an Irish lass on his bedpost. It was flattering and made her feel good.

She had grown fond of Betty, too, with her zest for life and men, just not Ben. He was a dear old fellow but still missed his wife, trying desperately to keep her alive by referring to her all the time. Perhaps his daughter had sent him away so she could have a break from him.

Sylvia was an enigma, Jenny decided. She was outspoken and oozed sex appeal, a real hit with the men. She herself would never wear such tight-fitting dresses, but Sylvia got away with them.

They'd met on the corridor earlier and Sylvia had started telling her about her daughter: 'I can do nothing right and she can't wait to get away from me. Rebecca's still living at home but keeps insisting that as soon as she finishes university next summer she's going into a flat on her own. No more sharing for her – she fancies a penthouse somewhere chic. I decided to turn the tables on her and told her I needed to get away from her for a while, hence this cruise. For a change I didn't leave a full freezer. I gave my home help two weeks off and I didn't let her do any ironing last week. Maybe that girl will finally understand what it's like to look after herself and might just appreciate me when I get back.'

'The poor thing. How old is she?'

'There's nothing poor about her. She's been spoiled rotten by me, by her father, who now buys her anything she asks for because he feels guilty about the divorce, and by her grandparents, both sets, who dote on her too. Rebecca's been indulged all her life. She'll be twenty-one in December. Before I left, I phoned them all and told them on no condition are they to rescue her while I'm away. My mother said I was being very harsh.'

'Well, you obviously know your daughter better than anyone else. Your mother's probably being overprotective,' said Jenny.

'What's really rich is that this is the woman who sent me for plastic surgery on my eighteenth birthday to take the bend out of my nose – she told me it was ugly.'

'She didn't!'

'She did. All I got from her was "You're no beauty – your nose is ugly. It's too Jewish," which was rich too. From the time I reached puberty the other thing she kept telling me was that I must meet and marry a nice Jewish boy. A nice Jewish boy wouldn't have minded a nice Jewish nose, would he? But, no, I had to change it. When I found one and became pregnant, that nice Jewish boy was no longer acceptable and they had him sent away. Is it any wonder my daughter and I are a mess?'

'My mum died three days after my eighteenth birthday. I've never quite forgiven her, even though I know that's stupid. My father remarried very quickly afterwards and I haven't quite forgiven him either.'

'I wonder if we'll make the same mistakes they did.'

'Probably.'

'Families, eh? They think they have a licence to say anything to other family members. I bet your mother wouldn't have told anyone else they were no beauty,' said Jenny, thinking that a nose job for an eighteen-year-old was a bit extreme.

'Oh, she would, trust me!'

Jenny found herself admiring Sylvia for the single-minded way in which she seemed to have dealt with life. She had let slip that she had an apartment in Cyprus and was going to meet her lawyer when they docked there: she was considering upgrading to a villa. Money seemed to be no object.

And there's me, she thought. Just over two months ago she was still married. Now she was cruising on her own, not knowing what she was going to do with her life. Richie, her brother-in-law, was right. She'd have to finalise things with Fergus if she were to move on. Being angry forever wouldn't solve anything. She'd go to a solicitor when she got back and set things in motion. She hoped Leslie had told their brothers what had happened. She couldn't face doing that, and knew they'd want to murder him for hurting her.

Sixteen

EARLIER THAT EVENING THE BUTLER HAD arrived at the Mistral Suite. He had pushed a trolley into the sitting room and, with a flourish, set the small table with starched linen and gleaming silverware. Sonny and Bud had been in the next room downloading the photos they had taken over the previous few days.

'Would you like me to come back when you've finished and clear away?' the butler had asked.

'No, thank you. You can put the do-not-disturb sign on the door on the way out.'

'Well, hon, what do you make of the honeymoon so far?' Sonny asked, putting his hand on Bud's knee.

'It's been pretty perfect, apart from that episode in the casino the first night.'

'Oh, give it a rest, Bud. I was just making conversation with the guy, being polite.'

'The guy's name is Juan, and you were giving him the once-over. I was there, remember, and you were definitely coming on to him.'

'Because I asked him where he was from?'

'It was written on his badge, under his name, with his country's flag beside it.'

'I hadn't noticed that, and we've been over this already.'

Bud was determined to make his point. 'Had he ever been to Vegas? What difference would it have made if he had?'

'That was just being friendly too.'

'So you say.'

'It's the truth.'

'So that's why you stayed on after I'd changed what I had left, just to be friendly?'

'We've been through all this before. I stayed because I was having fun, and because I was winning,' Sonny said. 'I like winning.'

'You're greedy. You want it all, don't you? You have me now and already you're looking around for someone else.'

'Oh, please, Bud, don't be so melodramatic. Let's eat.'

'I can't, not with you anyway, but you enjoy your dinner because I'm going to the buffet for mine to see what I can pick up there. And I might even go to the casino after that and try my luck.'

'Good, because I can't take any more of your childish fantasies. It was bad enough the way you treated the wedding planner, practically accusing him of trying to seduce me. Maybe we should have gone to a convent for our honeymoon, somewhere there'd only be some old nuns around to distract me.'

Bud picked up his key card. 'You needn't wait up for me.' The door slammed behind him.

Sonny was furious and got up to follow him, then changed his mind. Bud's outbursts never lasted too long and he couldn't let the lobster go to waste.

They'd met at a post-production party of a film Bud had been making in Nevada. Sonny had been there as a plus one for one of the makeup artists. He was a stylist then – for one of the most exclusive men's shops in New York. As such he always knew who was in town and what events they were likely to be attending. Above all, he was discreet in his work and private life. Because his discretion could be depended on, he'd soon got work as personal stylist and shopper to the A-listers who lived in or visited New York. He was probably one of the few people who could tell with any degree of authority whether George Clooney was gay or not, but he wouldn't. Since that first meeting, which Sonny had almost cried off attending because the makeup artist had become too possessive, he and Bud had been inseparable, if you didn't count the innumerable times they had fallen out over Bud's irrational jealousy and Sonny's need to flirt.

Seventeen

DOUG WAS ON THE BRIDGE. IT WAS TWO A.M. and all was quiet. He wasn't on duty but he couldn't sleep. Normally he loved this time of night, when fishing and cargo boats moved silently on the inky water and the odd cruise liner passed at a safe distance, its lights twinkling like crystals. The sea was calm. He was not.

His number two said nothing as his commander strode about. It wasn't the first time he'd made these unscheduled visits, blaming insomnia.

The latest email Doug had received from his wife an hour earlier had caused his blood pressure to rise further. What was he expected to do from a ship almost two thousand miles from home? Andrea wasn't coping. She hadn't been since Lewis was born. She was drinking too – he knew that from the tone of her email and from the time at which it had been sent. He had taken extended leave when their son was six months old to help her with her post-natal depression. They had gone from one doctor to another but nothing had seemed to help. They were told it would take time. Her mother had moved in for a while, but Andrea had thrown her out because she'd discovered her daughter's hidden supply of gin in the laundry basket. Andrea had said she had got rid of her because she was plotting to take the baby away and planting booze to make her look like an unfit mother.

In hindsight it was apparent that Andrea had been drinking heavily all the time Doug had known her, but she was clever, having learned how to conceal it publicly. Doug drank socially, but never while he was in command. He had done his fair share as a junior officer, but he had seen its effects and how it destroyed careers, and he was ambitious.

Andrea had been cunning, and in their early days Doug had never suspected anything, enjoying and sharing her popularity and gregariousness while accepting them as part of her role. It was only when she had lost her job with the other cruise company that he realised her outgoing nature was a front. She had managed to lead a double life for a long time, but in the end, her craving had overtaken her willpower during the long shifts she worked. She had been discovered charging drinks, even bottles of wine, to guests' tabs. She had been under surveillance for a while before they told her. Her reputation had been untarnished previously and she was given a warning instead of her notice, with the proviso that she took advantage of staff counselling. Within weeks of being back on board, she was caught again. She had been told her dismissal was effective immediately and was asked to hand back her uniform and phone. She was kept under virtual ship arrest until they docked close to an international airport from which she could be repatriated. She was relieved they didn't press charges and drank more to forget her humiliation.

The cruise world was a small one. Many crew members had friends or family serving on other ships and in other lines, and with the immediacy of emails and mobile communications, Andrea's disgrace wasn't a secret for very long. Doug had worked through it, his colleagues not referring to it, but it hung unsaid in his presence, in the staff dining room and on the bridge. That was almost harder to bear because he was aware that everyone was talking about it. It would have been good to unburden himself to someone, but it would have been disloyal to do so.

For a time Andrea had hidden from the world. Guildford, where they had bought their house, was new for both of them and they hadn't had much opportunity to make friends. They hadn't considered this an issue when they had fallen in love with the period house. A few months after her dismissal, and after Andrea had spent three months in rehab, she had become pregnant. Doug had just signed up with a new company. He was looking forward to the challenges ahead, although deep down he joined his ship and command with trepidation.

Children hadn't been a priority. They hadn't discussed it much, assuming they would come along in time, but not quite yet. She had stopped drinking for the duration of the pregnancy. Now they were faced with post-natal depression and it wasn't long before she turned to alcohol to try to lift her spirits.

She'd attempted suicide the day after he'd joined this ship and he had had to be relieved on compassionate grounds. Lewis was only six months old. His sisters had come to the rescue, taking turns to mind the infant when Andrea was admitted again to rehab, a different facility this time. There she was to address her drinking and have her depression managed. Afterwards, when she returned home, she had seemed to be back to her old self and he had felt confident enough to go back to his command. But he still had concerns.

'Is it natural not to bond with your baby?' he had asked his mother.

'It's not normal, but it does happen. Not everyone is cut out to be a mother. Some people don't like small babies, but as they grow and start responding they are usually won over. Andrea's been through a lot. Give her time. She'll come around.'

He'd wanted to believe her, but now, six months on, she was drinking seriously again and he was too far away to do anything about it. He'd spent hours trying to figure out if her suicide attempt had been a cry for help, or a rehearsal.

'How do I know she'll not try something like that again?' he'd asked her counsellor.

'No one can answer that. But if you worry about it all the time, you'll never be able to rekindle your trust in her.'

'But what about our child? How can I protect him when I'm not there?'

'You can't police her around the clock. All your families can do is make sure that there is a good support network. That's the best way to ensure that any behavioural changes won't go unnoticed.'

'Am I overreacting?'

'Not at all. You have every reason to feel like this, especially as you work away from home, but generally post-natal depression decreases with time and Andrea is being well monitored and medicated.'

But if Doug was honest with himself, he never had rekindled any trust in Andrea and wondered if he ever would.

Tonight's email had read, *I've had enough. I can't take more of this. You off enjoying your cushy life … forgotten …* There was nothing else. If Andrea were merely drunk she'd probably be more rational in the morning, but if she'd passed out and Lewis was crying in his cot for her … or if she'd taken too many pills … He reached for his mobile and rang their landline, which was beside their bed. There was no reply. Then he dialled Andrea's mobile. She didn't answer that either so Doug called his mother.

'I'll have to take some time off,' he said, after apologising yet again for waking her.

'If you do that, you'll get a reputation for not being reliable or up to the job,' she said.

'Lewis is more important than my job.'

'Oh, Doug, I know he is. I'll go around there now. You've worked so hard to get where you are. Don't do anything hasty to jeopardise that.'

'I'm not worried about me being hasty, I'm worried about Andrea being incapable.'

'We'll sort something out between us until she gets better again.'

'If she gets better.'

'She will, with the right help. I've been thinking perhaps we could get an au pair to stay with her for a while. That way you'd know Lewis was being taken care of in situations like this. I'll bring it up with her, if you like, and see what she says. She might be more comfortable with a stranger around her. Maybe she'd feel less threatened. It can't be easy always having your mother-in-law or sisters-in-law looking over your shoulder.'

'Mum, when did you get that halo? She threw her own mother out.'

'I have a thicker skin. Didn't I raise you three? Look, I don't mind interfering a bit, and between us all we'll manage, so don't worry.'

'I don't know what I'd do without you.'

'That's what families are for. I'll go around now and check things out.'

'Should you go on your own? What if she gets violent? Ring Maxine. You will let me know what's going on, won't you? Text me when you get there, please, will you?'

'I will.'

'And sorry again for waking you up.'

Half an hour later a text arrived from one of his sisters: *We're at yours. Everything fine! Lewis coming for a little holiday to mine. Don't worry – will mail you in the morning M xx*

Doug felt as if a weight had been lifted off him. He'd just been given a reprieve. Maxine was a natural mum and loved Lewis as she did her own children. His son would be safe now, for the moment, but he wished he could say the same for his wife.

Eighteen

ALTHOUGH IT WAS SCARCELY THREE hundred miles from Israel to Cyprus there was a sea day between the two – time to relax and enjoy the amenities of the ship. The News and Pursuits bulletin for day six was filled with events and activities, from vodka-tasting to dance lessons. There was a carnival atmosphere on board that day, with the officers involved in providing a poolside buffet. Doug watched from the top deck as ice sculptures were wheeled out from the galleys, depicting mermaids and seahorses. They began melting almost immediately, but the trickles of water snaking across the decks quickly dried in the Mediterranean sun. The food stations were decorated with carved melons and pineapples.

One chef created animals and geometric patterns that stood out in relief as the different colours of the fruits were delicately exposed. Some of the officers cooked steak, chicken or fish. Another carved a suckling pig, which had been spit-roasted in advance. All added their own national garnishes and accents to the dishes and touted unashamedly to the passengers to try their wares. The aromas were fantastic and there was a great buzz as people queued to sample everything.

'That's a great party down there,' one passenger said to Doug.

'We aim to please. And I think the crew enjoy it as much as the guests. Have you tried any of the dishes?'

'Not yet. We wanted to take a few pictures first. Can we have one with you?' the wife asked.

'Certainly.' He signalled to one of the waiting staff to take the photograph of the three of them together.

'You must try some of our maître d's speciality. It's called Kaiser's Mess,' Doug said. 'It looks a mess, but it tastes divine. That's him there – he's got a crowd around him already.'

From their vantage point they looked down and saw the corpulent officer playing to the gallery, adding alcohol liberally to whatever concoction he had made.

Noticing Doug watching him, he raised the bottle and saluted his captain. Doug laughed and saluted back.

John interrupted Jenny's daydream. When his shadow fell over her she instinctively sat up and reached for her sarong.

'I've secured a table over there. Ben and Betty are holding it for us. I'm going to see if I can round up any of the others to join us.'

'I saw Marcus earlier. He's reading in the shade.'

Then Jenny spotted Hamish coming down from the upper deck where he liked to sunbathe. She waved and caught his attention. Sylvia was still toasting herself, making sure there would be no strap marks with her low-cut swimsuit. She had hardly moved all morning. Hamish went over and splashed her.

The gala deck lunch was a noisy affair. They stayed chatting at their table for more than two hours. Gradually people left to take siestas and a break from the heat. Ben was the first to leave, telling them all, again, that he had diabetes and would have to have his dinner early because that was his routine.

'Well, Ben, we'll see you around,' said John.

When he'd gone, Betty said, 'Not if I can avoid him, I won't. I came away to try and meet someone with a bit of life in them, not someone who's married to the memory of his dead wife and sets his clock around his medical regime.' She caught Hamish's look of disbelief. 'I told you, young man, I may be in my seventies but I haven't forgotten what life is about.'

'Obviously not, and for the record I think you're marvellous! And you're playing hard to get.'

'What about the rest of you? Did you hope to meet someone on the trip?'

'Yes,' Sylvia said. 'I enjoyed being married and would risk

it again. I'm ready to start a new relationship, and they say it's easier to do that on holiday.'

'Do you really think so? I'd imagine it would be harder to get to know the real person in a situation like this. It's an unreal world,' said Marcus.

'Isn't love an unreal place too?' asked Betty.

'Probably. I'd never thought about it like that.'

'If you find it you should hold on to it,' John said with conviction. 'Would you agree, Jenny?'

'I'm not sure. Sometimes it destroys people. It can turn from love to possession, obsession, hurt and even hatred.'

'Wow, Jenny, that's dark,' said Sylvia. 'I live in hope that I'll get it right the next time – that there's a knight in shining armour just waiting to find me and carry me off to his castle, or whatever, and we'll live happily ever after.'

'That's the spirit,' said Betty. 'If you believe it, it can happen.'

'I'm not sure I want a next time,' Jenny said, and flushed as she sensed John stare at her. He said nothing. Neither did anyone else. She felt churlish: she had changed the tone of a pretty perfect lunch, and she hadn't meant to do that. She had sounded like a disillusioned woman. 'I'm sorry. I don't know where that came from. Excuse me.' She stood up, anxious to get away before the tears spilled.

John put a hand out, but Sylvia restrained him. 'Let her go.'

To avoid meeting anyone in the lift she ran down the stairs and along the corridor, holding back until she got inside her stateroom, then she let go and sobbed. She cried over her pent-up anger at her husband. She cried for what he had turned her into – a bitter, angry woman. She cried for the way he had broken her faith in people. The old Jenny would never have been so cynical, but then she realised she wasn't cynical: she genuinely felt she could never trust anyone again. She had loved Fergus unconditionally and he had crushed that love. She knew that most men were good and kind, like her brothers, her brother-in-law and her friends' husbands. She'd just been unlucky.

How was she going to face the others later? Maybe she'd just order room service. She toyed with the idea of ringing her sister. Leslie's voice would calm her, but she knew she'd only make her worry and decided against it. Eventually she fell asleep.

She woke at four thirty, feeling drained. A moment later she thought she heard a gentle knock and something being pushed into her door slot. She lay still and waited a few minutes before investigating. She wasn't ready to face anyone just yet. Eventually she got up, opened the door quietly and took the envelope from the slot. She tossed it onto the bed, then went to wash her face before looking at its contents.

Inside there was a voucher for the spa, a hot-stone massage, in thirty minutes' time. There was a note: *My treat. Enjoy. Betty. X*

Nineteen

HAMISH HAD SPREAD THE BROCHURES OUT on his bed. He liberated a bottle of whisky from the stash in his sock drawer and poured two generous measures.

'A splash of water, is that right?' he asked Sylvia, taking a bottle from the fridge. They'd be in Cyprus the following day and he was going to see the hotel his friends had recommended he should consider as an investment. He also had a few apartments to view. When he'd discovered Sylvia had property there, he'd decided to pick her brains and had invited her to his stateroom. 'I'm in a wee bit of flux at the moment. I'm trying to decide on selling my business, buying abroad and keeping a bolthole somewhere at home, and I'm beginning to wonder if I'm mad to consider getting involved in so many ventures at the same time.'

'Why do you have to do them all at once?'

'I have a few classic cars I like to tinker with and rally sometimes. Currently I keep them in a disused warehouse. If I relinquish that space it'll cost me a fortune to garage them.'

'How many have you got?'

'Eleven or twelve,' he answered, 'and I've had enough of wet and windy Scottish weather, so it's decision time. I developed this facial-neuralgia thing so, whatever happens, I won't spend another winter there. I've put my place in Edinburgh on the market, and as soon as I get rid of it, hopefully before the winter, I'll rent for a few months while I tie up the loose ends.'

'If you bought into the hotel you'd obviously have accommodation in Cyprus whenever you'd want it, I presume. So that might be the best of both worlds, get a *pied-à-terre* at home and have warmer winters in the Med.'

'I have a few places in Ayia Napa. I bought them years ago when my father died, but I never stayed in them. I have them with a letting agency and they oversee everything for me. If I do go into the hotel, I might sell them, but if I decide against it, I might just buy a wee den in Cyprus for just myself.'

'I get great use out of my place and I prefer to come over in the winter when there are fewer tourists. I try to make it every November with some of my friends and in March with my daughter, but Paphos is lovely any time. I'm actually considering something more permanent for myself, and am meeting my solicitor there tomorrow. He's a good friend. If you wanted to ask his advice, I'm sure he'd be honest with you. Where exactly is the hotel development? Is it near the historical sites?'

'It's further down, overlooking the beach.' He took the map out and showed her.

'That's only minutes from the place I'm going to see.'

'We'd be neighbours, then. Or you could marry me and we'd just have to buy one place. That would be a good compromise!'

She threw back her head and laughed at him. 'Nice try, but I'd be hoping for a more romantic proposal than a money-saving one.'

They talked on about tax implications and rents, and he explained, 'Longevity is not an asset the men in my family seem to enjoy. Who was it that said, "There's only one thing worse than growing old and that's dying young"? My father and his three brothers all died in their forties and early fifties. They had never taken a week off work in their lives. I think it's very sad that not one of them had ever made time for a wee bit o' fun. They all died wealthy and they left it all behind them. I don't want to be the same. I want to be decadently lazy, somewhat naughty,' he said mischievously, 'and self-indulgent, see a wee bit more o' the world and enjoy myself a tad before I go.'

'Don't we all! You don't seem to be doing too badly. Anyway, you've no guarantee that you'll have the same fate. You could live to be a hundred.'

'Aye, I could, so I might as well do it in places I like. You know, Sylvia, recently I realised I was doing exactly the same as they'd done before me, working all the hours that God sent, always trying to best my competitors. It's a cut-throat business and failure was never an option. My father built the company up from a fleet of three to a sizeable one of road trains and hiliners that go all over the continent. Don't get me started. I'm on my holidays! Apart from the cars and the rallies, I never went anywhere, and hadn't been abroad since my ex-wife died. Crazy, isn't it? And what's even crazier is that I don't know why I stopped. I used to love to travel. Then, out of the blue, my main rivals in business made an offer to buy me out. It was a very good one but I scoffed at their cheek. I never had any intention of retiring but it got me thinking.'

'So did you accept?'

'Not yet. They've upped the offer since, and I'm still trying to decide what's best. That's why I came on this cruise, that and the itinerary. It's great to have more than a few hours in a place and I was planning to come over to Paphos anyway.'

'You wouldn't have to retire – you could always start a new business, maybe even do something completely different.'

'I like to be busy and I have a few things in mind, new ventures and all that, but I have a young nephew working with me and I don't want to give away his birthright. I'm not quite convinced whether he's in it for love of the haulage industry or as a means to a sure legacy when I keel over – there'll always be a demand for road freight when you live on an island.'

'That's cynical.'

'Aye, and true. He's just like me, a chip off the old block and all that malarkey, and that's what I'd have been thinking at his age, so I know. If I do agree to the buyout it would have to be conditional on him having a share and a place in the new company.'

'It sounds as though you get on well together.'

'We do. He's a capable lad and he shares my passion for the old cars – he likes nothing better than tweaking and tuning them with me. He's just acquired one of his own too, a Triumph TR6. She's a beauty. As I have no bairns of my own he's the next best thing.' He folded the map.

'Boys and their toys, eh?'

'Something like that. Can I top you up? We can take them out on the balcony.'

She nodded and went over to slide open the door.

He stretched and smiled. He liked her gutsiness, and she was a looker, but he wasn't sure if the Dane had already made a move on her.

Twenty

BETTY HAD GONE TO THE SPA AFTER JENNY'S abrupt departure from the lunch table. She had seen something of her young self in her. She was fragile. Betty had been hurt enough to recognise it. She was convinced that loving someone, and all that it entailed, was not worth the pain that followed when it went wrong. Her first love had been a bully. He wooed her, spoiled her, married her, humiliated and belittled her. It had started subtly enough and she had refused to admit to herself that something was not right with their relationship. After the rows, which he made her feel were her fault, she had tried even harder to please him. In her early-married days women's liberation hadn't yet become headlines.

You belonged to your husband. Women were expected to stay at home and be good little housewives. It wasn't done to talk about your marriage or your problems. If you had any, you kept them to yourself. Magazine articles told you how to look attractive for your husband and how you should have the toys put away, the children bathed and ready for bed, your hair combed and your lipstick on by the time he came home, tired from a taxing day at the office.

Betty, with other women who had been fifties and sixties brides, had officially become 'a housewife' once she had married. That was the category on driving licences and census forms, and she had complied wholeheartedly. She had put aside her teaching qualification so that she could be a good wife and mother, making sure the house was always spotless and welcoming, that his favourite meals were always ready for him. 'What's this disgusting offering?' he'd often ask, when she'd spent hours preparing something different. 'Aren't I giving you enough housekeeping money to put a decent meal in front of your husband?' He'd stand up and leave it untouched.

Sex was sex, not the lovemaking she craved, but a duty, with no thought of pleasure or satisfaction for her. It was all over very quickly. No tenderness, no imagination, always the missionary position, followed by a post-coital smoke. Orgasms hadn't been written about then either and the G-spot was unknown.

His death from a brain haemorrhage seven years into their marriage had brought letters and cards of sympathy from work colleagues, neighbours, relatives and friends, all consoling her on her tragic loss, saying what a lovely man he had been. She wore mourning black for six months, told her children how good their daddy had been and how much he had loved them, which he had in his fashion, and planned ways to make her life better.

His pension and frugality had helped. She could manage quite comfortably. But she never grieved his passing, never missed him beside her in their bed. She never told a soul that she had been relieved when the policeman had come to the door to tell her he had died. He'd collapsed on the pavement outside his office and had succumbed on the way to hospital. Once the shock had worn off and the funeral was over, she felt as though a huge cloud had blown away. She had felt liberated and free, as though she owned her life again and had a second chance to do it her way. She'd got work teaching in the local girls' school and, as they became old enough, she even had her own girls in her classes.

For some strange reason Jenny had been the catalyst in dredging up these memories. Something about the hurt look in her eyes when she'd announced, 'I'm not sure I want a next time,' had brought them flooding back to Betty. She had been there, and it was a very dark place while it lasted. But she had found love a second time, with a wonderful, warm, responsive and caring man, a headmaster in the local boys' school, who had embraced her daughters as his own. When he had died they had mourned him with love and happy memories. It was those contrasts that prompted her to go to the spa and book a treatment for her. Jenny was fragile, and Betty felt she was a kindred spirit. She hoped she'd learn to trust again, as she had done.

*

Jenny lay in the darkened room, the pling-pling spa music washing over her while aromatic essences tickled her nose. Her immediate reaction had been to cancel the appointment, but that might have been ungracious. She couldn't let Betty pay for this treatment; she'd sort it out with her later or return the compliment.

Before she'd begun, the Filipina masseuse had slathered her with oil. 'The stones give their power and warmth to tired muscles, promoting peace and tranquillity.' As she worked on her back Jenny felt herself relax properly for the first time in ages. She hadn't realised until then how tense she had been, and by the time her seventy-five minutes were over she was revived and ready to face the world.

'I wish I could bring you home with me,' she told the masseuse. 'That was fantastic.'

'Well, spoil yourself. Come back again for another before the end of the cruise.'

'I might just do that,' she replied, and meant it.

Twenty-one

RECONCILED, BUD AND SONNY HAD SPENT
the afternoon on the top deck, basting each other and basking
in the hot sun. Bud was reading and rereading a script.
He'd promised to give his verdict on it when he got home
from Europe. He'd been gripped by the storyline, with a
few reservations, and he'd been happy to have it go to the
screenwriters. Now he wasn't so sure. He'd always gone with
his instincts and they'd never failed him up to now, but this
was outside his normal genre and he felt the main female
character didn't ring true.

'When I read this I keep thinking of Katharine Hepburn,'
he said to Sonny. 'The main character reminds me of her.

She was constantly cast in roles that she didn't grow into. She didn't suit any of those romantic leads she was given.'

'I never saw any chemistry on screen between her and Spencer Tracy.'

'They were both under contract to Metro Goldwyn Mayer, and it made economic sense to use them as much as they could. Besides, Tracy didn't want their relationship to become public.'

'How do you know all these things or, more importantly, how do you remember all that trivia?' asked Sonny.

'Film school. Anyway, this woman,' he said, waving the script around, 'is supposed to be in shock. She's discovered her perfectly respectable husband is a paedophile. She's devastated, yet when he's accused she sits beside him in court, holding his hand. I just feel that's totally out of character. Would she be able to behave like that towards him after she'd found out something so devastating? I'd imagine, if I were her, that I'd have chopped his balls off. Wouldn't you? This is her final scene and it's just not working for me. Would you read that passage and tell me what you think about it?'

'Bud, you know I'm hopeless at that stuff. Ask me what she should be wearing for the scene and I'll tell you.' He saw Bud's look of disappointment and said, 'Give it.' He read through the selected pages and said, 'You know what this needs? A woman's eyes. Why not get Betty, Sylvia and Jenny to read it? Ask that woman who was with us on the coach the other day, the one with the scary eyebrows, too. Just give them the bare outline of the story and a bit of her character and ask them what they make of her from those pages. You couldn't find four more different women, so if it works for them it'll work for a general audience.'

'You're a genius, husband. But would it be very cheeky to ask them?'

'I don't think so. Let's get them together for some pre-dinner drinks in the suite and do it.'

'Today?'

'This evening.'

Bud was up like a shot. He donned his bathrobe, stashed his sun-screen in his bag and, script in hand, said, 'I'm off to have this photocopied. Leave voice messages on all their machines if they're not there. Thanks, gorgeous,' he said, blowing him a kiss.

Betty sent her second daughter a text message: *Hope everything and everyone good at home. Have met a very interesting bunch of people who make mealtimes most enjoyable and entertaining. One of them described us as delightful misfits and I think he was right. Ship lovely. Food great. Delighted I came. Off to cocktails now in a film producer's suite! Love to all. Mum xxx*

Her daughter replied: *Mum! We always knew we could let you go out on your own, but remember what happened the last time you met 'interesting' people on a ship!! I think we're all too old for a new stepfather, never mind a misfit one. Xxx Your worried daughter!*

Betty laughed. It didn't need a reply. She and three of her daughters were very close. It was the eldest she had problems with – or, rather, who had problems with her. Betty put her hand to her side. She was unaware that she did this every time she experienced a dart of pain. The last one had been bad. She'd go back to her stateroom and take some tablets.

*

Sylvia dressed in a clingy devoré number that accentuated her ample bosom and curvaceous bottom. She fastened her jewellery around her wrists and neck, and only then remembered her fob chain. She'd hate to lose it. It had been a gift from her grandfather for her bat mitzvah. He'd taken her into the dingy office in his pawnbroker's shop and opened the large safe to reveal his personal riches. It was a true Aladdin's cave of treasures. Little trays held rings that glittered with diamonds, sapphires, emeralds and other precious or semi-precious stones that she hadn't yet learned to recognise. Other drawers contained fobs and pendants, pearls and charm bracelets, while the watches were separated in different trays for men and women. He'd allowed her to choose a piece that she would wear when 'you become a lady'. She'd picked a more modest slimmer chain with finer links and a little pearl, but he'd insisted on her taking the chunkier one.

'Some people are superstitious about pearls – they think they represent tears, and we can't have that. I don't want my little girl having any more tears in her life than she has to.'

That visit and the chain had inspired in Sylvia an interest in jewellery that would eventually lead her to go to work with her father. He had inherited the business and her grandfather had lived to see her grow into the lady he'd envisaged. Together, all three had refined it from a pawnshop to a very successful high-end jewellery boutique.

Although in value the fob chain was hardly significant, it was priceless in terms of sentiment and memories. She treasured it and, despite the significant cache of gems she had amassed over the years, no other gift had ever meant as much to her.

She couldn't believe she'd lost it. She searched through her pouches but there was no sign of it. She even took her suitcases out from under the bed to look inside them. I'm sure I was wearing it when I flew to join the ship at Athens, she thought. Perhaps not. Maybe it's at home. I'll report it anyway, in case it slipped off without me noticing. It may have been handed in.

She completed her makeup, gave her hair another spray of lacquer and headed off to Guest Relations.

The attendant was called Jack, his name-tag told her. He flashed a white smile and went off to fetch the book where everything that was handed in was recorded, but there was no entry for it.

'Don't worry. It may well turn up. Sometimes people find things and forget to bring them to us until the next day, or only remember it when they're passing on their way out for an excursion, so please check back with us again.'

'I'm not even sure I lost it on the ship.'

'Well, fingers crossed you did, and we'll find it for you.'

Sylvia thanked him and took a lift up to the Mistral Suite. She was intrigued by Sonny's message. It promised proper Manhattans in exchange for some professional advice. She didn't know what she could contribute to the party but was curious. She was delighted to see that Betty was already there, getting a lesson in cocktail-making from Bud. She hadn't met Heather before and they eyed each other suspiciously.

Jenny was the last to arrive. She'd bumped into the older couple she had met the first afternoon on the bridge. 'You both look very glamorous. Is today the anniversary?'

'Yes,' he replied. 'Rose and I are having drinks with our family and friends in the cocktail lounge and then we're dining in the Ravello restaurant.'

'That sounds lovely.'

'It is,' Rose chuckled, 'but I feel tipsy already – the captain sent us a bottle of champagne earlier.'

'You deserve it. It's not every day you celebrate forty-five years together.'

'It's gone by so quickly, hasn't it, Matt?'

He nodded. 'I think our children have a few surprises in store for us.'

'Well, I look forward to hearing about them and the party. Have a great evening.'

'We will,' they replied in unison, and headed for the lifts.

Sonny answered the door and ushered Jenny onto the balcony in time to hear Betty announce, 'If there's to be a casting couch I demand to have my agent present. And it had better not be an epic as I might not be around long enough to see it finished!'

'Don't talk like that,' Jenny said.

'Do you really have an agent?' asked Heather.

'No, but I'll get one if I'm going to Hollywood!'

'Ladies, I'm not sure about Hollywood. Sonny and I asked you here to get your honest opinion on something that relates to my work. I hope you won't think I'm taking advantage of your good nature.'

'For Manhattans like these I'll give anyone my opinion,' said Sylvia.

Bud explained his dilemma, gave them a sketchy overview of the storyline, then asked them to read the pages he was going to distribute.

'What will you do if we don't like it?' asked Sylvia.

'You don't have to like it. Just give me an honest reaction.'

'So, no pressure, then,' muttered Jenny, and the others laughed.

When they'd had time to read and digest the piece, opinion was divided among the women. They debated back and forth, and had more cocktails, before Bud declared, 'Well, that was very worthwhile, thank you, ladies. I'll go back to the scriptwriters and get them to tweak the final scene. Now, how are we doing for time?'

'I wish you'd wear a watch. You ask me that at least a dozen times a day.'

'Well, I usually use my phone, but I've given that up for the honeymoon. Ladies, Sonny is to timepieces what Imelda Marcos was to shoes!'

'Like, that's no exaggeration.' Sonny laughed, and told them they were all late for dinner.

Jenny caught up with Betty on the way and thanked her for her spa treat.

'I'm glad you enjoyed it. Now, not another word about it.'

'But it's—'

'I said, not another word. It was my pleasure. That little get-together was fun, wasn't it? Now, let's see if those nice men have kept any space at their table for us tonight.'

They had, and were seated with an empty chair between each one. They'd left two together for the Boys.

'Some of you haven't met my husband. He can be quite witty company, on a good day. Just don't get him started on his yacht, or horses.' Heather said as she went off to join Will at their usual table after issuing an invitation to them all for drinks on their balcony next time.

'Have I met her husband?' John asked.

'He's the guy who came over and asked me to dance the other night. Will, in the nightclub, remember?'

'We thought you'd got fed up with our company,' said Hamish as Sylvia made an issue of sitting between him and John.

'No, we were just having a pre-promo-production meeting for our new movie.' Betty giggled. 'How many Manhattans did I have? Sonny, you have a very heavy hand.'

'So I've been told. That's one of my virtues.'

'It's my fault we're late,' Bud explained. 'I called an impromptu meeting of my new executive all-female editorial team.'

'We got a bit carried away,' Jenny said. 'The prospect of the silver – or should that be hi-definition multi-coloured? – screen, the mention of Hollywood and all that. But it was fun.

I'd love to read the whole script, if that isn't against copyright laws or anything.'

'Be my guest,' said Bud. 'I'd value your comments.'

It turned out that John was a bit of a movie buff and knew Bud's movies very well.

'Maybe you'd like to back this one,' Bud said.

'Let's talk about it another time.'

This exchange wasn't lost on Hamish, who muttered to Sylvia, 'Christ, where did that young buck get his money from?'

Marcus admitted he never went to the cinema, preferring documentaries on television to fiction. The Boys promised that if it got as far as being premièred they'd all be invited along to London or NY. It would be a great excuse for a reunion.

Dinner over, they progressed to the nightclub where the dance hosts were already busy with the unattached. Chad came over and said hello to everyone. 'He still looks familiar to me, but I just can't place him,' John said, in an undertone, to Jenny. Kathy, the computer woman, was there too, and Jenny wondered where and with whom she now dined. She hadn't eaten with them since the first night, although she waved when they met.

Will joined them, without Heather again. 'She's gone to get ready for me,' he joked. They all danced a little, laughed a lot and thanked their gods that they still had eight nights left, to enjoy more of the same.

Twenty-two

DOUG WAS AT THE HELM WHEN THE SHIP dropped anchor off Paphos. Cyprus was a favourite stop with passengers and for the next two days he'd watch them come and go as they liked, enjoying a little of what the island had to offer. The old port was too small and too shallow to accommodate the ship, so they tendered the guests back and forth. That'd keep some of his crew busy.

Tendering in the lifeboats was a new experience for Jenny and many of the guests. 'Let's hope this is the only reason we'll ever need to get into one of these,' they said to the crew, who smiled. They'd heard the same remark more times than they could possibly remember.

'These things look much bigger when you're inside them,' someone said as they sat down.

It took only minutes to ply the waters to the port and the cruise ship, which had towered over them when they moved away from it, quickly shrank into the distance.

Jenny wanted to go off exploring on her own: she had to do this to get a sense of where she was. However, the woman she was talking to said, 'I'm heading to see some of the ruins.' That had been her intention too. She'd caught a bit of the Destination Lecture on the television in her stateroom and had learned that the island was the territory of Aphrodite, the Greek goddess of love. She couldn't leave the other woman without being rude, so she walked along beside her. They ended up meandering in and out of the remains of temples and villas, marvelling at the clarity of the mosaics and how they had survived the centuries.

'Are you enjoying the cruise?' Jenny asked.

'I'm loving every minute of it. We haven't done many, but each one gets better and they're all so different.'

'Are they?' Jenny was surprised. 'In what way?'

'Well, according to the people at our table, veterans although they're in their thirties, this one has a slightly older clientele because of the three-day stopover in Israel. Lots of family groups are making pilgrimages to their Promised Land. On the last Med cruise we did, it was party time the whole way, dancing under the stars, fancy dress and themed evenings. It was quite wild. And terrific fun. Have you a nice crowd at your table?'

'Definitely. They're an interesting bunch and we have great conversations, no holds barred.'

'I wonder what Aphrodite would make of all these tourists traipsing around her island.'

'She'd probably think she was in Hell, her paradise overrun with foreigners.'

They laughed and the woman looked at her watch. 'I promised my husband I'd meet him for lunch. He's not interested in history, unless it's to do with sport. It was really nice talking to you, Jenny.'

'You too. We'll bump into each other again, no doubt.'

Jenny detected a very different sense of history here from what she had encountered in Israel. She felt carefree and happy and … optimistic. She still had no clear vision of where the future might lead, but she was open to opportunities. It might be time to do a bit of travelling, she thought. She could probably keep doing her translations and maybe even teach English too, if she felt like it. She'd always wanted to see South America, and maybe now was the time to plan it.

It was stiflingly hot. Despite her straw hat, flimsy blouse and linen shorts she was baking, so she decided to have lunch by the sea to enjoy the breeze. As she strolled along, waiters cajoled and coaxed passers-by into their restaurants. She found one that she liked the look of and it had a free table in the shade. She ordered a cool drink while she considered what to eat.

She wondered what was happening at home. She knew what the papers had been saying about Fergus recently, and wondered if anyone in the media knew she had left him for good. After her miscarriage, one tenacious reporter had speculated she was away convalescing. But the tabloids could put a spin on anything if it made good copy. No one would believe that she had known nothing about his disreputable business dealings or his underworld connections. Neither would they believe that she had walked away from her marriage with no material possessions. All she had taken with her was a feeling of liberation. She wanted none of his ill-gotten gains. In any case, Richie had pointed that if the accusations against him were proven to be true, much of what Fergus owned could be frozen by the Capital Assets Bureau.

After she ordered she looked around her at the other tables. There were couples talking, a little girl sleeping in her buggy under a lace-fringed parasol, friends laughing, everyone in holiday mood. The sun did that to people, but she was more aware now than ever before that a smile could fool anyone. By the law of averages she reckoned that most of these people had had close encounters with reprobates and stubborn relatives. Some would have lost friends, jobs, husbands or wives, babies even. Others might be going though chemo. No one could escape their fate. It was all part of life and you had to accept the bad with the good. She sighed with contentment as her food arrived. This was what holidays were supposed to be about and she was more determined than ever to enjoy every minute of it.

She spotted Sylvia and Hamish walking along the promenade, accompanied by a bearded young man. They waved at her and she waved back. They seemed to be in a hurry to get somewhere. The afternoon stretched in front of her and she decided to go back to the ship for a swim and a rest. En route she wandered in and out of the little shops. An artist with a range of unusual ceramics caught her eye and she ended up buying two square pieces for her sister. On impulse she picked up a plate with an olive motif painted on it and bought it for herself. It would symbolise the start of her new life.

At the pier, she accepted a glass of juice from an attendant at the tendering station. She had just missed a boat, but she could see another on its way from the ship. They looked like squat orange and white beetles buzzing along the top of the aqua sea.

While she waited she considered her sister's embargo on communications, and decided to ring her anyway and fill her in on the trip so far.

Leslie's reaction was predictable: 'Are you all right? There's nothing wrong, is there?'

'Absolutely nothing!'

'So, tell me all. What's the talent like and where are you?'

'It's wonderful and I'm wonderful. What's happening there?'

'Never mind that – what's this about the talent?'

'There's nothing to tell – yet! I'm saying no more, but I've never had such a hectic social life. I'm enjoying every minute. We're in Paphos for a couple of days and I've spent the morning improving my mind. Now that I'm cultured out for the day I'm switching off for the rest of the afternoon, by the pool.'

'I'm really envious,' her sister said.

'You should be. It's terrific! The tender's here. I have to go
– love to everyone.'

A seaman took her elbow as she stepped into the boat. There
were only a dozen or so people in it. They were discussing
what they had done and comparing their leather purchases.
Jenny hadn't noticed them on the ship, but she immediately
recognised their accents: they were from Ireland. She hoped
they wouldn't recognise her as Fergus Ruddy's wife. She didn't
want to start apologising for her husband.

Twenty-three

JACK WAS AT GUEST RELATIONS WHEN MR Mercer emerged from a lift. Jack winked at Marina and got ready to do battle in whatever new war this testy man was about to wage. Mr Mercer was bare-chested, wearing only striped shorts that exposed a generous overhang of beer belly. He was sunburned, hot and bothered, so it was no surprise to those at the desk when he said, 'I'd like to make a complaint.'

'Really, sir? Perhaps you'd like to come inside. Guests are not supposed to be in these areas in poolside dress.'

'There's nothing wrong with the way I'm dressed. I was like this all day on the island.'

'Quite, sir, and you caught a good bit of the sun too, I see.

You'll want to mind that. The Mediterranean sun can be very sneaky. You don't realise how hot it is. Anyway, sir, you're off the island and we do have a dress code, which is actually very relaxed. If you'd feel more comfortable we could let you have a T-shirt with the ship's logo on it to put on.'

'Well, then, maybe—'

'And we'll bill it to your room. What size would you be?'

'Look, sunshine, I didn't come down here to be conned into buying your merchandise. I came here with a complaint.'

'Then, as I said, you'd better come inside. We mustn't risk offending the ladies' sensibilities,' he said, indicating a group of elegant women who were sitting in the foyer, enjoying some colourful cocktails while listening to the afternoon piano music.

Mercer had been stopped coming back on board at the security check. He had attempted to bring four bottles of wine with him. His wife and sons had had two each as well. 'There's nothing that says I can't spend my money how I like.'

'Absolutely right, but I think you'll find there is something about bringing alcohol on board, sir, but with so much to take in people sometimes miss that – or get carried away with the cheaper prices in some of the places we visit.'

'Well, they confiscated our drink as we were coming back on, and they can't do that.'

'No, sir, indeed they can't. But I think you'll find that it hasn't been confiscated. It's just been put aside for when you've finished your holiday. It'll be given back to you intact as you leave. They gave you a receipt, I trust, sir?'

'This is disgraceful,' he blustered, choosing not to answer that.

'It's company policy. I'm sure we have everything on the ship. We pride ourselves on our comprehensive liquor offering. It's one of the best on the seas.'

'I'm going to write to your head office when I get home. This isn't good enough.'

'Well, of course, that's your prerogative, sir, but let us know if there's anything else we can do for you while you're with us.' He held the door open to let him exit. 'May I just tell you, sir, that sometimes we've had guests who've ended up leaving their bottles behind when they realised how heavy they weighed. I'm sure you'll agree it's not really cost-effective to pay airline excess-baggage charges for cheap booze.'

'I'd break them first.'

Mr Mercer stomped off. Jack winked at Marina again and took his log from the shelf. He recorded his latest encounter with the Mercers, who were steadily working their way up his black list, the one that made it to Head Office. He went back outside to the desk and the next query. Life was never dull out there.

Marina was doing some paperwork when her pager went. It was from one of the medical officers. 'Emergency, Trade Winds Suite.' She immediately said, 'Alpha, alpha,' quietly on the public announcement system, and within seconds a red light showed in response. That code was only used in life-and-death situations. She passed on the message, then alerted the captain.

'Keep me posted,' he instructed her.

'I still get shivers down my spine when I get a call like that,' she said to Jack, looking at her screen to remind herself of who was occupying that suite. 'It's that lovely couple who celebrated their wedding anniversary yesterday. They're travelling with a party of eleven. I'd better try to locate some of them.' She made a note of their stateroom numbers and asked Jack if he'd check to see if any of them were on board. That task was easy as the key cards held by every passenger were recorded when they departed from and returned to the vessel.

Medical emergencies happened routinely and it wasn't unusual for a passenger to die at sea. The ship was equipped with its own infirmary and medical team, but occasionally more serious emergencies in inaccessible places necessitated the back-up services of a helicopter. The spectacle of one of these arriving, hovering, then landing on the helipad tended to reassure onlookers, instilling in them an added sense of security that should they ever need such assistance it would be readily on hand.

Unfortunately for today's patient it was too late for further intervention. Marina alerted the captain.

'Oh, what rotten timing for them. Matt and Rose had their celebrations yesterday. I saw them before dinner. He seemed fine then, having a right old time,' Doug said.

Matt appeared to have had a heart attack. He had been fully dressed and lying on the bed when it had happened. 'He said he didn't feel well at lunchtime,' Rose had told the medics, 'and our son and daughter insisted we take it easy for the rest of the day.'

'It was our wedding anniversary yesterday,' she told Marina now.

'Of course it was,' said Marina.

'And we had a great party. He really enjoyed it.' She began to cry as though she had just realised there would be no more parties for them, no more anniversaries to celebrate together. Marina let her talk.

'I went out for a walk to let him sleep for a bit, but when I came back he wasn't breathing. I can't believe this is happening. What do I do? I don't know what to do now.'

'We'll take care of everything for you,' Marina said gently as she took her through to her sitting room, where cards and flowers and two large purple balloons bore witness to the previous day's festivities. One of the ship's doctors sat down beside her. Another stayed with the body.

It was obvious the shock hadn't really set in as Rose fiddled with her phone. 'I can never remember anyone's numbers any more.'

'Neither can I,' Marina said soothingly. 'That's the problem with speed dialling. Can I help?' Together they found the relevant numbers for her family and some of the friends with whom they were travelling.

'They've all gone ashore to do some shopping, looking for bits and pieces for my grandchildren. Oh, my God, how will I tell them they've lost their granddad? That they won't be seeing him any more.' Her shoulders shook and she sobbed again.

A discreet knock announced the captain's arrival and Marina took this as her cue to leave. 'I'll be back in a few minutes. I'll just get us some tea,' she said as she left them together and went off to make the calls. Before she did so, she went to each of the cabins to make sure none of the group had come back in the meantime. Then she phoned Matt and Rose's son, telling him that his father had had a turn and perhaps they should make their way back as soon as they could. He assured Marina that he'd tell the others as soon as he'd gathered them up – it would take just a few minutes. The women were in a cluster of shops close by and the men were having a beer across the road. She could hear their laughter in the background. She hated this part of her job, knowing their world was about to shatter.

She paged Jack and told him to alert her as soon as any of the ill-fated group returned. She organised some refreshments and made her way back to Rose, and told the captain that she'd stay with her until her family arrived, but he insisted he would. She was grateful to him for that. He was a hands-on type of guy and it meant a lot to people to feel they were valued: that what happened in their lives was important to others too.

'You know, Captain,' Rose told him, 'one of the highlights of this trip for him was being allowed up on the bridge in Athens. He never imagined he'd be invited up there, and he wrote about it on the postcards he sent to everyone from Haifa.'

Marina was glad they had another night at anchor in Cyprus – at least it gave the family a little time to decide what to do. She'd have to deal with the paperwork and the authorities. The body would have to be removed to a hospital and a post-mortem arranged. Sometimes if departure was imminent, relatives had to pack all their belongings in haste if they wanted to leave the ship and stay with their loved one until he or she could be repatriated. If it happened at a weekend or on a public holiday it could be a nightmare. If they had to sail immediately, she always felt as though they were abandoning the bereaved just when they seemed most lost.

The family arrived back, concerned but not expecting the worst. Marina escorted them to the Trade Winds Suite, where they were given the news.

'We'll do everything we can to help with any arrangements,' the captain told them.

The son kept saying, 'But he wasn't even ill.'

'He was, love,' his mother consoled him. 'He was only given a few months, but he swore me to secrecy. He knew he was on borrowed time. We both did, and that was why he wanted to do this cruise. It was supposed to give us some lovely last memories together with all of you, and it has, hasn't it?'

Their daughter was distraught. 'Why didn't you tell us?'

'What good would that have done? You'd all have been faffing and fussing around him, and you know how much your dad hated that. He died as he wanted to. We made our anniversary, and not many people have that much time together. The last few days have been a lovely bonus. Isn't that true?'

'You're being very brave, Mum,' her daughter said, hugging her.

'I've had a little while to get used to the idea, but it's still a shock when it happens. I'm just glad he didn't have to spend weeks in hospital. He would have hated that.'

'What do we do now?' asked the son.

'There are some procedures that have to be followed,' Marina explained, 'but we can talk about them later, if you'd like a little time together first. We'll leave you now and you can call me when you're ready.' She put a card with her number on a side table and left, so that the family could come to terms with what had happened. You never knew what was going to happen on a ship, she mused, and she enjoyed the challenges. No two days were ever the same.

Twenty-four

SEEING THOSE IRISH PEOPLE ON THE WAY back to the ship had unsettled Jenny and she found herself checking to see if they were about before she sat by the pool. Until then she had been revelling in the anonymity of just being herself, not Fergus Ruddy's wife. Since she'd joined the cruise there had been short periods when she'd forgotten that part of her life, which now she was determined to put behind her. Whatever fraudulent activity Fergus had got up to in his business dealings, it was insignificant when she set it against the hurt he had done to her, and to how he had behaved when she'd lost their baby.

Her idea of travelling for a year or so had taken hold. She

could go anywhere she fancied. She got into the pool, letting the water envelop her, and lay there, floating on her back. In this unreal world of pure escapism she felt untouchable and protected.

John had wandered where his feet took him. Years of work-related travel, with all that that entailed, had taught him to enjoy time on his own. He had had his fill of the enforced niceties and politics of being pleasant to everyone, especially to people he knew he would never meet again. He had spotted Jenny earlier. She had been alone too, but he respected that and had gone off in another direction. He was taken with her, which surprised him. He wasn't looking for romance and felt she wasn't either, but that didn't stop him thinking about her from time to time. He sensed that whatever had happened in her recent break-up was holding her back from being completely open with him. But he also felt that if he were patient she would confide. He sensed a connection that he didn't often feel with people he had just met – a feeling that they were both doing the same thing, sizing each other up. In an approving way. He had gleaned that she was widely travelled and an accomplished linguist. She seemed to understand the pressures of the sort of high-flying lifestyle in which he'd been involved and why he needed to escape them for a while. He felt drawn to her and found he might just be willing to talk to her about his life.

He took the coastal road that led to some of the larger

hotels in Paphos, with extensive private terraces and their own beaches. He stopped for a coffee in a café that overlooked a sandy cove and was canopied with gnarled vines. The sun dappled through the leaves and made patterns on the gingham cloths.

It was great to be able to sit here and just be, he thought, people-watching, creating internal documentaries of the lives of everyone around him. He noted that there were remarkably few young people about. They had probably partied all night and would surface in the late afternoon to top up their tans. There was no shortage of the middle-aged and overweight, couples mostly, who had come here to catch the sun. Many of them looked like over-cured leather.

He phoned his father as he always did, and got the usual response: he wondered why his son was wasting time and money in a place like that. 'When will you be home? The end of next week?'

'Are you missing me?' John asked, knowing his dad could never say so even if he was. His phone beeped, telling him its battery was about to die, but their unspoken protocol meant his father should end the call first, or John would be silently accused of never having time for his old man.

'Nice of you to ring even if you can hardly spare a few minutes of your valuable time while flitting around the world.'

John was saved the rest of the litany by the familiar ring of the chime doorbell in the home where he had grown up.

'There's someone at the door. I have to go. Bye, son.' His father terminated the call.

John continued his walk and on impulse decided to go into one of the five-star establishments. He could have waited until he got back to the ship and charged his phone, but decided against that. He produced a credit card as he made the request to use the business centre. The receptionist escorted him there, logged on to one of the terminals, entered the password for the day and left him alone.

He keyed in Chad Tayloe-Stuart and got no matches. He changed the spellings to Taylor and Stewart, added history professor, historian, teacher. Still nothing. Then he tried universities in the States. Intrigued – there was nothing criminal in pretending to be something you weren't but it was an odd story for a dance host to fabricate – John was still convinced they'd met before. Perhaps Chad had a different story for every cruise, but he had said he hadn't done that many. Maybe he was just trying to find out which profession impressed the ladies most. He logged off, still puzzled. *Maybe I should give it a go. I could pretend to be a TV producer, a psychologist or a physicist.* A false trail might spare him making excuses for his wealth.

The hotel terrace overlooked the bay and he decided to have lunch out there. He'd got used to a life of leisure, but was fast approaching the stage where he would miss having some structure to his days. It was great to know that money wasn't an issue, but he wanted to do something challenging and satisfying. The old man had been right – you could get tired of enjoying yourself.

His thoughts turned to Jenny, as they seemed to be doing

quite a bit. He acknowledged that he was attracted to her. He found her interesting and entertaining too. She remained a mystery. She reminded him of a wounded animal that wanted to trust but was too wary of strangers to do so. Time was moving on, though, and if he was going to get to know her better he had to increase the pace.

As he was leaving the hotel, he paused at the desk to ask, 'Can you recommend a good restaurant that the locals frequent? I want somewhere with atmosphere but not a touristy place, somewhere with character and charm.'

She could, and even offered to book a table for him. He decided to take a chance that Jenny would agree to go with him and let the receptionist make the reservation. Then he wandered back towards the port.

In another café, Sylvia and Hamish were looking at plans with an estate agent and her solicitor. They had been to an exclusive development of seven villas a few kilometres outside the town, and had then visited the hotel development that Hamish's friends were hoping he'd invest in. They were sitting under a huge umbrella and Hamish was number-crunching in a well-worn notebook. The agent offered him a calculator, which he waved away. 'I prefer this method. It gives me time to think as I do the sums, and I don't like to do anything in haste.'

'That's very wise,' the agent agreed. 'It's just that you're here for such a short time.'

'I have friends who got their fingers burned buying in a hurry off plans in Bulgaria and Spain.'

'The market here is very different,' the solicitor told them. 'I have clients who were stung with those investments too.'

The agent intervened, 'I know you're thinking of having somewhere for your own use, but leave that aside for a moment and consider the advantages of buying into a hotel. We have winter sun, and every year our numbers go up. More and more visitors come and stay here for several months to avoid not only the cold but heating costs back home.' He slid some figures across the table for Hamish to study. 'You won't lose money on this investment. These are the Hotels Association figures for bed–night occupancy over the past five years and, as you can see, they rise every time, despite the recessions in Europe.

'You've already had experience of time share,' he said to Sylvia, 'but I honestly think that's run its course. It's too restrictive, having to travel at the same time very year. It was different fifteen, twenty and thirty years ago, when air fares were more expensive and people only took one break a year. Now they prefer to be able to take advantage of good deals and be free to do so when it suits them, not when their time-share slot demands it. We've bought a lot of them back in the last few years.'

'I'm glad I sold mine when I did,' said Sylvia. 'I'm seriously tempted by one of those villas you showed us this morning.'

'Look, we've got plenty to think about,' Hamish said, giving nothing away, 'and I think we should go now and digest it all for a wee while. Can we call you tomorrow? We don't sail until the evening.'

'Certainly, and if you want to see the properties again, let me know. I'd be happy to take you there, or answer any questions about the hotel development. We can always fly you back out for another look.'

Sylvia shook hands with the agent, who strode away confidently. She turned to Hamish and said, 'We're going to have lunch, a late one at this stage, on the terrace of the Elysium. Please join us.'

'I wouldn't like to be an interloper.'

She laughed. 'It's not a tryst. We did all that years ago, didn't we?' She exchanged a knowing look with her solicitor. 'Now we're just very good friends. Come on, Hamish, I want to know what he really thinks of these places, without the sales pitches and the jargon.'

Twenty-five

JENNY SENSED HIS PRESENCE BEFORE HE spoke. When she opened her eyes John was standing behind her lounger, two multi-coloured cocktails in his hands. 'I thought you'd like to try today's speciality,' he said. 'It's called Cyprus Caprice.'

'I'll be an alcoholic by the end of this cruise.' She laughed.

'Not on these you won't – they're mixed fruit juices.' He sat down on the next lounger and said, 'I thought I'd save the alcohol until this evening. I've taken the liberty of making a reservation for two at a little taverna, in the hope that you'll join me.'

'I'd love to,' she said, delighted with this development.

He raised his glass in a toast. 'Only plastic ones by the pool. It's not quite the same when they don't clink, is it? Cheers to us, anyway.'

'To us,' she repeated, and wondered, with a frisson of anticipation, was there, could there be, an 'us'?

They chatted for a while as more of the seats filled around them, with travellers back from excursions wanting a dip or a rest. A band set up on the stage at one end of the pool and began to play.

'You'd probably get tired of this if you could do it all the time,' she said, 'although I'd love the chance to see how long it would take.'

'I reckon four or five months.'

'Until I was craving normality, or my money had run out? Or until I'd outgrown my entire wardrobe?'

'Possibly the wardrobe problems would come before cabin fever set in,' John said.

They saw Heather walking along the upper deck in her leggings and fleece – on the way to the gym for her Pilates class and workout, no doubt. 'Now, that's a timely reminder to go and work off my lunch before dinner. I have a bet on with myself that she'll kill the young instructor with her stamina and enthusiasm and I want to be there to see it. She insists on two back-to-back sessions.'

'Why does she take it so seriously? You can see her ribs through her clothes.'

'She's an exercise addict. Maybe she's not happy and it's

filling a need. She probably pigs out on chocolate when no one's looking. Both release the same endorphins.'

'I'll never have that problem, at least not the exercise part, but I'd have no difficulty with the chocolate. I've met her husband and he looks as though he enjoys the good things in life. And now you're both making me feel guilty. I didn't do my deck mile today.'

'There's no time like the present. The afternoon one is about to start. See you at eight.'

'Tyrant,' she muttered as she got up. She watched him disappear inside and realised she had a big grin on her face.

*

Bud and Sonny had taken a tour of Cyprus. Bud never quite switched off from his work, no matter where he travelled. He was always on the look-out for locations and clicked away happily on his digital camera, capturing road signs, views, angles, the familiar and the unusual, how the light fell on street corners, or on ruins and even, occasionally, allowing someone to catch a shot of the two of them together. Sonny teased him about having to be surgically removed from his camera when he went to bed at night, but Bud insisted, 'This way it's easier to keep a record of what we've done and where we've been, and everything's in chronological order, so I don't need to make notes.'

'I think the mind is your best photo album. There you can enhance and improve the images, make the sun shine and taste the wine. You can't do that with a print.'

'True, but they're the next best thing. Besides,' he said meaningfully, 'there are things I'd rather not commit to camera – intimate things that hopefully both of us will always remember.'

'You betcha,' he agreed. 'So can I assume that you might just put the camera away when we get back and we can capture some more of those moments?'

'Let's go. We can come back into town later on and check out the action.'

Twenty-six

ANDREA LOOKED OUT OF THE WINDOW AT THE
rain and then at the calendar. Doug would be in Cyprus for
two days. She poured herself a drink – gin over frozen lemon
slices from the freezer. She always kept the little tins of tonic
in the fridge. That way it didn't matter if she ran out of ice.
She'd been relieved that her mother-in-law hadn't taken the
bottle away with her when she'd left. She'd been there all day,
blitzing the house, making her eat breakfast and lunch, sorting
through Lewis's clothes, separating the ones he'd already
grown out of and putting them aside for the charity shop.
Doug's sister had taken him to stay with her, to give Andrea
a rest, and had left with another pile, plus a stack of nappies,
bottles and formula in another bag.

'With my two now in secondary school, they're rarely in before dinnertime, what with school clubs, sports and the drama society. I'm suffering from empty-nest syndrome and they haven't even left home yet,' Maxine had told her. 'Can you imagine what I'll be like when they move out eventually?'

'You really love kids, don't you?' Andrea had commented.

'I'd have liked a few more, and I still haven't given up hope. It's not too late. We've had all the tests done and they can't give us any medical reason why it's not happening any more.'

Andrea hadn't known this, but she reasoned they probably hadn't told her because she had other things on her mind, like post-natal depression.

Now they were all gone: her mother-in-law, her sister-in-law and her baby. The place was too quiet, and Andrea felt exhausted. She just wanted a drink to make her sleep and keep her asleep for a while. Sleep had become an obsession, and the more she worried about it the less it happened. She wanted to sink into her pillows and shut out the world, without listening in the dark for the first shuffles and snuffles that prefaced her little boy's waking cries. She wanted to sleep for ever and wake up fresh, like she used to, ready to embrace every day. She wanted her old life back, the life she'd had before she'd ruined it, but that could never happen. Even if she never had another drink, the shame wouldn't go away.

Doug was off enjoying that life, her other life, and she was left to look after their baby. Sometimes she thought it was worse because she knew what he'd be doing at every minute of every day. She could see him in his work environment, to which many wives were never privy. She could see him having his time off in exotic places. She knew from his schedule that today was a port day so he'd probably have done his paperwork early and gone ashore for a meal with some of his colleagues. They usually went up the coast a bit to avoid meeting the passengers. That way they could let their hair down without feeling they were being watched.

In her more rational moments she understood that Doug had no choice in being the centre of attention. It was his job. She'd known that when she'd met him, but it didn't stop the resentment rising within her. She could see him meeting, greeting and entertaining the guests, smiling, always smiling, and looking sexy in his dress uniform, master of his ship and of his glittering world, a world that she should still be part of, but would never be again. She didn't like the bitterness she felt against his life. She knew how hard he had worked to achieve his position of power, and although she was very proud of him, she now begrudged it to him. She couldn't make those feelings go away.

She needed another drink to clear the fog and blur the future. Lewis was hers, theirs, and she loved him; she kept telling herself she really did. But the thought of having to be responsible for him for almost eighteen more years was just too much. She felt freaked and panicky when her mind went down that path, and now she felt guilty because she'd allowed him to go away for a little while. That would make Doug think she couldn't cope, and she could. She knew she could. Maybe when she'd had enough sleep she'd feel differently.

She sat down in the clean kitchen and was grateful to Doug's family. They could always be depended upon in a crisis and this must be one because it had brought them all running. Her mother-in-law was coming back the following day to take her to the hairdresser.

'I need to get my colour done too, so we'll make a day of it. Hairdresser first, then a nice leisurely lunch somewhere, and afterwards we'll go to your doctor and get that prescription renewed.'

Andrea had accepted she needed to talk to her doctor, but she had already decided that she wouldn't allow her mother-in-law to go in with her: she wanted to discuss having her tubes tied and she didn't want her to know that. She'd feel she had to tell her son and it was none of her business, or his, come to think of it. It was Andrea's body and her decision to make. She'd never have any more children, whether Doug wanted them or not.

The silence was unnerving and she realised that she was missing Lewis, missing holding him, missing watching the clock and counting the time since the last feed. She phoned Maxine to see how he was getting on and was relieved that he'd gone down for the night. Maxine told her to have a long soak in the bath and an early night to take full advantage of the break. And she promised she would. Before she turned off the lights she filled a glass with ice, prised some lemon slices apart and took the bottle upstairs with her. While the

bath was running she emailed Doug: *I'm having a baby holiday.*
Lewis is already in bed at Maxine's and I'm looking forward to
having a really deep sleep tonight, all night long and longer, I hope.
Andrea xx

On the ship Doug had come back to his quarters. He'd
had to make an appearance earlier that evening at a loyalty
cocktail party for the regulars. He'd presented a bouquet to an
American couple who were taking their twenty-fifth cruise
with his line, and whom he'd greeted like old friends, joking,
'You could probably steer the ship to its next destination better
than I could by now.'

After that he'd paid another visit to the Trade Winds Suite to
check on the bereaved family. Matt's body had been discreetly
moved to a hospital on the mainland for a post-mortem. Doug
had sent one of his officers to accompany the family, one who
could speak Greek, although that hadn't been necessary.

Rose had tried to enlist Doug's help in persuading the
family and their friends to continue their voyage, arguing that
that was what her husband would have wanted. He preferred
not to get involved in such matters: he knew from previous
experience that such discussions often caused family rows at
a time when everyone should be pulling together. Rose was
adamant that she and her son would stay on in Cyprus and fly
home with Matt's body but that everyone else should enjoy
the rest of their holiday.

'Matt loved life, as you all know, so the best way to honour and remember him is to go on with your holiday as if he were still with us, instead of moping,' Rose had told the rest of the family and their friends. 'We'll have his funeral when you all return, and give him a proper send-off.'

Doug had been impressed by how remarkably positive and decisive she was at such a difficult time. He was impressed, too, by the respect her family showed her in allowing her to be the decision-maker. In the end they had given in.

He had stayed with them for a while longer. Then, satisfied that they were coping, he had taken his leave. He had wanted to check his email, always alert for any nuances in his wife's that might herald problems on the home front. He preferred to do this in private: the crew were discouraged from using their mobiles in public, and he liked to lead by example.

He would have been concerned by his latest communication from Andrea, if it hadn't been followed almost immediately with one from his sister: *Mum to the rescue – she should be in the fire brigade. Andrea in v. good form today. They're off to the hairdresser and the doc tomorrow. House sparkling. Lewis is asleep, upstairs, at mine. He's adorable! Don't worry!! XXX*

He replied to Andrea first:

Delighted to hear you're having a little break. Hope you have sweet dreams and a really good rest. I was going to call you, but I'll wait until tomorrow. I don't want to disturb you. We lost a passenger today – you know all that that entails so I didn't get to go ashore and buy your almondy Cyprus delights so if I don't get them tomorrow you'll have to make do with the ones they sell on board, unless I can get around one of the pastry chefs to make some for me. Meanwhile take care. You know I love you, Doug.

He then wrote to his sister:

M

Not only Mum to the rescue, but you too. I owe you both, big time. I can't begin to describe the panic I feel when I get those emails from A. The one tonight for example told me she was going for 'a deep sleep tonight, all night long and longer, I hope'. If I hadn't had yours immediately after it I'd have assumed she'd taken an overdose. Sometimes I think I'm going mad. I miss the old A so much. We were a great team and I thought that would go one for years. Was I deluded or what? Thanks for being there, sis, for us all, and give Lewis a big hug from his daddy. XX

Twenty-seven

BETTY HAD HAD A BUSY DAY. SHE'D GONE TO
Nicosia: she'd wanted to see where the island was divided.
The guide was good, but it was tiring trying to concentrate,
especially when the odd mispronunciation got in the way. She
was glad to be back on board to rest before dinner. She was
suffering for sitting for four hours on the coach. The pain in
her side hadn't abated after she'd had her painkillers, and she
wondered again if it was time to go on to the stronger ones
she had in her safe.

There was open seating that night in the dining room,
many of the younger passengers eating early so that they
could sample the nightlife on offer in Paphos. Others had

set off for Limassol. She spotted Ben being seated at a table with four others, and the maître d' directed her towards them. Ah, well, new people to talk to, she thought, as she said hello to everyone. She was relieved to find that Ben's hearing aids were turned on but, as it happened, he would not have needed them because the other people at the table with them were the Mercer family, who were rather loud.

'What do you think of it so far?' the burly man enquired, but before she or Ben could answer, he boomed, 'The food's not up to much in Paphos, is it? Everything's smothered in olive oil and they give you loads of bread to fill you up and keep the portion sizes down. These foreigners rob you blind. A right rip-off.'

He looked around the table for agreement.

'I had a perfectly lovely lunch today in Nicosia on my tour. Typical Mediterranean food,' Betty said.

'You did a tour? That's another rip-off. You don't need to do one of those, just walk around by yourself. There's not much to see here. Just a load of ruins, and they don't have English beer.'

'I found it all fascinating, so many cultures and millennia of history to explore. Are any of you interested in history? But you must be to have chosen this cruise.'

That quietened them for a bit, but she was on a roll. The teacher in her recognised that this idiot had probably never even heard of ancient Greece or the Roman Empire and it was clear that the word 'civilisation' was not in his vocabulary.

'My only regret when I travel in Europe is that we learned

only French and Latin at school. Younger people have so much more scope now. I'm always impressed by the way other nations speak so many languages, while I stand there open-mouthed. I'm sure you young men are proficient in a few. Are you?'

Mr Mercer replied, 'No, they aren't. They were more interested in other things.'

'Well, such interests usually come from the parents, I find. What about you?' Betty asked the wife.

He jumped in again: 'No, she doesn't.'

Betty asked about Ben's day while the orders were being taken. He had found some people for a hand of bridge and they had gone ashore afterwards for a drink.

'Oh, that's great. I must play some time. I saw it on the programme, but there's so much to do that there isn't enough time for everything.'

Ben agreed.

Mr Mercer blustered on: 'Are you two together?'

'Oh, no. We met on the ship. You run into such nice people on these voyages, don't you? Have you travelled much?'

'We went to Egypt four years ago.'

'Ah, your love of history again ...' She let that hang in the air.

'And Mallorca, don't forget Mallorca,' his wife said.

'That's right. We went to Mallorca, not on a boat, though. I'm not sure if we'd do this again. We've had a lot of trouble. We didn't like the people they put us with in the dining room the first night so we had to ask to be moved. Russians, I think they were. Foreigners, anyway.'

'But we're the foreigners here. We're the outsiders.'

The family looked at their patriarch for his response to that observation. There was none. 'Then they confiscated our wine.'

'Bad luck follows you. Have you ever thought of having your chakras checked? They might need to be unblocked. Wouldn't you agree, Ben? They may just need to clear your path to positivity.'

The two young men sat in silence.

'They don't say much, do they?' Betty asked their mother. 'Have they special needs?'

Ben almost choked on his soup.

Mr Mercer's voice rose a few more decibels. 'Special needs? What do you mean? Tim's twenty-four and he's an accountant. Fred's twenty-seven and he's just got his master's in counselling.'

'Well, they're certainly old enough to travel independently,' she said, thinking of her grandsons, who had travelled the world by the time they were twenty-one. 'Oh, to be in my twenties again. It's such an exciting time, isn't it?' she addressed the young men. 'Don't you find having your mummy and daddy with you a bit stultifying?' Neither answered. 'I'd have hated that at your age, but then I had four daughters and was widowed by thirty.'

'I hadn't realised,' said Ben.

'Oh, that's all a long time ago. These young folk don't need to hear about that. What's the nightlife like on board? I'm too old to try the disco, although I'm sure I'd love it. Have you met anyone nice? Do you go the nightclub? I'm sure you're out on the town tonight.'

The main course arrived and Mr Mercer poked at his steak. 'I thought this came with greens.' He snapped his fingers. 'Let me see that menu again. I know it said this steak came with greens.'

Betty asked, 'May we start?' and began to tackle her lobster. Ben cut through his steak, which nestled on a bed of creamy, garlicky spinach. He said to Mr Mercer, 'I think you'll find the, eh, the greens are underneath your meat.'

Mr Mercer clicked his fingers again and shouted, 'Forget it,' to the baffled waiter, who had just come back with a menu.

The ever-vigilant maître d' had been observing from a distance and came over. 'Is there a problem?'

'No.'

Betty drew herself up in her chair. 'Yes, I'm afraid there is. May my friend and I move to another table, please, for two?' She stood up. 'Before I go, young men, you should move away from that tyrant of a father. Your mother is afraid to speak, but I suppose she's stuck with him. You're not. It's time to grow up, form your own opinions and see the world for yourselves.'

With that, she followed the maître d' to another table, with Ben in close pursuit.

'What an obnoxious bully,' he said, with more animation than she had seen from him before. 'You were magnificent.'

She smiled. 'I was rather, wasn't I? I enjoyed it.'

'So did I!' He chuckled. 'Very much.'

Twenty-eight

'WHAT DOES IT SAY ABOUT ME THAT THE FIRST date I go on in years starts with a trip in a lifeboat?' Jenny said. 'I hope it's not an omen!'

'So do I,' John said, helping her as she stepped into the craft. Her pale green linen dress blew against her legs.

'It's another life since I've been on a date.'

'I'm afraid I can't make the same claim, although I've never needed the lifeboat on one before either.'

They came around under the bow of the ship and the lights along the coastline were in view. As they got closer, snatches of music wafted towards them. Behind, the lights of the ship twinkled and reflected on the water.

'Do you feel like walking? It's about fifteen minutes away. If not, we can grab a taxi.'

'Let's walk. I love these balmy evenings.'

The restaurant was in a side street, hidden at the end of a cobbled alleyway. 'I'd never have found it if I'd been on my own,' Jenny remarked.

'Neither would I, but I had a bit of help from a local, and it came with her highest recommendation. It's a family-run establishment.'

The bill of fare was neither lavish nor long, like that on the ship. There were just three choices, written in chalk on a blackboard. The kitchen was clearly visible at one end and the commander-in-chief seemed to be a diminutive grey-haired woman sitting on a high stool directing operations. The patrons all seemed to know her and shouted greetings as they came in. Her toothless husband was the chef.

John asked for a wine list but a waiter presented him with the already opened evening's selection – 'Here the chef make the food and he decide what make best with it.'

'Well, I can't argue with that.' John laughed. 'Six years' studying wine and for what?'

'Did you really?'

'I've got some certificates somewhere to prove it. Working in the drinks industry, the distilling end, that is, involved a lot of wining and dining, so I felt it was a necessary adjunct to my job. I enjoyed it too. It's something you never get tired of, but you have to be careful not to become a bore about it.'

'So how does this taste? I like it, but my knowledge extends to phrases you see in comedy sketches. Is it long on the palate, a fruity little number, or has it a good nose and legs?'

'Don't let the oenophiles hear me saying this, but I honestly don't think it matters, as long as you like it, and I do. It's very pleasant.'

'Pleasant?'

'Yes!'

The conversation between the two never waned. They talked about their families, friends, holidays, but they both knew they were not being totally candid. She felt that if she opened up to him she'd seem pathetic and helpless, hopeless even, and he was harbouring the secret of his quite recently acquired riches and had yet to divulge that to anyone in case it got back to his father before he had had a chance to tell him.

He was an interested listener, and Jenny entertained him with stories of some of the trade missions she'd been on and of how language difficulties often brought levity into an otherwise dull succession of meetings and depositions. She told him about her father remarrying so soon after her mother's death.

'I can never understand why men can't cope on their own when their wife dies. Women get on with their life, often keeping the family together, no matter what, but men seem to seek out a replacement as soon as they can.'

'It's not one of our finest traits, I'm afraid. I've managed four years post-marriage. Is that some sort of a record?'

'Almost. In our case the new Mrs P. J. Rahilly arrived in

less than a year and a half and she's only a few years older than me.'

'P. J. Rahilly, the portraitist? He's your father? I was at the opening of an exhibition of his in London a few years ago. His style is quite unusual.'

'Then you've probably seen him more recently than I have.'

'How weird is that?'

'Did you buy anything?'

'No, the prices were outrageous, but I love galleries and wander in and out of them wherever I am, speculating on what I'd buy if I were an investor.'

'An investor? I'd buy because I liked something, not because it could be valuable. Believe it or not, I don't have one piece of my father's art. My sister and brothers have a few between them. He did a portrait for my eighteenth birthday.'

'What was it like? Was it very formal and posed?'

'Not at all. It was of me reading a book on a riverbank with a parasol. Very Renoir. He used to enjoy doing that, putting his subjects into settings that could have been painted by Monet, Lautrec and the likes.'

'What happened to it?'

'I'd just lost Mum, and that time had such awful associations for me, for us all really, that no one got around to hanging it anywhere. He took it, and all the other art in our house, after he remarried and sold the place.'

'That must have hurt.'

'It didn't then. There was just one piece I loved, a portrait of me in a pink tutu, holding my cat, Blackie. I'd been given her on my eighth or ninth birthday. I can remember that one in vivid detail, because it was so personal, I suppose, or maybe because I loved the cat. Come to think of it that was very Degas. I never thought of that before. He probably sold them all years ago.'

'They'd be worth a fortune now if he's held on to them. Maybe he's keeping them to leave to you when he dies.'

'I don't think he knows if we're still alive or not, and he cares even less. In fact, I'd go so far as to say he has forgotten us. I don't remember when I saw him last.'

'That's really sad. Were you close growing up?

'We were lost somewhere below Francis Campbell Boileau Cadell and Andy Warhol. He admired the first's versatility and deplored what he saw as the gimmick of the latter. I don't think he ever granted his offspring the same degree of scrutiny. Don't get me wrong, he wasn't a bad man or unkind, just detached. We were background noise. He didn't come to my wedding. Oh, he said he wanted to, but he had an exhibition to finish and he didn't need the distraction. Mind you, he did pay for it, but my eldest brother gave me away.'

'I was very lucky with my family. I just have one brother and he's a right regular guy. My folks adopted me just after I was born, after years of waiting, and then, bingo, eleven months later Colin arrived naturally.'

'We call siblings born within the same calendar year "Irish twins".'

'I never heard that before.'

'I don't think it was meant to be complimentary when it

originated. I believe it goes back to some time after the famine when families emigrated in their thousands and Irish Catholic ones had dozens of children, frequently with two born in the same year. Anyway, are you and your brother close?'

'Very. He's a great guy and we couldn't be closer if we were blood brothers. Our father would say he's the reliable one. He's in management. He married the girl from the next road, settled down in a nice semi, with two children, one of each. They live in Manchester. He's totally dependable and your stereotypical good family man.'

'Does he envy you your success?'

'Not a bit. He's very happy in his world and, if I'm really truthful, I'm the one who envies him.'

'Would you like to settle down?' she asked as he topped up their glasses.

'I thought I had when I got married, but it's only now that I've taken time to step outside my life that I've realised I was leading an unrealistic existence. It was like being on a colourful carousel, one you could jump off anywhere you wanted and hop on to the next thrilling adventure. It was marvellous, exciting and challenging, but it didn't give me any time to be real. I now know what a lonely life my ex must have had – I'd taken her away from her home in Malaysia to a strange country and culture where she had to make new friends and fit in with my family. Then I'd go off again and all she had was a phone call or text messages for weeks at a time. Then I was back and we'd have passionate reunions, packing weeks of longing and missing each other into a few days, and the cycle would start again. Is it any wonder that she sold my dog?' He laughed.

'So you retired. Wasn't that a bit extreme? Did you do that to counteract your lifestyle – or what?'

'To take stock and maybe begin again. Can you understand that?'

'Probably better than you can imagine.'

He paid the bill, and they walked back through little streets till they reached the seafront. There was a completely different feeling to the place by night. Music assaulted their ears as they drifted past bars and cafés, where people were still eating outside under coloured lights. John took her hand and squeezed it. She squeezed back and smiled at him. He leaned down and kissed her softly on the lips. It was balm for past hurts, a promise of things to come. He put his arm around her shoulders and drew her closer. She could feel the heat of his body through his shirt and smell the tanginess of his aftershave as they stood close together. A frisson of excitement ran though her veins. 'I've had a really lovely night,' she said. 'Thank you for inviting me out.'

'So have I, Jenny, and it's not over yet,' he replied, 'but we'd better get back or we'll miss the last tender.' They continued to walk in contented silence.

'Well, look who we have here, the wee Irish lass and the young Sassenach, all cosy together!' said a voice behind them.

Hamish, Sylvia and Marcus were heading in the same direction and it was clear from their laughter that they had had a good night somewhere too.

'Your timing is as impeccable as ever.' John slapped Hamish on the back.

'Don't be such a tease,' Sylvia said to him, but Hamish was clearly having too much fun to stop.

'I thought we'd be planning Betty and Ben's nuptials, and I was wrong there, but an Irish wedding will be a great excuse to come to Dublin.'

John and Jenny laughed. He had interrupted their moment, but John kept his arm protectively around her. As the tender bounced its way over the waves going back to the ship Marcus suggested they go to the nightclub for a drink. John glanced at her, and she said, 'I'd love to, but I've had far too much to drink for one evening, so I won't, thanks.' She didn't want to lose the closeness they had had all evening by joining the others.

Sylvia lowered her voice to ask, 'How did you manage to snare the best bachelor on board? You probably have other plans and don't want us spoiling them.'

'I have not!' As she answered, she realised that that was probably what they all thought. And John? Had she given him that impression too? Back in the foyer they hovered and John offered to walk her to her cabin.

'I'm fine, really. You stay and have a drink with the others and I'll see you all tomorrow.'

If he was surprised he didn't show it. They all hugged her, and she kissed John's cheek, then whispered, 'Thank you again for a lovely evening.' He held her hand for longer than was necessary and she didn't pull away from him.

She was still awake an hour later, playing and replaying the sequence in her mind. Would she have allowed him in for a while – or maybe to stay the night? Was that what he'd wanted too? Was she imagining the chemistry between them? She definitely liked him. Had she been too abrupt in refusing to allow him to walk her back? Would he have taken it as rejection? What would she say when she met him the next day? Would it be awkward?

With these anxieties buzzing in her mind, she eventually fell asleep.

Twenty-nine

SYLVIA HAD ALREADY SPENT AN HOUR IN THE sun on her balcony, after her late breakfast had been delivered. She couldn't get enough of the heat and, though she knew the risk of skin cancer and the damage that ultra-violet rays caused, she didn't look too wrinkled so far, and she loved having an all-year tan. Anyway, she always had the surgeon who performed her breast augmentation to call on if she needed a little pucker tightened. She'd met him socially a few times and then he'd asked her out. 'Before I answer that,' she'd said, 'I need to ask you something. What would happen if we were dating and I wanted to call on your professional services?'

'I wouldn't do it,' he replied. 'I won't operate on friends or family.'

'In that case, I'll have to say no, with regret, to a date with you,' Sylvia said, 'but everyone tells me you're the best there is and I'm going to need all the help I can get in that department very soon!'

Two weeks later she booked an appointment, and within another two she had emerged bruised but with more bust and thinner thighs than when she'd arrived at his private clinic. Soon she was recommending him to her other friends. He'd cautioned about sunbathing topless for at least a year, as that sometimes darkened the scars. They were almost invisible, and the way things were going on this trip, she was probably going to be the only one who ever saw them.

Reluctantly she left her balcony and dressed. She was meeting Hamish and the estate agent again. They'd decided to view the villas a second time: they seemed a good buy. They were the sort of places you read about in Sunday supplements — *Looking for a home in sunny Cyprus, in the historic city of Paphos? Then look no further. Visualise yourself in this exclusive enclave of just seven prestigious villas overlooking the sea, and with its own private beach.*

She already was. They were gorgeous, so much nicer than an apartment. She'd promised her solicitor she wouldn't make any rash decisions, but she knew she'd end up buying there. She'd spent half the night walking through the rooms in her mind, imagining how she'd furnish them, seeing herself cooking a barbecue for the friends who'd come to stay with her, and swimming in the clear sea water. But she was a clever enough businesswoman not to let the estate agent know she was already hooked. She'd play him along, pointing out the drawbacks. The previous evening she'd asked Hamish if he'd go back with her that morning. He was more inclined to put the money into the hotel development, but was going to mull it over.

'I can always stay with you if it's fully booked,' he'd joked.

'And I can have free drinks any time at the hotel if I tell everyone I know one of the backers.'

'Seriously, I think it's a good buy, and if the other option wasn't on the table I'd be in there, although what a bachelor like me would want with such a big place I don't know.'

'You mightn't always be a bachelor, and whomever you meet, assuming you do take someone's fancy, will in all likelihood have a child or two.'

'Someone like you, you mean?'

'I do not!' she said.

'Oh, God, rejected again. Life gets very complicated. And I thought I was going to find somewhere here to escape all that.'

'You can never escape life, unless you're dead.'

'That's very profound.'

'And very true, too.'

Now they were on the tender, going back to the island. 'You were very naughty last night, interrupting Jenny and John,' Sylvia said.

'It didn't take much to separate them, did it? And as I'm

getting nowhere with you, perhaps there's a chance for me there.'

'You were doing a good job of annoying Marcus too at the bar.'

'Would he be your type? Somehow I see you with a more fun-loving, spontaneous guy – someone dashing and charming ... someone you may have overlooked.'

'Oh, go away.' She pushed him, and in doing so caught a glimpse over his shoulder of Betty and Ben getting into the boat together, helping each other. 'Look over there. I might be needing a new wedding outfit yet!'

By the time they landed at the pier Sylvia had persuaded the older pair to come with them to see the villas. The agent was waiting by his SUV and they all climbed in together.

'This trip is turning out to be full of unexpected surprises. I don't know when I've enjoyed myself so much,' Betty said as they drove along.

'Me neither,' said Ben. They both missed the look that passed between the other two.

When they had completed their inspection Sylvia knew she wanted in; she knew which villa she wanted too, and although they were all pretty much the same, those at each end had a bigger wrap-around patio to catch the morning and evening sun. She told the expectant agent that she'd talk to her solicitor that afternoon and they could thrash out the finer details.

'The terms are the ones I gave you yesterday, with the discounts we discussed,' he pointed out.

'Nonsense, man,' said Hamish. 'If the good lady was negotiating from the UK you'd be offering to fly her out here again and again to sign papers and organise finance, pay for her accommodation and meals. You'd be quite happy to spend five thousand euro on her to secure a sale, so I think a wee reduction in that area would be quite in order.'

He'd obviously struck a chord because the guy never flinched. 'I'll have to go back to the developer and see what he has to say.'

'You do that, but remember, we're sailing this evening.'

He dropped the four off at a busy little restaurant, where Sylvia insisted, 'Lunch is on me. I feel like celebrating. You'll all have to come and stay when I'm here.'

'How exciting. If I were a bit younger I'd do the same myself, get away from cold winters and layers of sweaters. If I ever do, you can do the negotiating for me, Hamish,' Betty said. 'You had that poor man on a griddle.'

'You're even better at it than I am,' Sylvia said.

'Well, you know what they say about Scotsmen and their pennies! Now, you two,' he addressed Betty and Ben, 'tell us what you've been up. It seems ages since we saw either of you.'

Thirty

JENNY HAD LOST THE CONTENTMENT OF THE previous night and was becoming apprehensive. How would John react when they met? She finally decided that he probably had no interest in her other than as someone with whom to share an evening in a foreign place. If he had had other thoughts, though, had she brushed him off? That certainly hadn't been her intention. From what he had told her, he was used to meeting new people, being charming and polite, then saying farewell. Having told herself this, several times, she went up on deck to do her mile. She met Will up there.

'Not going ashore?' he enquired.

'I went to the markets earlier, when it was a bit cooler. Although I love this heat, I just wilt in it.'

'Me too. Why don't you come down and join us for an afternoon cocktail? It's as good as any siesta. We might even have that game of Scrabble we talked about. I must warn you, Heather's a bad loser. Say about three?'

'I'll look forward to it,' she said, and continued her walk. She liked Heather's eccentricity and that she was her own woman, not caring what anyone thought of her. She couldn't imagine her losing at anything. She dressed as she pleased, in classic clothes that could have come out of the carefully co-ordinated closets of Wallis Simpson or Mary Quant, the sort that actually made the wearer look androgynous. She could easily picture her hosting a *Come Dine With Me* dinner party. The guests would be totally intimidated, afraid to ask where she'd learned to make her turducken.

Jenny wondered how she came across to the others. She wasn't strident. She wasn't a pushover either. It was clear to her after last night that she was completely out of practice at reading signs when it came to dating the male of the species. Looking back, she accepted she hadn't needed much practice in that department in recent years. She was always comfortable in male company, and would have thought that growing up with four older brothers would have prepared her for anything, but she was wrong.

She took lunch from the salad bar, choosing from an appetising array of seafood, and sat at a table at the back of the vessel. When they were moving she loved this spot, watching the ship's wake gurgle and boil, leaving its foamy trail to spread out for quite a distance behind it, like an embellished bridal train. She found the sound of water soporific. When she'd finished, she went to join the trivia quizzers. It was obvious from the familiarity with which some of the teams interacted that they had been doing battle against each other at every opportunity over the past few days. She joined a team called the Casuals, made up of three young Americans, a Scottish couple and herself, and was delighted when she knew the first few answers.

When some questions elicited boos from the teams, the host would say, 'It's not *Mastermind*. Everyone knows these answers!'

The hecklers shouted back, 'We don't!' and the hour degenerated into a raucous free-for-all, with queries, contradictions and teams saying wrong answers out loud to steer others in the wrong direction.

The Casuals came joint second and they all got ballpoint pens as prizes. The winners got luggage labels, presented with the dignity of Oscars and received with cheers, clapping and more heckling.

'It's not what you win, it's the honour that counts,' the host said.

'Will you join us again?' one of the Americans asked.

'I'd love to. That was great fun. If you'll excuse me I have something else in my social diary – an appointment for a game of Scrabble. I've never been as busy in my life.' Jenny laughed.

She freshened up and headed for Will and Heather's Sirocco

Suite. She passed a steward with a plate of chocolate-covered strawberries under cling film.

'They look nice.'

'They are.' He laughed. 'Would you like one? I'm sure it wouldn't be missed.'

'Don't tempt me.' She smiled.

'Who's tempting you?' asked Will as he opened the door.

'No one. Let the battle of the words begin.'

'Should I be scared?'

'I doubt it.'

'What'll it be? A cocktail? A G-and-T? There's a full bar, so choose your poison. I'm having a whisky.'

'I'd love some sparkling water.'

'Well, take a seat. The board's all set up for us.' It was, complete with a large dictionary beside it.

'Don't tell me you brought that in your case with you.'

'I'm not that much of a fanatic. It's from the library here.'

'I'm a bit rusty. I haven't played for a while.'

'Oh, you don't forget – it's like riding a bike. Do you know all the two-letter words?'

'I think so, but it's the three-letter ones that stump me. I hadn't realised they had added *qin* the last time I played and was beaten when my opponent tagged a seven-letter word to my *qi*.'

'I did that once with *zo*. I had a great word ending with *d* and put it down making *dzo*. Funny how you remember those coups, isn't it?'

The board was set up with only two racks. There was

no sign of Heather, and she wondered if she was in their bedroom having a nap. She sat on the sofa and Will took the other end.

'Let battle commence,' he announced as they drew a tile to see who would start. They chatted between moves and were pretty evenly matched. Jenny took the first game with a lead of just twenty-five points.

When Will suggested another, she asked, 'Will Heather be joining us this time?'

'No, she's at Pilates, and I've treated her to a spa appointment for some hot-stone nonsense. Won't be back for hours. Did you ever have one? It sounds sensational and very sexual. I might give it a shot myself.'

'I did, the other day, and it was fantastic, although I wouldn't have thought of it in those terms, but I came out walking on air.'

'Now, what about a real drink before I get my revenge? Champagne or a glass of wine?'

Jenny was beginning to feel a little uneasy, but she had misread signs last night too. Was she being paranoid? What was wrong with her? Had Fergus really made her suspicious of men? There was nothing suspicious in playing a word game with someone. If the occasion had arisen while she was still married she wouldn't even be having these thoughts.

'Heather likes to exercise a lot,' she remarked.

'We're complete opposites. She doesn't do sun. She's an exercise freak. She lives by the dictate that a woman can never be too rich or too thin. She's already done the deck mile and contortions or something or other. She looks good on it, though, and it keeps her happy, although I personally prefer the more rounded, voluptuous woman.' He was looking at her in an appraising way. 'Well, what's it to be?'

'I'll stick with the sparkling water. I had a lot of alcohol last night so I need to be a bit careful today. I'm still a little hung-over,' she lied. She told him about the restaurant they had gone to and mentioned John's name a few times, creating the impression that they were very close. He brought the drinks back to the table and sat down again. They began their game, but she was finding it hard to concentrate this time.

After a few gap fillers, like *ted* and *ulu*, he put down *urubu*. 'What on earth is that?'

'A vulture, I believe, and it's a great way of dumping a plague of *u*'s – three in one move.'

'I'll have to remember that one.' She played *euoi*, using one of the *u*'s he had played and he challenged it.

'That's my way of getting rid of a clutch of vowels. I haven't a clue what it means,' she confessed, 'but I know it's allowed.'

'Then let's look it up and we'll know the next time.' He reached over for the dictionary. 'Ye gods, it says here it's "a cry of impassioned rapture in ancient Bacchic revels".'

They laughed. 'I wouldn't have thought that would be allowed because it's Greek,' he said, 'but if it's in Chambers it's permitted, right?'

'That's the Bible, according to Scrabble buffs.'

He dropped the dictionary onto the sofa between them, reached over and put his hand on her leg, squeezing it. 'I'd love to hear you make cries of impassioned rapture with me during Bacchic revels or any other sort of frolics.'

She laughed but didn't move, waiting for him to take it away, but instead he leaned over and moved his hand higher. She jumped up and her letters flew all over the place. 'What do you think you're playing at?'

'Jesus, woman, I was only joking. Will you relax?' He started collecting the letters and putting them back on the rack, as though his behaviour had been perfectly normal and they would continue the game regardless. Again Jenny wondered if she had misread the signs or read more than had been intended into that gesture.

'Sit down. No harm done, but you're seriously sexy and I wouldn't be a normal red-blooded male if I didn't think that, or fancy a bit of the other with you.'

'You're making me very uncomfortable so I'm leaving now.' Her key card had fallen off the table. She didn't stop to pick it up. She'd go and get a replacement at the reception desk. She walked towards the door, but before she could get to the handle Will grabbed her from behind and pushed her towards it with his full weight. She felt his rapid breathing on her neck, which he nuzzled, working himself into a full frenzy of arousal as he rubbed himself from side to side against her buttocks, one hand clenching her breast with a vice-like grip.

'You're hurting me,' she said.

'Don't you women like a bit of rough play?' he answered, and as he pulled at her clothing, she heard her blouse rip. She tried to push him away but he had caught her off guard. In pinning her to the door he had trapped her arms in front of her. His breathing became more intense the more agitated he got, and she could feel him opening his trousers. She shouted for help. He jerked her head around roughly and tried to kiss her to stop her, but when he couldn't reach her mouth he pulled her around to face him and latched on sloppily to her lips. He smelt of whisky and food. She bent her knee but couldn't get it up high enough to stop him. Instead she kicked the door repeatedly with the full force of her heel as he fumbled at the opening of her trousers. Suddenly there was a knock and she could hear the steward asking, 'Is everything all right, Mr Pembry-Travers?'

He clamped his hand over her mouth and held it there. 'Fine, thanks. Sorry about the noise. Just moving something about.' He looked flushed and frightened. She could feel his erection die as he stayed pressed against her, but he didn't move away for what seemed a long time. She could feel his breath against her cheek and wanted to vomit. Then he spat, 'If you say anything to anyone, I'll tell them that you came here offering sex for money and you'll be off the ship before we sail tonight. Now tidy yourself up, you frigid bitch, and get out.'

She stared at him. She couldn't talk. Or cry. She straightened her clothes, tucking the ripped shirt into her trousers as best she could. She wiped her hand across her mouth, and shivered when he went back to get her key off the floor. As he handed it to her he said, 'We're quite clear, aren't we? Nothing happened. Nothing at all. Now get out.'

She didn't remember going back to her cabin, or putting the do-not-disturb sign out. She just knew she needed to be alone. She tore off her clothes and stood under the shower, soaping and shampooing for a long time before she felt clean. She hadn't given him any signals. She knew she hadn't. She didn't cry – she was too angry for that. Had he planned it? He'd sent Heather to the spa for the longest treatment on the list. Would anyone else have taken it as a bit of fun and enjoyed an illicit mid-afternoon romp?

Her mind kept spinning. She eventually fell asleep on her bed. The phone ringing on the locker woke her, but she decided to ignore it. It rang several more times. She didn't answer those calls either. It was well after seven when she sat up and told herself, you have two choices. You can let that creepy bastard spoil your holiday or you can forget him and get on with it. She'd never see him again after the cruise so why should he have any hold over her? He shouldn't, she decided.

She showered again and dressed carefully, having decided to go upstairs for something to eat, even though she had no appetite. She wasn't going to hide. She had done nothing to be ashamed of, even though she felt she had been violated. She played her phone messages with some trepidation in case Will had had the gall to call her. She discovered John had left one asking if she'd care to join them all for dinner. She was relieved because he sounded his usual genial self. They'd be going ashore at seven, he'd said, so she'd missed them. The next was from Sylvia, saying she had something to celebrate and hoped she'd be seeing her later on. Sonny had left an enigmatic one: 'We have something for you.' The last was from Betty: 'Call me a nosy old lady, but I'm worried about you. You know where I am if you need me for anything!' And she'd left her stateroom number.

So much care and kindness – there was no way she'd allow that vile creature to spoil it. Taking a deep breath, she left her cabin and walked into Sonny and Bud, who were coming down the corridor, looking as though they were going out on the town.

'Where have you been all day? We've been looking everywhere for you,' said Bud. 'Have you been hiding from us?'

'Of course not – I got your message a few minutes ago.'

'We saw the sign outside and decided to ring you instead because we have something for you to remember us by.'

'Am I likely to forget you two?' She laughed, delighted to see their friendly faces.

'Come back and we'll show it to you.'

She followed them down the corridor, and when she was seated in their lounge, Sonny took a box off the coffee table. It had tissue paper spilling out. 'There,' he said, 'take a look, but be careful, it's delicate.'

She peeped in gingerly, and saw a piece of glass nestling among the folds.

'You can touch it – it's not that fragile,' Bud said, removing a beautiful Murano vase similar to the one she had left in her former home. It was the same vibrant red with a trim of the signature Murrine lozenges around the rim and base. He handed it to her.

'It's beautiful, but I can't possibly take it. It's far too much.'

'We want you to have it, and whenever you look at it, you're to remember that you promised to visit us in New York.'

'To meet your straight friends and your Bernese mountain dog, whose name I can't remember, and Martha, who cleans for you, and Scrooge the concierge?'

'He's Bruno – the dog, that is. See? You feel you know them all already.'

'I do, but seriously this is too kind.' She didn't know she was going to cry, but when she did she couldn't stop.

Bud sat down beside her and put his arm around her. 'It's not such a big deal, Jenny. We spotted it at the market and remembered you told us you used to have a red piece that you liked. We'll have it shipped for you so you won't have to worry about transporting it home.'

'You will not,' she snuffled.

Sonny brought some tissues and, baffled by her reaction, he said, 'Jenny, is there more to these tears than gratitude? Has this gift touched a nerve for you, or some unpleasant memory? If it has, we can get you something else.'

'It's not that, really. I love it. I'm sorry, really I am. It's just – you're too kind, and look, Bud, I've ruined your shirt with my mascara.'

'It'll wash, but why are you so upset?'

'Something horrible happened today.'

They were incredulous when she had finished telling them what she had been through.

'He'll have to be charged. That's assault and could have been rape if the steward hadn't come along.'

'He threatened that if I made a complaint or told anyone he'd say I'd offered sex for money.'

'That's nonsense. Who'd believe that?'

'Who'd believe me? To all intents and purposes he's a happily married man, travelling with his wife. I'm a recently separated woman, on her own, who had gone to his rooms voluntarily while his wife was off for a lengthy session in the spa. Who would you believe if you didn't know me? And you don't really, anyway, do you?'

'She does have a point there, not about believing you but about the way it looks on the surface. But, Bud, he can't get away with this. What he did is a criminal offence. Let's have a think about it, Jenny.'

'Please don't do anything. It'll only make matters worse,'

'We won't,' they said.

'But he won't get away with it,' Sonny added. 'We'll see to that.'

'That unfortunate wife of his, do you think she knows what he's like?' Bud wondered.

'Please don't tell her.'

'We won't, although it's more than he deserves.'

'I've ruined your evening. Were you going ashore for a meal?'

'Yea, but that doesn't matter. You haven't eaten either. It's not too late to get something in the dining room, or we could order room service. Which would you prefer?' asked Bud.

Her hesitation confirmed what they thought. 'Room service,' said Bud, going to a side table to fetch the menus.

Sonny took the vase and put it back in its box, tucking the tissue inside the neck. 'We'll find you another gift. This would only have unpleasant associations.'

'No, don't do that. It's lovely.'

'I will. You won't have to look at it ever again. Now, let's eat something and we'll open a bottle of champagne – I always find there's nothing like bubbles to block out nasty things. You're safe here with us, Jenny. '

'I know that,' she said, and meant it.

Thirty-one

MARCUS WAS GETTING READY TO JOIN THE others to go ashore for dinner. He resisted the urge to check his emails. I'm finally starting to relax with this odd bunch of people, he thought, but it's not the same as travelling with Malena. Maybe if he'd used call girls on his trips abroad it would have been easier. Sylvia was interested in a bit of a fling. She'd said it a few times. Maybe tonight he should put Malena out of his mind and get on with his life. He closed the door to his suite and made for the foyer.

'I wonder what happened to Jenny,' Sylvia said later, in the bar on the seafront. 'I left her a message, but I never said where we were going.'

'Maybe she's off somewhere with her gay buddies,' said Hamish, looking at John, wondering if he'd had anything to do with her absence.

'Or she could have stayed on land and not bothered coming back to the ship earlier,' said Marcus, who had seen her earlier that day when the walkers had done their circuits of the upper deck. He had been reading in the shade.

'It's a pity. I would have liked her to be here to celebrate.'

'Do you think you've rushed into it a bit too quickly?'

'Oh, Marcus, if you'd seen the villa you'd have bought it yourself,' said Betty. 'Besides, Sylvia knows the island and had done her homework before this trip, so it's not as though she'd just landed, run to an agency and bought somewhere, is it?'

'I agree,' Ben said. 'If I were ten years younger and a good deal richer, I'd buy out here myself.'

Hamish pointed out the illogicality of such an argument. 'None of us knows how long we have so we should do everything when the opportunity presents itself, irrespective of what age we are. I've outlived all the men in my family and I'm not yet fifty, so you could say by the law of averages I'm on borrowed time, but I'm going to make the most of what I have. That's why I'm on the cruise. I have to pay for the usual everyday expenses no matter where I am, so if I'd be happier in a sunny place then it makes sense to go there.'

'Did you decide to invest?'

'Ah, now, John, I'm a cautious Scot.' He laughed. 'However, I'm seriously considering my options. Anyway, a toast to

Sylvia and let's hope she'll be very happy there, and that the invitations to visit will arrive in the post – frequently.'

'I'll drink to that,' said Betty, and they clinked their glasses.

At the end of the evening Sylvia called for the bill only to find John had already settled it. He'd left his credit card at the desk as they arrived. There were protests from everyone.

'Hey, lad, there was no need for that. You're putting up the bar a wee bit too high for some of us,' Hamish said to him as they walked back into the street.

'No need to feel like that, Hamish. It's not a competition. I had a bit of good fortune recently and there's not much pleasure knowing it's in the bank when it could be used on evenings like this.'

'Laudable sentiments, I'm sure.'

'It's a bit of a liability, actually,' John said.

'I'd like to have the chance to see how I'd cope with such a liability,' said Ben.

'Well, I'm still learning,' John said, closing the conversation and leading to Sylvia's conviction that he must have won the lottery. In a way, he supposed he had. They walked back briskly to the tender station, without much time to spare.

'I'm going on deck to watch as we sail away,' said Sylvia.

'I'll join you,' said Marcus.

Ben and Betty decided it was time to turn in. Before John could say anything, Hamish said, 'Come on, lad, let me buy you one of those special malts.'

'Good idea.'

He was still wondering what had happened to Jenny and

whether things might have progressed the previous evening if they hadn't met the others. He knew he hadn't said anything to offend her, and that if she'd had his message, she'd have replied to it, if only to tell him she had already made other plans.

'I think she's sweet on the Dane,' Hamish said.

'Who, Jenny?'

'No, Sylvia.'

'Well, good luck to them. I hadn't noticed. Now, what are we having?'

After a while Hamish said, 'Do you mind me asking you how you made your money? You seem too young to retire. You've travelled the world with the drinks industry, but it's not that well paid, is it? If it is, then I'm in the wrong business.'

John smiled. 'I don't mind you asking me at all. I made a good living, but that didn't make me rich. A quirk of fate did, but I'm not going to tell you what. It's not that I don't want to, it's more a matter of loyalty.'

'It sounds mightily intriguing.'

'Believe me, it's a lot stranger than that.'

A few decks below Sonny and Bud escorted Jenny back to her cabin. They'd finished the bottle of champagne, opened another and managed to make her smile. The bubbles had certainly made her giddy. She promised to get straight into bed and, to make sure she did, they waited on the balcony until she was in it before leaving her to fall asleep.

They had helped her put the incident out of her mind

temporarily, but they had no intention of letting that man get away with what he had done.

'She asked us not to say anything to anyone.'

'The captain's not anyone.'

'Sonny, you can't go to him.'

'Why not? The buck stops with him. And I'm not letting it lie until tomorrow.'

'He's probably up on the bridge, right now, directing operations.'

'Don't worry, I'm not going to try and break through security to get at him. I'm going to Guest Relations to request a meeting.'

'Then I'm coming too.'

The ship was not as busy as it was most nights. The majority of the passengers who hadn't already retired were up on deck for the sail-away, waiting, watching and dancing as the lights of Cyprus faded behind them. The desk was quiet, as it often was before a sea day, and Jack had only another hour to go before he could sign off. He had switched his shift with one of the other team members who had wanted to meet up with some friends that afternoon. He smiled as Sonny and Bud approached. He had noticed the flamboyant duo before and they were always polite and non-confrontational.

'What can I do to help, gentlemen?'

'We have rather a delicate matter that needs to be addressed. Is there somewhere more private where we can talk?'

Jack was surprised, but he was professional enough never to register his first impressions. 'We won't be disturbed in there,' he said, indicating an office to the side. 'I'll open the door for you.'

He was incredulous when they told him what had happened. This was a first for him. He often had complaints when amorous or rejected suitors tried to gain access to the objects of their passion, but usually a caution and the threat of expulsion from the ship were enough to cool their ardour. This, though, was in a totally different category.

'You do realise I have no authority to act in this matter.' They nodded. 'It would be up to the captain to set an enquiry in motion, if he felt he had the grounds to do that.'

'We understand that perfectly, which was why we wanted formally to request a meeting with him. As soon as possible.'

'Gentlemen, it's past midnight so it will have to be tomorrow.'

'We can't be sure that the man won't try to bother Jenny again during the night. We wanted her to stay in our suite but she refused. Is there any way you can keep an eye out for her?'

'We can certainly make sure he can't use the ship's phone to annoy her, and we have CCTV at strategic points around the vessel, so we'll monitor any movement from his suite to her corridor. Now, will you excuse me for a moment? I need to log this complaint while you're still here.'

He left the office, convinced the men were telling the truth. They had no reason to lie. He looked at the clock. It was half past midnight. He had to act on what he'd been told. It wasn't his place to decide to leave it until morning. He called the duty officer and was told that Captain Doug was still on the bridge. He'd just handed over to his second-in-command.

'I do apologise for calling you at this late hour, sir, but there's been a sexual-assault complaint against one of the guests, and I have the complainants down here in the office.'

'No need to apologise, Jack. I'll pop down and have a word. Do you need any medical or security back-up?'

Within minutes he had arrived. 'Do you think this is a genuine complaint?'

'I'm afraid I do, sir.'

'Well, Jack, your instincts are usually right. Let's see what it's all about.' If he was surprised to find two overtly gay men making the complaint he didn't show it, but when they had finished recounting the episode, as Jenny had told it to them, he was quite disturbed.

'You were right to bring this to my attention. I'll need to speak to Jenny Rahilly in person, though, before I can approach him. Leave it with me. You can be assured we'll deal with this as is fit and as soon as we can. And you can rest assured that he'll not bother her again.'

Thirty-two

JENNY WAS USUALLY ABLE TO BOAST THAT she'd never had a hangover, but after last night she'd never be able to say that again. She woke with a heavy head after a coma-like sleep, and as she drew the curtains back the bright light caused her to recoil. Then she remembered Will's attack. Don't, don't, don't, she told herself. Forget him. He's not worth it.

It was only half past seven and she decided some sea air and a brisk walk might help. She pulled on some shorts and a T-shirt and went upstairs. A few others had obviously had the same idea of starting the day with some pep in their step. She was relieved to see Heather in the front bunch so she wouldn't have to talk to her. Then she spotted John running on the other side of the ship. She waited for him to come around. He slowed to walk with her, his singlet wet with sweat and his skin glistening. He was hardly out of breath although he'd obviously been exercising for a while.

'We missed you last night,' he said. 'Sylvia had just put a deposit on a new villa so we were celebrating with her.'

'I didn't get your message, or hers either, until after you'd all left, and then I was led astray by Sonny and Bud. They have a creed that bubbles cure everything, but they neglected to tell me that the cure came with its own side effects and I'm suffering this morning. It's true, champagne really is the worst. I think the bubbles go straight into the bloodstream.'

'I hope whatever you were trying to cure was nothing too serious.' She felt herself tense and shivered. If he had noticed, he made no comment. 'I was led astray by Hamish – although, to be truthful, I'm not sure who was doing the leading by the end of the night. I didn't see you around yesterday and I wondered if you were avoiding me.'

'And I wondered the same about you, but I can assure you I wasn't.'

'Neither was I. So, what next?' he asked, looking intently into her eyes.

'What are your plans for today?' she asked, and thought, what a stupid thing to say!

'I thought I'd have breakfast, do a session in the gym, eat and drink some more, have a break, maybe a swim, do a bit of reading, eat and drink some more. It's the formal dinner tonight and then maybe I'll go dancing, if I find someone to come with me,' he said meaningfully. 'Oh, and I plan on giving Hamish a wide berth – my constitution isn't up to it. What about you?'

'Much of the same, without the gym, but maybe with a quiz instead. Yesterday's was a bit of fun. I might go dancing, if the right person were to ask me to, and if that doesn't happen, there's always that dance-host fellow with the fancy name, Chad Tayloe-Whatever. Right now, I fancy pancakes for breakfast, not those big thick doughy American ones, but dainty crêpes with lemon and sugar. They should help the hangover.'

'Can I join you? '

'Of course. I thought you'd never ask.' She smiled at him, happy to be back on an even keel.

'I'll just nip down and have a quick shower. Meet you out on the terrace in ten, fifteen minutes?'

He's so normal and so nice, not like that other creep. To push thoughts of Will out of her mind she counted the pictures along the corridor before she reached her stateroom. It had already been made up in her absence and there were two envelopes on her bed, along with the daily newsletter. The first contained a note from the Boys: *Hope you had a good night's sleep. We need to talk to you, sooner rather than later. It's important. Call or come down to us when you get this. B&S.* The second was on official paper requesting that she contact Guest Relations as soon as possible. The Boys could wait: they were probably just checking up on her. But the second note puzzled her, and the more she agonised the more puzzled she became. Could Will have made a complaint about her or, worse, had there been bad news from home? She couldn't wait until later to find out. She'd go down straight away.

Marina had been briefed on the situation and came out from behind the desk to talk to Jenny. She took her into the same office where the Boys had been the previous night. No, she assured her, there had been no bad news from home. So it had to have something to do with Will.

'Let me get us some tea and I'll explain,' she said, making a call. 'The couple from the Mistral Suite have made an accusation about one of the passengers and your name was mentioned in this context. Because of the nature of this the captain was informed and he'd like to join us.'

'I told them not to say anything,' Jenny protested, but a little part of her was relieved that it was out in the open. Growing up, although she was independent by nature, she had always had her brothers to look out for her, and now it seemed Bud and Sonny had taken over. Out of her own environment, she was glad of their support. 'Does everyone know? I'd hate to think everyone was talking about me.'

'You needn't worry about that. They don't and they won't. Only those who need to know have been told and that's the way it will stay.'

Relieved, she asked, 'Does – that man know there's been a complaint made against him?'

'From our end, I can assure you definitely not.'

A knock announced Doug's arrival, with another officer and a steward with a tray.

The captain greeted Jenny, not with the hip-bumping of the previous occasions when they'd met but with a formal bow. He waited until the steward had left the room, then said, 'Let me introduce you to Officer Shaun Shannon. He's our security officer, and if you have no objections I'd like him to be present to follow protocol.'

Jenny felt she was being swept along on a wave she couldn't control and, as though sensing her bewilderment, the captain said, 'I know this is all very intimidating but it's necessary. Whatever you tell us stays within this room. No one else need be involved.' He gave her a moment and Marina filled it by pouring tea for them all.

'I'm very disturbed by what I've heard and I appreciate that it must be very upsetting for you to talk about it. Would you mind telling us what happened? You do realise that I'll also have to speak to the …' he hesitated slightly '… the guest in question too, Mrs Rahilly?'

'Please call me Jenny,' she said. Used to taking minutes, writing notes and doing instantaneous translations, she told him what had happened exactly as it had occurred, with no frills and no digressions, her voice faltering a few times, especially when she recounted his threat to tell people that she had gone to his room offering sex for money. No one interrupted.

'I feel a fool, being so naïve, but I never suspected Heather wouldn't be there, or that he might have had other intentions.'

'Whatever his intentions were in inviting you there, or your reasons for going, they don't change what he did. It's a criminal offence to assault someone, Jenny, and we have to treat it as such. However, maritime law is very blurred and convoluted and it's often difficult to get a clear conviction. Factors like where the ship is registered, whether it was in territorial waters or deemed to be on the high seas, where its next port of call is are all subject to different regulations,' the captain explained. 'If we can get a confession from the man we'll have him taken off the ship tomorrow when we dock in Rhodes. It would be up to you to decide if you wanted to pursue him when he's back in the UK, and if you do, we'll help you all we can.'

'I've no intention of doing that. I want to forget it ever happened. I don't fancy bumping into him around the place, but I'm reluctant to sacrifice my holiday for him.'

'I can appreciate that. But let's take it one step at a time. If we don't get a confession from him, we'd be willing to facilitate your leaving this cruise, if you feel uncomfortable about staying on, and we could put you on a similar one whenever it suited you. You don't have to make decisions about any of that just yet.'

'I've made some really nice friends over the last few days and I don't see why I should feel awkward staying put. He's the one who should feel guilty and ashamed. Not me.'

'We all wholeheartedly agree with you,' said Marina, 'and you mustn't feel isolated. If there's anything we can do, or if you want to talk to any of our medical team, just call me and I'll arrange it.'

'We'll make sure there's extra security on his movements too, so you needn't worry that he'll come bothering you again,' the other officer said.

'Thank you, but I've been through worse. I'll survive. I'm just grateful the steward came along when he did.'

The captain stood up. 'I'm sorry this happened. Believe me, it's not something we often have to deal with. I'm sorry we had to drag you away from whatever you had planned this morning too.'

'I had a date with a plate of crêpes,' she said, remembering that she was supposed to have met John for breakfast.

'Then let me escort you to the buffet.'

'Won't it be closed by now?'

'There's not much point being in charge if you can't throw your weight around sometimes,' he said, and she laughed, feeling much better.

'Thank you for being so kind. It's one thing being independent, but there are times when it's nice to have people around too.'

'We all need that,' the captain said, opening the door for her.

There was no sign of John when she got back to the terrace restaurant. She wondered what he would make of her latest disappearing act. She looked around in trepidation. There was no sign of Will either. Noticing, the captain said, 'I quite fancy a pancake myself. Could you do with the company or would it tarnish your reputation to be seen eating with a sailor?'

She laughed. 'I'd love it, but it might be your reputation that's at stake.'

'I'll take my chances. Now let's get those pancakes.'

*

Later that day Jenny stationed herself by the pool in the hope of catching John and explaining what had happened that morning. Instead she encountered the Boys – or, rather, they found her. They'd been waiting for her to contact them. Bud hunkered down beside her. 'Honey, I hope you're not offended, but we just couldn't do nothing.'

She told them what had happened and about her meeting with the captain, and assured them, 'I'm fine, really fine. Everyone was so nice and I appreciate what you did, honestly, I do, but now I just want to forget about it.'

'Right. Well, it's formal night tonight so we'll expect to see you all glammed up later on.'

'I can't wait to see the pair of you in your tuxes – have you co-ordinated your colours?'

'Now, pretty lady, you'll have to wait and see,' Sonny said theatrically. 'We're going to the spa.'

Ben and Betty sauntered by. Betty smiled. 'There you are. I was looking for you everywhere. What about a coffee or an ice cream on the terrace? Ben's going off for a lie-down, thank God.'

'Shush.'

'Oh, he can't hear me. The hearing aids are turned off again.'

'Well, I've had enough sun for the time being so I'll go and get us a table.'

'I'll just tell him and follow you up.'

When she arrived, Jenny had two frothy cappuccinos waiting and Betty began, 'A little birdie told me you were seen up here with a dashing young man, one with several stripes on his epaulettes. What have you been up to?'

Jenny replied, 'Curiosity killed the cat.'

'Well, it hasn't killed this one yet! Come on, what's going on? I don't want to pry into your business, but I get the feeling that something isn't quite right.'

'I know, and I appreciated the message you left me last night.'

'If you need someone to confide in you can count on me. Now, what about that mid-morning assignation?'

'Betty, you should be writing novels with that fertile imagination of yours. It wasn't an assignation, as you so delicately put it. We were simply talking. We'd been doing a bit of business and I missed breakfast.'

'Is that "bit of business" a euphemism for something else?' she asked with a mischievous look. 'And was that "bit of business" why you didn't join us last evening?'

'Betty! No, it most certainly was not!'

'It's difficult to hide on a ship. Sylvia told me the two of you were laughing and chatting and that you looked very comfortable together.'

'So that's who your little birdie was! Well, you can tell her there's nothing to tell.'

'You can tell her yourself. Here she comes.'

'Well, you're a bit of a dark horse, first you snare John and then you throw him over for a man in uniform – the captain, if I'm not mistaken, and a married man at that.'

'You're reading all sorts of things into an innocent breakfast, and I did not throw John over, as you put it.'

'I met him earlier and he said he'd been stood up.'

'Something cropped up,' Jenny said.

'I bet it did,' said Sylvia. 'Well, he's obviously not too upset. He's invited us all to drinks on his terrace before dinner tonight and he told me to pass on the invitation if I met any of you.'

'And it's posh-frock night too,' Betty said.

'I didn't tell him I'd spotted you with the top brass. Would it have mattered if I had?'

Jenny didn't answer. Betty put a hand on her arm. 'Did something happen?'

Jenny looked from one to the other, sensing they knew more than they were pretending.

'We met Sonny and Bud and they just said we were to keep an eye out for you today, that you might be in need of some extra tender loving care,' Betty told her.

'Good God, is nothing sacred on this ship? It's worse than a goldfish bowl, and for your information, it has nothing to do with John.'

'Don't worry. They didn't divulge any secrets and we didn't mean to intrude, but we're here if you want to talk to us. Isn't that right, Sylvia?' After a few seconds, Betty added, 'You were missed last night.'

'I have a bit of news too,' Sylvia said.

'Of course, the villa! Tell me all about it,' said Jenny.

'No, not the villa – Marcus and I.'

'No – really? You two?'

'Yes, truly, last night after sail-away.'

'You minx,' said Betty.

Sylvia tossed her hair coquettishly. 'I knew it would happen sooner or later. He's really very sweet, if a bit intense, but I can work on that. You know, I wouldn't mind getting married again – to the right man.'

'Did you tell him that?'

'Not quite. I didn't want to scare him off so soon.'

'He hasn't taken his eyes off you since that first lunch,' said Jenny.

'Neither have Hamish and Ben!' Betty added. 'And a few others around the ship.'

After those revelations, talk moved on to Sylvia's new property and to the formal evening ahead. 'Let's all go and get our hair done,' Sylvia suggested, 'and we'll knock them out tonight. If you're up for it, girls, I'll make the appointments now.'

They were, and she left them chatting.

'Betty, you look tired. Maybe you should stay out of the heat for a while. It's going to be a late one tonight.'

'You're right. I'll go for a little rest after lunch. I can't have you young things showing me up.'

Thirty-three

JENNY WASN'T THE ONLY ONE WHO HAD woken up that morning feeling muzzy-headed. In Guildford, Andrea had the mother and father of a hangover. She had done serious damage to the contents of the gin bottle. She picked her way through the clothes and towels she'd left where they had dropped. I must get this tidied up before Doug's mother arrives, she thought. She plunged her hand into the cold water from the bath she'd had the night before and pulled the plug out. Then she cleaned the tub until it shone. She rooted in the bathroom cabinet for some painkillers, took some paracetamol and a shower, and dressed and made up her face with care.

She checked her emails and saw one from Doug. Did he honestly think some almondy Cyprus delights would make up for leaving her behind with a demanding baby? She shut her laptop and took the laundry downstairs. She programmed the washing-machine, switched on the coffee-maker and went back upstairs to fetch the gin bottle and glasses. She topped up the bottle with water and replaced it where it had been on the sideboard the previous day, then emptied the bin, in which she'd discarded the lemon slices. Once she'd had a strong shot of caffeine, she rang Maxine to ask about Lewis.

'I didn't want to call earlier as I knew you'd be caught up with the school run. Was he good for you?'

Maxine's kids were past the age of being delivered to and collected from school, but she let that pass. 'He was a little angel. He slept all night and he's guzzled his bottle and food this morning. He's a great little eater. Did you get a good rest?'

'I slept like the dead. It was wonderful. I'm just waiting for your mum to arrive. We're off to get our hair done.' She shouldn't have mentioned that she was being collected – it only reminded people that she'd lost her licence for being over the limit. 'We're lunching out too. It'll be great to have a meal without a baby in my arms, thinking he's going to need changing soon or a bottle. Outings have to be planned and plotted for.'

'It's impossible to have a proper chat with them around, isn't it? Wait until you have two and you'll look back on these days as being positively halcyon! Go and enjoy your little break. I'll hold on to him for a few days, maybe until

Monday, as the kids love having him and they can spoil him at the weekend.'

'That would be terrific. I can see your mum pulling into the driveway.'

An hour later, Andrea and Doug's mother were in the hairdressing salon, waiting for their highlights to develop. Andrea was working out in her head what she'd say to her doctor. Would he be sympathetic? If he suggested any of that counselling nonsense she'd go to someone else. She'd had her fill of that in the rehab place. She knew what she wanted and it certainly wasn't more children. She wanted her depression to go away, too, and although she knew, somewhere deep in her psyche, that she needed to give up the booze, she didn't want to do that, not yet.

'That looks wonderful,' the stylist said. 'It really was in need of a good reshaping, and the highlights bring out your eyes.'

'You look terrific, Andrea,' her mother-in-law said.

'You don't look half bad yourself. Come on. Let's have a lovely lunch somewhere.'

They went to a bistro on the corner, which was already filled with ladies-who-lunch and a few businessmen with electronic gadgetry beside their plates. The two women chatted easily. They had liked each other before all the other business had happened. Doug's mother had been good to Andrea and never made comments when she could have, no matter what she was thinking, and she loved her little grandson passionately. She even ordered wine without any discussion or guilt-tripping.

When they had finished, she drove Andrea to her doctor.

'I'll stay in the car and wait for you. You don't need a minder with you.'

Andrea was relieved. She and Doug had met Dr Tatton when she was discharged after her first stretch in rehab and they had taken to him immediately. He was younger than most of the old fuddy-duddies who had treated her before, and seemed to understand her need for drink. He'd even managed to get her to stay off it for the whole of her pregnancy. He wasn't a pushover, he could be quite harsh, but she trusted him. He monitored her depression clinically, adjusting her medication frequently, and it certainly made her better able to cope knowing he was just a phone call away. There was only one other patient in the waiting room. They nodded at each other, then looked away. She picked up a magazine and realised she'd just read it at the hairdresser's. She put it down with a sigh and sat there fidgeting with the strap of her handbag and tossing her new bob occasionally. It felt good.

The man was called in and she picked up the magazine he'd been reading – a glossy one about trucks. Who'd read, never mind write, such stuff? Curious, she flicked through the pages, which were filled with pictures of men sitting on tractors or standing proudly by precision-parked fleets, decorated with different liveries and logos. What did a monthly subscription to such a title say about her doctor or his clientele? She smiled at the thought and at that moment he opened the door to call her in.

'Well, Andrea, it's nice to see you looking so happy and well. How have you been?'

She had a consultation about her sleeplessness, her mood swings and how she was coping, and she lied so that he would think she was capable of making other decisions.

'I'd like to reduce your dosage a little and see how that goes. We'll start easing you off these things,' he said, writing her prescription. Then she broached the subject of sterilisation.

'I'd like to think you've discussed this with your husband,' he said.

'I haven't, and before you go off on a rant, I won't. A woman has the right to choose and I choose not to have more children.'

'I'm not trying to deny you that right, Andrea, but will you talk to him first? It's a very big decision to make, not one to be rushed into.'

'I've done my share of talking. I never want to go through post-natal depression again. I'm not maternal. I don't go gaga over babies and, besides, I've done the reproduction thing once and that's enough. I'm not rushing into this – I think of nothing else.'

'No two pregnancies are ever the same so there's no certainty that you'd go through the depression again with another, and we'd be prepared, unlike the first time. Having a tubal ligation is a very permanent form of birth control. There are other roads you could go down initially, in case you changed your mind in the future. Lewis is not yet a year old. Your body is still adjusting. Give yourself a little more time and come back in to see me in, say, three months' time and we'll talk again.'

'I won't have changed my mind.'

'Possibly not, but I'll be happier knowing that you've given it more consideration. It's a very big decision. Maybe by then you'll have discussed it with your husband too. He might opt for a vasectomy instead. Many men do, you know.'

'I'll be going ahead with it, whatever he says.'

'Well, let's make sure you have all the facts to think about in the meantime.' He handed her the prescription for her anti-depressants and mild sleeping tablets. Then he gave her some leaflets on sterilisation.

'How's the drinking these days?' he asked as he stood up to open the door.

'Fine. Don't I look fine?'

'You certainly do. Is Doug abroad at the moment?'

'Of course – off doing his Captain Fantastic thing, charming the ladies and making the men envious.'

'It sounds very glamorous, but it must be quite a responsibility.'

'Oh, it is, and it beats being stuck in a surgery all day, listening to patients moaning, or being chained to a baby, having to make feeds and change nappies *ad nauseam*, doesn't it?'

'Well, when you put it like that, it probably does,' he agreed. 'Now, you look after yourself and that little fellow of yours and I'll see you soon.'

She'd been gone almost an hour, but her mother-in-law was quite relaxed about it. 'I was enjoying listening to a talk with that young American tenor, Noah Stewart. He has a heavenly voice. Now, I need a few things from the supermarket, but I can drop you home first if you want, or do you need to get anything?'

'I have to pick up my prescription. Doug's ringing at six too, or Skypeing me, depending on the reception.' She needed more gin and more small cans of tonic water, but she'd have to order those online when she got home. Bottles were heavy, and not having a car meant she had them delivered. Normally Lewis's buggy was a perfect vehicle. She could buy some in the supermarket and alternate between the off-licences in her area, but she couldn't take an empty buggy for a walk, could she?

Thirty-four

JOHN WAS BAFFLED BY JENNY. HE KNEW enough about women to be able to tell when they were interested in him, and she certainly hadn't given him any signs to the contrary. She didn't seem the inconsiderate type, yet she hadn't turned up for their breakfast and he had waited quite a while. He'd been to the gym after that and had seen the woman with the mad eyebrows pounding the treadmill as though she was trying to power the ship. She seemed to spend hours in the place. He saluted her and she smiled back. With his routine completed, he went back to his balcony with his laptop for company.

He'd told everyone he was retired, which was true in one

sense, but not in another. He'd retired from his very lucrative contract with the drinks company, despite the inducements they'd offered him to stay on and develop the growing Japanese and Chinese markets. They'd told him that if he changed his mind in the future they'd take him back. He was a recognised connoisseur and would have no trouble walking into that or another similar position if he wanted, which for now he knew he didn't. He had other fish to fry, as his mother would have said. His father just kept telling him, 'That's not the way we brought you up. Jobs aren't easy to come by any more. I don't know what your poor mother would have made of this nonsense if she were here now.'

For the umpteenth time he wondered how she would have taken the turn of events that had seen him become a multi-millionaire overnight. He would have been able to tell her about it straight away, but his father was a different matter. She'd probably have been delighted for him once she'd got over the shock. She wouldn't have felt threatened. She wasn't that sort of person. He knew the time was fast approaching when he'd have to tell his dad in case it leaked out and he heard about it from someone else. That would only make the situation worse, if that were possible. He hadn't discussed it with anyone, although he'd had a strong urge to tell Jenny when they were having dinner in Paphos. He wasn't sure if they'd have another like that, the way things were panning out, but he decided it was worth another shot. He'd see how she acted when they all came for drinks later and make his mind up then.

Once more he typed in Marcel F. Tingue and waited until the entries popped up, then read about the winery, the family and its long history.

*

Marcus had spent the night with Sylvia, in a mad, passionate and very satisfactory way. She was an ardent and creative lover and he'd had no trouble in matching her, once he'd put Malena out of his mind. This cruise was full of surprises. When he went back to his suite early that morning he automatically checked his emails. At least, that was what he told himself, but in reality he was checking to see what Malena was up to. She had been working on a complicated company law case, which was going through the courts right now and was making daily headlines in the papers and online. It involved a global investment institute and its bank. Several of the big guns had already been indicted, but when one had turned state's witness and made accusations of insider trading against the investors, the bank had decided to appeal the previous convictions, which had scapegoated them wrongfully, they claimed. The opposing legal team was being led by Germund, the man who had cuckolded him right under his nose, and taken his wife from him.

He hadn't been prepared for what he read. The popular press was having a field day.

It's not all war for legal eagles. Although they may be battling it out in a merciless war across the courtroom floor, when Malena Nielsen and Germund Poulsen leave the barbed arguments and cutting snipes behind them in the confines of the chambers they declare a truce as they go back to their love nest. College sweethearts, this pair found each other again quite recently and left their spouses to set up home together. Malena was married to industrialist Marcus Harms, who is believed to be holidaying abroad. Poulsen's wife is designer Ada Pedersen. Both lawyers are immersed in what is predicted to be the courtroom battle of the decade. The last time these two giants met head to head was when Poulsen defended Mr X, the man behind Denmark's biggest sex trafficking scandal involving several hundred eastern Europeans. Nielsen lost that time.'

He opened YouTube and found images of them arriving separately at the courts, surrounded by their teams. He then went to Facebook and discovered a thread there. He flicked down through the comments:

Can these lovers really be impartial?

Will the outcome be decided on whether she gives him breakfast in bed before going to court?

Those lawyers should be jailed for defending those white collar criminals.

Would you want your fate decided by a couple on opposite sides of the fence but not of the duvet?

Is it legal? I wouldn't allow it.

No matter who wins they win. Nice work if you can get it!

He closed the laptop, glad he was away from home. Malena was history. All this publicity might or might not damage her practice, but he told himself that he really didn't care any more – although she still made him angry when he thought about her. This wasn't like a business contract that had gone wrong, one from which he would have to cut loose before going in search of a replacement order. He wasn't able to move that quickly and forget their shared past, and he knew he'd have to face up to a few things. The divorce would be straightforward enough – she had said she wanted nothing from him, but that didn't mean there was nothing to legalise. There was the house, the yacht, the cottage by the sea. He'd get on to all that when he got home. He resisted the urge to contact his office. For now he was going to concentrate on Sylvia and enjoy himself.

Hamish and Marcus bumped into each other on the top deck. Both were on a mission to find Sylvia. Separately they had walked by the rows of loungers on the pool deck scanning them for her well-endowed form. Then they had gone up a deck to the more secluded area, the only place from which the helipad could be seen at the ship's bow. This was Sonny and Bud's favourite place to sunbathe, and there they were, faces down, oblivious to the rest of the world. Marcus had given up on finding Sylvia and stopped to lean on the railings overlooking the pool deck. That was where Hamish came upon him.

'Great life this, isn't it? Nothing to do and all day to do it,' he said. 'I could get used to it.'

'It's taken me a little time to switch off completely, but cruising certainly is a relaxing way to do it. Being surrounded by people who are having a good time is quite infectious.'

'Aye, I suppose it is.' Hamish agreed, thinking, you'd enjoy it all the more if you'd loosen up a bit.

They observed the goings-on below where little knots of people had gathered. They were watching some of the galley staff carving sculptures from enormous blocks of ice. It was too soon to see what they would be when they were finished. A steel-pan band, wearing brightly patterned shirts, provided catchy calypso music. That had even tempted a few people off their recliners to dance in front of the stage. Waiters wove in and out, doing practised balancing acts with trays of colourful cocktails. The place was buzzing.

'Have you seen Sylvia about,' asked Hamish, 'or the others?'

'Not since last night.'

Betty and Ben were in the games room where several serious hands of bridge were being played. There were no beginners, only the committed players who couldn't live without their fix wherever they travelled. Betty looked around. People said bridge was a social thing, but any onlooker would have thought there was nothing social about this gathering: they were all out to win and show the others what good players they were. She had played all her life and enjoyed the mental stimulation.

She had played with Heather, whom she had met at the Boys'
script brainstorm, and had made a loose arrangement to play
with her today, but there was no sign of her so she partnered
Ben instead.

He was growing on her. He was well read but poorly
travelled. In him she sensed a lonely old man who had been
totally devoted to his Esther, but whose horizons hadn't
stretched very far. Now he was at the edge of discovering
things he'd never done, or expected to do, and it seemed to
her that he was almost afraid to admit he was enjoying it.

Thirty-five

HEATHER HADN'T TURNED UP FOR HER GAME with Betty because all hell had broken out in the Sirocco Suite as the day unfolded. Will and Heather had ordered breakfast in their room. It was delivered at precisely nine o'clock and their steward, after asking if they would like it served outside, had set it out for them on a table in the sitting room. Heather, wrapped in a heavily embroidered silk kimono, was busy counting her vitamin pills before washing them down with carrot juice when Will opened an envelope that had been delivered on the tray. He read the note it contained.

'What's that?' she asked.

'Oh, just an invitation to a cocktail party – trying to sell us another cruise. They can get nothing right. It's only addressed to me,' he said, and threw it onto an armchair.

'How boring – we can skip it,' she answered, turning her attention to her sugar-free muesli and low-fat milk.

Will made a big deal of buttering his toast, then playing with his grilled bacon, poached eggs and tomatoes.

'Not hungry?'

'No, and as I've often told you, it's a mistake to order the night before because you never know what you'll be in the mood for the next morning. I prefer to choose at the buffet.'

'I hate facing people first thing. I like to ease my way into the day. This is much more civilised, don't you think?'

'No, I don't.'

'Oh, don't be such a grouch, Will. We're on holiday. What's put you in such a foul mood?' She finished her muesli and went to change into her exercise things. He still hadn't touched his food when she was leaving, but she was going to work off what she'd eaten.

As soon as the door closed he retrieved the envelope and took the card out. It stated: *Please make yourself available for a meeting with Security Officer Shaun Shannon. He will call at your suite at 10.00 a.m.* It was signed by Captain Doug Burgess.

Jesus Christ, I'm ruined. The Irish bitch must have complained. If Heather believes them I'm finished. She'll leave me. Shit, shit, shit, what am I going to do?

He got dressed, then paced up and down, trying to work out a plausible story. He was sweating so he went back into the bathroom to apply some more antiperspirant and wipe his forehead with a damp flannel.

The knock came. He was surprised to find a posse outside. Security Officer Shaun Shannon introduced himself, then Marina from Guest Relations and finally the captain, who said they could have the meeting elsewhere, if he preferred. He declined. Heather wouldn't be back for another hour and a half at least, if she had a sauna as she usually did. He offered them a seat, but the captain remained standing behind the sofa, surveying the room.

The security officer did most of the talking. 'I presume you know why we're here?'

'I expect it has something to do with the mad woman who came here yesterday. She threw herself at me, and when I pushed her away she tore at her clothes and threatened to tell my wife I'd attacked her. She asked me for money to keep quiet, but I called her bluff and sent her packing. I'm no fool.'

'Well, Mr Pembry-Travers, we've had a formal complaint so I'm sure you understand that we have to follow it up. Perhaps you'll give us your side of the story.'

He could feel the sweat soaking the underarms of his shirt. He wiped his forehead with the back of his hand. 'A complaint. *She* made a complaint? Can you believe that?'

'How did you meet the lady in question?'

'I don't know. I think my wife met her and she came here for drinks the first evening at sea.'

'On her own?'

'There were a few other couples, but she was on her own.'

'And have you met her since? At dinner, on a tour, or in the nightclub, for example?'

'No – yes. I might have danced with her once or twice, I can't remember, but I never thought she was on the game. Just shows – you can't really tell, can you? She was very pleasant when we bumped into each other on the ship, I mean, you can't miss anyone here, can you?' he said, trying to lighten the tone. 'It's like swimming in a goldfish bowl. Isn't it?'

'Did you invite her here yesterday afternoon?'

'Of course not! She arrived at the door and I thought she'd come to see Heather, my wife.'

'But your wife wasn't here, was she?'

'No. She'd gone to some exercise class, as she does most afternoons, and then to the spa. I didn't want to seem unfriendly so I asked her in. I even offered her a drink, which I now realise, in the light of the way she came on to me, was probably the wrong thing to do. Come to think of it, she didn't have one, but I had no idea that she was going to make a pass. I mean, you don't expect that sort of thing, do you?' He knew he was talking too much and slowed down, trying to read their expressions. He should have moved the bloody Scrabble board before they came. Maybe she hadn't mentioned that, but it had certainly drawn the captain's attention and he stood with his gaze fixed on it.

There was an uncomfortable silence, which he felt he had to break. 'She has some nerve making a complaint when I'm the one who should have reported her.'

'Why didn't you?' Marina asked.

'I didn't want to upset my wife, make her feel she'd have to avoid anyone. I wonder how many other men the little schemer will try that trick on before the end of the trip. I'm sure some people would be naïve enough to pay her to say nothing in case it might damage their reputation. No smoke and all that.'

Marina nodded.

Doug addressed him for the first time: 'Yes. That's why we have to be so careful about accusations like this. We have to look at them from every angle. We can't tolerate any such behaviour. Passenger safety and peace of mind are paramount to us and to what we represent. It's a nasty business, being wrongly accused, and it's hard to get a reputation back once it's damaged.'

'You're absolutely right there,' Will agreed, sensing the interview was coming to an end and that he had somehow managed to deflect any blame from himself.

'You have some interesting words on the board there,' Doug said. 'I've never heard of half of them before – I'm a "cat" and "dog" man myself. It's no wonder I always lose. Is it you or your wife who has such a quirky vocabulary?'

'I like to think we both have, but she might disagree.' He laughed.

'What is an *urubu* and an *euoi*?'

'The urubu's a vulture, and it's a great way of dumping a plague of *u*'s – three in one move.' He hesitated. 'You'd have to ask Heather about the other one, I can't remember.'

Doug looked knowingly at his security officer and Marina.

Then he turned back to Will. As he did so, the door opened, and Heather strode in, wearing her singlet and leggings, a towel draped casually around her shoulders. Will turned white, but before he could say anything, Doug greeted her: 'Ah, the wordsmith. I'm delighted to meet you. I'm intrigued by your knowledge of obscure words and was wondering what *euoi* means?'

Heather looked at the board, clearly puzzled. 'I haven't a clue. I've never heard it before. It must be one of Will's. What's this? Surely you're not trying to sell us another cruise when we're scarcely halfway through this one. Things must be bad if they're sending the top brass canvassing from door to door.'

Doug smiled at her, 'Thankfully, we don't have to do that, but I'll let your husband explain why we're here.'

Will stood there, incredulous, but said nothing. He didn't know where to begin. He'd blown it and he didn't know how to get out of the situation in which he found himself. If he admitted what he had done, he'd lose his marriage. For one wild moment he thought of making a dash out onto the balcony and jumping over the rails: that way he wouldn't have to face the consequences.

'Well, Will. What's this all about?' she asked.

He still said nothing.

'There's been an incident, an accusation involving your husband,' Marina said.

'An incident? What sort of incident? Will, what the hell is going on?'

Will realised it was more important to convince his wife

than the others. 'It's just a misunderstanding. Nothing to worry about.' He turned to Shaun and said, 'I won't take it any further. The woman is obviously disturbed.'

Ignoring his bluff, Shaun addressed Heather. 'There has been a serious accusation of assault against your husband by a female passenger. We have spoken to both parties and have no reason to disbelieve her. Fortunately for your husband, she has not yet asked that we report this to the relevant authorities so if I were you, sir, I'd count my blessings and run while I still can. If she does, it will be an entirely different matter and out of our hands.'

Will was speechless. There was nothing to say that would improve matters. He was trapped and there was no one to blame. There was no point now in trying to deny it.

'I'm afraid we're going to have to keep your husband under ship arrest until the next port,' the captain said, 'where he'll be disembarked as soon as we dock. He's free to use room service at any time in the interim, but not to leave these quarters. You are welcome to stay on board with us, madam.'

'What do you mean, ship arrest? Is this some kind of joke?

'I'm afraid it's no joke, Mrs Pembry-Travers.'

'This can't be true. Oh, dear God, no, not again, not on the ship.' Her voice shook. 'Will, I warned you after that episode with the groom at the Grangers' house party. We're through. Pack your bags and go, but I shan't be going with you this time.' She pulled the rings off her wedding finger and put them on the table beside the Scrabble board. 'I won't be wearing those again.'

'Please, Heather, there's been a mistake. It's all lies and an – an injustice. Let me clear my name. Let me explain.'

'You've done enough of that in the past. You just can't keep it zipped up or your hands to yourself, can you? Well, you've gone too far this time, and I was a fool to believe you could change. I don't need to hear any more.' She turned to Marina and said, 'I'm so sorry. I really am. Please tell the woman, whoever she is, that I'm sorry.'

Marina put an arm around her and gave her a hug.

'Do I know her?' No one answered. 'Have you a spare cabin? It doesn't have to be a suite. Anywhere. I can't stay in this one.'

'Are you sure? We'll leave you to talk things over.'

'I'm certain. I've done all the talking I intend to do. Now, please, any size of cabin will do. I'll get my things together straight away. Can someone stay with me while I do?' she asked, shooting her husband a filthy look.

Shaun offered to wait on the balcony.

'We can bring in someone to help you,' Marina suggested.

'Thank you, but I'll be quicker doing it myself.'

Doug and Marina left together and she whispered to him, 'How were you so certain?'

'From the Scrabble words. No one could make that story up with those obscure words. Then there was the steward's account of events. He said he met Mrs Rahilly on the corridor before she went in there yesterday and it was clear when Will opened the door that he'd been expecting her. He wouldn't have been if she'd just turned up to try to get money out of him. He also said that the noise that had attracted him had sounded like someone kicking the door, trying to get help. It stopped as soon as he knocked. A few minutes later he saw her leaving the stateroom in a distressed state and we have that on CCTV. But most damning of all was his wife's reaction. It had obviously happened before. Besides, I believed Mrs Rahilly all along, but I had to be sure.'

'So did I. I feel so sorry for his wife. He had some nerve, trying to brazen it out. Jenny Rahilly told us that he'd been quite specific about what time he expected her. I checked with the spa and he'd made the booking for his wife, so he knew she'd be out of the way for a good while.'

'He hadn't even moved the Scrabble board and it was exactly as she had described it. He even used the same words she told us he'd used when describing the vulture thing as a great way of "dumping a plague of *u*'s".'

'I noticed that too. If she had gone there to solicit, she'd have been too busy setting him up to remember any of that with such clarity. She'd never have remembered the words they played either. In fact, I can't see them playing at all, if that had been the case.'

'Nor can I. It doesn't strike me as a great seduction move.'

'Do we have to organise onward transport for him?'

'We're not obliged to, but I think we might, if you don't mind, Marina. Make sure it goes on his credit card.'

'I'll get on to it. His wife's very brave, deciding to stay on without him.'

'She's a formidable woman. You wouldn't mess around

with her,' he said. 'You know, I thought this was going to be an uneventful Mediterranean trip, but there's been plenty of excitement so far.'

'And we've still four days to go,' she said, and they laughed.

'Keep me posted if there are any more developments. I'd like to let Jenny know that he'll be gone in the morning and under surveillance until then.'

'I'll do that for you,' Marina said as she headed back to Guest Relations.

Thirty-six

THAT DAY THE BEAUTY PARLOUR WAS BUSY, the spa was booked out and the nail bar had a waiting list. At sea, pampering took on a new urgency, especially on days when they were not docking anywhere. There was so much time to enjoy everything that self-indulgence had to be factored into everyone's programme.

Sonny and Bud had had a session in the couples' therapy room. That involved twenty-five minutes in a flotation tank, followed by a lime and lemon ginger salt glow treatment, where warm oils were drizzled over them and they were given a vigorous massage. They had agonised over whether they had been right to make the complaint on Jenny's behalf, but after meeting her and discussing it they were happy they had.

Betty had persuaded Ben to try a neck and shoulders massage, even though he protested vociferously that Esther would have considered it a waste of good money.

'Well, Ben, Esther isn't here to see you spend it, and you can't take it with you, so live a little, man. Start spoiling yourself!'

'My daughter will think I've lost my mind.'

'Then don't tell her, although she might be delighted you have!'

He grinned. 'I doubt that very much, but I'll give it a go.'

Marcus was no stranger to looking after himself. He had been in earlier for a deep-tissue massage. Skiing, sailing and cycling meant that old, and not so old, sports injuries often gave him twinges, so massage was a regular part of his health regime, both at home and when abroad.

Hamish had decided that a Swedish massage sounded too good to miss. He hadn't been in the least put out when the masseuse turned out to be a diminutive Thai and not a tall Swede. But he had been sceptical when she asked, 'Would you like light or firm pressure?' From her size, he decided that light would probably do no more than tickle him, so he answered, 'Firm.'

He had to stop himself crying out for mercy when she started on his shoulders, her tiny hands pummelling him like a methodical sledgehammer. But, determined not to be perceived as a wimp, when she asked if the pressure was all right, he replied, 'Fine, just fine,' and steeled himself for more of the same. He felt battered and bruised by the time he left, and anything but relaxed. On the way out he saw John in the solarium and went over to him. 'I need a beer.'

'Perfect timing. I was lying here contemplating getting one but I was too lazy to do anything about it. Let's go outside.'

Sylvia, Jenny and Betty were sitting in a row having their hair blow-dried. There were no mirrors in front of them, just windows to the open sea. They waited until they were all finished and left together. They were laughing. Sylvia was a few inches taller than when she had gone in, her red curls piled high in a heavily lacquered sculpture.

'My God,' Betty said, 'you look just like Sybil from *Fawlty Towers*.'

'I do, don't I?' asked Sylvia. 'I just said I liked it dried fuller rather than flat.'

'Well, she took you at your word. In fact, we all look like extras from *Dallas* or *Dynasty*,' Betty added.

'We do, don't we? They obviously do their training in the States.' Jenny giggled.

'I'm going back to my cabin to tie a sarong over mine and see if it'll flatten it. I'm afraid that if I put a comb to it it'll snap off. It feels like she used glue to keep it in place,' Sylvia said. 'Come with me and we'll see what we can salvage.'

Jenny said, 'Maybe they thought tonight was fancy dress, not the gala.'

'Then we'd be in with a chance as the Ugly Sisters.'

When Captain Doug had suggested to Jenny that she could leave if she felt inclined and take a different cruise whenever it suited her, she had considered doing just that and going home. Despite her best efforts at blocking out what had happened, she kept remembering. She wondered what Will had said when, or if, he had been confronted. What would she do if she bumped into him? Would he still be on the ship? Despite that, though, she had enjoyed the afternoon much more than she had expected to.

The first thing she noticed when she got back to her stateroom was another bottle of champagne sitting in fresh ice. The one she had been given on her arrival was still on the sideboard, waiting for an occasion to open it. She immediately assumed it was from the Boys. It would be so typical of them – bubbles as a cure-all. Then she spotted an envelope and her heart constricted. It was about yesterday.

The card inside read:

Jenny, I hope you are feeling better. I am happy to say that we have had a positive conclusion at this end to our problem. If you care to contact Marina she'll fill you in. Meanwhile, try to enjoy the rest of your holiday, and if we can do anything to make it better, do please let us know.
Doug Burgess

She couldn't wait to get down to Guest Relations to find out what had happened.

Marina told her about their confrontation with Will. 'He didn't actually confess, and he made a half-hearted attempt to deny he did anything. Anyway, the upshot is, he's confined to his suite until we dock tomorrow morning, so you needn't worry, you won't have to see him again.'

Jenny wanted to ask how his wife had taken it, but felt it wasn't her place to do so, but she was curious just the same.

Relieved, she headed off to dress for John's pre-dinner drinks. She had a shimmering full-length silver dress that hugged her in the right places. Her strappy shoes and red clutch completed the look. 'Not bad, not bad at all,' she muttered to herself as she closed the wardrobe door and got a glimpse in the long mirror. 'Now, let's see if I can get through tonight without a *faux pas.*' She took the chilled bottle of champagne with her and was surprised to find she was the first to arrive.

John was buttoning his dress shirt when he opened the door. 'Wow, you look stunning. Come on through.'

'Am I early? I thought Betty said to come at half past,' she said, putting the bottle on a table. She had actually waited until twenty to so that she wouldn't be the first to arrive.

'No,' he smiled, 'you're fine. I'll be with you in a mo. You didn't have to bring that.'

She felt awkward. Should she explain what had happened? If she did, she'd only get upset again. As though he were reading her mind, he asked, 'What happened this morning? My rapidly expanding waistline isn't thanking you for making me eat your pancakes as well as my own at breakfast. I made the mistake of ordering for the two of us.'

'John, please forgive me for that. Not for having to eat the pancakes, but for not turning up. Can I ask you to trust me? I promise I'll tell you what happened, but not tonight.'

'You said that the night we met too.'

'This is different, much different, but I'll tell you everything, I promise.' There was a knock, and John's steward came in with a large tray of canapés, which he took to the balcony.

'Now, where have the others got to?'

'I'm not expecting them until seven, but let's open the bubbly,' he said, looking at the label. 'Nice brand.'

'It arrived this evening with the captain's compliments.'

He laughed. 'My complimentary champers is far inferior to that. What did you do to get into his good books?'

'I'm sure Betty told me half past six.'

'And I'm sure she was matchmaking again.'

'She wouldn't do anything that blatant, would she?'

'She just did and we fell for it,' he grinned at her, 'but I hope we don't need intervention from a third party to be friends, or more, do we?' He stretched out his hand to her and there was a loud knock at the door.

She took it briefly and smiled. 'No, of course we don't.'

'It sounds like they've all come together,' he said. He leaned down and kissed her lightly on the forehead. 'We'll continue this discussion later.'

They arrived on each other's heels, the women elegant in formal numbers of varying lengths, showing off tanned arms and shoulders, the men authoritative and debonair in their dress suits. Sylvia had managed to tame her hair and Ben had decided to break his self-imposed curfew on late dining. Sonny and Bud made their entrance in matching, but different-coloured, striped silk waistcoats and almost as much jewellery as the ladies. Sonny's pocket watch glinted as it caught the evening sun. Marcus had left his red bow-tie undone in a casual way, and procured a seat beside Sylvia, which didn't go unnoticed by Hamish or Betty.

'No kilt, Hamish?' Betty remarked.

'Now, Betty, apart from the fact that I don't have the legs for it, it's far too breezy on deck to be walking around in that. A sudden gust of wind might shock some of the old ladies.'

'Less of the "old ladies", thank you,' Betty said.

'Forget the old ladies. I don't think I'd withstand the shock either,' said Sylvia.

They stayed outside until the sun had sunk beneath the horizon in another dramatic exit, leaving the sky pink- and orange-streaked in its wake.

Doug changed into his dress uniform before phoning Andrea. He used to look forward to their chats, but of late they had taken on a new edge. He never knew when he was dialling how she would be. If she was too exuberant, he knew she had taken her medication. If she sounded distant and slow, she hadn't. If her voice was slurred, she'd been drinking. Today he was pleasantly surprised by her tone.

'I've been looking forward to your call all day,' she told him. 'What's happening on the tug?'

He smiled. That was how they always referred to the ship. It had become a private joke, whose origins they had now forgotten. 'Just the usual madness. What have you been up to? I hope you've taken advantage of a break from Lewis to get plenty of rest.'

'I've had a lovely day. Your mother treated me to the hairdresser so you won't recognise me when you get home in a few weeks. I've got a new look.'

'I liked the old one.'

'You'll love this even more. We had a fabulous lunch and I had my check-up. You'll be pleased to hear that Dr Tatton, who liked my hair by the way, is very pleased with me. He's reduced my pills and he was asking after you too.'

'That's good news.'

'Your mum drove me to Maxine's on the way home to see Lewis and give him a cuddle. He's fine and doesn't seem to be missing me at all. I hope you are.'

'Of course I am. It's much harder being away now that we're a family. I feel guilty leaving you with all the extra responsibility.'

'I'll get used to it. I'll have to, won't I? What have you been up to – another peaceful day at sea?'

'I wish. We had a sexual-assault case and the culprit is now under close arrest in his suite until we get shot of him tomorrow in Rhodes.'

'That's awful.'

'Fortunately the woman doesn't want to take any action so that eliminates a lot of red tape at our end. The man's wife won't have anything to do with him. She's staying on for the rest of her holiday on her own. Apparently it's not a first offence.'

'Wise woman. I'd do the same. Any receptions or events tonight?'

'It's gala night, so I have to do my happy-clappy bit. I'm hosting a table of American travel writers. They're doing a Europe-in-ten-days thing. It should be a bit of fun, actually. They're only on for three days and have almost drunk the bars dry already. One asked me earlier on if they had running water in Greece and would their cell phones work there? Can you believe it?'

'I can. I was in the front line for long enough. Do you remember the couple who wanted to know if they should take toilet paper with them when they went to Barcelona?'

'Nothing would surprise me.'

'Well, enjoy your night and we'll talk tomorrow. Be good.'

'I always am. You look after yourself, Andrea, and remember I love you.'

'Love you too.'

He put his phone down on the table, feeling more relaxed about his wife than he had been for ages. If the doctor had decreased her medication she must be feeling a lot better.

The ship took on a different ambience on a gala formal night. Official photographers captured wedding anniversaries, engagements, birthdays and special moments between old and new friends. Merry after their pre-dinner drinks, the solos party from the first lunch squashed together with the Boys for such a memento, then were escorted to their table.

The style was glamorous, makeup perfect, hair beautifully coiffed and jewellery sparkling. Opulence hung in the air. Dinner on such nights was served with style and grace. The tables were set with precision and panache. Cutlery and glassware gleamed, and the menus tantalised. The choices were numerous. The sommeliers were kept busy recommending wines to go with the seafood medley, the lobster, the red snapper, the rack of lamb, the Châteaubriand steak. The ship's orchestra, in cream jackets and red bow-ties, played in the background.

After dessert had been served, the executive chef appeared on the staircase. He was followed by his team of sous chefs and a selection of staff from the galley, all togged out in pristine whites. He gave the guests the staggering statistics of how many bread rolls, eggs, kilos of beef, litres of milk and cream, and bottles of wine were consumed in a typical cruise, each raising a cheer from the tables. When he finished introducing the sous chefs – the pastry chef attracting the loudest applause – he conducted a parade of his staff through the dining room, the passengers waving their linen napkins above their heads. When the excitement had died down, Hamish said, 'Well, what's it to be? The casino or dancing under the stars, Ben?'

'I think I'll go upstairs and have a look.'

'Well, don't get too excited about it,' Hamish said, giving Betty a nudge. 'You could be on a promise there.'

'Behave yourself.' She laughed. 'And what about you, letting all the eligible ladies slip through your fingers?'

'Betty, that's the story of my life, but I'm prepared to sit by and wait until they discover that the others aren't anywhere close to matching my charm – and come running. Maybe that mousy little computer lady would take pity on me.'

'She keeps very much to herself. She's like a moth – she just comes out at night for a twirl or two with those dance fellows and then disappears,' said John.

'She's a little short in the personality department,' said Marcus.

'That's a diplomatic way of putting it.'

'I tried to draw her out about Brisbane, where I have lots of friends and business dealings, but she clammed up. She's very hard to talk to.'

'I agree,' said Hamish, with a grin. 'That could be a bit of a challenge, though – a mystery woman or a woman with a mystery!'

'You'd think your Scottish accent should charm anyone,' Betty observed.

'Well, it's obviously not working on this trip!' he replied, looking pointedly at Marcus.

Marcus had staked his claim on Sylvia and had made it plain that he didn't want to share her. 'Can't we just get away from everybody and talk, get to know each other properly? We could go back to my place.'

She nodded. 'I'd like that, but can we dance for a bit first?'
He agreed reluctantly. He was a bit more serious than the type
of man she usually went for, but last night she had set out to
change that. She'd never been with a Dane or, for that matter,
a gentile before.

'Those dance fellows have a great job,' said Ben. 'That one
looks a bit like a circus act with his moustache and oiled hair.'

'He does. But think of all the rich widows and desperate
divorcées you'd meet. One of them might sweep you off your
feet,' John teased.

'I don't think I'd have the stamina for it,' Ben replied, and
they all laughed.

Betty and Ben danced for a while until he retired. After
that she almost wore the dance hosts out, between partnering
Sonny or Bud. Chad had been effusive in his compliments
and had obviously heard that Bud was in films: every chance
he got, he made some reference to Hollywood.

'Does he think I'm casting for a Fred Astaire role? Look at
the way he shows off every time he passes us. Hasn't he enough
single women without bothering ours?' Bud wondered.

When he danced past again, he stopped, and said, 'Ladies,
you look divine, and you gentlemen are equally fetching. You
all look like film stars.'

Betty groaned. The others were on the floor, and she asked
Hamish to escort her to her quarters. 'You're some woman,
Betty. Are you trying to prise me away from the lovers?'

'Was it that obvious? I must be losing my touch.'

He took her arm and led her to the lifts.

John and Jenny danced close together, laughing and joking, and several people noticed that something was developing between them.

'Our damsel in distress may have found her cure,' Sonny whispered to Bud.

'That's exactly what she needs and he seems to be a genuine guy.'

After he'd seen Betty off, Hamish came back to try his luck with Kathy, the computer woman. He didn't get anywhere. She hadn't said anything except 'Yes,' 'No,' and 'Yes,' when he asked if she was enjoying herself, finding her job a challenge and if she would do it again. In between he could have marked her absent, except that she had stood on his toe once, reminding him that she was there.

Bud got mad with the adulation a waiter was heaping on Sonny and threw a tantrum. 'You've ruined a perfect evening again, haven't you? I'm going to bed and you needn't hurry back.' They both disappeared but the spat didn't last long, and soon they were back on the dance floor. Eventually they said good night and went to their suite to make up in private.

Once they were back in their suite, Sonny let out a shriek. 'My watch! I've lost my grandfather's pocket watch. It's gone.'

'It can't be gone. Are you sure you were wearing it?'

'Positive. Don't you remember Sylvia commenting on it when we were at John's?'

'You're right. Maybe someone found it and handed it in.'

'Is it likely that the lost property office would be manned at this hour?'

'I'll try Guest Relations.' He dialled, only to be told that it had not been given in during the past hour. He should check the following day: it may have been found earlier, but the shift had changed and the attendant now on duty had no access to the office at this time. They went back to the bar to ask there and got the same response. Bud tried to console him. They retraced their steps and rang John, but he hadn't yet returned to his suite. Finally, realising that there was nothing they could do until the morning, they went to bed.

John was pleased that the evening was going so well. Whatever had happened earlier in the day with Jenny was obviously not important. Tonight had been perfect and he knew they were back on course. He planned to take her ashore the next day in Rhodes. If they could get away from the others, they would recapture what they had felt that night in Paphos. He didn't want to rush her. She reminded him of a kitten learning to trust humans for the first time. She'd come close, scarper away, then come a little closer. He had to allow her to bridge the final gap when she was ready. If he moved too quickly he'd drive her away. They danced the last dance together, a slow number. Then he walked her to her stateroom and kissed her, light but demanding too. Neither said anything.

Then: 'Will you come in?'

'I thought you'd never ask.'

They stood at the rails on the balcony, gazing at the stars.

'They never seem so bright back in Dublin.'

'It's the same in all cities – too much light pollution.'

A shooting star caught their eye, followed quickly by another. 'Make a wish,' he said.

She closed her eyes and did as she was told. 'When we were small we believed that a shooting star was a soul going to heaven.'

'Do you still believe that?' he asked.

'Not for a minute. Did you wish?'

'I did.'

'Do you think it'll come true?'

'Ask me tomorrow,' he said, smiling before drawing her to him and kissing her. 'What about you?'

'There's a distinct possibility, but you can ask me tomorrow too.' She grinned.

John didn't get back to his suite until the early hours of the morning. He hadn't rushed Jenny, but they had reached a new level in their friendship.

They had kissed again when they came in from the balcony, his hands gently exploring the curve of her back and her bottom. She had moved closer, pressing herself to him. He nuzzled her neck and she moaned softly. He slid one of the slinky straps off her shoulder and she put her hand up to stop him, but not in a way that made him feel rejected.

'John, sit down, please.' She sat on the bed and held out her hand to him. 'I want to make love to you so much, but I don't think I'm ready for it just yet.'

'I don't want you to feel you have to.'

'I don't. It's not that at all. It's just …' Her voice trembled.

He reached for her and held her close. 'You don't have to feel—'

'It's not about what I'm feeling. It's just that – well, I'm afraid. I had a miscarriage a little while ago and I haven't made love since.'

Then the tears flowed, tears she had been holding for months.

John sat cradling her, rocking her back and forth until the sobs subsided and she could talk again.

They lay down together and talked more.

'There's a lot to tell you but not now. You must think I'm a neurotic creature. Have I frightened you off?' She smiled at him.

'Never. We have all the time in the world for talk. Would you like me to go and let you have some rest?'

'No, I'd hate it. Please stay.'

Even though their kisses became more tender, more ardent and then more demanding, he held back. This was not the right time and he was surprised when he heard himself say, 'I'm prepared to wait, Jenny, no matter how long it takes.'

Thirty-seven

SONNY COULDN'T SLEEP – HE WAS SO UPSET over his loss. His grandfather, whose initials he shared and which were engraved inside the cover, had promised him that pocket watch when he'd realised he was gay. 'Be proud of who you are,' his grandfather had said. 'Never let anyone shame you, or be ashamed of you. That way you can always hold your head up high – and wear my watch with pride!' And he had done so until last night. He slipped out of bed without disturbing Bud, pulled on some tracksuit bottoms, a T-shirt and some flip-flops, then let himself out quietly. It was still before seven o'clock, but he wasn't the only one up and about.

Cleaning teams had already washed down the decks, the handrails had been polished, the windows were gleaming and all the loungers had a rolled-up towel and cushion placed on them. Some early birds were getting their wake-up coffee from the buffet, while others were taking them back to their staterooms.

Heather stood at the rails on the top deck as the ship glided gently to a halt, inches from the pier at Rhodes. She marvelled at the skill of those involved. They had to be highly trained to be able to manoeuvre such a monster with such precision into such a tight space. She remembered the captain telling them at one of the cocktail parties that the two extensions on either side of the bridge gave them a clear view of the length of the ship and that through their glass floors they could see to the edge of the harbour, to prevent them crashing into it. Now she was witnessing it for herself.

The yellow light from the rising sun lit the beige stones on the ramparts and the ruined walls. The lofty vessel dwarfed these once majestic buildings, as well as the men who were fixing the ropes to the capstans down below. She had slept, worn out from the emotion of the previous day. She'd eaten her dinner in her new stateroom two decks below the one the suite was on. The beaded coffee-coloured outfit she had bought for the gala dinner hung unworn in the wardrobe, the matching shoes still in their box. She had called room service and dined alone on her balcony.

She had had good years with Will – it would have been seven the following month. It wasn't a love match, but it had suited her and he had let her live her own life, pretty much. He had given her the position and social life she had always enjoyed, both before and during her first marriage, and he had seemed to care for her, but he was a randy old goat, like most of his horsy-set friends. In return she had run his houses, orchestrated his dinner parties, segregated his different groups of friends and acquaintances – business, equestrian, golf and sailing – and charmed them for him, massaging egos when necessary. In the country he saw himself as a munificent squire, in the yacht club as a would-be commodore and in London as a man of position in the City. He had understood and agreed to the rules. She had made it clear from the start that if she was to be his wife she was never to be humiliated by sordid affairs and call girls. There had been whiffs of scandals and indiscretions in the past, before they had married. Yesterday had been too much: she had come in to a contingent of officialdom – his accusers – and he had looked defenceless, pussy-whipped and so guilty. He couldn't even make eye contact with her.

Now he was leaving her life, and she his, and she had mixed feelings. She wondered, not for the first time, who the victim had been. And for the umpteenth time she decided she was probably better off not knowing. She hadn't yet decided whether she'd tell everyone the reason that their marriage had come to such an abrupt end. She was in a strong position to bargain with him if she kept quiet. She didn't need his money: she'd inherited quite a lot from her own family, but she had a competitive spirit and she'd enjoy the power struggle that was sure to follow. Meanwhile she felt a little sorry for the stupid man.

She'd never understand why some men thought they could have sex whenever they wanted it, wherever and with whomever they fancied. She'd always thought it was overrated for the fuss they made about it. She'd had many passionate encounters in her time but never felt the compulsion to ravish every good-looking man she met, and knew that several of her girlfriends felt the same. Maybe the right man had just never come along. Perhaps that was why she took such satisfaction from her antiques, her music, her houses and her exercise regime. Whatever, she'd miss some of the life they'd shared, but he had thrown it away, carrying on under her nose.

Will had been told to have his things packed last night, apart from his toiletries and whatever he wanted to wear the next day. At seven a.m. a porter collected his bag and took him downstairs. He hadn't spoken to anyone. He hadn't even asked to talk to his wife. He knew there was no going back where Heather was concerned. He had thought several times of jumping overboard during the night, but he had lacked the courage. He needed to put distance between them for now. If she talked, he'd be blackballed from his clubs and he'd never be accepted at Ascot. He'd be a laughing stock in his circles. And all for a fumble with that stupid Irish bitch. When they had married, Heather had insisted on a pre-nuptial contract.

It covered all sorts of transgressions, but sexual assault had not featured. Despite that, he knew he had broken more than the rules and was lucky to be getting off without a prosecution, although they had warned him that that could still happen.

He was escorted to the staff exit on deck four and across the wide pier to a Customs office, where he showed his passport. Officer Shannon witnessed his leaving, waiting until he'd got into the taxi they had organised for him. Will didn't glance back at the towering ship. If he had, he might have seen his wife on deck, watching his ignominious departure.

Jack arrived on duty at seven o'clock precisely, with three more of the Guest Relations team. It was going to be a busy day. They were docked here until ten that evening, and as the town was only a few hundred metres away, traffic on and off the ship would be constant. With no tendering, there was no urgency about disembarking those who had tours booked. He was just checking the night records when Sonny appeared. He explained about his pocket watch. Jack checked the register of lost and found, but nothing had been entered there. He was explaining that sometimes it took a day or two for things to appear, when he overheard the woman at the next station saying, 'I know I had it on me when I went for dinner. It's in the photos we took. Look, you can see it there.' She produced her camera as evidence.

'I'll make a note of it and we'll let you know as soon as we hear anything. I'm sure it will turn up.'

'I sure hope so. It's of very special sentimental value to me.'

By ten o'clock Jack was uneasy. A pattern was emerging. There were too many reports of missing jewellery – all valuable pieces. They had recorded six already and another woman was making a report at the desk. This was no coincidence. He rang the duty officer and asked if he could see the captain as soon as possible. He was summoned to his quarters and went there immediately.

'Jack, why is it that when I hear you want to see me I know I'm not going to like what you'll tell me?' the captain asked.

Jack smiled. 'I wish it were otherwise, and I hate to be the bearer of bad news, but I know you're definitely not going to like this. I think we have a professional thief on board.' He read the list recorded since the beginning of the trip: 'Two necklaces and a bracelet until last night.'

'That doesn't seem excessive.'

'It's not, and the bracelet turned up, but we've had eight reports this morning so far.'

'That sounds serious. Are you thinking along the lines of someone who lay low until formal night, when the bling and tiaras had an outing?'

'I'm afraid it's looking that way, sir.'

'Have we any leads, anything at all to go on?'

'Absolutely nothing. All we know is that these victims are women, except the guy with the pocket watch, and most, including him, were wearing their jewellery last night. And they all noticed they were missing at the end of the night when they were getting ready for bed.'

'Well, that's something. At least no one's reported anything missing from their stateroom. We need a list of anyone who requested extra or replacement key cards. Let's get Shaun Shannon up here and decide on a plan of action. We can't afford to delay. Whoever has stolen these things may have an accomplice waiting to take them from him or her in Rhodes. That way we'll never recover anything, but we might be able to stop it happening again.'

'I never thought of that. I've heard of this sort of thing going on, but it's never been a problem on any ship I've worked on until now.'

'Let's hope it doesn't become an even greater one. We have those journalists on board – they're leaving us today but they spent the whole night in the bar so I think we can probably count them out. Are any of those people aware that others are missing their valuables?' the captain asked.

'I don't think so.'

'Great. Let's try to keep it like that. Tell your team to take anyone else into the office to get a report or rumours will fly and we don't need that.'

'Certainly, sir. I'll get on to it straight away.'

Thirty-eight

BEFORE JOHN HAD GOT INTO HIS OWN BED he had noticed the flashing light telling him he had a message. It was from Sonny, asking him if he'd found his pocket watch. He'd gone outside to where they had had their drinks earlier and looked around, but there was no sign of it. It was too late to call and tell him, so he turned off the light and tried to sleep, but he couldn't.

Something he couldn't identify was bothering him. In the half-awake interlude before he fell asleep he tried to work out what it was. He knew it wasn't anything Jenny had told him. By the morning he had forgotten about it. He and she were going to explore Rhodes together. He had a guidebook that recommended a walking tour and that was where they would begin. It suggested going with a guide because there were around two hundred lanes, streets and alleyways that didn't have a name, and that was in the old medieval town alone. It added that getting lost was almost to be expected, and advised that when, not if, you did, you should try to make for the fountain in Sokratous, the closest thing to the main street.

'I believe the tour takes about an hour and a half, so when we lose our way we'll have all day to find it again,' he told Jenny, when they met as they'd agreed on the pool deck mid-morning.

They left the dock and walked to the tourist office. From there a guide shepherded them through various gates to ruins and monuments, crumbling temples and mosques, along parts of the old walls of the citadel and past shops filled with postcards, scarves, hats, sunglasses and gaudy plastic replicas of antiquity. They looked at each other, smiled at each other, laughed, held hands, and touched the way new lovers do. The history lessons were lost on them, although both were aware of their exotic surroundings: the deep-blue sky, the tantalising smells and the vivid colours of the flowers.

The tour finished close to Symi Square where they found themselves outside the entrance to the Municipal Art Gallery. He noticed Jenny's interest.

'Would you like to have a look inside, or shall we have lunch first?'

'I'd love to go in, and it would give us a chance to cool down a bit. I'm wilting, and I'm not hungry yet.'

The entrance was posted with flyers and notices of upcoming and current cultural happenings on the island.

'You certainly wouldn't get bored if you lived here,' she remarked to John as he paid for the tickets.

'I'm not familiar with many modern Greek artists, are you?'

'No, I don't think so, but maybe we'll recognise some as we go around.'

They spent an hour inside, discussing the works. They agreed on some and didn't on others. It was way past lunchtime when they came down the stairs leading out to the cobbled streets and into the heat. On the way Jenny stopped suddenly in front of a poster of a painting she recognised. John saw her turn pale. Intrigued, he came back to see what she was looking at. It was a notice for an exhibition in some other gallery and the artist's name was printed boldly in black, P. J. Rahilly: her father. Later, she told him it wasn't the name that had first caught her eye but the illustration on the poster. It showed a portrait of a young woman with a parasol reading a book on a riverbank.

'That's my portrait, the one my father painted of me for my eighteenth birthday. What's it doing here?'

'It's a great likeness. Did you know he had an exhibition here?' She shook her head. 'Well, that's one hell of a coincidence. It's running for the month, in wherever this place is. I'll find out.' He came back with two flyers and directions.

'It's a highly reputable gallery, run by the Municipal, and it's only five minutes away. Would you like to go and see it?'

'I need to think. Let's have a cool drink first.

She told him she didn't know whether she was more upset at suddenly being thrown into her absentee father's sphere or by the fact that he was selling the portrait.

'It was mine. He gave it to me. I've never really forgiven him for taking it when he left.' He could see how shocked she was. 'I don't know why I should be surprised. He was always selfish. I don't remember if I told you, but very shortly after Mum died he just upped and left with his new wife, and he's hardly ever bothered with any of us since.'

'Maybe he needs the money. He might have fallen on hard times.'

'I doubt that very much. Any time you read about him in the papers it's when a new royal portrait or some such is being unveiled, and they don't come cheap.'

She hardly touched her drink, then she said, 'Yes, I want to go to the exhibition, if only to see what I'm worth in my father's eyes.'

'I'm glad, because I think you'd regret it later if you didn't.' He paid the bill and they made their way to the Gallery of the Knights. At the entrance John said to the attendant, 'Does the artist live in Rhodes?'

'Some of the time, yes,' the woman told him. 'He usually comes here during the winter and stays for a month or so. I think he likes to move about. It probably gives him inspiration.' She handed them a catalogue each with titles, numbers and prices. 'He was here for the opening with his wife last week, but he flew out the next day. I'm not sure where. Do you know him?'

'I used to,' she replied.

The space was cool and cavernous with a ribbed arched ceiling and lots of nooks and crannies. It looked as though it might have been a refectory in times past. The paintings were well hung and lit, giving them the respect they deserved. There were several family groups, depicting smiling siblings, patriarchal men, beautiful and plain women. Others were just head-and-shoulders oils and watercolours in the style that P. J. Rahilly had made his own. John watched as Jenny came face to face with the portrait of herself, *Jenny at Eighteen*. He stood back and, looking at the catalogue, saw it was marked 'Not for Sale'. She stood in front of it for a while before moving on. Another painting seemed to hold her interest too. It was titled *Self-portrait with Elena*. He came up behind her and said, 'Is it a good likeness?'

'It's just him, with a few more lines and the same untidy hair. It's like standing here in front of him in person.'

'The detail is fantastic. Look at the child's dress and her hair. You feel you could run a comb through that. Who's Elena?' he asked.

'I haven't a clue, but she's cute, isn't she?'

'He's extremely talented, and expensive too. There's the same little girl in a ballet dress, over there. Number twenty-eight. It's called *I Own the World*.'

'That isn't the same little girl. That's me, in my pink tutu, with my kitten – and I did own the world back then. It used to hang on the landing in our home. I always loved it. It's not for sale either.' She went back to his self-portrait and studied the child. 'That's definitely not me – the clothes are wrong and he's much older in it. Yet the child has a great resemblance to me. I didn't notice it before because I was concentrating on his features.'

He looked from one to the other and said, 'You could be sisters.' It was clear from her expression that Jenny had just come to the same conclusion – her father had another daughter. Elena was her half-sister.

'I don't think I needed it, but if I did here's the proof. Look at these.' She led him into the next alcove where there was a triptych, executed in Madonna and Child fashion, called *Growing Up*.

'That's Sophie and Elena.'

'Is Sophie your stepmother?'

'I never thought of her as that, but I suppose she is. I can't believe he never told us about the child.'

'Maybe he felt you'd be annoyed that he'd left one family to start another.'

'I'd like to think he had that much consideration for us. It's more likely that he never even thought he should. My father doesn't do lateral thinking. He never did.'

'Have you seen enough?' John asked gently. 'Or would you like to go around again? I'll wait outside for you.'

'I'd like you to stay.'

She glanced around. The attendant had left the room so she quickly took photos with her phone. Satisfied, she slipped it back into her bag. John put his arm around her shoulders and gave her a hug and they did the exhibition again, in reverse order this time, then went outside and into a small café.

'Families can be very complicated,' she remarked as she looked at the menu. 'Is yours, or were your parents the stereotypical boy met girl, married, had children and lived relatively happily ever after till death did them part?'

'They thought they were,' he answered.

'What does that mean?'

He paused. 'You've had enough excitement for one day. We'll leave my family exposé to another.'

'Ah – a man of mystery. I'm not sure I can wait.'

'Well, I'm not giving you a choice.' He leaned over and took her hand. He was about to kiss her when, as though on cue, Hamish appeared from the crowded street followed by a woman hidden beneath an umbrella, sunglasses and a wide-brimmed hat.

'It's the lovebirds again. May we join you?' Hamish asked. 'We're archaeologied-out. I never want to hear another date and I'm in need of a wee drink.'

'Hamish, your timing, as ever, is perfect,' Jenny said, 'but we'd love your company.'

John agreed. 'Sure thing, pull up some chairs.' The 'we' turned out to be Heather, the woman John kept meeting in the gym.

Hamish asked her, 'Have you met everyone before? This is Jenny and John.'

'I see John in the gym and I know Jenny. How are you?'

Hamish said, 'We met up on the walking tour and decided we'd had enough, so we bunked off and here you are. It's a nice spot, isn't it?'

Jenny said nothing, just stared at the woman.

'Are you OK? Shall I get some water? You've had quite a shock this morning,' John said quietly to her.

'You're not wrong there,' she replied.

*

Later when John looked back on the day he felt that had been when it had gone wrong. Jenny had taken her father's surprising revelation of a half-sister, even if she'd had to find out through his paintings, pretty well. She had been relieved that he wasn't selling her portrait and glad that he had held on to the one of her and her kitten. After Hamish and Heather had joined them, though, she had kept looking around, agitated and completely different from how she had been previously. Had she expected her father to arrive round a corner? Or had the other woman upset her somehow? Admittedly Heather was eccentric, and her eyebrows were weird. She even suggested that Jenny should have hers tattooed on to emphasise her eyes – she could have her lip line done too. Jenny was not amused and showed it.

Jenny had called him mysterious, but he wasn't half as mystifying as she was. She couldn't be carrying a torch for the roguish Scot, could she? Or was she jealous of Heather? He couldn't imagine why she should be, but something had tipped the equilibrium of the day when Hamish and Heather had joined them. And he hadn't a clue what it was.

He'd never understand women.

Thirty-nine

MARCUS AND SYLVIA HAD TAKEN THE HOP-on-hop-off bus tour of the island. They had left it at a sandy beach, whose name they hadn't noticed, and were sitting on a low wall eating ice cream. They had spent the previous night together in Marcus's suite and were still in the afterglow that follows a new coupling with someone attractive and attentive. They wanted to know everything about each other.

'This can't go anywhere,' she told him. 'Long-distance relationships never work.'

'Absence makes the heart grow fonder,' he argued.

'And gives both parties a chance to wander.'

'You're very cynical,' he said. 'They're not like they used to be. You don't have to wait for weeks to get a reply to a letter – there's Skype, email and Facebook – and no shortage of flights between Copenhagen and London.'

'You've thought it all out, haven't you?' she teased.

'Yes, I have,' he said seriously. 'I like you, very much, and I'd like to think we could see each other after the holiday ends.'

'I'm very flattered by that, Marcus, so let's see how things go in the meantime.'

'Don't look so scared. I'm not proposing marriage, only friendship,' he said.

She laughed. 'What a pity! I might have said yes.' He looked so shocked she added, 'I know that! Neither was I.'

'Good. It's important to be on the same wave.'

'Wave length,' she corrected.

He laughed this time and said, 'Yes, that too … I have to tell you something that may affect our friendship.'

'You're not single?'

'No, it's not that, but you're Jewish and …'

'Is that a problem for you?' she asked. 'It didn't seem to be last night.'

'No, not in that way, but what I have to say may be a problem for you.'

Sylvia was fascinated. She hadn't a clue what he was about to reveal and wasn't prepared for it when it came out.

'Although I'm Danish, my grandparents and mother were German. My grandfather was an officer in the SS. We never knew and it was never discussed in our home. I found out by accident and I've never told my sister or brother.' He paused for her to digest this. 'Will that stop us being friends?' he asked, with a worried look. 'I felt it would be dishonest not to tell you.'

'Thank you. It can't have been easy. I never met anyone before who admitted anything like that.' He didn't say anything. 'My mother's father lost his three sisters, a brother and all their families in the Holocaust, but although we'll never forget, nor should we, you don't have to take the blame for any of your ancestors.' She grasped his hand.

'Thank you,' he said, squeezing hers. 'Normally I don't think about it too much, but this trip, being in Israel and now getting to know you, has made me think about it more than I ever have before.'

'Well, it was a different time. My paternal grandfather, who was a very wise old man, and had also lost members of his family, told me that it was very hard to move on, especially as the dreadful details kept emerging after the war was over. He never forgot, but he learned to forgive sufficiently to be able to enjoy his later years. He was very fair, and he used to tell me stories about his relatives. They were mine too, I suppose. I used to go down into his shop – he lived over it – and sit with him for hours, letting him talk.' Subconsciously she put her hand to her neck and remembered she still hadn't come across the fob chain he had given her. 'He always stressed that not all the Nazis were evil. Many of them were just frightened young boys, who had no choice but to go into the army and obey orders.'

'That was very charitable. Unfortunately my grandfather

wasn't one of the good ones,' Marcus said. 'He killed himself shortly before the war ended.'

'No more apologising for your relatives. I don't know what mine might have been up to in the past. And you should meet my mother! I'd disown her if I could.' He laughed, and Sylvia said, 'Being surrounded by all this antiquity and talking about the war is making us morbid. Let's go for a walk along the beach. I need to buy a little present for my daughter, although she probably doesn't deserve anything. She's a spoiled little madam, though I say it myself.'

Sonny was still distraught about his pocket watch and it had taken some persuasion to get him to go ashore at all.

'Moping isn't going to bring it back.'

'You think I don't know that, Bud?'

'Let's go out, and it may have been given in by the time we get back. If not, you'll just have to accept that it's gone.'

'You can be so cruel sometimes.'

'And sometimes that's the kindest way to be, instead of clinging to false hopes. If it's gone it's gone. It's not life-threatening, and we still have each other.'

'I suppose you're right,' he agreed reluctantly, but despite having phoned the desk three times already, he insisted on going past before they disembarked.

Jack was on duty and sympathetic. 'We'll keep looking for you. When you come back from your outing, perhaps you'll pop in to us and give us an account of where you were last night. Which bar, the casino, the theatre, that sort of thing. It might help us trace it, and we can tell the cleaning and serving staff to keep an eye out.'

The Guest Relations team had already been given instructions from Officer Shannon to compile a dossier on all the reported losses, which now amounted to ten. That way they might just be able to pin down the thefts to one area of activity and, hopefully, the culprit.

'I'll do it now,' said Sonny, 'before we go out.'

Jack took them into the office and began to take notes. Bud and Sonny retraced their movements.

'We had drinks in the Windward Suite – I know I was wearing it then because one of the ladies who knows her jewellery, Sylvia Rosenblatt, admired it. We stayed there until it was time for dinner and then we went straight to the Explorers' Restaurant.'

Bud interrupted, 'Oh, and we stopped on the landing outside to have that photo taken of the group. There were nine or ten of us and we had a bit of pushing and shoving to get the pose just right. Remember? The guy had to take a few before we'd all stopped pulling faces. Maybe it fell off there.'

'Or maybe the picture will show if you were still wearing it then,' Jack suggested.

'Good one. We sat at our usual table by the windows and immediately afterwards we went up to the top deck. We stayed there until about half past midnight, the whole lot of us dancing like things possessed. We'd had a lot of champagne by then.'

'Can you give me the names of those you were with? We'll ask them to check, too, in case they remember when they last noticed you wearing your watch.'

'That's a great idea,' said Sonny, happy they were taking his loss so seriously.

'Did you go anywhere else during that time, back to your stateroom perhaps?' Jack asked.

'No, I don't think so. A visit to the washrooms probably, but nowhere else.'

'Right, leave it with us,' said Jack, winding up the interview. 'You go off and enjoy your day. Rhodes is a beautiful island and there's loads to see and do. I wish it was my day off.'

They thanked him and left.

＊

When Jenny got back to the ship she left John, saying she'd see him later. She wanted to talk to her sister, but she needed to get over the shock of having Heather thrust upon her in the town. Could Will be back on board? Heather hadn't mentioned him and she hadn't wanted to ask. If he was back, she'd leave the ship as soon as possible, that night, if necessary.

She pressed speed dial and got through immediately.

'Well, you've obviously heard! How do you feel about it?' Leslie said, by way of greeting.

'Heard what?'

'About the injunction. You did know …? Oh, Jen, I'm sorry. I thought that was why you were ringing.'

'Slow down. What injunction?'

'Fergus's company. There's been an injunction served and everything is frozen. It's in all the papers and on the radio. There's a warrant out for his arrest, but he seems to have gone into hiding.'

'I'm glad I'm away from all that. I'm honestly beyond caring what happens to him.'

'Do you really mean that? I'd feel so much happier if you were. It would be less heartache for you.'

'I honestly do. Believe me, I have no feelings for him of any kind.'

'But, Jen, if his assets are frozen you'll get nothing from him.'

'I don't want anything from him. I told you and Richie that.'

'What if he goes to jail?'

'If the things they say about him are true, that's where he deserves to be.'

'But what about you? You're entitled—'

'I took the only thing I wanted – my freedom – and I'll never give that up again, so let's talk about anything else.'

'OK. Have you met someone? Tell me everything!' Leslie gushed.

'Possibly, but be patient! A lot's been happening, most of it very good, but I have some news for you. I think we have a half-sister.'

'What?'

'And she's called Elena.'

'How the hell did you find that out?'

She filled Leslie in on the coincidence of the exhibition being on while she was in Rhodes, on the portraits that had been in their home, and that their father had been on the island earlier in the week.

'She looks exactly like I did when I was a child, the same unruly blonde hair.'

'I can't take it in. I mean, what are the chances of finding out this way?'

'As soon as I finish talking to you I'm going to forward the photos I took on my phone. They're a little dark, but you'll see the resemblance for yourself.'

'Send them straight away and I'll call you back after I've looked at them.'

Jenny did so, and when Leslie rang back, her verdict was the same. 'There's absolutely no doubt about it – she could be your twin. By the way, I sent them to Richie at the office and he agrees. Now what are we going to do? Will we try to contact Dad and tell him we know, or will we wait until he tells us, if he ever does?'

'I don't know. I've parked that until I get home – let's decide then.'

'What about this "someone"? Tell me all.'

'There's nothing to tell yet. It's too soon, but it's promising.'

'I'm delighted for you. By the way, Richie wants to know if you'd like us to keep the newspapers for you about Fergus and all that.'

'No.' She decided against telling Leslie about the Will episode. She'd parked that too, although her priority now was to find out if he was back on the ship. The only way to do that was to talk to Marina or Jack at Guest Relations.

At the desk she found Marina, who assured her that Will had left and could not return. In fact, she added, he would be blacklisted in future from all the ships in their fleet.

'But I met his wife earlier.'

'She chose not to leave with him. I shouldn't tell you this, but I don't think she'll be going back to him. It appears his assault on you wasn't an isolated incident.'

'The poor woman – but does she know it was me? She never said anything.'

'He didn't tell her, and we wouldn't divulge that information, even if she asked, unless you wanted us to.'

'It gave me quite a shock seeing her in the town, and I kept waiting for him to appear. It was horrible. I never felt like that before. It was quite threatening, really.'

'Well, you can relax. He should be back in England by now. I know it's easy for me to say, but do try to forget it and enjoy the rest of your holiday with us.'

'Thanks. I promise I will.'

Betty had taken another tablet. The pain had got worse, but they had warned her that it would. She had stayed in bed all morning and tried to read, but her head was fuzzy. She'd overdone it last night, with all that dancing, but she'd had a great time. This was the first day she'd taken the stronger medicines she'd been prescribed, and she fell in and out of a light sleep. When she'd mentioned taking the cruise, three of her daughters had encouraged her. The eldest had been violently opposed to it.

'What happens if you get ill on the ship? Who'll look after you?' she'd asked.

'I'm not going to the moon. I'm well insured, and if I die I'll ask them to drop me overboard, no fuss, no mess and no funeral for you to worry about.'

When Betty had said this to her second daughter, later on, she had said, 'Mum, don't talk like that. She just means it would be terrible to be ill when you're away on your own.'

'It's no different from being ill on my own in my house, with one of my daughters living less than five minutes away by car, but who finds that journey too difficult to make. I see more of Denise and she lives in France.'

'She's very busy, Mum. Her lifestyle is crazy.'

'So crazy that when she does ring it's to tell me that, and when she comes round, I can't see her behind the flowers she brings. Then she sits with her phone and that tablet thing on the table between us in case someone important is looking for her. That's not a visit. It's a duty call. I don't make many demands on you girls, you know that, but is one visit a week too much to expect in the circumstances?'

'I'll talk to her.'

'No, don't, because that will only make her feel bad later on. She's so taken up in her world of high finance I doubt she'd even know what you were talking about. I'm sorry. I shouldn't be putting all this on you. Pay no attention to me

– I'm just being grumpy, but sometimes it annoys me. You've always been there for me, sweetheart.'

'And I will be, Mum, you know that. We all will. And for what it's worth, I think you're entitled to be a little grumpy now and then.'

'Am I mad to be going away?'

'Not if you feel up to it. You love travelling and the blue skies and sunshine will do you good. I'd come with you if I could.'

'I know that, but you do more than enough for me already.'

She lay for a while remembering this conversation. Her girls were so different, and always had been. The eldest took after her father, and didn't like cuddles or intimacy. The others were like her own family – tactile, caring and loyal.

Eventually she felt a little better and decided to get up. When she left her stateroom, there were very few people about, most having gone ashore. She made for the buffet and chatted with one of the staff. They all seemed to know her now and she always had a smile for them, asking where they came from. To their delight, she was usually able to tell them she'd been there at some stage. A few officers sat at a table, enjoying a little respite from their duties.

'It's wonderful to be so spoiled,' she said, to the man in front of her at the buffet, as she selected some salmon and an assortment of salads. 'Wouldn't it be great to have this at home, endless choice every day, without having to cook?'

When he replied, 'I wouldn't want so much foreign stuff,' she recognised him as the awful man whose table she had left a few nights before. 'Is there any ketchup?' he asked the attendant. Then he stretched back in front of her to get something he'd forgotten, and sent her glass of water flying. She tried to step out of the way but her food slipped off the tray, followed by the cutlery. As she made an attempt to rescue something, anything, she lost her footing and slipped on the wet floor. She knew immediately she had broken something.

Within seconds she was surrounded.

'Don't move her,' she heard someone say.

'That wasn't my fault. I didn't do anything,' Mr Mercer said. 'The floor's wet and she slipped.'

'No one's blaming anyone. Stand back, please. Get the medics up here,' another voice said, above Betty's head.

The four officers had come from their table to help. One was mopping the water around her with a pile of linen napkins, another hunkered behind her, propping her up, and towels appeared miraculously to keep her warm.

'My goodness! If I'd known that was all I had to do to attract a bevy of good-looking sailors I'd have done it on the first day,' she said. They laughed.

The medics arrived with a stretcher and splinted her leg. 'I'm afraid we're going to have to X-ray that. There may be a fracture.'

'I think so too,' she agreed. 'I felt something snap.' She asked them to let Jenny and Sylvia know what had happened to her, in case she didn't make it back in time for the sailing.

Minutes later she was on her way to Rhodes General

Hospital, one of the ship's doctors in attendance. He sat beside her in the ambulance and said, 'You're very brave – that must hurt like hell.'

'It probably does, but can I tell you something in complete confidence?' He nodded. 'I'd just taken some morphine.'

'We may have to mention that in the hospital,' he said.

'I don't mean them, I mean anyone on the ship. I don't want them to know.'

Ben was running around like a demented chicken. He had been in town earlier and had had his lunch at the precise time his diabetic regime dictated. After that, he'd walked about until the heat had driven him back. He was usually afraid he'd get lost in unfamiliar places, but had no such fear here because the ship could be seen from everywhere. No matter where you were, there it was, framed between buttresses, crenulations and arches. As he had come back along the pier an ambulance had pulled out from the gangway, frightening the life out of him by putting its klaxon on as it drew level with him.

He didn't know what plans Betty had made for the morning, but she had promised to be his bridge partner that afternoon and she hadn't shown up. He'd phoned her stateroom and left a message, but nothing. Maybe they had changed the venue: they did things like that sometimes, moving the location of the quizzes. Sometimes he'd missed the first round by the time he'd discovered where he was supposed to be, so his score sheet wasn't eligible for inclusion in the final count. He'd missed his bridge game now because he'd waited for Betty, and everyone was already partnered. Esther would never have done anything like that, but then Betty was more … flighty, that was it. She was more flighty than Esther, but he found he now missed her when she wasn't around.

Doug took a taxi to Faliraki Beach to snatch a few hours on his own. He liked to get away from the crew too, and felt they were more comfortable without bumping into him on their down-time. He was in mufti and had taken his swimming gear with him in a gym bag. He walked the five-kilometre stretch of the sandy beach, and back again. He asked an older couple to keep an eye on his things while he had a swim, and came out of the water refreshed. He spoke to his mother, who told him that everything at home was under control. There was no need to check: he'd hear from them soon enough if anything went wrong. Then he rang his sister.

'I can hear Lewis in the background. He sounds happy. I'm missing the little fellow like mad. I'm sitting here on a beach full of families and keep imagining him running in and out of the water, swimming, maybe even going fishing with me.'

'Give him a chance, Doug, he's only ten and a half months old.'

'Yes, but for the little I see of him I'll be paying his college fees before I know it.'

'You'll be back in a few weeks. He might even start walking then. Maybe you and Andrea should go away somewhere for a few days. It would do you a lot of good, I'm sure.'

'In an ideal world, but not if she's still drinking. Besides, I want to spend that time with Lewis too.'

'Maybe she just needs to be made to feel a bit special.'

'I thought it was fathers who were supposed to get jealous of mothers spending so much time with their young, not the other way around.'

'Let me tell you, brother dearest, where families are concerned there's no such thing as normal.'

He called Andrea. She, too, sounded in great form. 'I'm going shopping today with Mandy. Remember? We used to work together.' He remembered Mandy only too vividly. 'She's come to stay for a few days so we're going to hit the shops. Don't worry, I won't go mad.'

Doug wished it had been anyone but Mandy. She and Andrea had been known as 'the Party Girls'. He knew he had to curb his negativity. She was entitled to enjoy time with her friends. He couldn't deny her that. In fact, it might help break the cycle of isolation she had been in since she'd made a mess of her career, and since the birth too. He had to admit, though, that it was a relief to hear her sounding so normal, happy almost. Knowing her penchant for footwear, he said, 'Treat yourself, you deserve it. I'll pick up the tab for a new pair of shoes to match whatever you get.'

'Doug, you spoil me.'

'If I stop, you can start worrying.'

A taxi dropped him back at the pier and he felt a sense of pride in the gleaming vessel docked alongside – his other baby. There was an ambulance parked halfway along, which brought him firmly back to reality. What now? It pulled away before he got to it. He reached into his pocket and took out his pager.

Forty

JOHN WAS SITTING IN THE LOUNGE, WHERE they all gathered before dining. He was earlier than usual and there were lots of empty places. 'Gin-and-tonic, please,' he said, when a waiter came up to him.

A group arrived and sat on the sofas near to him. The Irish accents caught his attention. 'I'd put money on it she's the wife. I saw them together several times at functions and I'd know her from the papers. I'd recognise her anywhere. She was up on the top deck with the walkers this morning.'

'Well, they won't be going cruising if he's sent to jail.'

'He ought to be. It's that respectable white-collar craftiness that got the country into the mess it's in. Knowing how to bend the rules, and paying the politicians to play along with them.'

'I heard she'd left him.'

'Not a chance. She'd never walk away from his money. That's probably a ruse – she'll be off somewhere hiding it in offshore banks or in overseas property. In fact, if that was her you saw on the ship, that's probably what she's doing.'

'Shut up, the lot of you. Here she is. Pretend you don't notice.'

John looked towards the entrance and saw Jenny approach. Had they been talking about her? Maybe it was just their accents that had made him think so. He stood up but something stopped him kissing her. She didn't seem to notice. 'Betty's been taken to hospital,' she said. 'She's fractured her fibula.'

'Oh, the poor woman. How did that happen?'

He noticed the group behind him had stopped talking, possibly hoping to glean information that might fuel their speculation, so he ushered her towards a larger table at the other end of the room when he saw Marcus and Sylvia arrive. Sylvia told them the sketchy details. Guest Relations had given her a message from Betty, saying she had been taken to Rhodes General Hospital after she'd slipped. That was all they knew.

'I met Ben earlier and he was frantic because he couldn't find her all afternoon. She hadn't turned up for an assignation,' Jenny told them. 'When he heard where she was, he wanted to go and see her. It took a bit of persuading that she mightn't appreciate seeing anyone just yet. I told him she might even be in theatre. He only relaxed when he knew that one of the medics from the ship had stayed with her.'

'Where is he now?'

'He's waiting downstairs by the gangway for her to come.'

'Poor old fellow. What a terrible thing to happen to Betty, and she was having such a good time too. She's a great character,' said Marcus.

'Anyway,' said Sylvia, 'the latest news is good. I've just been told that she's had the bone set and is on her way back to the ship.'

'At least she doesn't have to stay in Rhodes on her own,' John said. 'Will she be able to walk?'

'Probably on crutches, but we can take it in turns to look after her. They have wheelchairs on board. I've seen them somewhere,' said Jenny.

When Sonny and Bud joined them and heard what had happened, Sonny said, 'We'll have to turn our chaperoning duties to Betty as Jenny doesn't need us any more.' He tilted an eyebrow towards her and John, who just grinned back.

Hamish was the last to appear, with Heather in tow. 'Do you mind if my new friend joins us for dinner? Her husband had to go home suddenly – business commitments – so she's been left high and dry.'

John studied Jenny's reaction. Her facial expressions went through a whole spectrum before she gave what appeared to him to be a very forced smile. There was definitely something going on that he didn't know about. Bud and Sonny talked together quietly, shooting Heather and Jenny meaningful looks. Had Heather something to do with the conversation he had overheard outside? Were she and her absentee husband anything to do with Jenny and moving money about? Jenny had told him nothing about her life in Dublin. It was time to step aside a bit and see what he could learn.

There was great excitement when Betty arrived back, groggy but apparently quite happy and pain-free. She had an enormous cast on her leg and ankle, with painted toes peeping out at the end. The crew had settled her into a wheelchair and brought her to their table, with a relieved Ben at her side. They shuffled their chairs around to make space for them and she announced, 'No cocktails for me tonight, I'm afraid, alcoholic ones anyway. I'm drugged up to my eyeballs on whatever they gave me.'

'Shouldn't you rest?' Ben asked.

'By the look of things, that's all I'll be able to do for the remainder of the trip and the next several weeks, so I may as well enjoy this while I can.'

Dance-host Chad, the maître d', the computer woman, some of the waiters and several others stopped to talk to Betty and give her a hug. Captain Doug came over and asked if he could join them for a bit. They shuffled up some more to fit him in.

'He's probably terrified you'll sue,' Bud muttered, not bothering to keep his voice down.

'Don't be so crass,' said Sonny, in disgust.

'I love Americans,' the captain said, taking it on the chin. 'They're always so direct. We British hide everything in innuendo.'

'In Denmark we accept that cobblestones are often uneven and that sometimes we're at fault if we fall,' said Marcus.

'Oh, I'd never sue,' said Betty. 'It was an accident. I slipped. It was no one's fault. These things happen, and I'm getting so much attention it was almost worth it.'

'You're very kind,' the captain said. 'I hope you've been properly looked after. Do you need us to contact anyone for you?'

'There's no need to worry anyone at home. It's only a broken bone. They'll find out soon enough. I must say, though, I'm very honoured that the captain has come to see me.'

He bowed graciously. 'Well, maybe you'll return the compliment and do me the honour of gracing my table for dinner.'

'The honour would be all mine.' She bowed back. 'Thank you, kind sir.'

Before he left, he added, 'And all of your friends, of course.'

Sonny said, 'Betty, you're such a flirt! You had that poor man eating out of your hand.'

'Can I get some lessons from you?' Sylvia asked.

Betty chuckled. 'I don't think you need any.'

'Like Bud said, he's probably still terrified you'll sue,' Ben said.

'I won't,' reiterated Betty.

'Do you think he meant it, the invitation, or was he just being diplomatic?' asked Marcus.

'He meant it, all right. He wouldn't have mentioned it otherwise,' said John. 'You can look out for the gilt-edged invites.'

'I can't go. I'm not one of this group,' Heather said.

'Well, you don't have to. It's not a royal command,' said Jenny sharply. Sonny and Bud nodded. If Heather noticed she didn't show it, but John did.

'You've all been together since the first lunch, haven't you?' Heather continued. 'I'm fascinated – what's the common thread between you all?'

'It's simple,' said Betty. 'We like each other.'

'That's all very well, but it's time to get you to bed,' Jenny said.

'OK. I *am* fading. Too much excitement for an old bird like me. Thank you all for your concern. You're great.'

John knocked the brake off the wheelchair and pulled it back from the table. They clustered around to say goodnights. Something glinting on the carpet caught his eye. It was a gold chain. 'Oh, that's mine,' said Betty. 'I can't have put it back on properly in the hospital. I'm so glad I didn't lose it. I've had it a long time.'

John escorted Betty to her stateroom, then Sylvia and Jenny helped her get ready for bed. Betty had refused to go to the hospital infirmary overnight. 'I know how to use my crutches if I have to get up. Besides, I can ring if I need help.'

The minute she was tucked up in bed she fell asleep. The two women decided that one of them would stay with her and bunk down on the pull-out bed.

'You go back to John,' said Sylvia.

'No, I'll stay. Too much has happened today and I need a bit of time on my own.'

'Are you OK? Is he rushing you?'

'No, that's not it. He's a perfect gentleman. It's far too long to go into now.'

'I have all night.'

'Marcus will be waiting for you. I'll see you tomorrow.'

'He probably hasn't even noticed I'm not there. They were all going to see that conjuror, the one who used to be on telly all the time a few years ago. He's very good.'

'I doubt Marcus would put a conjuror before you. Go on, get out of here.'

'I really like him, you know.'

'I noticed.' They laughed quietly.

'You have my number if you or Betty need me during the night. Promise you'll call.'

'I will.'

Jenny pulled a light blanket over her legs and lay down. Her mind raced. When she'd told one of her colleagues at the publishing house that she was going on a cruise, he'd said, 'It'll be great to get away and switch off from everything for a bit.'

If only he knew the half of it, Jenny thought. An injunction against her husband, with the distinct possibility of an immediate arrest, the discovery of the lost family portraits and a new half-sister, a sexual assault against her, and sharing a dinner table with her assailant's wife. And there was John.

Switch off, indeed!

Forty-one

BETTY DIDN'T WAKE UNTIL AFTER FIVE A.M. and was delighted to find that Jenny had stayed. They had some tea and croissants delivered and chatted for ages, opening up to each other. Jenny told her what had happened with Will. She was horrified and said she had sensed something was not right.

'I was terrified when Heather turned up so unexpectedly when I was in Rhodes Town. I'm sure I was rude to her, but I didn't know if she knew it was me he'd attacked and if I was the one who'd complained. I didn't know where he was either, if he was going to appear any minute too. I suppose I should apologise.'

'I wouldn't, dear. If she doesn't know it's you, finding out would only add to her pain and embarrassment. She must feel terrible. Can you imagine her shame?'

Jenny told her about her father and how she'd come across his exhibition, and about the significance of his paintings of her and Elena. Betty told her about her daughters, especially the one she had never got on with, no matter how hard she tried. 'You shouldn't have to make such an effort with your child. It's not natural.' They agreed on that.

Then Jenny told her about the miscarriage and what had happened afterwards. It was then that Betty told her about the pain and the prognosis.

After Jenny had helped Betty to get dressed, and left her to rest for a while longer, she went up on deck to enjoy the panorama. They had left Rhodes overnight and were arriving at Marmaris in Turkey. The port was beautiful. The marina was endless, with yachts and boats rivalling those at Monte Carlo in grandeur and opulence. The white sprawl of the town faded into a verdant backdrop of mountains that enveloped the whole area in a horseshoe. The nearby islands looked as though they were floating on the water. It was magnificent.

She didn't know what she had expected, but this was not the image she had had of Turkey from before. She had only been to Istanbul, and it was hot, dusty and too busy. It had also been Ramadan so the cafés and restaurants were completely empty until sundown. She had been one of the interpreters who formed part of an international mission that was looking into conditions in the sweatshops. They had visited textile and footwear factories, where the fumes cut your eyes, and you could hardly breathe for the smell of glue. The noise, the stench and the heat were unbearable.

Here, at Marmaris, she was witnessing the other side of Turkish life. This picturesque pleasure park for the rich and famous had come a long way since the days of Suleyman the Magnificent. She couldn't wait to explore a former bastion of the Ottoman Empire. She dashed back to shower and change, realising she was still in the clothes she'd worn the previous evening.

Hamish and John were enjoying the view, too, while they had breakfast outside.

'Did you notice any tension last night, or in town yesterday, when Heather joined us?' John asked.

'Aye, I did. Jenny definitely wasn't her usual breezy self. Heather's not the easiest person. She's very edgy, but I felt a bit sorry for her, her husband just upping and leaving her on her own. If he's such a big shot, surely he'd have a wee underling who could fix whatever needed fixing for him.'

'I agree. Holiday time is sacrosanct in my book.'

'If you don't mind my saying so, John, from where I'm looking your whole life seems to be a holiday. I know you were in the drinks business, but I thought you said you'd left it. What is it you do?'

John laughed. 'Not a lot!' He had wondered when Hamish would ask outright again. He'd hinted and skirted around it so many times. 'Well, it's like this. I was in the drinks business, which is rather ironic considering what's happened—'

'There you are. I was hoping to find you up here.'

Jenny's arrival interrupted their conversation. 'Ben and I were going to take Betty ashore and stroll along the marina into the old town. I know she wants to do a bit of shopping. We've been told it's flatter here than it is in Mykonos, where we'll be tomorrow. They don't recommend we bring the wheelchair there at all.'

'Aren't you the organised one!' Hamish said.

'Feel free to join us, if you'd like, or if you'd prefer, you guys could go off and do your own thing, and we could meet somewhere for lunch. What do you think?'

'If it weren't for Betty's accident, I'd think you were avoiding me,' John said.

She put her hand on his. 'I'm not, I promise.'

An hour later the five of them were setting off along the waterfront. A group of off-duty crew were getting ready to go cycling.

'Where are you headed?' John asked one of girls from the casino.

'Over there. Since I joined this ship they keep telling me about the mountains and now they're taking me to see them.'

'Did you hire the bikes?'

'No, they belong to the ship.'

'I'd love to be able to join you,' Betty said, 'but I fear my cycling days are over.'

'It's great freedom to get out on the open road when

you've been cooped up for a while,' said one of the waiters. They waved at another group of their colleagues, disgorging themselves from the bow. 'Look at them! They're off like swarming locusts to the Internet cafés.'

'It's a whole different world,' Betty mused. 'It's so easy to be left behind, isn't it, Ben?'

He nodded. 'It's all happened so quickly. I used to be considered well informed, but now I'm a has-been.'

'Will you listen to the pair of them? They've probably forgotten more than I'll ever know,' Jenny said.

Ben muttered that he hadn't a clue what his grandchildren were talking about, with their 'twittering, tweeters and texting'.

'It's really not that complicated,' John said. 'I'll give you a lesson and you can impress them when you get home.'

'That'll surprise them all right. It's all gone by too quickly. Only two more nights. I can't believe it,' he replied.

They meandered along, admiring the yachts, some of the larger ones with uniformed crew, others with workers busily polishing, repainting and varnishing. Further along, some fishing boats were having their engines overhauled. In another smaller dock, the skeletal ribs of a new vessel were being crafted with precision, while from above seagulls wheeled and dived, keeping their beady eyes on all that was happening below.

The women went off shopping, with Ben in tow. John waited for Hamish to tackle him again about what he did. He didn't have to wait long. Within minutes Hamish suggested they stop for a coffee.

'You were saying about being in the drinks industry ...'

'I retired from that some months back, and now I'm seeing the world on my terms, and not at the behest of those who were paying me.'

'But you seem far too young to be retired.'

'That's what everyone tells me,' he said, playing Hamish along. He paused and stirred his cappuccino. 'But it won't be for much longer.' He kept stirring. He wondered how Hamish would bring the conversation back.

'Aye. I'm at a bit of a crossroads myself at the moment. I don't know which direction to jump. But I suppose we're lucky to have options in today's climate. I've a takeover bid on the table for my company, and if I accept, I'll be like you. I always said I'd like to retire by the time I'm fifty-five and if I accept the offer I'll be redundant by then. And you're much younger than I am.'

'Forty-two,' John volunteered.

'Aye, I thought you were about that. I don't know if I like the idea of having nothing to do. Did you find that hard?'

Something had caught John's attention. The dance host and the mousy computer woman were coming along the promenade, but they parted at that instant, and she walked back the way they had come, as though, having spotted John and Hamish, they didn't want to be seen together.

'Sorry, Hamish, I got distracted there. You were saying?'

'I was asking if you found being retired difficult to deal with. I'm not a golfer, and think there's something senile about all those grumpy old fellows and bridge ladies sitting around fusty clubhouses replaying their best shots or hands. I mean, who cares?'

John laughed. 'There are other options, you know.' Before he could expand, Jenny, Ben and Betty appeared with enough bags and parcels to suggest that they had been good for the Turkish economy.

A little later, they met Sonny and Bud for lunch. 'We have a surprise for you, Jenny, but you won't get it until you're back home – we had it shipped in case it got broken in your luggage.'

'You shouldn't.'

'We should. We love your company and we wanted to get you something to remember us by.'

'I don't think I could ever forget you two. You've been so good to me.' They had also been spending money on designer clothes, and they warned the others to stay away from the jewellery vendors.

'Sonny can spot a knock-off a mile away, especially the fake Rolexes.'

'I never found my pocket watch,' he said sadly, then explained to Betty and Ben that he'd lost it on the night of the gala dinner.

'That's weird,' said Jenny. 'Betty almost lost her chain last night and Sylvia is convinced that she's lost one too.'

'They took all my jewellery off in the hospital and gave it to the medic who was with me while they were setting my leg. I obviously didn't fasten the clasp properly. I was so happy John saw it. Now, I'm keeping all of you from exploring this place. Once we've had lunch, pop me in a taxi. I'll go back for a rest and you go your own way. And lunch is my treat.'

Everyone objected, but by the time they had finished, almost two hours later, John had taken care of the bill and paid for Betty's taxi. Hamish tried to chip in, but John was having none of it.

Before she left she said, 'That's it. I won't talk to any of you unless you allow me to book one of the speciality restaurants for tonight – I'll let you know which one later. Indulge me, please. I want to do it. I've so enjoyed all your company so let's enjoy our penultimate night together. I'll see you there at eight, and that includes you, Ben. Forget your diabetes for one night, or have your snack whenever you must, but I'll expect you there! Please tell Sylvia and Marcus too, if you see them.'

'Can we make it seven thirty? If no one objects, that is. We're always last to leave the table and we never make it to any of the shows, not that I'm complaining, but we'd like to go to tonight's. It's big-band music and we love that,' Bud said.

'That's no problem. I love it too,' said Betty.

When the others set off, John and Sonny were deep in conversation.

'Go on, we'll catch you up,' he called, and the two walked off in the opposite direction.

They sailed away at seven, enjoying the views as they left, leaving the sloping hills of southern Turkey behind. The restaurant that Betty had booked specialised in Mediterranean cuisine – Sylvia and Marcus had asked to be excused. The soup came in bowls made from herbed bread and that set the standard. It was another meal of revelations, stories and laughter.

Their main courses were served under shining silver domes. When they all had one a team of waiters lifted them in a synchronised movement to reveal plates of decorative beauty.

'Did I tell you about my first mud-wrap experience?' Betty asked. 'It was in Hungary, not long after the fall of Communism, and it was all quite utilitarian and brusque. The women working there would have beaten Charles Atlas with their muscles. You had to strip off and they put you on a wet sludge-coloured sheet. They scooped handfuls of thick, gloopy green stuff onto my legs, stomach, shoulders and arms. Then they wrapped me up and left me there, without saying a word. I thought my woman was just being sensitive by not spreading the mud all over me so I did it for her, under my sheet. When my time came I had to stand in a corner while a young fellow of about seventeen came in with a power hose to rinse me off. Well, you should have seen his face when I dropped the sheet. I only found out afterwards that you're not supposed to put the mud near your reproductive organs or your breasts. And there I was, covered from neck to toe, and it was his job to make sure it was all washed away. I'm sure he's still in therapy.'

'Aren't they supposed to be bad for your blood pressure, those mud baths?' Ben said.

'Oh, Ben! There's no hope for you,' said Hamish. Their

laughter attracted attention from a table in the corner, whose occupants were staring at Jenny.

'It *is* her. I know it is,' one of the guests insisted. 'Look at her, wining and dining in style. You'd never think her husband's going to be in prison soon.'

'Oh, give it a rest, will you? If Fergus Ruddy was clever enough to get up to the stuff he's accused of, he probably never told her a thing. I know I wouldn't have told anyone, even you, my darling wife. Now let's forget them. We took this holiday to get away from the doom and gloom at home, not to bring it with us.' The others agreed with him and the conversation moved on.)

John asked Jenny, 'Am I going to get you on your own later on?'

'Definitely,' she replied.

As they left the restaurant, Betty whispered, 'Have you seen the eyebrows woman today?'

'No, thank goodness. She must have found some other new friends, although she probably spent most of her day in the gym.'

'She was at bridge this afternoon, when I hobbled by, but she didn't see me.'

'I know I'm being horrible, but she just reminds me of – of it all and of him, even though I know it's not her fault.'

'I shouldn't have mentioned it. Have you told your young man?'

'No, and he's not my young man yet.' She grinned mischievously.

'He would be if you'd let him.'

'I know.'

✳

They couldn't all get seats together in the theatre, which suited John and Jenny perfectly. They stayed near the back and left early. The *Sing It and Swing It* show had the audience clapping to the rhythms of some well-loved old tunes, classics all.

'You can't beat a dash of nostalgia to get the happy memories going, can you, Betty?' Hamish asked as he and Ben saw her to her cabin.

'I'd thought my memory bank was just about full, but the people I've met this week have added lots more to enjoy when I get back home.'

'That's a nice way of looking at things,' Ben said.

'Aye, it's important to keep adding new ones.'

John and Jenny went out on deck for a while, then to his suite.

'You promised you'd tell me all about yourself,' he said, 'but you haven't. There's so much I want to know about you. Is tonight the right time for confessions?'

'John, I'm so mixed up at the moment I wouldn't know where to begin. Why don't you tell me about your life?'

'I will, but first can I give you a starting point, perhaps?'

Surprised, she turned to look at him. 'You know about Will?'

'Is Will the man you were married to?'

'No. He attacked me the other day.'

'I haven't a clue what you're talking about. When were you attacked? Where? On the ship? Is that why you disappeared? And who are those Irish people who keep watching you and whispering about your husband?'

'What Irish people? Where?'

'This could be a long night.'

It was.

Forty-two

JENNY FELL IN LOVE WITH MYKONOS WITH ITS clusters of traditional windmills and flat-roofed white houses uniformly decorated with blue shutters and doors. Those in Little Venice had balconies overhanging the water, and looked as though they might topple in at any minute. She and John walked into the town, where the streets were so narrow that island transport had had to adapt. Deliveries were made in noisy little vehicles no wider than a motorbike with a sidecar. Even then, pedestrians had to jump onto the steps leading to the houses and shops to avoid being squashed.

'I can see now why they warned us we wouldn't be able to take the wheelchair here.'

The alleyways were paved with huge, irregular-shaped slabs, and the walls were festooned with vibrant bougainvillea, while the jewellery shops seemed to specialise in black diamonds.

'This is like walking through a painting. Everything's bright and sunny and you want to see what's around the next corner. It makes you realise how dull we are.'

'There's nothing dull about you.'

'Flatterer. But you know what I mean. The colours and contrasts beat Killiney Beach on a wet day.'

'They probably come to our part of the world and love our contrasts and countryside, our seasons and clouds.'

'We're never satisfied, are we?'

'Sometimes we are.' He smiled pulling her to him and kissing her forehead. 'I'm glad you told me everything last night. I feel so much closer to you now and I hope you feel the same way about me.'

'I do and very relieved too. I wanted to tell you, but I was afraid you'd run a mile. I hated the idea of being thought of as needy or as a victim.'

'Nothing could be further from the truth. You've had a bad run and hopefully you − we − can put that behind us now,' he said squeezing her hand, 'if I'm not being too presumptuous.'

She squeezed his hand back and smiled at him. 'You're not!'

They sat in a square drinking beer while some of the local feline population came by to see what was on offer. As they weren't eating, the cats soon moved on to pester the people at other tables.

'Now, when we go back I need to leave you to your own devices for a bit. I have to do something.'

'That sounds serious.'

'It is, but it's nothing for you to worry about.'

Back on the ship, Jenny was sitting by the pool when she saw John talking earnestly to Officer Shannon. Not for the first time, she wondered if he had something to do with the cruise company.

✳

That evening when the solos, Bud and Sonny went back to their staterooms they all found gold-embossed invitations from the captain waiting for them. He had invited them to a private dinner in the Drawing Room the following night.

To Bud and Sonny's delight, a local troupe came to the pool deck that evening to entertain and teach everyone to dance like native Greeks. The moon was full and the loungers had been stowed away. The solos found tables and dragged extra chairs over so that they could be together. They hadn't seen much of Sylvia and Marcus that day, but they joined them, looking very pleased with themselves. There was no sign of Heather. Betty was comfortably seated, her crutches stowed out of the way of the dancers.

Jenny had noticed John rubbing his wrist and flexing his

hand several times during dinner and again now. 'Have you hurt yourself?'

'Just an old sprain that flares up every now and again.'

They chatted a little about the private dinner the next night. They had to get most of their packing done beforehand, as their cases had to be outside their doors for delivery to the pier early the following morning.

'We've canny wee Betty to thank for the invite.'

'No, you haven't. We have that ignorant boor who caused me to fall.'

'I thought you said it was an accident?' said Ben

'I wasn't going to tell the captain about that ignorant galoot, who spilled my water on the floor.'

'What's a galoot? I've never heard that before,' Jenny wondered.

'Haven't you? In my book it's a clumsy, awkward, lumpen troglodyte!'

'You don't like him very much, do you?'

'And neither would you!'

John said, 'I'd better not get on your wrong side.'

'There's no chance of that, dear. If I were forty years younger you'd be my ideal man.'

'Madam, please, spare my blushes. Jenny, help me.'

'Back off, Betty. I saw him first.'

'OK. Now, will you stop looking after me, the lot of you, and get up and dance. I need a laugh,' said Betty.

'I'll stay with you.'

'Hamish, I forbid it. Get up there and show me your moves. You don't need a partner for this.'

He obeyed, and the dancers began to teach some traditional steps. Large circles formed as they swayed and moved back and forth to the hypnotic rhythm. Chad came over to sit with Betty. Kathy, the computer woman, stopped to enquire about her leg, but before she'd finished hugging Betty, Hamish saw her, came over and grabbed her hand, whisking her into the nearest group. The music quickened, the noise level rose and dancers fell about, laughing at their desperate efforts to keep up with the professionals.

On the top deck a few passengers and officers watched the shenanigans, grinning widely. But Captain Doug and Jack weren't smiling. They had something much more important to do than watch others enjoy themselves.

John looked up and the captain nodded at him. He whispered to Jenny, 'I may be a while. If it's not too late I'll call you. Otherwise I'll see you in the morning.' Before she could say anything he was gone, leaving her more mystified than ever.

'Trouble in Paradise?' asked Hamish, seeing her baffled look.

'Not at all.'

'If the young buck's deserted you, perhaps we can have a wee twirl before he gets back.'

'I'd like that.'

An hour later, there was still no sign of John and she eventually went back to her stateroom alone. She went straight out onto her balcony and stood there for a long time, looking up at the sky. When she saw a star shoot across it, she didn't bother to wish.

Frustrated, she went to bed. They had only one more day and night and it seemed they were being thwarted in their efforts to get closer to each other.

Forty-three

IT WAS THREE THIRTY IN THE MORNING. John and Doug Burgess were sitting at a circular table. There were numerous items of jewellery spread before them, including an inscribed gold pocket watch and a chunky fob chain. Jack, from Guest Relations, was checking them against the lost-and-found register.

'Everything seems to be here, except one diamond stud earring, but that probably just fell out somewhere. I doubt even that pair would target someone's ears.'

'I wouldn't put it past them,' Captain Doug said. 'They're professionals and brazen.'

'You know when you said the dance host was a magician? I

have to admit I wondered if you were involved, and you were just putting up a smoke screen,' Shaun Shannon said.

'Thanks! I knew I'd seen him before, but I couldn't place him until Ben, the old guy at our table, made a comment about his waxy moustache and oiled hair. I immediately had a vision of a ringmaster in a circus and then it clicked. He used to call himself the Ringmaster because he could remove rings, bracelets, watches and necklaces from his stooges without them knowing. At the end of his show he'd give them all back.'

'I don't think that was Chad Tayloe-Stuart's intention this time,' Jack said.

'I agree. They used to keep repeating the programmes on some satellite channel and I watched them when I had jet lag. I never could sleep when I was supposed to, and there weren't too many channels in Dubai and Malaysia that I could understand, apart from round-the-clock news bulletins, and they're even worse than sleeplessness.'

'We're going to have some very happy passengers in the morning, John, thanks to your insomnia,' the captain said. 'Put that lot in the safe, Jack, and let's get to bed.'

It had taken a while, but Chad had eventually confessed to being the thief on board. He had also told them his real name was Mitch Stuart. Only then did they search his cabin, his luggage and his safety-deposit box. They found nothing, only a modest amount of cash and his credit cards. It was Jack who suggested that he was working with an accomplice, but Chad had strenuously denied it, yet he wouldn't tell them where the stolen goods were hidden, or if he had already got rid of them.

'Let's watch that CCTV footage again,' Captain Doug had said, 'the bit where he takes the watch John planted.'

They watched the solos go to join all the others who were trying to learn the steps of Zorba's Dance. John had stood aside to let the others out and, flexing his hand several times, had taken off his watch and put it on the table. Moments later, Chad had appeared and sat down beside Betty.

'Look! He deliberately kicked the crutches out of the way, and when he bent to move them, he pocketed the watch. Rewind that, please,' Officer Shannon said.

They watched it again and again, stopping and starting it, and, sure enough, he could be seen taking it off the table. Satisfied they let the video run. It was then that Kathy came into the frame, bending to give Betty a hug. As she did so, Chad slipped something into her bag. It was over in a second.

'I thought it was odd,' John said, 'the way she always hugged people, because she's the coldest person I've ever known. Her face is like a mask. She did it to Betty the other night when she came back from the hospital and – do you know something? – she was trying to take her necklace. I swear that's what she was up to. It was on the floor when I moved her wheelchair.'

Kathy was brought in for questioning, without Chad present. She kept her mask-like expression while denying everything. 'Anyone could slip something into my bag. I'm not responsible for that.'

'Well, then, you won't mind us doing a search of your stateroom,' Officer Shannon said.

'You need a warrant for that.'

'We don't if I authorise it. I'm in control here,' Captain Doug bluffed. 'But you can be present.' They led her to her quarters. They found the stolen items in her safe and in a beach bag in her wardrobe.

She and Chad were later taken down to staff quarters and put under ship arrest.

Forty-four

SONNY AND BUD WERE SAD THAT THEIR
Mediterranean honeymoon was almost at an end. It had
surpassed expectations. When Sonny was summoned to Guest
Relations he couldn't believe it when he saw his pocket watch
glinting on the desk. Reaching for his wallet, he said, 'I'd like
to give a reward to whoever handed it in.'

Jack, who was feeling a little like Santa Claus, replied,
'That's unnecessary, sir. We like to think all our passengers
would have done the same if they'd found it.'

Sylvia was thrilled when she was told her fob chain had
turned up. 'I was beginning to think I was going mad,
imagining I'd been wearing it because it's like my talisman

and I never travel without it. You don't know how happy it makes me to have it back.'

One by one the other pieces were reunited with their owners, and Jack rang John to tell him he could collect his Rolex.

He laughed. 'Jack, I bought that Rolex in Marmaris for twenty euro as a lure. Sonny did the bargaining. I know he thought I was a bit cracked because I put my own in my pocket first. But he didn't ask and I didn't say anything. Then I did my damnedest to show it off by faking that wrist injury. I don't want it back.'

'I'll give it to one of the stewards the next time they bring me a midnight snack.'

'You do that,' he said, and he set off to find Jenny. Time was running out and there was still so much to say to her.

Her reception was less than warm when he came across her reading by the pool. Betty and Ben were beside her.

'I'm sorry about last night,' he said.

'No need to apologise. You're a free agent.'

'It's not like that. Let me explain. Let's go and have a coffee. Please.'

She said nothing, but she pulled a wrap over her bikini and followed him. When he had finished his explanation, she said, 'If I didn't know you, I'd think you'd made that up!'

'I couldn't tell you in case it was all a mistake, and Doug asked me to say nothing.'

'Oh, it's Doug now, is it?'

'You can talk. He sent you really good champagne!'

'I still have a bottle.'

'And he buys you pancakes for breakfast.'

'Who told you that?'

'I have my sources.' He laughed. 'So, are we friends again? There's something else you should know.'

'Oh, no!'

'Oh, yes. Remember I said my family revelations could wait? Well, I think I need to tell you. Let's find somewhere quieter. What about my balcony? We could have lunch there.'

She agreed.

When they were seated at lunch, John began. 'You remember I told you I was adopted? Well, recently I found my father's family.'

'Is that not a good thing?'

'Yes, it is, but it's given me a huge problem. I never went searching for my birth-parents because I was happy with my adoptive ones and my brother, Colin, their natural child. My mum, who died a few years ago, would never have minded if I'd wanted to know, and often told me so, but it was a huge bone of contention with my dad. His attitude was that I was theirs and that was all there was to it. When they took me, no one had ever thought that in the future I'd have the right to find out anything about my past. He thought this legislation was a real invasion of privacy and that everyone was better off letting things lie.'

'I can see how that could be awkward. So what did he say?'

'I haven't told him yet.'

'Why on earth not? When did you find out?'

'About three months ago.'

'Does your brother know?'

'Nope. I haven't told him either.'

'I don't understand.'

'It's not quite as straightforward as it sounds. My folks, my adopted folks, are humble people. I've just found out that my natural parents were anything but. My mother was a language student, staying with a French family, when she became pregnant by their son. She was Irish, from Cork, I think. He was their only child. She had gone over for six months, and came home with more than just good French. She was due to start at university, so she gave me up. I only recently discovered she died in a car accident when she was twenty-three.'

'That's so sad. What about your father? Did he know about you?'

'Apparently so, but not until after I had been adopted. His name doesn't appear on my birth certificate.'

'How did you find him?'

'I didn't. He found me, or at least a legal firm did. He died last year with no other descendants and he left me his estate, a hell of a lot of money, a bloody enormous vineyard in Burgundy, with a grand château, three estate houses and a mobile wine-bottling company.'

'What's that?'

'Exactly what it says – it goes about the wineries and provides a bottling service to suit their needs. That on its own is an extremely lucrative business.'

'But you studied wine, didn't you?'

'That's the irony. I did. Dad thought I was being fanciful, getting above myself, when I did my exams.'

'Maybe it's in your genes. Have you gone over there yet?'

'I did, and I was blown away by it all. And I felt so guilty. I know I have to tell Dad and that he's going to feel totally undermined.'

'He might be delighted for you.'

'I doubt it. It'll be like a slap in the face.'

'He might surprise you. Maybe he could get involved – give him a new focus in life.'

'I doubt that too. He's very set in his ways. You know, the funny thing was that my French father, Marcel Tingue, had obviously kept tabs on me as I was growing up.'

'It's not Château Tingue you're talking about?'

'One and the same.'

'But their wines are known the world over.'

'Isn't it sad to think we could have been friends? He knew all about me and my career. He left me a very moving letter, with some photographs of my mother too. He told me he'd never loved anyone else. We would have had so much to talk about, but he respected my family too much to interfere.'

'Do you wish he had?'

'Sometimes, yes, but at others, no. I had a really good life and home. I never wanted for anything.'

'You have to tell them. There's nothing to be achieved by keeping it from them any longer.'

'I've made up my mind to do it when I get back from the cruise.'

'Will you keep the vineyard and all the trappings?'

'That's why I took time out. I needed to think about it. And I'm still doing that, but I'd be mad not to.' He was quiet for a bit. 'It's very beautiful. I'd love to show it to you. Would you come over with me to see it?'

'I'd be honoured to. I love France. But tell me something, these wines of yours – do you like them? Are they good ones?'

'Oh, yes,' he grinned, 'they're very … pleasant. Very, very pleasant.'

Forty-five

THE DRAWING ROOM, WHERE JENNY HAD first bumped into Heather, had been transformed for the captain's private dinner party. The furniture had been replaced with a long table set for twenty, ten at each side. Silver gleamed and the glasses sparkled against the snowy tablecloth and napkins. There was a row of flower arrangements running along the centre, low enough to talk over, but not small enough to disappear. Several tall candelabra towered over the setting and cast gentle shadows.

Captain Doug came forward to greet them all in turn. He looked suave and dashing in his navy uniform. He knew most of their names now, and the places had been arranged beforehand.

There were a few other couples, whom no one knew. Sylvia was placed between Hamish and the chief engineer. Her cleavage was defying gravity this evening and had not gone unnoticed by any of the men around the table. As always, she flirted outrageously. Jack's Day-Glo teeth flashed every time he smiled, and he did this a lot to Sonny, who was beside him, wearing a black velvet waistcoat, a Kelly green shirt and his pocket watch. The ship's surgeon, a strikingly good-looking Norwegian called Andro, was on his other side.

A rather large woman, in baby pink, was sandwiched between Bud, in a black velvet waistcoat and cerise shirt, and Marcus, who was sombre in a grey suit. The staff officer sat between a serious-looking man, who turned out to be great fun, and Heather, who was wearing a beaded coffee-coloured dress. If anyone was uncomfortable with her being there, they didn't show it. Ben met a fellow Londoner, and they reminisced about the war and rationing throughout the meal. The food and beverage officer plied the woman on his right with too much wine, and everyone looked away discreetly when she had to be helped back to her stateroom before coffee had arrived.

Betty took her place beside the captain, who had adjusted his stride to keep in sync with her crutches. Jenny was on his other side, next to John.

When Captain Doug had helped Betty to sit down, he turned to Jenny and said, 'I'm sorry about a certain guest being here. My maître d' assumed I'd meant to invite all of you at the table the other evening, but of course I hadn't. I only realised when I saw her arrive. I hope it won't upset you too much.'

'Don't worry, I'll take care of her,' John said. 'We're delighted to be here.'

Captain Doug stood up. 'Relax, there'll be no speeches. I just want to tell you that you're most welcome. I don't do this on every cruise, but sometimes there are special people on board who deserve special treatment, and from what I hear you all fit into that category. Besides, I wanted a night off.

'I apologise for making you leave your packing to be here and I hope it will be worth it. You can talk about religion, money, sex and politics, but no one is to ask me who is driving the boat, and there are to be no Costa jokes. We have HEARD them all B-E-F-O-R-E! Now enjoy yourselves.' And they did.

Different wines accompanied the *amuse-bouches* and the gourmet dishes, each introduced by the executive chef and the chief sommelier. This was their moment to take centre stage as a double act and they did it with aplomb.

Conversations started and were interrupted. Jokes were told and punch lines forgotten. Glasses were raised and cards exchanged. There was something bittersweet about the last night of a cruise. Tomorrow the ship would arrive in Athens and they'd all part. But none of them would forget the trip for so many reasons.

'I don't think I'll ever forget tonight,' Betty said. 'It's been wonderful, Captain Doug. Thank you so much.'

'I can honestly assure you, Betty, that the pleasure has been all mine, and I mean that. How will you manage getting home?'

'Ben is on the same flight and he's promised to look after me, and that nice lady at Guest Relations has organised wheelchairs at the airports for me.'

'I hope we'll see you again.'

'I don't think you will, but it's been very special, very special indeed.'

As they queued to say good night, Heather singled Jenny out. 'It was you, wasn't it?'

'Yes.'

'How dreadful for you. I'm so sorry.'

'And I'm sorry for you, too. What will you do?'

'I'll start a new life, but not before I make him suffer a bit for humiliating me like that, never mind what he did to you.'

'Good luck.'

'You too, and I'm so sorry again. You didn't deserve it.'

'Neither did you.' The women hugged warmly.

'Well, Captain, it looks as though I'm going home still single,' said Hamish, tipsy from the generous quantity of wines and liqueurs. 'That was a marvellous night, and I'm off now to pack my floral shirts and cut-off shorts. On reflection, though, I've had a bloody marvellous time, even though I didn't pull. Maybe I'm getting too old for that sort of thing. I'll be fifty in three months' time.'

'Maybe you should go on another cruise to celebrate,' the captain suggested.

'What a marvellous idea. I might just do that.' He slapped Captain Doug on the back. 'Thanks again – you run a tight ship.'

Bud walked in front of Sonny. 'You were! You spent the whole meal chatting up that Norwegian surgeon. You were flirting with him all night and you know it.'

'Oh, shut up. You're just being melodramatic again, you divo,' Sonny replied.

'I thought it would be different once we were married.'

'It will be, if you keep this up.' They argued all the way back to their suite.

Sylvia waited for Marcus to finish thanking the captain, and was surprised when he left her at her door to go and do his packing.

'Will I see you later?'

'I don't think so,' he replied. She felt as though he'd thrown cold water over her: he'd had a good time and it was over. Time to get back to reality. She wanted to run down the corridor after him and ask what she had done to upset him, but her pride wouldn't let her. How dare he treat her like that?

Marcus had found himself looking around the glittering table, remembering dinners and functions he'd been to with Malena, his sophisticated and accomplished wife. He looked across at Sylvia, with her deep and flagrantly exposed cleavage, and thought, I let her go too easily. I should have fought for her. I just let her slip away. I have to try again.

John and Jenny were the last to leave the Drawing Room.

'I bet you'll be glad to see the back of us,' John said to Captain Doug.

'I'm not supposed to agree with you but, yes, it's been one to remember. In lots of ways. Tonight was a good way to end it.'

'Well, I've had a wonderful time, despite everything, and thank you for your kindness,' said Jenny.

'Thank you for yours, and for your understanding. You could have made my life very difficult if you'd wanted to prosecute.'

She put out her hand to shake his, but he shook his head. 'Remember, no hands,' and they bumped hips, much to John's amazement.

Jenny and John agreed to meet in half an hour when their packing was done and their cases outside their respective doors for collection.

They didn't do too much talking that night. She snuggled up beside him in his bed. 'I think I'm ready,'

And she was. Their love-making was tender and fulfilling, with the promise of much more to come.

Doug went up to the bridge for the changeover of watches, then said goodnight to his colleagues.

He made his way back to his quarters. It had been a good night. He hadn't enjoyed himself so much for a long time. He took a shower and clicked on his computer as he always did before turning in.

There was a message from his sister: *Andrea has taken an overdose. She's in intensive care. Call me when you get this. Maxine xx*

'No, I don't think she did it deliberately. There's no note or anything. She probably just forgot she'd taken them. She was out drinking with that friend of hers, Mandy. I think they'd been at it all day.'

'And Lewis? Is he safe?'

'He's fine. He's still with me.'

'We dock in a few hours' time and I'll be on the earliest flight I can get. I'll let you know. Ring me if you hear anything.'

'Of course.'

The next day, as soon as the Greek authorities had given clearance for disembarkation, a waiting car brought Doug to the airport.

Changeover was streamlined, with passengers being directed in batches to various colour-coded sections in the hall for baggage retrieval. The green area was almost cleared when a booming voice was heard shouting, 'Mind that bag, you clumsy woman.' This was followed immediately by a heavy thud and the sound of glass splintering. 'I told you the handles wouldn't hold on that thing.' An ever-increasing pool of red wine haemorrhaged around the bag onto the floor. The man said, 'I knew that'd happen. What a poxy holiday. I'll never cruise again.' He gathered up his belongings, left the mess behind and marched out, followed by his wife and two sons.

Forty-six

FOR MANY OF THOSE WHO HAD LEFT ATHENS six and half months earlier on that eventful cruise, it had simply joined their other holiday memories, and came to mind when Israel, Rhodes or anywhere else they had visited in the Mediterranean popped up on the television or in conversation.

For those who had gone to that significant Solo Travellers' Lunch, the memories were more enduring.

Betty survived the three months she had been given before the trip. She succumbed to the pancreatic cancer she had known about for longer than that, but had kept secret from almost all of those she'd met. She had told Jenny the night she'd stayed with her after her accident and they'd been in constant contact. 'The outcome is inevitable. Drugs might prolong my life but they won't make me better. I've lived long enough and well enough. Let's just obey nature and allow me to go when the time is right.'

She had refused chemotherapy, insisting that she just wanted to make the most of every day. And she did.

Her leg hadn't mended, but morphine helped both conditions, and the end came exactly as she would have wished, gently and with no fuss. She just fell asleep, surrounded by her daughters and family. Ben had been a regular visitor and she had enjoyed the time they spent together. She even had him talking about his next holiday, and persuaded him to buy new hearing aids.

'I wish you could come along as well,' he'd said. 'It won't be the same without you.'

'Well, Ben,' she teased, 'what would Esther have to say about that?'

'Betty, it was you who made me realise that she's no longer here and I have my life to live. Thank you for that. Nothing I do now will change what she and I had together. You made me realise how boring I'd become.'

'Not boring, Ben, just too settled. Far too settled.'

He visited her four days before she died when they reminisced and laughed about the cruise. Both knew they were saying goodbye, but that wasn't mentioned. He kissed her forehead before he left, and she held his hand for longer than was necessary. They didn't need words. They understood each other.

His daughter couldn't believe the change in him. He no longer resembled the ageing, morose, rigid father whom she had pushed into the holiday to give her some respite. She was grieving for her mother, too, but he hadn't seen that, and so were her children. When he'd come to see them, all he had talked about was how things used to be. He must have driven her mother mad when he retired, although she'd never complained. Now he arrived with brochures and itineraries, and was full of talk about places he wanted to see.

'I think I might give the Caribbean a go, although I need to find out when the hurricane season is.'

'There's a cruise around the Baltic – now that one could be really interesting. I'd love to see St Petersburg.'

'Maybe we could all go on one together some time.'

If he'd suggested that a year ago she'd have said a definite no, but now, with this newer version of her father, they might think about it. He was often out now when she rang, visiting some old dear he'd met, or at the library using their computers – researching, he told his grandchildren. The oldest had been almost impressed when he'd received a tweet from his granddad to say he was definitely going on another cruise. Soon.

*

Heather was in Argentina. She hadn't seen Will since he'd been sent home, corresponding only through their lawyers. After the cruise she had gone to stay in their country house.

She had instructed her lawyer, 'Get an injunction issued that he's not to come here for as long as I need to stay. If he's anywhere near the place, I'll go public on what happened. Never mind the gossip columnists' versions of irreconcilable differences, I'll give them the truth if he tries to contact me, and no amount of money will buy him out of that.'

Will wrote to her a few times, but she burned the letters unopened. He settled an enormous sum on her. She left instructions with an estate agent in Kent to find her a suitable residence, where she could show off her antiques to their best advantage. She looked up an old friend, Carlos, whom she frequently met in England at equestrian events, and who was a guest in their private box at Royal Ascot every year. 'I need to get away for a while, so I'm going to take up your invitation to that ranch of yours. This time I'll be alone, but don't read anything into that.'

'As if I would. You're as subtle as ever.' He laughed. 'I'd heard there were rocks in the marital bed.'

'There is no marital bed.'

'Better and better.'

He was between wives three and four – or was it four and five? She couldn't remember. His *estancia* was thirty miles from Buenos Aires.

'Carlos, where's your taste? What's happened to all your

lovely antiques, and your library? What did you do with your books? This place is like a barn.'

'Gloria, my last wife, who only lasted a week longer than the interior designers did, got rid of them all. She had the place *feng shui*ed or something, and decided the positive energy in here was being blocked by books and old furniture. I was in England for a month and when I got back they were all gone. So I sent her packing too.'

'And has it made a difference to your energy levels?'

'I never had any complaints in that department. What do you think? I'm as much a goer as I ever was!'

Heather agreed. She'd found that, with time and proximity, she was beginning to look at him in a new light. 'You have to get them back, make this place a home again.'

'If the urge is so strong, why not do it for me – or with me?'

'Why do you keep marrying them?' she asked.

'I'm an optimist.' He grinned.

'Or a fool.'

Bud was being petulant again. Sonny had been spending time – too much time, he thought – with the star of the latest Hollywood blockbuster. It had out-grossed the main competition within weeks of its première and its leading man was the hottest property for a decade. He had heard about Sonny and asked him to style his wardrobe for his tour and his guest appearances. He was on every talk show across the

US and was preparing for another tour to coincide with its European release. When he asked Sonny to go with him, Bud blew a gasket.

'You go and our marriage is over.'

'Bud, you're letting jealousy get in the way of my life. I don't flip when you go to Hollywood or to your meetings, charming the pants off any millionaire who might invest in your latest production.'

'That's different.'

'What's different about it?' Sonny asked rationally.

'I don't flirt and send out those come-hither looks that you give every good-looking male.'

'This isn't about me. It's about you. Your problem is that you don't trust me. If you really try to stop me going to Europe, then it's over between us, because I can't live with your never-ending suspicion. This is my biggest break and you want me to give it up.'

'I'm sorry, Sonny. I can't help it. I'm so afraid I'll lose you.'

'Well, you certainly will if you keep up those antics. I'm telling you, I'd like to go.'

'And I'm telling you, I wouldn't like you to.'

The stalemate lasted for three days. When Sonny got home from work each evening, he announced his arrival by slamming the front door, then the bathroom door and often the bedroom door. Bud ordered take-outs for one, voicing his opinions to Bruno, their Bernese mountain dog. Sonny answered through him too.

'Someone's in a temper then, isn't he?'

'Maybe we need a little break from someone's hissy fits.'

'Wouldn't it be nice – just the two of us here on our own for a while? We could go for long walks together in the evening.'

'Do you think he'll go to France, Bruno, with that pin-up?'

Sonny broke the impasse. 'I had an email from Jenny. Betty died.'

'Oh, my God. That's so sad. When did you hear?'

'At lunchtime, and I've been thinking. Hear me out. Life's too short for this sort of carry-on. I'm going to Paris next week. I can't not go – it's too important to my career. If the roles were reversed you'd do the same. So, I've been thinking – why don't you fly over in two weeks' time and join me in the South of France and we'll have a few fabulous days together?'

Buddy looked at Sonny for a few seconds and took him in his arms. 'I'm sorry. I've been despicable, haven't I?'

'You have, but I forgive you, divo, just this once. Now, let's make up for lost time before I have to go.'

✳

Sylvia hadn't got over the way things had ended or, rather, had been left hanging between herself and Marcus. He had treated her abominably. That 'good night' on the corridor after the captain's dinner had been their farewell. He hadn't even come down to say goodbye before she'd left the ship. *Boy, did he know how to make a woman feel badly about herself.* No one had ever made her feel so used when they'd dumped her.

She wondered sometimes if he'd pretended to be single so that he could have it away with her. It wouldn't have bothered her so much if she'd been playing the same game. The sex had been good and she knew that that was what she should remember – not their parting. *But I really liked him and thought he liked me.*

She also wondered if he'd tried to get back with his wife or she with him.

She had no pictures of her and Marcus together. He had never allowed anyone to take any, always saying he hated photographs and taking the shots instead. She had the group photo taken at the gala – John had bought them all a copy – but Marcus was standing between Hamish and Ben and his head was turned sideways, as though he hadn't wanted to be seen there. She often wondered if the yarn he had told them about Malena was just that, a yarn. Yet he had confided the secrets of his German past to her and she felt he wouldn't have done that to just anyone. Would he? She'd never know, and she wouldn't try to find out.

Today she was leaving her general manager in charge of the jewellery boutique. Her cases were packed and she was off with her daughter to her new villa in Cyprus. She'd just about finished furnishing it and had a few things to bring over. And she'd arranged to meet up with Hamish, who would be on the island. They'd kept in constant contact since the cruise and he'd been so good about Marcus, sensing her hurt.

'He wasn't right for you. You need a real man, one with a bit of life in him – someone you can have a laugh with.'

'Someone like you, Hamish?'

'Well, you could do a lot worse.'

'I'll give it serious consideration.'

'I wouldn't hang about – you might have competition.'

'I'll take my chances.'

He'd sold his business and handed over the care of his classic-car collection to his nephew. He'd wintered on the island and met a widow at the hotel he'd stayed in. He'd told Sylvia that they'd become more than just good friends.

'I feel, despite all my good intentions, my bachelor status in in danger!'

'Good God,' Sylvia exclaimed. 'She must be something special.'

'Aye, she is. Wait until you meet her. I know you'll love her. Now, the thing is, we'd both value your expertise because we're looking to buy a place together.'

'Nothing would give me greater pleasure. I'm looking forward to meeting the lady. Does she have a name?'

'Laura.'

'Well, you can be our first dinner guests, when Rebecca and I arrive. She's studying for her finals and as she has actually been doing a bit, I decided to let her have a break'.

Marcus went back to Copenhagen and to work. Despite his concerns his business hadn't gone under while he'd been absent. In fact, it was thriving. Malena and Germund were still making headlines over the case they were fighting in the courts from opposing sides. He'd wait until that was over to meet her and come to an arrangement about their divorce.

Twice while the court was in session he'd gone in to sit at the back and watch the proceedings. They were ruthless. You could have cut the vitriol and sarcasm with a knife, it was so thick. They scored any point possible. Media speculation had switched from the content of the trial to the personalities of the two warring lawyers. There was conjecture as to whether both egos would survive when one was defeated.

The trial lasted another two weeks, and Malena's team were the victors. Marcus sent a congratulatory yellow rose to her chambers, something he had always done when she'd won a case, and this had been her biggest to date. She didn't acknowledge it, but he hadn't expected that she would.

He was too busy to do anything about the divorce and kept finding excuses to put it off. He didn't think much about Sylvia at all and when he did, it was to compare her with Malena. He still hadn't given up hope of reconciling with his wife, although nothing suggested that it might be feasible.

About a month after the trial had concluded, he came into his office to find a yellow rose on his desk. His PA said it had been delivered but there had been no card.

'I know who it's from.' He punched in Malena's number.

'Can we talk?' she said.

'Yes, but let's meet, somewhere neutral.'

'I don't want a fight,' she said. 'What about that little place in Klampenborg on Saturday? About ten.'

When they met they shook hands, as formal as strangers, but after ten minutes it was as though the past nine or ten months had never happened. They walked along the beach they had walked along hundreds of times in the past and ended up spending the weekend in their cottage, as they had done hundreds of times before.

'I was mad. I got swept away. I'm so sorry for hurting you. I never stopped loving you.'

When she asked him if he had met anyone in that time, he shook his head. 'No one. I never stopped loving you either.'

'I know I don't have any right, but can you ever forgive me?' she asked.

'I can try,' was his reply.

Doug had flown home from Athens to be with Andrea. She was still in intensive care when he reached the hospital. They were hopeful, as she had drifted back into consciousness for a few minutes earlier that evening. Later she convinced them all that it had been a mistake. She hadn't meant to commit, or even try to commit, suicide. She had forgotten that she'd taken her tablets. She admitted she had been drunk and agreed to go into therapy when it was suggested she was not fit to be in charge of her child.

Maxine stepped in again, taking Lewis. He went back to his ship, joining halfway through a cruise. He was worn out with anxiety. He wanted to take compassionate leave for a few months because he was worried that he'd make a mistake at work and mistakes could cost lives. His mother persuaded him to wait until he saw how things worked out before putting his job on the line. 'She can't do any harm where she is.'

In that knowledge he tried to get on with his job. His family didn't tell him she had signed herself out on the day he left, deciding they would keep an eye on her until his scheduled leave, in a few weeks' time. Just before he came home his sister warned him that Andrea wasn't coping. She wouldn't let anyone into the house.

'How bad is it?' he'd asked.

'I may as well as be truthful with you, Doug, because you'll see it for yourself soon enough. If Lewis was there and Social Services came in and saw it, they'd take him from her. The house is filthy. There are bottles and piles of dirty washing everywhere. It even looks neglected from the outside. I brought the kids over to cut the grass one day and Andrea screamed profanities out of the bedroom window at them. She didn't even come out to see Lewis.'

'Oh, Maxine, I'm so sorry to have dragged you into all this. I can never thank you enough for taking him. That's what's kept me sane.'

'He's like our own. We'll be heartbroken if he leaves us now.'

It took some persuasion and a lot of intervention to get Andrea to agree to go into rehab again. She stayed three days and then signed herself out, stopping at the off-licence on the way home. She opened one of the bottles on the street and drank deeply from it.

Doug was tidying the garden when he heard her coming up the path. Her first words to him were, 'It's all right for you and your fancy lifestyle, swanning around the world doing your Captain Wonderful bit, while I'm wasting away here, tied down in this hellhole with a screaming baby, shitty nappies and no life.'

He'd had enough. Normally he never accused her or tried to say, 'I told you so,' but there was more than a broken relationship at stake here: there was the safety of their child. He went into the kitchen and she followed him. She got a tumbler, poured herself a large quantity of gin and sat down at the breakfast bar. She didn't add a mixer. He sat across from her. It was only eleven o'clock in the morning.

'Andrea, I'm tired of pussyfooting around you. It's time for some straight talking.'

'Don't lecture me, Doug. I'm not one of your minions.'

'I know that, but I've done everything I can. I'm not lecturing you and I never have. You knew my working conditions when we met. You knew I'd have to be away. I've done everything to make your life easier when I'm not here. I tried to get you help for your drinking. I got you help with Lewis, and help in the home. My family have taken over the care of our little boy and still all you want is another bottle.'

'It's easy for you,' she argued. 'Everyone loves you. Charming Captain Marvellous in his sexy uniform. Who cares about me?'

'Don't try that on me, Andrea. You were the life and soul of the ships you worked on. Christ, I used to be jealous of all the attention you got. You messed your life up. You can't blame anyone else for that. Can't you see that you lost your job because of drink? Now you're very close to losing your child and ... your marriage.'

'I don't care.'

'You haven't even tried to fix things.'

'I was going to tell you something too,' she said, slurping more gin. 'I never wanted a child, and I certainly don't want any more. I've been to Dr Tatton. He's arranging everything for me. I'm having my tubes tied, and there's nothing you can do about it. It's my body and my decision.'

Doug was incredulous.

'And I was going to tell you something else. It's over between us. I was going to tell you that,' she said, pushing her fingers into his shoulder.

He was about to remonstrate, then realised there was no point. He didn't care any more. All he had been doing during those months at sea was trying to convince himself that he still did, but the truth was that his concern and love were only for Lewis and his welfare.

'Well, as you have it all figured out so nicely, let's do it legally. We'll go to see a solicitor this afternoon. All I ask is that you try to be sober for that, as I'd hate to be accused later of talking you into something when you were out of your skull with booze.'

After the meeting she moved out. She got a solicitor to deal with everything and went to London. No one had heard from her since. She didn't remember her child at Christmas. Doug and his sister were awarded joint custody of Lewis. Doug put the house on the market and left instructions that her half of the equity was to be sent to her solicitor when it sold.

*

Jenny had had a manic six months, and was unlikely ever to forget the cruise. She didn't need the beautifully decorated glass ewer that Sonny and Bud had sent from Marmaris to remind her of it. It arrived a few days after she'd got home, and she'd sat holding it, running her fingers over the embossed gold detail, remembering everything in minute detail.

She had contacted her father through the email address at the bottom of the flyer for his exhibition. It had taken him three weeks to phone, and when she challenged him about Elena, he just said, 'I didn't think you'd want to know.'

'But she's our half-sister. How could we not want to know?'

'I never thought about it like that.' And she knew he hadn't. That was her father. He never thought about anything like that. He was the centre of his universe, and always had been. Everyone else was a mere satellite that happened in and out of his orbit by chance or by design.

'I'd love to meet her. Are you coming to Ireland any time soon?'

'No, but we'll be in London. I'm preparing for an exhibition over there.'

No invitation. Nothing. 'Maybe Leslie and I will come over for the opening, if you'd like that.'

'If it suits,' he replied.

Annoyed at his lack of enthusiasm, Jenny decided to get

something else off her mind. 'You know the painting of me with Blackie when I was young? Could I have it, please?'

'I didn't think you'd want it.'

'Well, I do. It reminds me of my childhood,' she said, feeling she was dealing with a stranger, someone who had never shared any of those great moments with her.

'Very well. I'll have it shipped over to you.'

Knowing it would probably take him months to get around to that, she said, 'Send it to Leslie's address.'

'Are you moving?'

'No, Dad. I left Fergus when he became violent and beat me up after I lost our baby. '

'Quite right, too. I don't hold with that sort of carry-on,' was all he said.

What was it about the man that he couldn't engage with any of his children?

The painting duly arrived with no note, no compliment slip. Nothing.

Leslie and Jenny read about the upcoming exhibition in an interview in the *Sunday Times*. When he was asked how many children he had, their father answered, 'A daughter, Elena.'

Neither mentioned this to him when they turned up at the opening. It was very crowded, and they saw their half-sister leave with a foreign-looking woman, whom they presumed was her minder. They didn't talk to her. Their father greeted them as he did everyone else – a quick 'Hello, you're very welcome, thank you for coming.' He was immediately swept up by some demanding patron. That was it: the audience had been granted and executed. It had lasted less than five minutes.

As they waited for a cab to take them to John's penthouse, Leslie said, 'I bet that little one doesn't even know she has us and four half-brothers.'

'I'm sure she doesn't.'

Fergus had been arrested and bailed while the police prepared a file for the director of public prosecutions. He had had to surrender his passport. It was inevitable that he would be sent to prison. When his assets were frozen, he and Jenny weren't divorced so the house was deemed a joint property and left alone. Jenny still wanted no part of it. She had moved on, but was happy that Fergus would have something to go back to. It didn't seem right that the home his parents had worked for and kept all their lives should have to be forfeited.

The first weekend she went over to London she told John more and more about what Fergus had put her through. He had been shocked.

'What a coward. We're not all like that,' he told her gently, and she believed him. The more they saw of each other, the closer they grew, and she missed him when he wasn't around because she couldn't hear his voice or smell his aftershave, his clothes, him.

John and she had visited Bud and Sonny in New York for Thanksgiving weekend shortly after the cruise had ended. She had met Bruno, their Bernese mountain dog, Martha, who cleaned for them, and Scrooge, the concierge. She later told them, 'Guys, I have to say it was over pumpkin pie that I realised I was in love with John. When he was sitting at your gloriously overladen table, steeped in traditions, trying to pretend he loved it, not wanting to offend, I knew that I wanted him in my life, to make our own traditions and be together forever. And when I saw the way your dog trusted him I knew I did too.'

'Does this mean we'll have a wedding to plan?'

'Not yet!' she replied. 'Divorce takes years in Ireland, but we're going to move in together – officially. And you can come and visit us in France.'

John told his brother first about his natural father, the inheritance and the estate, and together they went to see their father. His reaction was as John had feared.

'Well, you were always inclined to act above your station. Now you can really swank.'

'Dad, I didn't look for this. I never wanted any more than you gave me. In my eyes, there was never any doubt that you were my father and Mum was Mum, and you couldn't have been better parents.'

'I know that, and she was right proud of you, always telling everyone where you were, and how well you were doing for yourself.'

John and Colin exchanged glances. They both knew that that was the nearest he would ever get to praise from their dad.

'I couldn't have asked for a better or a nicer brother, either,' John said slapping Colin on the back.

Colin laughed. 'Hey it's you who's come in to money not me – there's no need for this sort of palaver.'

Strangely, his Dad didn't seem to be affected to learn that John's natural father had known all about him. It might have been different if John had done the searching himself. When the three of them went to France together, he admitted, 'You've fallen on your feet, son. Your mother would have loved it here.'

'It's my home now and you're welcome any time. We might even turn you into a wine-maker. You could have your own place here on the estate or stay in the château. God knows it's big enough.'

'I think I'll stick to the ale. But I've always fancied seeing myself playing *boules* in a village square. Maybe the darts team would come over.'

'I never imagined you playing boules. That's quite a revelation, Dad.'

'Let's hope that's the end of yours,' his father replied.

'Actually, there's one more. I've met someone and I'd like you to meet her.'

'Not another of your foreign women.'

'Yes, if that includes the Irish.'

'They're not foreign. They're our neighbours. Your birth mother was Irish.'

How had he known that? John wondered. The sly old fox, maybe he'd known all the time and was letting him stew.

So when John next saw Jenny, he told her, 'It's time you saw what you'll be letting yourself in for if decide to stay with me.'

'I don't need to see all that to make my mind up,' she said, hugging him. 'Just try to get rid of me.'

When they drove to his dad's house, Jenny turned to John and said, 'I'm anxious that they'll like me.'

Colin and his wife and their two children were already there.

'Of course they will.'

She needn't have worried. His father was charm itself and when he said after about only ten minutes, 'You know Jenny, you remind me of the boys' mother', they knew everything would be all right.

'Jenny and I are going over to France the week after next to get to know it all a bit better!' John said to Colin. 'Half-term is coming up so why don't you come along and bring the kids with you. You too, Dad. We can enjoy exploring it together.'

Two weeks later, John and Jenny were en route to his estate. 'The whole place inspires me now that I have someone to share it with, although it'll be madly busy as I learn the ropes. The agents Marcel put in place will be there for just a few more months.'

'I'll help. I can work from there too, but you'll have to educate me a bit first. I can't sit with wine buyers and producers,

swirling and spitting and just saying that their wines are very
– very – well very pleasant.'

'We'll turn you into an oenophile in no time at all.'

'What – no turrets?' she'd exclaimed, when they reached
the top of the long driveway the first time she saw the château.

'No turrets. Is that a deal breaker?'

'Oh, it might have been, but I've just spotted the corner of
a swimming pool over there.'

The château was imposing but manageable, made of cut
stone with pale turquoise shutters on its numerous windows.

'It's perfect,' she exclaimed as they followed the rotund
housekeeper inside. Vases of fresh flowers brought life to the
rooms, and the furnishings were a mix of antique and modern
pieces. 'It's so French. I love it. Marcel had very good taste.
There's nothing to do but move in. It feels so homely and
welcoming.'

'I'm sorry I never had the chance to meet him.'

'So am I, for your sake.'

'Do you think you could you be happy here with me – or
is it too soon to ask you that?'

'I could be happy with you anywhere, and no it's not too
soon at all.' She walked into his arms and kissed him.

Together, as they fell more in love with each other, they fell
more in love with the place – its rolling hills, river valley, duck
pond and sprawling château they would come to call home.

They spent the next few days exploring the properties,
meeting the staff in the various enterprises, eating in the
nearby towns and in the cream and blue dining room. She

watched as John charmed everyone, just as he had done with her. He exuded a quiet and confident air of authority, but never appeared cocky.

'I didn't know you spoke the lingo,' she said.

'There's a lot you don't know about me yet.'

'I'm beginning to realise that, but I know we'll be happy here together.'

'So do I,' he said, wrapping his arms around her. 'I'm so glad I found you.

'So am I.'

Today was the beginning of another Mediterranean cruise. It started from Athens and was going to Israel, Cyprus, Rhodes, Marmaris and Mykonos.

Captain Douglas Burgess welcomed his handpicked guests as old friends, then led them towards a side table on the spacious bridge. There, they saw an array of canapés. A uniformed waiter served champagne.

'You might have noticed that we don't shake hands here, but that doesn't mean we're unfriendly,' the captain said. 'We knock elbows or touch hips as we pass, just a little precaution to avoid passing on germs. If you get sick, we'll feel sorry for you. If we go down with something, it's not sympathy we'll get because no one will be going anywhere.'

That got a laugh from everyone, as it always did.

'So, before we hit the high seas, why don't you get a bit of practice at the how-de-dos and say hello to each other?' The guests looked at each other. He walked over to the two people nearest him and they bounced hips. He touched elbows with another. That was the cue for them all to began raising elbows or gyrating – 'Hello, hello, hello.'

'Now I'm going to ignore you for a bit. We've work to do,' the captain told them. 'Although you may not see much of us during your time with us, we're a bit necessary up here, especially First Officer Lars Carlsen over there. He can read the maps and the dots on the radar screens. Meanwhile, may I ask you all to be very quiet for the next few minutes, and please don't talk to any of us until we clear the harbour. This is a pretty tight one and, as you can see, there's lots of traffic so we need to concentrate. After that, we're all yours.'

He was back in form.

Acknowledgements

A book is a team effort and without the always helpful and cheerful Hachette Ireland team this one would not be in print. Special thanks, however, have been well earned by my editor, Ciara Doorley, for her words of wisdom, prosecco and champagne chocolate truffles.

To my copy-editor, Hazel Orme, for her eagle eye and astute suggestions.

To Joanna Smyth, editorial and publicity assistant, for her ever prompt attention to my requests, and to those behind the scenes who never get a mention. Thank you all.